THE POLICY

THE POLICY

PATRICK LYNCH

A DUTTON BOOK

DUTTON
Published by the Penguin Group
Penguin Putnam Inc., 375 Hudson Street,
New York, New York 10014, U.S.A.
Penguin Books Ltd, 27 Wrights Lane, London W8 5TZ, England
Penguin Books Australia Ltd, Ringwood, Victoria, Australia
Penguin Books Canada Ltd, 10 Alcorn Avenue, Toronto, Ontario, Canada M4V 3B2
Penguin Books (N.Z.) Ltd, 182–190 Wairau Road,
Auckland 10, New Zealand

Penguin Books Ltd, Registered Offices:
Harmondsworth, Middlesex, England

First published by Dutton, an imprint of Dutton NAL,
a member of Penguin Putnam Inc.

First Printing, September, 1998
10 9 8 7 6 5 4 3 2 1

REGISTERED TRADEMARK—MARCA REGISTRADA

LIBRARY OF CONGRESS CATALOGING-IN-PUBLICATION DATA:
Lynch, Patrick.
  The policy / Patrick Lynch.
    p.   cm.
  ISBN 0-525-94340-4
  I. Title.
PR6062.Y596P65   1998
823'.914—dc21   98-15442
                                                              CIP

Printed in the United States of America
Set in Garamond Light

PUBLISHER'S NOTE

In memory of Edward James Humphreys

ACKNOWLEDGMENTS

I would like to thank the following for their generous help with this book:

Michele Van Leer of John Hancock Mutual Life Insurance Company, Robert Ryan of Boston Mutual Life Insurance Company, and Joseph Thompson of New England Mutual Life Insurance Company for explaining the issues and showing me how the industry works; Agnes Bundy of Fleet Bank in Providence for her reflections on life in Rhode Island; Dr. Rupert Negus and Dr. Helena Scott for their help with the genetic science and medical elements of the story; and actuarial refugee Cathy Gibaud for convincing me that it could all really happen.

CONTENTS

DECEMBER THIRTEENTH

Snow was drifting in the gutters, swirling and skimming over the dark road. The first fall of the season, fine and hard, like white sand.

The cabdriver coughed and zipped his windbreaker up to his chin. "Five below freezing," he said, as if somebody had just asked him. "Wind veering northwesterly. Coming down from the ice cap."

Sitting huddled in the backseat, Michael Eliot pulled his raincoat tighter about him. He should have worn something warmer. He'd been at home all afternoon, working up a sweat in the den, trying to get it finished before Margaret's father arrived on the weekend and told him what he was doing wrong. He hadn't planned on going out. But then an hour after supper the phone rang. It was Harold Tate. They had to meet right away, he said. Something that wouldn't wait. And it had to be at his office. He wouldn't say why.

"Five below freezing," the cabdriver said again. He gave the heater a nudge with the flat of his hand. "Black ice all over."

It was half past ten and the Old World streets of the East Side were empty. The kids at Brown had gone home for the vacation, the only remains of their partying a festive string of colored lights hung up over the entrance to the Wriston Quadrangle. On the radio a cheery voice announced that there was now a seventy-six-percent chance of a white Christmas in the greater Providence area, as if that was just what everybody had been praying for. As they crawled down the hill towards Benefit Street, Eliot couldn't help reflecting for a moment on what a white Christmas would actually mean: the road accidents, the crippling falls, the deaths among the old from pneumonia and hypothermia, not to mention the occasional skater falling through the ice and the house fires that wouldn't be reached in time. Somewhere in the company they would have the figures on that. The actuarial department had the figures on everything, and the man who ran it knew most of them by heart. All Eliot knew was that a white Christmas meant a snowstorm of checks, because his department would be writing them. And each check was a life.

They crossed the river at the end of College Street and followed the neat granite quays south towards the interstate. Clouds of steam were rising from a line of low-rises on Friendship, obscuring the cluster of floodlit tower blocks that passed for the Financial District. The driver looked like he was new at the job. He kept leaning forward, squinting through the windshield as if he didn't recognize the road. A street map lay open on the seat beside him. Eliot wondered if he knew the way. Tate's office was seven miles away in Warwick, on the edge of some high-tech industrial park, near Kent County Memorial Hospital, he said. Eliot had never been there before. He hoped they weren't going to have to stop and ask for directions. He wanted to get there. He wanted to find out what it was all about.

Twenty-five years ago he and Harold had been roommates in college, and for a while, when Eliot first moved to Providence, they'd been regular guests at each other's dinner parties. But that didn't happen anymore. Eliot had yet to even meet Tate's new wife, Suzy. Tate had gotten to know her at work, where she had been a lab assistant for a while. Apparently Suzy didn't go down very well among the East Side wives. She wore too much lipstick and showed too much leg—or so he'd heard.

Maybe Harold was having trouble with Suzy, thought Eliot. Maybe that was why he'd called. Tate's voice had struck him as strange, shaky even. It sounded like he'd been drinking. Perhaps Suzy had upped and left him. Margaret had always said it wouldn't last, that Suzy was just after a meal ticket. A girl like her was never going to fall for a man like Harold. She was loud and shallow and he was quiet, thoughtful—a biologist, for God's sake. Maybe that's all it was: a domestic crisis. Perhaps he just wanted to talk. They weren't exactly close friends any-more, but did Harold really have any close friends? He'd never been the gregarious type, and Wickford was hardly a humming metropolis. Maybe it wasn't anything to worry about after all. Maybe it had nothing to do with the tests.

The snow was starting to stick as they approached exit ten. A mile away the airport was a ground-hugging cloud of sodium orange. An-other few hours and they would shut it down. At the bottom of the ramp they passed a squad car by the side of the road, its red and blue warning lights turning noiselessly. A Pontiac was stopped a little farther on, one wing wrapped around the crash barrier. The driver, a woman, was standing in the beam of the headlights, hugging herself, staring at the damage as if she couldn't believe what she was seeing.

"Should've fitted them winter tires," said the cabdriver, shaking his head. "Folks always leave it till they damn near kill themselves. Guess they think the bad stuff only happens to the other guy, right?"

The Medan Diagnostics building was an anonymous two-story block of brown brick with recessed rectangular windows and a large empty courtyard. Like most of the properties in the area, it was surrounded by a tall wire-mesh fence, but the main gates stood open, unattended.

Tate himself was waiting in reception. Eliot could see him through the glass doors, pacing slowly up and down, still wearing his white lab coat. He paid the cabdriver and went inside.

Tate did his best to look cheerful, giving a hearty welcome and shak-ing Eliot's hand as if this was just a routine social visit. But when he saw the expression on Eliot's face, the smiling stopped.

"Mike, I'm sorry about all the—"

"I'm not supposed to be here, Harold," said Eliot, glancing at the uniformed security guard behind the front desk.

"Oh"—Tate closed the door—"don't worry about that, for God's sake. My office is just down here."

The inside of the building was budget high-tech, with brightly painted tubular furniture and blown-up photographs of microorganic life hanging on the plain white walls. Eliot followed Tate in silence.

"What a terrible night," said Tate. "And they say there's more to come."

Tate was forty-six years old, a year younger than Eliot, although of the two men he looked much the older. His short-cropped beard had more than a trace of gray, and although he still had most of his hair, his high forehead was deeply lined, like the fragile skin around his eyes. With a little more color in his cheeks he could easily have passed for a navy man. Eliot's looks were gentler, his complexion smoother. And he had friendly brown eyes that created a beguiling impression of vulnerability. It was something women in particular responded to.

They walked down a long neon-lit corridor with yellow doors on the right-hand side leading into a series of private offices. A pair of bright red double doors on the left marked the entrance to the laboratories. Through the glass panels Eliot glimpsed workbenches, sinks, a computer terminal, and shelves loaded with flasks and beakers. Beneath one of the panels a sign read:

<u>CONTAMINATION RISK</u>
FACE MASKS AND GLOVES TO BE
WORN BEYOND THIS POINT

"I'm just through here," Tate said, punching a number code into a keypad and opening one of the yellow doors. "How's Margaret, by the way?"

Eliot didn't answer at once. He wondered what the hell Tate was playing at. Was he afraid of being overheard? If so, by whom? Except for the security guard, the whole place seemed empty.

"Fine," he said warily. "How's Suzy?"

"Oh, fine. Looking forward to Christmas, you know. She loves this time of year, especially when it snows. She's a real kid about it."

Tate closed the door. The office was large, with tables and filing cabinets along two walls and a desk at the far end. Potted plants, folders, coffee cups, and stacks of computer printouts competed for space on every surface. A window looked out across the parking lot to a dark expanse of ground that Eliot assumed was a park or a playing field.

"Is this about her, Harold?"

Tate looked puzzled. "Who?"

"Suzy. Are you two having problems or—?"

"No, no. Good grief, no. Why would you—?" He seemed to think better of the question, gesturing instead towards an upright chair beside his desk. "Please, Michael, have a seat. I'm sorry if you . . . It's turned into such a terrible night. Maybe we should have a drink. What do you say?"

Eliot took off his coat and sat down. It was bad news. It had to be. Bad news for him. He stared at the bundles of printouts lying on Tate's desk, and suddenly he didn't want to know any more. Not yet.

"I was in the den," he said. He looked down at his hands. They were still spattered with paint. "Trying to get it finished up there. You know, I'm almost a year behind schedule. It was supposed to be finished in the spring. I thought about hiring professionals—I'm no handyman, you know that—but you wouldn't believe what they cost. I mean the painting and rewiring alone. And you can forget about the floors." Tate handed him a glass of whisky, sat down at his desk, "The other day this character quoted fifteen thousand dollars. And—well, you know."

Tate forced a smile. "It looks like a lot of money."

Eliot nodded and took a mouthful of whisky. Swallowed. There was an awkward silence. Then Tate opened one of the files on his desk. More printouts. Green and white paper, horizontal stripes. The file was marked STRICTLY CONFIDENTIAL in red letters.

"Michael, I'm sorry to drag you down here like this, but I couldn't— I couldn't think of any other way. We wouldn't want Margaret to . . . And my place is even farther. I just thought it was better here, where I can explain it all. Where we won't be interrupted. So we can talk it all through, thoroughly. Look at all the options."

Eliot's stomach was jumping. The whisky burned.

"Talk all what through, Harold?"

"Well—"

"The screening? The tests?"

Then Tate was suddenly talking: "I'll want another sample of DNA from you, that's the first thing. It's essential to do a second test, to be sure about what we're looking at. I want to take that from you right now. I've got everything ready in the lab. That's really why we had to meet here, you see? We won't be sure until we've run it through the system a second time. Of course, normally we wouldn't bother. But normally it's—well, it's business. This is different. You're a friend, Michael."

Eliot looked down at the floor. He had an unpleasant feeling of weightlessness. He didn't want to ask any more questions. Let Dr. Harold Tate handle it. It was his damned test, his technology.

"Anyway, in the meantime, it's only right that you should know what the findings are to date." He reached into the folder and started to spread out the sheets of paper over the desk. Then he stopped, holding down the material with the flat of his hand as if afraid it might blow away. "I'm very sorry, Michael, but I'm afraid what we've found on chromosome four isn't good. It isn't good at all."

Two and a half hours later Eliot was riding back up to the East Side. Tate had offered to take him, but he'd ended up drinking more of the scotch than Eliot had, and was in no state to drive anywhere. No sense risking your neck for a lousy cab fare, Eliot had told him, and Tate had shaken his head sadly and looked down at his shoes. He became maudlin when he was drunk. Eliot had forgotten that. Maudlin but affectionate. Eliot thought back to their college days and it didn't seem like a quarter of a century ago. He struggled to think of what he had done with twenty-five years, of all the things that had happened to him in that time. But between the few landmarks there seemed to be nothing but a gray fog, year upon year lived with nothing to show for it, not even happy memories. He had wasted too much time.

The snow was no longer falling. The wind had dropped, and high above the white dome of the capitol building Eliot thought he could see stars. Perhaps the airport would stay open after all.

This time the cabdriver was a black guy, forty-something, with a bull neck and wiry gray hair. He hadn't spoken since they left Warwick.

"Tell me something?" said Eliot.

The driver looked in the mirror, impassive, tired probably.

"What would you do if you found out you had just a few years to live? Say, four or five years. Just four years maybe, and as much money as you needed?"

The driver grunted, half amused, half dismissive. They pulled up at a light on Memorial Boulevard. A solitary pickup crossed their path and headed downtown.

"How much money we talkin'?" he said at last.

"Plenty. No object."

"No object? You mean like a million dollars?"

The driver glanced up towards the East Side. It was the classy side of town, sure enough—all that white clapboard history and Ivy League grandeur—but it wasn't Millionaires' Row. Not by a long shot.

"Five million. Ten million. Say ten if you like."

The light turned green. The cab made a slow right turn, one wheel spinning for an instant as they hit the gradient.

The driver chuckled. "Man, if I had ten million dollars I know what I'd do."

"So tell me," said Eliot, keeping his eyes on the mirror.

"I'd do just *exactly* what the hell I wanted."

Margaret had left a light on outside the front door, but the rest of the ground floor was in darkness. Eliot tossed his keys into the rosewood bowl and was halfway across the hall when he heard her voice coming from upstairs.

"Michael? Michael, is that you?"

Weariness. Reproach. Shading towards anger. She'd probably been asleep. The creak of a floorboard was enough to wake her, and in this old house all the floorboards creaked.

"Yes, it's me."

"What time is it?"

She knew what time it was. She just wanted him to say it.

"Two o'clock." He didn't want to talk. Not now. Not to her. "Big data loss problem. At the office. Just had to stay till we sorted it out."

"Are you coming to bed?"

He walked to the foot of the stairs. "There's something I have to do first. I'll be up in a minute."

He could see her shadow on the wall of the landing. He heard her sigh. Then the shadow was gone.

He walked into his study and slumped down behind the desk. The alcohol was still buzzing in his head, but as he sat there in the half darkness, surrounded by the too familiar clutter of his life—books he'd never read, pictures he'd years ago tired of looking at, antique furniture for an antique house—he began to feel a strange sense of detachment, of calm. There was nothing here to hold him back. He'd thought about changing his life a thousand times. He'd dreamt about it. The world had so much more to offer than a view from the ninth floor, dreary corporate bonhomie, fifty hours a week behind a desk. He'd dreamt of sweeping it all away and starting again. But he'd never done anything about it, at least nothing serious. He'd been afraid of the consequences, afraid that if he broke the rules they'd make him pay. Sooner or later.

He reached into his jacket and pulled out the small bundle of papers he had stuffed into his pocket. They were computer printouts: horizontal stripes of pale green and white, like the ones in Tate's office. Eliot unfolded them. On each page were columns of numbers and letters. One of the numbers on the first sheet had been circled in red.

There had been a moment in Tate's office, about half an hour before Eliot left, when things had suddenly become clear, when suddenly he knew what he wanted. And he understood in that moment that he would have to act quickly. Because some people were going to be very unhappy when they got word. Tate had been out of the room, taking a leak, already half drunk. That was when Eliot had reached into one of his files and stolen the printouts. Of course, it would only be a matter of time before Tate noticed they were missing. He would put it all together and realize who'd taken them. But by then it would be too late. Besides, they'd been good friends once. Maybe he would understand.

Eliot folded up the printouts and put them away in the bottom drawer of his desk. Then he checked his watch. Half past two in the morning. That meant half past eight in Europe. There'd be someone at the bank at half past eight.

He picked up the phone and dialed. After three rings a woman answered. Eliot asked to be put through to the private client department. For a moment he listened to electronic silence. Then a man's voice. They exchanged a few words of greeting. Eliot identified himself, then gave his instruction.

"Liquidate my holdings," he said. "That's right, the full ten million."

PART ONE

TRUSTING TO PROVIDENCE

1

"Two hundred and thirty-nine dollars," said Ferulli, pulling a crumpled envelope out of the glove compartment. "Can you believe it?"

Alexandra Tynan took the envelope. CENTRALIZED INFRACTIONS BUREAU was stamped in bold black letters above the Hartford address. She pulled out the ticket and frowned.

"Monkey couldn't even write," Ferulli said.

But the numbers were clear enough. Scrawled across the Amount Due box: $239. Alex looked up at Ferulli and smiled. "Probably your attitude."

"I come over the top of a hill doing—what? seventy?"

"Says seventy-eight here, sir. Posted limit was fifty-five. You're doing sixty now."

He eased off the accelerator. They were traveling north on the I-95, skimming through the industrial estates south of Providence. It was the first working day after New Year and just above freezing. Heavy snow was forecast for the afternoon.

"Okay, doing seventy-eight. The road is—Alex, it's *empty*. Conditions are perfect. Jesus Christ, I'm about to cross the state line into Massachusetts where the limit is sixty-five. The cop is hiding on the other side of the hill and as I go past, wham, he zaps me with his ray gun."

They came off at exit twenty, and he had to brake hard for a red light. He looked across at her, appealing for justice with his nice-guy smile. Mark Ferulli was in his mid-thirties, with a head of thick dark hair, Sicilian hair he called it, and looks that verged on film-star handsome. His eyes made Alex think of Al Pacino, lightless eyes, steady and probing. When he smiled, laugh lines made them warm and sympathetic, but sometimes, like now for example, Alex thought they were like a politician's—sincere, full of humanity, but too watchful somehow, as though looking for the right reaction or an advantage. She smiled back at him in spite of herself. Maybe he was annoyed about the ticket, but she could see that he was also rather pleased—certainly not too worried about being thought reckless. It was just like him, the stupidity very much his own brand, but Alex found it attractive nonetheless. In the context of Providence Life, the company that paid them their salaries, the company they were racing towards, Mark's naughtiness was like a breath of fresh air.

"I'm not saying I wasn't going a little fast," he said. "But two hundred and thirty-nine dollars?"

Alex tapped the steering wheel with the envelope. "So this is turning out to be quite an expensive purchase."

Just how much he had paid for the car she had yet to find out. He had said good-bye to her on Christmas Eve the driver of a two-year-old Toyota, and reappeared on New Year's Day behind the wheel of a brand-new BMW convertible. He told her he had driven up from New Jersey with the roof down, his cheeks flaming, a smile stretching from ear to ear—like a kid with a new bike, he had said it himself. Alex knew the parents hadn't bought it for him. Mark's father drove a delivery van for DHL and his mom boxed Oreos for Nabisco.

The lights changed and Mark gunned the engine, pulling away from the intersection with a squeal of tires.

"So are you going to tell me?" Alex insisted.

He checked the rearview mirror, and smiled. "Tell you what?"

"How much?"

"Alex"—he looked across at her—"does it always have to be numbers with you? Do you even realize that it always comes down to numbers?"

Alex pushed out her bottom lip in a faked sulk. She knew she was a number nut, so there was nothing she could say.

"You know what Bernard Shaw said about actuaries?" he said, turning back to the road. "He said they were people who knew the price of everything and the value of nothing."

"It was Wilde, actually, as in Oscar. And he said that about accountants."

Mark shrugged. "Actuaries, accountants, what's the difference?"

There was a big difference, as Mark by now ought to understand. In the twelve months they had been going out, Alex had certainly explained it often enough. To her way of thinking, accountants were no more than bean counters, following their clients through the fiscal maze, flagging faux pas and giving advice. There weren't that many accountants she knew who could stomach the math involved in her daily routine. Calculus, probability, statistics. It ground people down. That was why there were only ten thousand actuaries in the whole of the U.S. Alex herself had majored in math at MIT and had started out wanting a job on Wall Street, seeing herself in financial engineering maybe, a wire-head in some department where she could apply her modeling skills. But stories of burnout and ruthless employers had put her off. A summer job at John Hancock in Boston had opened her eyes to the benefits of actuarial work: entry level salaries in the high thirties and, after five years of hard work, election to the Society of Actuaries with remuneration heading towards six figures. But it wasn't just the math that set actuaries apart. Actuaries were . . .

Alex looked up at the sky, her eyes reflecting the solid gray overhead. She had eyes the color of wet slate, and eyebrows and lashes that were naturally dark—surprising in someone otherwise so blond. The brows crimped a little now as she tried to think what it was that made her profession unlike any other.

"Death," she said after a moment.

"What's that?"

Mark put his foot down to beat the lights on Exchange Street. He was going way too fast. A truck pulling out of a side street lurched to a halt as they sped by.

Death in all its forms, thought Alex, seeing now, despite her efforts to shut him out of her mind, Michael Eliot. He had planted a boozy kiss on her mouth at the ProvLife office party less than two weeks earlier, and now he was dead, his mouth closed forever.

Mark nudged her with his shoulder. "Come on, sweetheart, lighten up. I was only kiddin' ya."

Alex leaned forward and pushed the envelope back into the glove compartment.

"You're going to kill somebody with your new toy," she said matter-of-factly.

"You gotta loin to take a joke," he said, lapsing into broad New Jersey. "Talkin' of which—"

"Which which?"

"Of jokeses, beeby." He worked himself deeper into his seat, getting set to deliver the punch line. "What's the difference between an introverted actuary and an extroverted actuary?" he asked.

Not missing a beat, Alex said: "An extroverted actuary looks at *your* shoes."

"Damn! You already—"

"I *know* them all."

The kid appeared out of nowhere.

One minute they were looking at open road, and the next a kid on a red mountain bike flashed out from the sidewalk, pedaling like a maniac. Mark yanked the wheel, but it was too late to do anything. The kid's right hand slapped the windshield and was gone—a name bracelet or signet ring made a hard sound against the glass.

"Jesus Christ!"

Mark braked, lost control of the car for a split second, and slammed up onto the sidewalk, where they slewed to a halt. Horns blared as cars swerved to avoid them.

Miraculously they were okay.

"Jesus!"

Alex's heart was pounding. "Did we hit him?" she said. "Did we kill him?"

Without saying a word Mark climbed out of the car. People had stopped on the sidewalk, where a trash can was over on its side. An old man pointed up a side street and said something to Mark she couldn't hear. When he came back to the car Alex could see that he was badly shaken up, the relief at not having killed somebody turning to anger.

"Jesus. Did you see that? He just—"

"It was *your* fault," said Alex. She was trembling despite her efforts to keep control. "You were going too fast to—to react. You always want to . . ."

She clutched at her heart and was surprised to find that she wasn't really angry but instead exhausted, drained. It was the news of Eliot's death. It had knocked her out of kilter. Her emotions weren't lining up properly.

"Are you okay?" said Mark. He was pale and there were beads of moisture on his top lip in spite of the cold.

Alex raised an eyebrow. "Sure, I'm just having my first heart attack. You know, the one that thirty percent of people don't survive?"

She waited for him to get back into the car. For a moment they sat in silence, listening to the traffic go past. There was a smear on the windshield where the kid's hand had hit. Alex hoped they hadn't hurt him.

"Mark?"

Jolted out of his thoughts by her voice, Mark leaned across and kissed her on the cheek. His mouth was cold from the outside air. "What is it?"

"Do you think he suffered?"

For a moment he looked confused. Alex squeezed his hand.

"Michael Eliot, I mean. Do you think, when . . ."

But she couldn't finish. She had only heard the news on New Year's Eve. There had been a terrible accident a few days earlier. Michael Eliot had drilled into a live cable while putting up shelves at home. He had been killed on the spot. Electrocuted.

"Listen, Alex, I . . ."

Again Alex squeezed his hand, trying to show him that she didn't need consoling. And it was true: she had only known Michael Eliot at work, never socially. She certainly wasn't ready to admit that, for a time, she had thought about something more. In any case she'd never done anything about it. When Eliot had kissed her at the office party—it was just under two weeks ago now, the last time she had seen him, in fact— she had been shocked, confused. And it was shock she felt now, not really grief or even sadness. Shock at the suddenness of it, the finality.

"It's terrible, I know," said Mark. "Just—ridiculous. But there you go." He shook his head. "That's life. I mean, it's the kind of ridiculous thing that happens all the time."

Alex pushed a tear away with the heel of her palm. "Five-point-seven percent of the time, actually. I mean, if we're talking electrocutions as a fraction of household accidental fatalities."

Mark blinked and tried to smile, but he could see she was not joking.

The headquarters of Providence Life stood on the corner of Dorrance and Westminster in the heart of downtown Providence. Like much of the city, the building had taken its lead from Europe—in this case the ponderous sobriety of the Medici palaces in Florence. But where load-bearing walls had obliged the Medicis to stop after a couple of floors, here the architect had kept on stacking, piling floor upon floor until he reached the twelfth, where he topped the whole thing off with a flourish of elaborately carved stonework.

Ronald P. Macintyre loved the old building. He had been with the company since the great flood of '38 and, like the brass plaque commemorating that event at the main entrance, he had seen better times. Over the years he had been pushed sideways a little by the introduction of dedicated cleaning and maintenance and security staff, yet he was still always the first to arrive in the morning. Newcomers to ProvLife puzzled over what it was Mac actually did for the firm, but pretty soon they got tired of trying to work it out—he turned up in so many places doing so many things—and accepted that, whatever it was, it had something to do with the mail room, the air conditioning, and an ancient but still functional boiler reputed to be in the basement.

When Alex Tynan came across the parking lot dabbing at her eyes, it was Mac who came out a side door to greet her. He put down the box of files he was carrying.

"Alexandra! Happy New— Say, are you all right?"

Alex did her best to smile.

"You're pale," said Mac. "You look like you've seen a ghost."

Alex touched her cheek. It *felt* hot. "Oh, I don't know. I . . . I could be better, I guess."

She blew her nose into a ragged Kleenex, and took in Mac's weather-beaten face. He had a streak of soot on his forehead and a cobweb across the front of his circa-1952 buzz cut. A plastic mask containing a scrap of kitchen towel hung from a frayed piece of elastic around his wattled neck. For a moment Alex considered getting into a conversation about Eliot's death, but then thought better of it. She didn't know what Mac knew, and didn't feel up to breaking such momentous news.

"Had a near miss coming in," she said. "Nothing serious. I'm a little shaken up."

Mac pressed his lips together, squinting. "It's that old heap of yours," he said. "I told you about that taillight."

Mac had been trying to persuade her to get rid of her '85 Camry for years. Alex claimed the car had sentimental value, but the truth was, with all the debt she was still carrying, she couldn't afford to replace it.

"It wasn't the taillight, Mac. I had that fixed last month. Anyway, I got a ride in with Mark."

Mac looked past her and narrowed his eyes at Ferulli, who was taking an attaché case out of the trunk of the BMW. He didn't like Ferulli. Once a good-looking young man himself, Mac didn't trust good-looking young men, and he had seen the way Ferulli was with the secretaries in the treasury department. In Mac's view Ferulli was overly familiar.

"I see," he said. "You have to be extra careful in those sporty jobs. Specially with the roads so bad and all."

This was said good and loud, mainly for Mark's benefit as he ducked in through the front door with a brisk good-morning. Mark knew exactly how Mac felt about him, and dealt with it by giving him a wide berth. Alex looked down at the box of files, trying to hide her smile.

"So what is it today? F?"

For the past few weeks Mac and a team of rawboned schoolkids had been engaged in removing old files from the basement and sending them off to a data storage company at Iron Mountain in Massachusetts. ProvLife had gone digital in the late eighties and was only now dealing with the problem of the old paper records. It was slow, dirty work, and Mac was hating it. To make matters worse, the company was taking the opportunity to strip out some asbestos insulation while the basement was in such a mess. Serious men in full face masks went to and fro with large plastic containers, treating the material like it was radioactive waste, and telling Mac and his team when they could or could *not* enter.

"If only," said Mac peevishly. "We're still on E. E today and for the rest of the week. Ebbsworth through Eyot via Ewing and all points East.

Old carbons, rotting dossiers, dusty box files. And it all has to be logged. I'll be glad when it's over."

"Oh well."

Alex started to back away. Once started, conversations with Mac were difficult to break off. Alex knew that, for Mac, the casual chitchat that punctuated the working day was the whole point of coming in. He had often said to her that people in the company used to have more time for each other. It was different in the old days, more friendly.

She found the seventh floor empty. In the galley kitchen next to the fire escape she set the coffee machine going and watched for a minute as the aromatic brown liquid started to drip through the filter.

The memory of the kiss kept coming back to her. She'd been about to go home—had just collected her coat, in fact—when Eliot had walked in, probably from another function somewhere else. She must have betrayed a flash of interest without meaning to, because he'd come right over. And before she could say anything, she'd felt his lips on her mouth, his hand sliding around her waist. It had taken her a moment just to realize what was happening. And then he was looking at her, smiling, as if that was all the communication they needed. As if they already understood each other. It was a look he had given her before, even as they'd exchanged small talk in elevators and corridors.

Back at her desk she shuffled papers for a while, struggling to get stuck into work that wasn't in truth very urgent. The last few weeks had been a slack time for her altogether. She had finished her last set of actuarial exams in November and had until February before she started preparing for May's. In the meantime she was supposed to be working on a set of industry healthcare figures, modifying them to fit the profile of ProvLife's target customers. It was a peripheral part of a much bigger project: after a century of offering only individual life insurance policies, ProvLife was considering the big step into healthcare coverage. If this step was ever taken—and the board were said to be split on the issue—it would represent a huge change in the size and scope of the company's operations. In the meantime a pilot plan had just been set up, the customers in this instance being ProvLife staff and their families. Everyone had been encouraged to participate, to apply just as a regular member of the public would, right down to the filling in of application forms. The plan was supposed to give the company a feel for the extra administrative and analytical needs involved. The only difference from the real thing, besides the number of policies being written, was that ProvLife was paying the premiums.

The man in charge of selling the plan internally had been Alex's head of department, Randal White. White was ProvLife's "Illustration Actuary"—a giver of light where there would otherwise be darkness. He signed off on all the company's projections and forward planning, using data both from ProvLife itself and from the industry as a whole in its various reports and studies. ProvLife prided itself on its underwriting abilities—knowing which risks to avoid and which to embrace— abilities that it employed in writing policies worth anything from $5 million all the way down to $25,000. And since the company's underwriting strategy, products, and marketing were based on the validity of its actuarial projections, Randal White was a man of considerable importance. Richard Goebert, the company's chief executive officer, a man who liked to make jokes and was not above repeating them, was apt to say that the company did not trust to Providence, it trusted to Randal White.

Not surprisingly, White's influence went beyond the actuarial department. He was one of only three executive directors besides Goebert on ProvLife's twelve-man board, the others being Walter Neumann, the senior legal counsel, and Newton T. Brady, who headed up Finance. There was a rumor in the actuarial department that once Goebert decided to retire, White would be moving into his office with its immense balcony—the papal balcony, it was jokingly called—that gave onto nothingness eight floors above Westminster Street.

Sipping her coffee, Alex clicked the e-mail icon on her screen and was surprised to see that there was in fact a message. For a moment she had an eerie feeling that Eliot might have mailed her from the other side. She gave herself a shake. She was being silly. The poor man was dead, that was all. She called up the message.

$$$Fifty-one thousand dollars!$$$

It was simple and to the point. Smiling, shaking her head, Alex punched in Mark's number.

"I do not believe you."

"So, don't believe me."

"I do *not* believe you."

"Okay."

"Mark, that's a lot of money."

"It's a lot of car, baby."

"But—but"—the words wouldn't come—"you can't afford it."

"Well, I am affording it, clearly."

Alex blinked. She didn't know all the numbers, but she guessed the IRS let Mark keep around fifty thousand a year. He already had commitments: a house in Cranston, a houseful of furniture. Add to that a couple of decent vacations every year—Mark liked scuba diving, so it had to be the Caribbean—and there wasn't a lot left.

"But how?"

"Sweetheart, as I've been saying to you for the past few weeks if you ever once listened, things are going pretty well for me up here in the engine room."

For Mark the treasury department was where ProvLife did its real business.

"Yes, but—"

"Newton has been very—" He whispered into the mouthpiece. "Alex, I have received *encouragement.*"

"Yeah, but to go out and splurge that kind of cash on a—"

"You're not hearing me, Alex. I'm saying specific kinds of encouragement."

Alex pushed back against her chair, listening more closely now. "What do you mean?"

"We have talked about my . . . advancement."

"Promotion?"

"Spelled S-V-P." He spoke the initials as though savoring each one individually.

"Senior vice president?" Alex's eyes grew wider. "Mark, I don't believe it. I mean, how?" She clapped her hand to her mouth, realization dawning. "My God. You don't mean—you're not taking—?"

Mark laughed softly.

"But he only died a few days ago," whispered Alex. Her mind was racing, trying to make sense of it all. A horrible thought occurred. "Mark, when did you buy the car?"

There was a long pause and then Mark said: "Right after I killed

Eliot, of course." Again he laughed. "Come on, don't be ridiculous. And no, to answer your question, I'm not stepping directly into the dead man's shoes, but I . . . I mean, I don't know what's going to happen. All I'm saying is I had an interesting talk with Newton a couple of weeks back, and he said should any openings come up he would want to talk to me about what I felt I could offer the company, et cetera, et cetera. I mean, at the time it was, as I say, just encouragement, but now . . ."

Alex's shoulders dropped.

"Oh, *Mark*. Aren't you being a little overoptimistic? I mean, they can't want you to run the whole treasury department. Not yet. That's a lot of responsibility."

There was a moment of complete silence.

"Mark, are you still there?"

"I'm still here."

Alex wondered if she had said the wrong thing. She hadn't meant to imply that he wasn't up to the job. It was just that it seemed so unlikely. She tried to make light of the issue.

"Well, if you're up in the fast lane, all I can say is: make sure you sign up for the company healthcare plan."

"Pardon me?"

"I'm thinking of all the extra stress. And that damned car. I'd say it's a classic profile for an early heart attack."

"I seem to remember *you* were the one having the heart attack."

"No, but it'll come. Just give it time. Avoid salty foods is my advice."

"I can't believe you have so little faith in me." Mark's voice was tight, almost angry. The fragile male ego. "Look, I have to go now."

"Mark, I—"

But it was too late, he'd hung up.

Alex called right back. A cool, velvety voice answered, which Alex recognized at once as belonging to Catherine Pell, the newest addition to the treasury department. Alex stiffened in her chair. Catherine had only been with the company for a month, but already everyone knew exactly who she was. Even Brian Slater, the nerdiest of the number crunchers in the actuarial department, had registered her arrival. It wasn't that she was especially pretty or curvaceous, or even bright; she possessed an intangible quality that it was hard to call anything other than *class*. It was there in the way she dressed, the way she did her hair, the way she carried herself. Next to her Alex felt like a hick. Add to

that the fact that the Pells were one of the oldest and most distinguished families in the state, and you were looking at a formidable
package—certainly not one the workaday world of the Providence Mutual Life Insurance Company was used to. Alex just wished the new
recruit hadn't landed a desk a few feet away from Mark's.

"I'm sorry, Alexandra," said the voice. "Mark isn't available at the moment. He's in a meeting."

"In a meeting?"

"With Newton Brady."

"Well, if it's not too much trouble, would you have him call me?"

"Surely."

Alex put the phone down and stared at it for a moment. She wondered what Mark thought of Catherine. He had been suspiciously silent
on the subject. Then she wondered what Catherine thought of Mark.
And what she would think of his new car. . . .

People started to arrive. There was a good deal of hushed talk about
Michael Eliot. At nine-thirty a memo came around from Goebert in-
forming everyone officially of what had taken place. It said that Michael
Eliot had been a consummate professional, and popular with all his colleagues. "In one sense or another we deal with death every day of our
professional lives," it rambled on, "but when it touches one of our own,
we feel it keenly."

When Alex called Mark at eleven o'clock, she was relieved to get
Kelly Davidson. She had been at school with Kelly, a person of size, as
the expression went, and one of the few serious smokers left in the
company. They talked briefly about Eliot's death.

"God, you can imagine what it's like up here," said Kelly. "It's like—
well, like somebody *died*. Newton came in this morning and his face
was *white*, I swear. I've never seen him look so upset. Liz hasn't even
called in."

Alex put her hand to her forehead. She was supposed to be having
lunch with Liz Foster, and she had completely forgotten about it.

"She's not in?"

"Nope. Catherine's taking her calls. I guess Liz must have heard the
news and is just too shaken up. It's understandable, I guess, her being
his personal assistant and everything."

"I guess that's right. I hadn't really—it hadn't really crossed my
mind."

"You knew Michael, didn't you? I mean—"

"No, not really," Alex said. "Well, you know. He came down to the department occasionally. I—I still can't believe it. I mean I just can't take it in."

"It's kind of eerie. A life company with a sudden death in it. Did you read Mr. Goebert's memo?"

Alex frowned. Kelly had a tendency to see patterns behind things, significance. It was extremely irritating to someone who was paid to contemplate chaos and impose her own, testable, meanings.

"Is Mark there?" she said.

"No, I'm afraid not. He's in with Newton Brady."

"He can't be. I called an hour ago and he was already in with Brady. What are they doing in there?"

"I don't know. He's been in and out of Newton's office all morning. Neumann went in a few minutes ago. I don't know what *he* wants." Kelly said *"Neumann"* as if she were saying the Slime Creature from the Black Lagoon. Everybody hated Neumann.

"Oh well. Just say I called."

Alex hung up and sat for a while thinking about Mark and about what he had said. It took her five minutes to start feeling bad. It had been wrong of her to scoff. Why shouldn't he be considered for promotion? And now he was too busy to answer her calls.

They were at a stage in their relationship—a year together, and going along pretty nicely, having fun—when an obvious next step had started to loom. Not marriage. Neither of them was contemplating that. Alex was only twenty-five and did not feel ready for sacramental vows, while Mark at thirty-four was used to being single. Alex and her cat, Oscar, lived on the top floor of a run-down clapboard house on Phillips Street about a mile from Brown. The lease was going to run out in two months and she had the option to renew it at a higher rent—a rent she couldn't really afford—or let it go. Mark knew all about this and for a while now had been talking up the merits of Cranston, saying how fashionable it was becoming, how much more fun than the stuffy East Side. An obvious question was in the air: should Alex move in? The approaching deadline had made them look at each other more closely than had so far been necessary. Inevitably, faults had been discovered, and Alex had found herself slipping into a pattern of hypercriticism followed by bouts of remorse. It was a pattern she knew well. It had destroyed at least two of her steady relationships. And here she was doing it again.

"You look as though you're being touched keenly."

It was Mel Hartman. He was one of the new intake, a mathematics wizard who obviously thought he was quite something. He had started hitting on her from day one.

"Pardon me?"

Alex stared at a tiny stain on his tie. Every morning Mel ate the pancake hi-stack around the corner in Gino's. Lots of maple syrup. Lots of butter. Alex had seen him do it.

"The memo, did you see it?"

"Sure. Yes."

"I love corporate expressions of grief, don't you?" Mel raised an eyebrow.

Alex realized she was supposed to be savoring his keen sense of irony. She found herself unable to smile.

"Hey, lighten up."

Alex stood. "Excuse me, Mel."

She stalked through to the staff bathroom. *Lighten up.* Everybody kept telling her to lighten up. Was she really so damned humorless? She tried a smile in the mirror, a warm smile full of humor, then stared at her green wool jacket. It was a pretty humorless jacket, that much she had to recognize. She slipped it off and hung it on the back of the door. Her pullover was gray, and so thick it dropped from her throat down to her hips in one flat block of cable stitch. And underneath she wasn't that bad. A little skinny maybe—Rosemary before she had the baby, Mark sometimes joked. She was considering what changes she might make in her wardrobe when she had an idea.

She chuckled all the way back to her desk. Lighten up? She would show them. She would show *Mark*. She tapped into the wealth of statistics put out by the Casualty Actuarial Society, and quickly established that 4.2% of the insured population owned convertibles or sports coupés. That was four people in a hundred—men, of course, most of them—picking up speeding tickets, knocking kids off their bicycles. She started to pull up statistics, trying to relate convertibles to untimely death. How hard could it be? You had a convertible, you drove too fast, you had accidents. You cut across other drivers, your girlfriend's hair blowing in the wind, provoking the guys in the saloons into fits of un-

controllable rage. They forced you off the road and shot you through
the heart. Or they forced you off the road, causing you to roll the car,
and you were decapitated along with the blonde. And then there was
pollution. You were lower than all the Broncos and Cherokees and
Rams—exposed to the air, breathing in all that lead. Brain tumors, lung
cancer, not to mention the sun and melanomas, and the heart attacks
from all the near misses. Loving her numbers, Alex tweaked and nudged,
cross-referred and braided. When company data wasn't enough, she
got onto the Internet, tapping into the property/casualty companies,
the actuarial clubs, the consumer groups, the manufacturers.

Humming softly, she gazed through the window of her computer at
a rising storm of bad luck. She was delighted by all the surprises. Of
guys dying in Mark's age group, 18% were being murdered. Almost one
in five. More people were murdered than died of cancer. Of course the
big C would start to kick in higher up the age curve. But down here in
the foothills of maturity, murder killed more people than anything else
apart from road accidents and—Alex smiled—*heart attacks*. According
to the biggest studies, heart attacks were responsible for one death
in five. This was surprising in itself. Thirty-something was young to be
dying of a heart attack. There was obviously a manufacturing fault
somewhere, probably a bum gene. Those pumps were just unreliable.

Alex leaned back in her chair and sipped at what was now cold coffee. It was time to get specific, narrow things down. Softtops and heart
attacks. She liked the sound of that. The two were of course completely
unconnected, but that was the beauty of it. Somehow she would *make*
a connection, like a conjurer pulling rabbits from a hat.

For the next step she turned to the most detailed records: ProvLife's
data on its own claimants. These she broke down by cause of death,
checking each category to see whether convertible ownership among
the victims was higher than the magic 4.2%. That was all she needed. If
more than 4.2% of murder victims owned convertibles then she would
be able to claim that, according to the numbers, owning a convertible
meant you were more likely to be murdered. And the same thing
would apply to heart attack victims. All she had to do was find the right
period—one year, two years, five years—or the right category by age or
sex. It wouldn't be the truth, of course. But it wouldn't be exactly a lie
either. As a claim, it would exist in the no-man's-land between people's

insatiable desire for hard information and their ability to fully under-stand it—a surprisingly well populated area, in Alex's experience. She would send her results straight to Mark via e-mail. She didn't expect him to roll around on the floor. But maybe by poking fun at her profession, at herself, she might get a smile out of him, make him forget what an idiot she could be sometimes.

It proved to be tricky. The Central Records computer seemed reluctant to play along with something so frivolous. When she finally fooled it into cooperating, the result was disappointing. For some reason—i.e., no reason—the effects were purely random. Cancer victims were a little less likely than the population as a whole to own a convertible. The same thing went for suicides. People who died in air crashes were slightly more likely to have sporty cars, but that wasn't much help. As for heart attack victims—Alex's first choice—they were right on the average for the population as a whole: 4.2% of heart attack victims drove convertibles. Frowning, Alex tweaked the time parameters, breaking the numbers down by year and going back over six years. A row of numbers flickered on the screen: 4.2%, 4.2%, 4.2%, 4.2%, 4.2%, 4.2%.

At first she thought there was something wrong with her screen. Such consistency, year on year, between figures that were in reality un-related was a virtual impossibility in a field of its size. She switched the monitor off and on again, but the numbers didn't change. The mistake was obviously hers. She backtracked, making a note of the databases she was sourcing, ran through the whole analysis again. But there it was: the same string of impossible numbers. According to Central Records, 4.2% of ProvLife's heart attack victims owned convertibles—*every* year.

Alex frowned, her fingers tapping at the edge of the desk. There was a glitch somewhere in Central Records, but how big a glitch? She went back into suicides. Over the ten-year period the figure for convertibles rose and fell just as she would have expected: 3.1%, 5.4%, 4.0% . . .

"Damn."

She was about to start over when the phone rang. It was Liz Foster. Alex checked her watch. Twelve-thirty. Lunch! She had been so en-grossed in the numbers, she'd lost track of the time.

"Liz, my God. I'm so sorry. Liz?"

"Yeah. Sorry for what?"

"Lunch. We were supposed to be having lunch. I completely—"

"Well, that's why I'm calling. I wanted to tell you I can't make it. I'm not coming in."

"Oh, right. Okay. You okay?"

There was a long silence, and then the sound of crying.

"Liz, honey?"

"Yeah, yes. I'm still here. I just . . ."

"It's all right, sugar. I understand."

"Understand what?"

"Well, about Michael. It must be real hard, working so close with someone and then—"

Suddenly Liz was weeping into the phone—openly, excessively it seemed to Alex, sobbing, struggling to catch her breath. "I'm sorry," she managed to blurt out. "I'm so sorry. It's just that—it's just that—" But she couldn't go on. Again she wept.

Alex looked around the office at the other actuaries. They were all bent over their work. It occurred to her that Liz might have had a crush on Michael Eliot. It wasn't uncommon for assistants to form close relationships with their bosses. Late nights working in the office, trying to meet deadlines, wives that didn't really understand the pressures. And Eliot hadn't been the kind of man to discourage flirtations. Alex knew that from her own experience.

"Do you want me to come over?" she said.

"Would . . . would you? I'd really appreciate it. I need to talk to someone."

"About Michael?"

"About everything."

2

Donald Grant walked into the autopsy room as if he owned the place. Slipping out of his overcoat, he dropped it onto one of the clean steel tables and parked himself on a stool three feet from where Sally Rudnick, the county medical examiner, was at work. She raised her head and eyebrows in answer to his greeting, but didn't interrupt her quiet for-the-record monotone.

"*. . . lividity unfixed and found primarily on the posterior body surfaces. Cyanosis absent. No sign of peripheral edema. Personal hygiene good.*"

Grant was in his early fifties and had a boyish, flushed face with bloodshot eyes that were a striking cornflower blue. A deep scar on his left temple looked as if whatever had caused it should have killed him. It made you wonder what those blue eyes had seen before he left security work and became ProvLife's chief claims investigator. In the office it was generally assumed that he had a military or police background—he certainly dressed like a G-man—but outside of the board and his own small investigations team, nobody had ever found occasion to ask. All most people knew was that he'd run a small security firm in the Boston area until Walter Neumann brought him on board in '84.

Grant lit a cigarette and watched Rudnick work, taking in her narrow shoulders and broad hips. He could see Michael Eliot's right foot, a blue tag on the big toe.

"Cold this morning, Sally."

"Yes, it is." Rudnick's head hunched down a little more. She didn't like Grant, and Grant knew it. *"Body hair of normal male distribution. Pupils are round, regular, equal, and contracted."*

She moved, exposing more of the body, and Grant shifted on his stool. He let out a low whistle. "Jesus Christ," he said.

"What is it?"

"Guy was hung like a friggin' donkey."

Rudnick stopped and snapped off the recorder. She turned to look at him from behind highly polished schoolmarm spectacles. "If you don't mind, Mr. Grant, I'm trying to do my job here."

"I'm sorry. It's just—"

She turned back to her work, pulling a light-pencil from her top pocket. "How much do you owe?" she said coolly, looking into one of Eliot's dead eyes.

"What's that, Sal?"

"Doctor Rudnick will be fine. How much does ProvLife owe? You know you never come down here unless the company's trying to worm out of paying up."

Grant massaged his throat. "Come on, Sally. I'm just doing my job, same as you."

"That's the tragic thing."

He took a long pull on his cigarette. It was cool in the room, but still warmer than outside. Rudnick was in a particularly bad mood. Grant watched her work and considered the spectacle of the dead man's body. He wondered what the hookers had thought about Eliot's generous endowment, then decided that it probably made no difference to them. Eliot had often made visits to the Holiday Inn after work. Since the construction of the convention center in the heart of Providence there had been no shortage of professionals around town. They did good business servicing the dentists and lawyers and salesmen, and they'd done good business servicing Michael Eliot. The Holiday Inn was right next to the convention center. Both were no more than five minutes' walk from the ProvLife headquarters.

Rudnick examined the inside of Eliot's mouth and waxed technical. Eliot had bitten into his left cheek in his dying convulsion. A tissue flap as big as a quarter was attached only by a hinge of delicate mucosal lining. He'd cracked a molar, biting down.

The face, Grant could see, was still distorted by the pain. Muscles stood out in the cheeks. Nothing would ever relax them. Grant tried to imagine what it must be like, being lit up like a Christmas tree, not being able to let go.

Rudnick stepped back from the table.

"Two hundred thousand dollars," said Grant matter-of-factly. "Standard in-house policy. The wife gets the money."

Rudnick nodded. "Well, you may as well get in touch with your bankers. Because this here's an accidental electrocution."

"Yeah, how can you be so sure, doc?"

She sniffed. "How can I be sure? Oh, years of experience. Half a dozen similar cases. Don't you remember that guy last year, the dentist?"

Grant just stared.

"You should. He cost you half a million, as I recall. Did the exact same thing. You came sniffing around then too."

"I did, huh?"

Rudnick shook her head in disgust. "You know you did. But you still had to pay up. Because it was an accident." She held up the corpse's limp right hand. "See that mark?"

Grant leaned forward and squinted at the yellow-gray elevated area of skin around a dry-looking lesion on the cheek of Eliot's thumb. He nodded.

"That's where he was holding the drill. That's where he took the shock."

"Oh yeah? You seen the drill?"

Rudnick cracked a sad, coffee-stained smile. "Of course not. I make all this stuff up."

She pointed across the room at a bench where a small metal power drill was wrapped in a plastic bag. Grant got up and walked over to it.

"What I don't understand is how you can be so suspicious of one of your own," she said to his back. "I mean, the average person, maybe—your clients, the people who pay the premiums, the people who pay your salaries—*obviously* you're going to want to screw them, that's what insurance companies do. But this guy? I mean, he was high up in the company. You knew him, right?"

"Sure."

"So, doesn't it feel a bit like cannibalism?"

"We're not eating him, Sally. We're just making sure—we just want to be sure that everything was kosher. We always do."

Rudnick put her gloved hands on her hips and turned. "You're saying you have reason to think he might have wanted to commit suicide?"

Grant picked up the bag with the drill. "His home life wasn't great. I know that."

"What does that mean, exactly?"

Grant shrugged. Rudnick looked at him steadily, making no effort to hide her contempt.

"I see," she said finally. "Well, all I can say is, if you want to commit suicide, there are plenty of easier ways."

Grant nodded slowly. "Easier, maybe. But not necessarily so accidental-looking."

Rudnick sighed.

"Looks old," said Grant, waving the drill at her.

"Circa 1960. Company went bust years ago. The insulation was shot. It's no wonder it killed him." She was holding a scalpel now, preparing to make the first Y-incision. "Sorry, Grant. From where I'm standing, ProvLife's gonna have to pay up."

There was a long silence. Rudnick drew in a breath and held it.

Grant usually turned away at the first cut. He could take the dismembered bodies, but the first broad slice from shoulder to sternum, the surprising revelation of the *inside*, the violation of the body—these things disturbed him. But this time he stayed. He stayed to watch as Michael Eliot, senior vice president, family man, pillar of the community, and whore chaser, lost his heart and lungs.

It was freezing outside. Wispy flakes of snow spiraled out of a gray sky. Grant pulled his lapels up around his throat and looked for the Pontiac. As he reached the bottom of the steps it came along the street and drifted to a halt.

Grant climbed in and shut the door. The lights had failed at the end of the street and a cop was directing the traffic.

"How'd it go?" said the driver, a slim man with sunken eyes and a bad complexion.

Grant made an O with his forefinger and thumb.

"Perfect," he said.

3

Liz's apartment was only a mile from the office on the other side of the interstate. It was an area of large, boxy clapboard houses packed together on badly swept streets, with yards neither in front nor back and windows that looked onto each other across narrow alleys of perpetual shadow. Built in the 1880s and 1890s to accommodate the sprawling families of Providence's new professional middle class, it was the kind of area that the lace curtain and the venetian blind were made for. Of course, the new middle class had long since become the old middle class and moved up to the East Side or out to the suburbs, but Alex couldn't help sensing the intrusion of its past: the self-conscious piety, the watchfulness, the crushing burden of all that New England respectability. It was one reason she stayed up on the hill, within reach of Brown. The university radiated a sense of liberality and openness that no amount of Puritan history could ever quite extinguish.

Liz's apartment was at the back of 7 Brighton Street, a typical house which somebody had painted an untypical color: the walls were pink, with doors and window frames picked out in red. From a distance it always looked to Alex like one of the strawberry candies her mom used to make. A child's animal mobile hanging in a first-floor window suggested that the effect might even have been intentional.

Alex walked up the concrete steps to the front door and pushed the buzzer. In one of the apartments upstairs a dog started to bark. Across the street a man in a blue parka was scraping ice off his windshield, watching her from under his fur hood. Since Liz's outburst on the phone, Alex had been giving the question of her relationship with Michael Eliot a lot of thought. Now, standing at the door, she couldn't help imagining Eliot's smart sedan turning the corner, pulling up outside the house, Eliot himself stepping out onto the sidewalk, hurrying past the stack of blue plastic crates with the WE RECYCLE logo on them. She wondered if he and Liz had ever slipped over here during the lunch break, just as she was doing now.

"Alex!"

For a moment Alex didn't recognize her. The smart suit and jewelry were gone, replaced by jeans and an old gray sweatshirt. Liz's hair, normally a sculpted mane of curls, hung down in a greasy straggle. Her face was tight with fatigue, her eyes puffy and swollen.

"Liz, my God—"

She sniffed and dabbed at her nose with the cuff of her sweatshirt. "I'm sorry, I haven't . . ." She stepped back from the door. She was wearing white tennis socks, no shoes. "I guess I'm a bit of a mess today."

"What is it, honey? Are you okay?"

Liz nodded and led Alex into the dimly lit hallway. A minitricycle with one wheel missing stood by the bottom of the stairs.

"Sure. My head hurts a little."

"Is it flu?"

"Glenfiddich." She managed a faint smile. "I always had a weakness for the good stuff. I'm making some coffee."

Alex followed her into the apartment, trying not to look too astonished. Like Liz, it was a real mess. The coffee table had been pushed over next to the television, and in the middle of the room were three large Delsey suitcases and a metal attaché case. Except for the attaché case, everything was opened up, clothes pulled out onto the floor.

"Sorry about all the . . ." Liz gestured helplessly at the room. "I wasn't . . . Milk, no sugar, right?"

She wandered into the galley kitchen. Alex sat down on the edge of the sofa, too stunned to speak. Here was something else Liz hadn't told her. It seemed extraordinary that she should be contemplating moving without having said anything.

"So, what? You're moving out?"

Liz gave a short, dismissive laugh. There were already tears in her eyes. She was in a bad way—one moment bitter, the next minute ready to break down.

"I don't know what I'm going to do," she said after a moment. "I don't want to do anything. It seems so . . . I'm sorry, Alex, I wanted to tell you. I wanted to explain everything to you and . . . and say good-bye. But I couldn't. Michael said I couldn't tell anyone, especially not anyone in the company."

Alex looked back at the jumble of clothes and realized with a jolt that there were men's things mixed in with the skirts and dresses.

"Liz, I don't understand."

Liz, about to pour the coffee from the pot, stopped and stared at her hand resting on the handle, as if the whole business of making coffee was suddenly unfamiliar.

"How long has this been going on?" said Alex.

"How long's what been going on?"

"You and Michael."

Liz sniffled. "It would have been a year and a half in February. Do you remember? I'd only been in the job a few weeks—moved up from Claims. The happiest eighteen months of my life." She looked up. "I loved him, Alex."

Then she was sobbing into her hands, her shoulders shaking. Alex rose and put her arms around her, held her. They stood like that for a couple of minutes, Liz sobbing, making a low keening sound.

"I can't tell anyone," she said through the tears. "That's the worst of it. I can't talk to anyone. They'll all be saying what a devoted, loving husband he was. Up on the East Side. They'll all be gathering around that bitch of a wife who never loved him—never, not their whole marriage—and comforting her in her hour of sorrow. And I have to sit here and pretend nothing happened, that it's none of my business. But I'm the one who's lost him, Alex. I'm the one who loved him. Nobody else did, nobody."

And she was weeping again, weeping on Alex's shoulder: Liz, the supercool, superefficient PA that everybody said should be running her own department, the way she had everything else organized. Who in a million years would have guessed that all that professionalism, all that dedication to her job, was driven by love? Good old-fashioned love.

Alex led Liz to the sofa and sat her down. Then she went back into the kitchen and poured the coffee, only to discover that it was stone cold. She set about making some fresh.

"Alex, you won't tell anyone, will you? Please don't tell anyone."

"Liz, of course not. I swear. I won't breathe a word."

"There's no point now, you see. People will say I'm dishonoring his memory. They'll say I'm being vindictive, or I want money or something. They'll all take her side."

She was right about that. It was a little late now for revealing infidelities. Whatever Michael Eliot had intended, the fact was he had done nothing to legitimize his affair with Liz. The family, the company, the world, none of them would recognize her right to mourn. As far as they were concerned, she would simply be an embarrassment—at best an expression of Eliot's human weakness, at worst a home wrecker.

"Does she—does she have *any* idea?" said Alex.

Liz shook her head. "I don't think so. She's so wrapped up in her own little world. Michael was going to tell her, but then he said there was no need. We could just leave her behind and let her work it out for herself."

Alex nodded, frowning. It sounded to her like Liz had been just a little bit gullible where Michael Eliot was concerned. Didn't unfaithful husbands *always* swear that they were going to leave their wives? Didn't they *always* make plans to escape with their lovers to some cozy, faraway place where the world couldn't find them? But when it came to the crunch, to the prospect of losing the house and half the income and most of their friends into the bargain, didn't they *always* decide they couldn't run out on their wives after all?

She took the mugs of steaming coffee over to the sofa and sat down at Liz's side. The attaché case lay at her feet, the set of suitcases opposite her by the fireplace.

"Liz, you mean all this"—she gestured towards the cases—"was really all settled? You really were—"

"Yes."

"Michael really *was* going to leave his wife?"

"That's what I said." Liz stared, indignant. "Why, you think I'm making it up?"

"No, no, of course not. I just thought—"

Liz reached over to a side table and held a pair of plane tickets up to

Alex's face. "We were already *packed*. Michael kept the cases here so that Margaret wouldn't see. Another day and we'd have been gone, for good."

"Gone where?"

Liz looked down into her mug as if it contained a mirage of some deeply cherished dream.

"Paris. Then the South of France. Can you imagine it? The Côte d'Azur."

Alex blinked. She couldn't quite believe what she was hearing. Michael Eliot was an insurance executive in a large-volume, low-margin insurance company, one that paid a little less than the industry average, as it happened. He ran the treasury operation—disbursements, short-term funds, money markets. He had a comfortable six-figure salary and a bonus from a profit-sharing scheme. In all, probably $200,000 in a good year, according to Mark. Someone like that didn't just up and leave the country. He'd be crucified. By the time the lawyers were finished with him, he'd be lucky to keep the clothes on his back.

"Did anyone in the company know? Michael must have said something about leaving. He wouldn't just—"

Liz shook her head emphatically.

"Nobody knew. *Especially* not the company." A thin smile formed on her lips. "Newton Brady was just supposed to walk onto the ninth floor after the holidays and find the office empty. No Michael, no Liz. *That* would have given him indigestion, all right."

That Michael Eliot had borne ill will towards his immediate superior was another surprise. Newton Brady was a corporate bruiser who stalked the finance department with a permanent scowl on his face, popping fruit-flavored antacid tablets between curt acknowledgments of his staff. On the other hand, Alex had heard it said that the chief financial officer could actually be quite charming if you got him on his own, and more than once she had seen Michael Eliot accompanying Brady to lunch at Federal Reserve or chatting good-naturedly with him in the marble-lined lobbies and landings. All that, it now seemed, had been mere office politics. But what was the use of politics if you were just going to up and disappear one day, and leave your employers to pursue you with a breach-of-contract suit? That wasn't going to get you a seat on the board.

"What am I going to do, Alex? I can't go back there. I can't go back and carry on, and pretend that nothing ever happened."

Alex put her arm around Liz's shoulder. "They wouldn't expect you to. They'll understand that you were—you know, close. Maybe it would be best if you asked for a vacation. They couldn't possibly refuse."

"And then what? Back to being PA for the next head of treasury? And who's that going to be?"

Alex thought about telling her Mark's news, about the *encouragement* he had received from Newton Brady, but quickly decided against it.

"I've no idea."

"I can't, Alex. I can't. I can't ever go back to that place. You know, when I walked out for the last time, when I walked out of there thinking I'd never have to go back, I felt wonderful. It's funny, you know? I was never really unhappy there. I always got on okay. But once I was out, I felt I was suddenly alive again."

Alex smiled, tried to understand.

Liz looked up at her. "I know it's different for you. You love it there, and you're doing really well and everything. You're going places, you've got it all planned. But I'm just a PA, and all PAs do is what they're told. I wanted to be free, Alex."

"On the Côte d'Azur, huh?" She gave Liz a squeeze. "I have to admit, it does sound dreamy. But then—honey, what were you going to do for money? How were you going to live? I mean, were you going to grow your own vegetables or something, breed rabbits like in *Jean de Florette*?"

Liz laughed, took a big gulp of coffee, wiped her mouth on her cuff.

"Sure, why not? Or carnations, like the peasant guy."

She drew her legs up and wrapped her arms tight around them. She looked like a little girl who didn't want to face the grown-up world anymore.

"I don't know what we would have ended up doing, but he said cash wouldn't be a problem. He said we'd have to live quietly, keep ourselves to ourselves, so that nobody would find us. But we'd have enough money for the rest of our lives."

"Well . . . I guess, if you lived simply enough."

"That's not what he had in mind. He said we'd get a boat. He was going to keep it at a place called Antibes. A sixty-footer. Big enough to sail around the Mediterranean. He always wanted a boat. A couple of times we sneaked down to Newport and watched them."

"A boat?" said Alex. "You mean a yacht? A sixty-foot yacht?"

"I guess. I told you: he said money wouldn't be a problem. He said we'd never have to work again."

"My God." Alex looked at the luggage, shaking her head. Then she became very still. "So . . . what's in the attaché case?" she said.

4

lex spent the rest of the afternoon in a state of shock. It was impossible to concentrate. She kept telling herself that it happened all the time, that PAs were always climbing into bed with their bosses. She had seen a survey in *Cosmo* claiming that eighteen percent of PAs admitted to having affairs with their bosses at one time or another, and that another quarter had fantasized about it (add to that the ones who *wouldn't* admit it and you pretty much had half). But Liz wasn't like that. At least, that was what Alex had thought.

At four-thirty Mark called her back and apologized for not having returned her calls earlier. Alex was relieved that he wasn't sulking. They arranged to have dinner together. At six o'clock she was already in the elevator.

Hemenway's was full when she arrived. She made her way up the stairs to the bar and found Mark with a couple of guys from the finance department drinking martinis. There was a pitcher on the bar, and they looked like they had already had a couple each. Ed Bergen, a soft-spoken southerner who took care of ProvLife's fixed-income investments, smiled when he saw Alex arrive.

"Here's someone to cheer us up," he said.

"We're having a little informal wake here," said Mark. "Care to join in?"

"Me and Michael used to come in here a lot," said Bergen, once Alex was installed on a stool. "He was . . ." He looked down at the olive in the bottom of his glass, and his smile disappeared. "I can still hardly believe it."

"It's been a hell of a day," said Mark, raising his eyebrows significantly.

Art Reinebeck, a twitchy red-haired man who worked alongside Mark in the treasury department, put his hand on Ed Bergen's shoulder. Alex could see that Bergen was actually quite drunk.

"The whole department's knocked sideways," said Reinebeck. "There's the emotional shock to deal with, and then the whole thing about who takes over from Michael."

"We used to come in here a lot," said Bergen to no one in particular.

"Yeah, it's going to take a while to sort things out," said Mark.

"It'll be okay, though," said Reinebeck, tapping the side of his nose. "Drew Coghill's gonna step in."

Alex looked at Mark and frowned. "Oh?"

"Sure," said Reinebeck. "He often covered for Michael when he was traveling. Been in the department for nearly twenty years. Great guy. Gave me my job in the first place."

"Twenty years?" said Alex, checking Mark's face again.

"Yeah," said Reinebeck. "I'd bet money on Newt choosing Coghill. He'll have to move pretty quick, though. Treasury is one place you can't let things drift."

Alex ordered wine and turned to Mark.

"What do you think?" she said.

"Coghill's okay," said Bergen. "Got the cork in a little tight is all."

Alex waited for Mark to answer.

"The smart money *has* to be on Coghill," Reinebeck insisted.

Mark shrugged. "Sure. I just don't know what Newt has planned."

"A little too tight in there," said Bergen, slurring his words.

"I saw you in with him today," said Reinebeck, ignoring Bergen. "Did he give any indication?"

"Not really. He's as upset as anybody about Eliot's death. But like you say, Arty, he's going to have to take a decision pretty quick."

"You don't want a question like that hanging over the department," said Reinebeck. "Before you know it, people start to have opinions."

"Fu-ckin' politics," Bergen said.

"Whoa there, big fella." Mark patted Bergen on the shoulder.

"He's right, though," said Reinebeck. "It can get a little partisan. But like I say, in this case it's clear-cut."

"That sounds pretty partisan to me," said Alex, wondering why Mark didn't speak up.

Reinebeck smiled. Then his smile froze. They all turned.

Catherine Pell was making her way through the crowd that had formed at the bar, a glass of white wine in her hand. She had on an expensive-looking tweed jacket cut in an evocatively equestrian style that pinched her narrow waist. She looked out of place next to a group of middle management insurance executives in their crumpled off-the-rack suits—or, rather, they looked out of place next to her.

"Catherine said she might join us," said Mark. He put his arm on Alex's shoulder as Catherine squeezed past Ed Bergen. "Catherine, have you met Alex?"

Alex shook the offered hand and did her best to smile.

"We spoke on the phone," said Catherine, showing Alex a line of perfect white teeth. Alex wondered if it was breeding or orthodontics.

"Yes," said Alex. "Of course."

She became aware that Mark was leaning forward slightly.

"Catherine's been helping us out today with Liz's work," he said. "By the way, have you heard from her at all?"

Alex pulled her eyes away from Catherine and looked at Mark's flushed face.

"What? Oh—yes. Yes, I spoke to her at lunchtime. I went over there."

"So? Is she sick?"

"She . . ." Alex looked at Ed Bergen. She hadn't really decided what to say about Liz. She wondered if anybody else, any of Eliot's close friends, had known about the affair. "She was almost in a state of shock."

Again she looked at Bergen, but he appeared to have drifted off into his own thoughts.

"We're all in shock," said Reinebeck.

"Well, I hope she'll be back in tomorrow," said Mark, trying to sound concerned.

Alex thought about the way Liz had looked standing in the doorway—then got a flash of the metal attaché case on the living room floor. What *was* inside? She had left Liz staring at it, slumped in an armchair.

Mark was pulling at her arm, the pager vibrating in his hand. Hemenway's used the system to let customers know when their table was ready.

"That's for us," he said. He looked at Bergen and Reinebeck, and then at Catherine. "We'll see you guys later."

From where he sat at the end of the bar, Donald Grant watched the two young people move down the steps into the restaurant area. He pulled out his mobile and punched in the number.

Snow blew along Phillips Street in hard gusts as the man in the black ski jacket made his way up to the front door of number twenty-nine. After almost an hour in the freezing dark he was glad to be moving again. The light coming from the downstairs room in number twenty-nine looked inviting and warm. Through cheap net curtains he could see the flickering light from the television on the face of an old woman wearing big seventies-style headphones. He figured she was either deaf or looking for better sound quality. Whatever the reason, it was going to make his job a lot easier. He checked the street behind him and then dropped the black nylon grip onto the doorstep.

There were two locks: a Schlage about a foot above the peeling doorknob and lower down a simple deadbolt. He pulled out the Mule Tool—an assemblage of bent rolled steel, plastic string, a pad of adhesive material, and a wedge—and knelt down in front of the door. It took thirty seconds to reach under the door, get hold of the deadbolt knob, and turn it. He moved up to the Schlage and pushed in the pick gun.

Inside the hallway he breathed warm soup-smelling air. Low, tuneless singing was coming from behind a new pine door. It took him a moment to work out that it was the old woman singing along to something religious coming through her headphones. *The Lord loves us all.* He moved up the stairs. The Tynan woman lived at the top of the house.

Alex stared out at the falling snow which was drifting thickly into the black gash of the Woonasquatucket River. Mayor Montanelli had spent a fortune on improving the quays and bridges and on putting in antique lamps, hoping to make of Providence the Venice of the Eastern Seaboard. He didn't like the way the tourists streamed past on the I-95 on their way up to Boston, rarely giving Providence a thought, rarely turning off to spend their dollars in his city. It just wasn't fair. Rhode Island might be the smallest state in the Union, but it had twenty percent of its National Historic Landmarks, and Providence had the lion's share of those. Not everybody in the city agreed with the expenditure. Among the higher-ups at ProvLife, there were those who thought Montanelli was an idiot. They never said anything, of course, but behind closed doors they talked about how long it would take him to bankrupt the town. Watching the snow settle on the ornate lamps, Alex was reminded of her own finances. She suppressed a shudder.

"What's up?" said Mark.

She turned to look at him. "Oh, nothing."

Mark was still flushed, and Alex found herself wondering if it was the effect of the martinis or Ms. Catherine Pell.

"So you were busy today," she said.

Mark smiled. "I was in with Newt."

"Newt. I thought it was Newton. You always called him Newton."

"He prefers Newt. Makes him feel like one of the guys."

"So? What did he have to say?"

The smile broadened. "What do you think?"

Alex gave a shrug. "I don't know what to think. He told you he was going to give Eliot's job to Drew Coghill?"

Mark laughed. "Sure, *right*."

"Art Reinebeck thinks that's the way it should be."

"Arty thinks Coghill's going to give *him* a leg up, that's what Arty thinks."

"So? Is he?"

Mark smoothed the red check tablecloth and slowly shook his head.

"Newt asked me if I felt ready to handle the department."

"My God."

"I know you don't think I'm the right man for the job, but—"

"Mark, I didn't say that. I was just a bit—when you told me this morning, I was a little taken aback. It's kind of too good to be true."

"Sometimes the truth is good."

"But—"

"But what?"

"Well—how is he going to sell it to the department? I mean, you've been with the company, what, five years?"

"Five and a half."

"Five and a half years doing cash management, and there are all those people that have— I mean, how's he going to sell it to people like Art?"

"A week from now and Arty will be saying, 'Mark is exactly what we need—a young man, an energetic man.' He's not stupid."

"And Coghill?"

"He's yesterday's news. He's still in the seventies, for Christ's sake. Alex, I don't know if you see it down in the actuarial department, but things are changing. The life market is changing." He leaned across the table, the excitement building in his voice. "With all this new technology—medical advances, genetic testing—the whole business of assessing risk is becoming unstable. In ten, even five years' time the life insurance market will be unrecognizable. And the old methods just won't cut it. Newt knows it, Neumann knows it—Christ, probably even Randal White knows it. Or he would if he ever got his nose out of those old mortality tables."

Alex drew her hands into her lap and pushed back in her chair. There was something unsettling about Mark's sudden enthusiasm for the business. Maybe it was just too soon after Eliot's death.

"If you're going to get the top job in Treasury," she said, "you'll need Randal White's approval. So you'd better not let him hear you say that."

Mark drained the last inch of his beer.

"Sure, Randal pisses with the big dogs, I know that." He wiped his mouth and looked around the room. "As a matter of fact he's going to speak for the company at the NIH forum at the end of the month. Did you hear?"

Alex shook her head. The National Institutes of Health forum in Washington was a big event. It was going to debate the question of whether or to what extent life and health insurers should be permitted to examine the genes of their potential customers—and discriminate accordingly. Most people in the industry wanted a free hand, but some politicians favored restrictions and even outright bans. They argued that genetic testing undermined the principle of shared risk and threatened to create an underclass of people who, through no fault of their own, were unable to get life or health cover. With federal legislation in the works, the stakes for the industry were sky high.

"Yeah, well, it's true," said Mark. "Our illustration actuary will be setting out the ProvLife position."

"Which is what exactly?" said Alex.

Mark shrugged as if it went without saying. "We want to test, obviously. I mean, as soon as it's economically viable. We *have* to test."

Alex took a sip of wine and watched Mark push a large piece of bread into his mouth. She wasn't sure she liked him this way: so cocky, so sure of himself. It was okay when they were talking movies or food or cars. It was fun then, most of the time. But this was business—hers as well as his.

"Do we?" she said. "Why?"

He swallowed. "Because if we don't test we'll get wiped out by other insurers that do. We'll be at a competitive disadvantage."

"So we have to test because other people might?"

"Of course. It's dog eat dog out there, sweetheart."

"But if Congress brings in legislation saying *no one* can, then everyone should be happy, right?"

Mark rolled his eyes, as if she were being perverse just for the sake of it. "Wrong. Because as long as people can check their *own* genes and find out in advance if and when they're likely to get sick, then *they* put *us* at a disadvantage. People with bad genes take out huge amounts of cover, and all the healthy people stay away. Come on, Alex, you know all this."

Alex was about to push the argument a little further, but then thought better of it. She decided to get back to less contentious ground.

"So when is 'Newt' going to break the news?" she said playfully.

Mark's shoulders relaxed. "Well, like you say, it has to be passed by the board. So maybe sometime next week."

"Here's to it," Alex said and raised her glass.

Mark raised his, but it was already empty.

Cheap furniture, cheap carpet starting to pill under the pine table where the woman probably crossed her feet, reading her big fat insurance books. And cold. He opened several cupboards before finding the boiler. No timer for the heating. She couldn't even afford to have a timer installed. And the boiler itself was in a terrible state. He was looking at the soot coming from the burner when something moved behind him. He jerked around, pointing the flashlight into corners, looking for the cat. Cats made him nervous, especially in the dark. It had withdrawn hissing under a chair as he came in through the door—a flash of gray eyes, then nothing. But there was no time for cat hunting. Grant had said forty-five minutes—in and out. No bugs, no wiretap, just a quick toss of the place to see if there were any connections.

He closed the cupboard door and walked back across to the table. No drawers. Then he saw a box file down on the floor next to the ratty old sofa. He flipped open the lid and smiled. Personal papers. Bills, bank statements, credit card demands. No airline tickets. He put the flashlight in his mouth and sat down on the sofa. For twenty minutes he sifted through the past four months of Alex's life. The story that came through was pretty clear. This was somebody struggling to get by. She had splurged at Christmas on a couple of gifts, but apart from that she kept a pretty tight hold on the purse strings. He put the papers back. If this was the whole story, then Alex Tynan didn't know about the money.

He let the beam of the flashlight play over the walls until he picked out a flash of glass, an ornate silver frame. He put the box file back on the floor and got up to take a look. A chest of drawers circa 1970. Tacky veneer peeling off chipboard. There were three framed photographs on top. An old black-and-white picture of a young guy in uniform. Tynan herself with an older lady, maybe her mom. No big family resemblance. Tynan got her good looks from dad, if that was dad in the uniform. Then there was a picture of Ferulli hitting a baseball, a big winner's grin on his face.

He pulled open the top drawer. Clean-smelling T-shirts. Another: pullovers, lots of thick pullovers. Probably what she used instead of decent heating. Then down at the bottom, underwear. Cotton, simple. Some too old, though, starting to go in the crotch. He pulled off a glove and pushed his fingers into the flimsy material, then brought a handful up to his mouth, breathing lemony soap smells. He caught a glimpse of himself in the mirror: flushed pockmarked face, hard eyes. He stayed like that for a moment, then put the underwear back. From what Grant said, Eliot would go for top dollar. Lace, silk, satin. Red and black. Then again, maybe he liked the schoolgirl stuff—as a change. He put the glove back on. Picked up the photograph of Alex with her mother, and thought that maybe Miss Tynan played on that innocence with her Mia Farrow hairstyle and big gray eyes.

Mark insisted on paying for the meal. Pulling out his credit card, he dropped a wad of receipts on the table. On one of them Alex saw a long list of four-letter words scrawled in black pen. Gathering up the paper to shove back into his billfold, Mark caught her expression.

"What?"

"Those words. Are you doing a crossword or something?"

Mark blushed a deep red.

Alex was so surprised, she immediately regretted having said anything. She waved her hand, laughing nervously. "No, no. It's none of my business."

Mark took the paper and flattened it out on the tablecloth.

"Look, I . . . It's a little embarrassing. What it is, is, Newt said"—he took a big breath and worked himself back in his chair—"Newt said I had to have a password to access certain parts of the Central Records computer. You know there are parts of the Central Records system that, um . . ."

"Ordinary staff?"

"That ordinary staff, unauthorized staff, can't get access to. It's a matter of client confidentiality, of course."

"Of course."

"*Alex.*"

"I'm just kidding. Listen, I think it's great you've been given the keys to the kingdom. Pending board approval, of course. I don't think it's any reason to be embarrassed."

Mark gave her a sidelong look. "Yeah, well, you can imagine what Art Reinebeck would say about it."

"Or Drew Coghill."

"*Exactly.* So it's not something you want to be waving around."

Alex looked at the paper. "So what have you got?"

"Nothing. I mean, it's not as if it matters, but I need to come up with something I'm not going to forget."

"What's wrong with your birthday?"

"Has to be letters, no numbers. Anyway, Newt said nothing like that. Nothing obvious."

"What about N-E-W-T?"

Mark smiled, but Alex could see that he was still uncomfortable. "That's probably what *he* uses. Or would, if it weren't so obvious. No, no names."

Alex took her pen. "How about this?" she said.

Mark watched her write.

"LIRA?"

"Sure. Celebrates your Italian heritage and all the money you're going to make."

Mark looked at the paper and then at Alex. He smiled.

"I'll think about it," he said.

Down in the street the man flipped open his mobile. Grant picked up on the second ring. Squinting into the lights of oncoming traffic, the man said, "I'm out of here."

Sitting in the bar of Hemenway's, Grant toyed with his steak dinner.

"So, do we have a problem?" he said.

5

Early each January Randal White took everybody in the actuarial department to *Le Villaret*, a restaurant famous for its Perigord dishes and fine wines. It was a tradition that dated back to the early eighties, but because of the sense of privilege White instilled, it felt like it had been going on since the company's incorporation. None of the actuaries was quite clear on what basis he undertook the expenditure. Other departments had lunches, certainly—Personnel considered it good for team spirit—but there was nothing to compare with White's *déjeuner*. A sideroom with views through double doors to the main restaurant was set aside for the function, and, with wine—White loved French wines, and would order only the *grands crus*—the eight lucky guests figured he had to be spending about sixteen hundred to two thousand dollars of company money. They loved it, of course. It made them feel that they were members of a club, an elite.

Despite some determined maneuvering, Alex found herself seated next to Mel Hartman, two places to the right of Randal White. As part of his ongoing campaign to get her to "lighten up," Hartman maintained a steady monologue throughout the meal while Alex tried to follow what White was saying to his nearest neighbors. The topic of discussion was the mayor. Sandra Betridge, an earnest, red-faced person who had joined the department along with Hartman, was maintaining that registered independents like Mayor Montanelli always turned into megalomaniacs when they attained high office. White refilled Betridge's glass and said something about independents being what Rhode Island was all about.

Alex watched him now as Hartman's stream of banter trickled on. There was something different about him she could not quite place. Then she realized what it was: his hair was longer. Normally carefully groomed, he had for some reason missed a visit, maybe two, to the barber and his hair curled over his crisply starched collar at the back. Though graying, White's hair still grew thickly, framing a head that Alex thought of as leonine. It was one of the things she liked about him—that and his intelligent, friendly eyes. They were delicately marked by years of laughter and suggested a man who lived for a great deal more than his work. Alex found that reassuring.

On this occasion, however, White seemed weary, as if the whole occasion was lacking something for him. Since the New Year, in fact, White had put in no more than two or three fleeting appearances in the department, and Alex had been obliged to send him an e-mail updating him on her progress with the healthcare figures and reporting the anomaly she had found in the ProvLife claims data. So far she had not had a reply.

Dessert came and went. Hartman said something mischievous and witty about Alex's car which she didn't quite catch, and then White was getting to his feet. Someone tapped a spoon against a wineglass, and, as though on cue, pale winter sunlight flooded the room.

"Well," said White, smiling around the table. "Here we are once again. Um . . ."—he glanced down at the tablecloth—"two shadows fall across our little gathering this year. We lost Ken Miller in the summer. I'd like to start by raising a glass of this great vintage to Ken. Like me, Ken loved his claret, and if he is up there watching, I hope he approves my choice. Ken did a great job heading up Data Systems and was much too young for a coronary."

He raised his glass. "To Ken."

Everyone drank in silence. Ken Miller had been a friend of White's— his closest in the company, people said. White wasn't the kind of man who showed his feelings, at least not where colleagues were concerned, but the news of Miller's death had shaken him visibly. According to Mel Hartman, he hadn't been the only one: most of the board had gone for medical checkups in the weeks that followed, their professional, arm's-length exploitation of death upset by its sudden arrival.

White cleared his throat and dabbed at his mouth with the napkin. As abruptly as it had appeared, the sun was gone again. The room seemed to darken for a moment.

"Heart attacks will kill you, of course," he said. "Diseases of the heart and circulatory system are, as you have reason to know, the superpredators that cruise the murky waters we make our study. Ken was just unfortunate to bump into one so early." He paused, his mouth squeezing into a line. Alex sensed that this was a painful memory for him, although he was determined not to spoil the mood of the party. "Electrocution is another matter."

It was as if the word itself carried a charge. The silence seemed to condense until Alex became conscious of her chest working to draw breath.

"Michael Eliot was—well, I think we all know what he was. I remember when he first joined us back in eighty-five. We were lucky to get him, and he made a big difference in the difficult years. It's no coincidence that we can date the start of our turnaround to 1990, the year Michael took over the treasury function. And now it seems . . ."

He frowned. Suddenly it was as if he had nothing else to say. A muscle twitched in his cheek. Without finishing his sentence, he raised his glass again, saying quietly: "To Michael, not forgetting those he leaves behind."

The toast went around the table.

"To Michael."

"To Michael Eliot."

People shifted in their seats. Alex watched White's hands. For what seemed a whole minute he said nothing. Then he looked around at the upturned faces. When his eyes came to rest on her, Alex felt a faint tingle of warmth.

"But *we* go on," he said. "Another year to live and breathe. No deep mystery in that, of course. Mathematicians have always done well in the great mortality sweepstakes. It was John Larus, I believe, who, in his study of the mortality of actuaries, 1889 to 1937, showed that the younger actuary enjoys an exceptional mortality advantage. The 1991 study by John Cook and Ernest Moorhead identified a similar trend. I refer you to *Transactions of the Society of Actuaries*, volume forty-one—please, Sandra, no note-taking."

He touched Sandra Betridge on the shoulder and, although she was not taking notes, her scarlet face declared that she had been thinking about it. She had a reputation in the department for extreme diligence, and at this typical good-natured teasing, everybody laughed.

White looked up at the molded ceiling of the airy colonial room until the laughter subsided.

"Why is that?" he said almost to himself. Then he smiled as his eyes came to rest on them again. "For what it's worth, I think it's because we have more fun."

"Hear, hear," said Mel Hartman.

"I think it was James Sylvester who remarked that the mathematician lives long and lives young. 'The wings of the soul do not drop off,' he said, 'nor do its pores become clogged with the earthy particles blown from the dusty highways of vulgar life.' "

Once more he raised his glass.

"The last time *I* looked, my wings seemed a little ragged at the edges, but they're still"—he gently dusted off his elbows—"still working, as I trust are yours. So this last is to us all, or more particularly to our wings."

"To our wings." They all raised their glasses and drank.

"I always knew you were a fly-by-night operation."

A man had come into the double doorway of the private dining room. He looked about fifty, well groomed with a winter-holiday tan. He wore a smart pinstripe and a dark red silk tie. He smiled at the silence he had created and then walked around the table to White, who greeted him. As they shook hands, Alex noticed the stranger's crisp white double cuffs and the gold cuff links.

"I don't want to interrupt your little gathering, Randal," he said, the condescension in his voice unmistakable, "but I didn't want to leave without wishing you a happy New Year."

"Why, thank you," White said. "Everybody, I want you to meet Charles Kenyon, Deputy CEO at Massachusetts General. What brings you down here, Charlie? I didn't think this was the cherry-picking season."

Kenyon laughed politely. "Just dropping in on the new team, Randal. See how they're shaping up. You know how it is."

White returned a neutral smile, but Alex could sense his irritation. Massachusetts General was one of the largest and most successful insurance companies in the region, and had recently opened plush new offices on Kennedy Plaza. In the life and health fields they were aggressively targeting Rhode Island's more prosperous residents—and part-time residents—around Newport and the smarter parts of Providence. They had also poached a number of middle-ranking staff from ProvLife, including two senior underwriters and a hotshot from Marketing. Alex had encountered some of Mass General's people in and around the Financial District. One of them she even remembered from her days at MIT. But he, like the others, had not been very friendly. To them ProvLife was a little too down-market, a little too workaday—a Kmart to Mass General's Tiffany.

"I heard on the grapevine that ProvLife's moving into health cover," Kenyon said. "Can that be true?"

White shrugged. "Now, where would you have heard that?"

"I have my sources, Randal. Not that I believe them, mind you."

"Really?" said White. "Why not?"

Kenyon laughed, not wanting to pursue the question. But White didn't oblige. He simply raised his eyebrows, awaiting a reply.

"Let's be honest, Randal," Kenyon blustered. "It's not really Prov-Life's thing, is it? I mean, it's—well—*highly* complex."

"Really?" said White, poker-faced. "*Is* it?"

Kenyon faked a chuckle. Brian Slater and one of the other actuaries at the table chuckled too, for no reason that Alex could see.

"I should have known better than to think you'd be giving anything away, Randal," Kenyon said, moving away. "Perhaps I'll have more luck in Washington. You are going to the NIH genetics forum?"

"Yes. I've been chosen for that dubious honor. You too, then?"

"Damned right. We've got a whole team going down. We've got to be sure the industry gets its message across, loud and clear."

"And what message is that?" said White.

Kenyon was almost at the door. He turned. "I'm sorry?"

"What *is* the message, as you see it? I'd like to know."

Kenyon's eyes narrowed. "The same as yours will be, I'm sure. We have to be allowed to test. It could cost us billions if we're shut out. Everybody agrees about that."

White regarded him steadily. "Everyone?"

"Well, don't you?"

White didn't reply. Suddenly everyone at the table was very still.

Kenyon brought a finger to his temple, struggling, it seemed, to re-main polite. "I don't know if you've studied the figures on this one—and if you're contemplating health insurance I suggest you do—but research on the human genome has quadrupled the rate at which dis-ease genes are being uncovered. Genes for everything from Alzheimer's to cancer. This is a tidal wave of information about life expectancy. Information for sale. To the public—"

"So what are you saying?" interrupted White.

"This is a seismic event for our industry, Randal," Kenyon said sim-ply. "We have to be able to test. If we can't test, we're wide open. We're underwriting in the dark. The state has to understand that."

White lifted his wine and sipped. His eyes smiled at Kenyon. Then he looked across at Hartman.

"What do you think, Mel?"

Hartman's mouth opened and shut. Then he frowned.

"It's a difficult issue," he said. "But basically what we're talking about is the nature of the risk-pooling system."

"Go on."

"Well, the whole point of risk sharing is to enable individuals who, on a random basis, may suffer an unfortunate outcome—a loss of one sort or another—to reap the benefit of the pooling system, which will in turn be paid for by other members of the class. The important thing here is that all the insured in a given class face a roughly comparable probability of loss. Only then will they be willing to pay a premium equal to their expectation of . . . bad luck. Otherwise what you're talk-ing about is a system of subsidy."

Kenyon was nodding. Hartman looked anxiously at his boss, but White was looking down at his hands.

"But surely," said White, "you have to balance the profitability of the insurance industry with the interests of the community at large, since we are a part of that community. You don't see a moral imperative there?"

"Well, if you mean there has to be a certain amount of risk shar-ing in society, regardless of the probability of loss, I'm not sure we—

the insurers, I mean—should be expected to pick up the tab for that."

White looked at Kenyon and smiled. "You see, Charlie. You have a convert already."

Hartman looked alarmed. "Well, I was just—"

"Come on, Randal. You're not really going to give the NIH all that crap about the community at large?" Kenyon's hands were planted on his hips. A disagreeable edge had crept into his voice. "A moral imperative? Don't you know that's exactly what the damned politicians and bleeding hearts want to hear? Coming from an insurer—even one like ProvLife—it'd be just the excuse they need."

White remained impassive. "I don't know if you've studied *the figures* on this one, Charles," he said, sitting down. "But there are at present forty million people in this country without insurance. Forty million people without access to decent health care. Do we really need to add to that figure?"

"That's an issue for government," said Kenyon. "Insurance is a business."

White looked around the table, his eyes smiling again. "Indeed it is. A very lucrative business with assets worth—I'm talking life insurance here—with assets worth around two *trillion* dollars. An industry that takes in premiums of some three hundred *billion* dollars a year, giving back not quite half of that in benefits."

"There's nothing in the Constitution that says you can't make money in this country," Kenyon said. "Not yet, anyway."

"And we do, don't we?" said White. "Of course, if we excluded all these people with unreliable genes, then we could make even more. Is that your idea?"

"Clearly, the industry needs to establish guidelines," Kenyon mumbled.

White nodded.

"Yes . . . yes. Well, when you're drawing up your guidelines, Charles, bear in mind that people at risk for certain kinds of genetic conditions are already turned down for either health insurance or life insurance or even employment." White shrugged and looked into his empty wineglass. "Of course, if they starved I suppose they'd be less likely to procreate, and so there *would* be a beneficial purging of the gene pool." He looked straight at Kenyon. "I think it's called eugenics."

For a moment Kenyon was speechless. A film of sweat had appeared on his brow.

"We can talk about this in Washington," he managed to say. "Maybe then we can have a serious discussion."

"They don't come more serious than this," said White.

He remained seated, watching as the other man left the room.

6

Phillips Street lay a mile and a half north of the Financial District, a few blocks short of Brown Stadium. It was not the best part of the East Side, and many of the rambling old houses were occupied by students. The lawns and verges were badly maintained, and a couple of the residents seemed to be in the process of stripping old automobiles in their front yards. On the other hand, the old-fashioned porches, the tall ashes and maples that lined the road, even the occasional twang of an acoustic guitar, lent the place a relaxed, easy-going atmosphere that appealed to Alex after a day of number crunching downtown.

Number twenty-nine was owned by an old lady called Maeve Connelly. About thirty years back she and her family had occupied the whole substantial property, but times had gotten steadily harder since then, and little by little, room by room, more and more of her yellow clapboard house had been rented out, until Mrs. Connelly herself occupied only a few rooms at the front. Alex lived on the top floor, half of which was taken up by an old storage room and a water tank that clanked and gurgled periodically throughout the night. The truth was, the whole building was badly in need of an overhaul. But the rent was cheap, there was a bus route at the end of the road, and the only way Alex was going to get anything better for the same money was to move miles out of the city or take her chances in the worst neighborhoods of South Providence.

She would happily have stayed in Phillips Street for another year or so, but there was a good chance the option wouldn't exist. Her lease was up for renewal in two months' time, and Mrs. Connelly was talking about raising the rent by at least a third. Her son-in-law was pushing her to demand even more. Apparently it was his opinion that with a little investment she could triple her income from the property, although why a lubricants salesman from Pittsburgh should be considered an authority on the subject was unclear. Of course, the simplest thing, the easiest thing—there was no getting away from it, the *cheapest* thing—would have been to move in with Mark. He had even suggested it once or twice, in passing. But Alex didn't feel that the time was right, and she wasn't sure Mark did either, if it came right down to it. Besides, she didn't like the idea of putting her love life at the service of her bank balance—or, as Liz Foster had once put it, squeezing a heart-shaped peg into a dollar-shaped hole.

For somebody more than two years into a steady job, Alex knew she wasn't exactly living like a highflier. It wasn't that ProvLife didn't pay her decently—although the good money would only start coming when she finally qualified as a Fellow of the Society of Actuaries—it was simply that circumstances had been against her. To start with, she'd borrowed heavily to get through MIT. Boston had turned out to be a surprisingly expensive town. In spite of evening jobs and weekend jobs and holiday jobs, the debts had just kept on growing. When, at her final interview with Randal White, she had been formally offered a place as a trainee actuary at ProvLife, it had seemed that she might be free of money worries at last. But Alex had only been in the job a couple of months when a new vortex of debt had opened up at her feet.

Her mother had decided one day to save money and clean out her own guttering, and had fallen from the ladder. She was lucky that the hood of her car took much of the impact, but a series of intricate operations were needed to repair the damage to her spine. And it turned out that she was badly underinsured. Alex had no choice but to take her new Volkswagen right back to the dealer, reclaim the '85 Camry, and beg Fleet Bank for another $20,000 loan. If it hadn't been for Randal White's effusive reference, she doubted very much if they would have given it to her. Now, eighteen months later, Alex's mother was back on her feet but, in spite of repeated attempts to put money aside, Alex herself was as deep in the red as ever.

Skimping on the medical coverage had been a disastrous false economy, but Alex couldn't really blame her mother for doing it. Money had been tight ever since her father had gone missing in action more than twenty years earlier. John Tynan had been an engineer in the air cavalry. He'd been aboard a Huey that had gone down behind enemy lines in Cambodia (it turned out), but nobody knew whether it had been a forced landing or a crash-and-burn. Alex didn't remember him. She hadn't even been born yet when he died. But her mother had never remarried, and the jobs she took once Alex was in school never seemed to last. To this day the service pension was pretty much all the income she had.

Alex shook the snow off her shoes and let herself into the house. A small stack of mail was waiting for her on the hall table, including a late Christmas card from Robby Halliday and a letter from the credit card company. The letter stated that she had failed to make the required payments, and that her card would be withdrawn "and the matter placed in other hands" if settlement were not made within thirty days. She had tried to be careful over Christmas, but with the presents and Mark's appetite for celebrations it had proved impossible. She'd comforted herself with the thought that once she passed her Survival Models and Construction of Tables exam in May she would almost certainly get a pay raise. The course would give her the final fifteen credits she needed for associateship—the halfway house to full qualification. Unfortunately, there was no guarantee she *would* pass, and any raise ProvLife did give her would be entirely discretionary.

She slowly climbed the stairs to her apartment, trying not to let her spirits flag, trying to think of something positive, something to look forward to. Under her door she found a note from Mrs. Connelly. It said simply: *Oscar caught a mouse.*

Oscar was a two-year-old of mixed origin—part Persian, part alley cat—with a sociable nature and fine black and white fur, which he deposited all over the apartment in little tufts and curls. He had the run of almost the whole house via a series of cat-flaps, but rarely strayed outside, contenting himself with a view of the world from the front porch or the rusty iron fire escape that clung to the side of the building. There was a chance that Oscar had made his kill in the backyard, but Alex had a horrible feeling that the mouse in question had been resident even closer to home.

She coaxed Oscar off the couch with a plate of Whiskas, and threw herself down on the cushions. Robby's card showed a wolf howling at wintry stars. Robby had a thing about wilderness. In the days when they'd been romantically attached, he'd insisted on getting out of Boston every weekend for long hikes. They'd even had a tent. He'd written all over the inside of it, his wacky scrawl covering every inch of space. It turned out he was now up at Ann Arbor, Michigan, talking over his latest money-making venture with some high-powered postgraduates in the natural sciences department. Since leaving MIT, he'd never had a steady job. He'd done the occasional spell of temporary clerical work, but only as a stopgap between more ambitious projects. Within a year of graduation he and a group of friends had set up their own small company, producing artificial intelligence modules for the software industry. The business had gone bust after eighteen months. Now he was getting excited about something else: software systems for analyzing meteorological data. According to the card, there was a big new market out there for up-to-date computer models of medium-range weather systems. He'd already decided on the new company name: Sunscape. Reading between the lines, Alex got the distinct impression that—just like the last time—he was looking to recruit her.

She shook her head and smiled. She and Robby had never really split up, at least not in the sense of having a definitive break—a lovers' spat or anything—but after leaving MIT they'd pretty quickly understood that they were set on following very different career paths. Then suddenly they had been living in different towns, doing different things. They had drifted apart the way they had drifted together in the first place. Whenever she thought about it, Alex told herself that it had been easy to separate because they had never shared anything very important. But every time she got news of him she was delighted. And the delight was always tinged with a shadowy regret.

Looking at his wildly plunging y's and g's, she tried to imagine what it would be like working with Robby Halliday on predicting the weather. It was tempting in a way: all the fresh air, all that freedom—and a branch of mathematics that was a shade more colorful than the one she'd decided to perch upon. The way he had embraced catastrophe and chaos theory at MIT had been remarkable. He was Mr. Volatility. And he was a lot of fun—relentlessly upbeat, always looking for new ideas, always ready to invest time and energy in whatever grabbed his imagination. But there were things that unsettled Alex too. It would have been unfair to say he was impractical, but there was something about his approach to life—his very optimism—that Alex had always felt she couldn't trust. He lived in the world of numbers, of hard facts, and yet there seemed to be some facts he was simply not prepared to acknowledge. Such as, that if you weren't sitting on a family fortune you needed to get a job and a steady income, or one day you'd be sorry. Or that starting up software ventures was a very shaky way of trying to make a living.

Alex put the card on the coffee table and reached for the phone. She punched in Mark's number. The line buzzed twice and then someone picked up.

"Mark? It's Alex. I just wondered how it's . . . Hello?"

There was a faint beep and then Mark's recorded voice came on, brisk and businesslike: *I'm unable to take your call at this time, but please leave a message after the tone and I'll get back to you as soon as possible.* What message could she leave? She wanted it to be something clever, witty, something Catherine Pell could never come up with. She heard the tone.

"Um, it's me. Alex. Just—just calling to see if you're okay, and um"— something *witty*—"I'll see you tomorrow, okay? Don't do anything—I mean, don't work too hard. Darling. Bye."

She hung up, let her head slump against her arm, jumped. The phone was ringing in her hand.

"Mark? How on earth did you—?"

"Alex? It's Liz."

"Oh. Liz." Alex let out a sigh. "Sorry, I thought—"

"I was Mark."

"Yes."

"Sorry."

"Don't be. It's just that I called him a moment ago, and . . . How are you, anyway?"

"Okay, I guess."

"You didn't come in again today. I thought maybe—"

"I took your advice. I called Newton Brady's office and asked for a few weeks' vacation. They gave it to me right away, no questions asked."

"Told you so."

"Yeah. He was real nice, actually. It was bizarre. He said the company valued me a great deal and would be looking to *enhance my role*, whatever that means."

"Liz, that's great."

"Yeah, well, I thought I may as well get paid while I think about what to do with my life."

Liz sounded a lot better than the last time: calmer, stronger, more like the cool PA she had always been in the office.

"That's good, Liz. I'm really glad to hear it. It can't hurt to keep your options open, can it? I mean, maybe if you moved to another department, it wouldn't be so bad. Just for a while. Anyway, it sounds like you're in line for a—"

"I opened the case."

Alex sat up. She'd wondered about the attaché case a lot the past couple of days, more than she cared to admit. Clearly she hadn't been the only one. For a moment she said nothing. Every time Liz mentioned Eliot, she got a flashback of the kiss at the party.

"You mean . . . Michael's attaché case?" she said eventually.

"I forced the lock."

"My God. Liz."

"I just couldn't resist it. It was sitting there in the middle of the room. I did it last night. It took forever."

"Liz . . . I don't know what to—"

"Alex, he was worth millions. It's all here."

Alex pressed the phone against her ear and held on tight. She had a vision of Liz sitting on the floor in her nightdress surrounded by money.

"What? In *cash*?"

"No. Ten thousand in cash. But there are records here. Bank statements. I think he had around ten million dollars, Alex. Numbered accounts in Switzerland, bearer bonds. And there are other papers I can't make out. A whole load of numbers and stuff. I don't know what they mean."

Alex was stunned. It didn't seem possible. How could Michael Eliot have had ten million dollars? How could he have had so much and yet spent so little? Unless it was money that somehow he couldn't spend, money that belonged to someone else. But maybe that was just what it was.

"Liz, are you sure you aren't getting things mixed up here? I mean, maybe this money is just something to do with the treasury department. You know, company investments or—"

"Alex, I know what bank statements look like." Liz's voice hardened. "And these have got Michael's name all over them. Money in, bonds purchased, bonds sold. Everything's here. Some of these transactions are only a few weeks old. I'm telling you, he had the money."

For a moment neither of them spoke. Alex felt suddenly uneasy. A man could be wealthy and not want the world to know, but this was different: Eliot's secrecy had gone way beyond discretion. His whole way of life had been a lie.

"Alex, do you think it could have had something to do with Michael's death?"

Alex didn't answer. Down below she could hear somebody climbing the wooden stairs. Heavy footsteps. She wondered if she'd remembered to lock her door.

"Alex? Are you there?"

"Yes," she whispered. "What do you mean?"

"I mean, Michael kept this money a secret. I'm sure he did. Even from his wife."

The footsteps reached the landing below, then stopped. What would she do if they kept on climbing? Oscar was sitting upright in the middle of the rug, staring straight at the door.

"How do you know that?"

"About a year ago she wanted to move to another house. There was this huge place that came up for sale on Blackstone Boulevard. Michael told her they *couldn't afford it*."

From below there came a jangling of keys and then the sound of someone unlocking a door. It was only Mr. Pavey downstairs.

"Well, maybe he didn't have the money then, Liz. Maybe somebody died and left it to him. That's probably what happened, isn't it?"

"I don't think so. He would have said something."

"Then ... I don't know, Liz. Maybe you're right. But I still don't see—"

"Suppose she found out. I mean, Margaret. Suppose she found out that Michael had all this money and that he was planning to leave her. She might have killed him to get her hands on it."

Alex sighed. This was too much.

"Come on, Liz. If she knew all that, all she'd have to do was divorce him. She'd get half the money at least, plus the house."

'You don't know her, Alex. She'd want more than that. She'd want revenge. Divorcing him would just have set him free."

"Liz, it was an accident. He drilled through a cable. That's a pretty hard thing to fake, you know, especially when your victim's bigger than you are. I mean, can you imagine? 'Hold this, honey, while I throw the switch'?"

"It could be done. You could find a way, if all you had to do all day was sit around the house thinking about it and planning it. She could plan anything. She planned Michael's whole life from the day she first set eyes on him."

7

Harold Tate put down the newspaper and looked out across the white expanse of the parking lot. Guy Pilaski was walking across the hard-packed snow in his long Christian Dior overcoat, an unlit cigarette between his lips. Tate checked his watch: twenty past seven, a little late for Guy. In spite of his position as CEO, he wasn't normally in the office much after six o'clock. Tate watched the Oldsmobile pull out of the parking lot and disappear into the traffic on Toll Gate Road. Another day of doing next to nothing, one day less to go until early retirement. How long was it now? Tate did the calculation in his head: four years, two months, and nine days.

Pilaski had been a surprising choice for chief executive. His scientific expertise was negligible—he'd once been finance director at a company that made industrial gases—and with his stocky frame, black moustache, and liking for splashy ties he looked more like the manager of a Florida night club. But the new shareholders had wanted him: someone less concerned with science and more concerned with the business end, someone who could be relied upon to run a tight ship. But Medan *was* a tight ship, and without the technology to worry about, Pilaski's much vaunted management skills were somewhat underemployed. Tate wondered what had kept him so late this time. He hoped it wasn't anything to do with Michael Eliot.

It was two weeks since Eliot's death, and so far there had been nothing in the *Providence Journal* to suggest that it was anything but an ordinary domestic accident. Tate had scoured the paper every morning and, beyond the original three column inches on page five, the incident had never again merited a mention. There had been no police investigation, no hint that the circumstances were in any way unusual. And they were *not* unusual, in themselves: as the *Journal* had pointed out, every year hundreds of Americans were killed or seriously injured making home improvements, many involving power tools. But then, the police and the reporters at the *Journal* didn't know that Eliot had plans, plans to make the best of the two or three good years left to him—plans that didn't include finishing the den.

Tate's first thought was that Eliot had actually killed himself. His old friend had taken the news well, he thought—had been strangely calm, in fact, after an hour or so—but maybe that was because it had taken time to sink in. Maybe over the days that followed he'd looked into what was waiting for him and decided it was better to take the short-cut home. Maybe he'd just wanted to get it all over with. Did that make Tate responsible? Eliot had known he was going to be tested. It certainly hadn't been Tate's idea; he'd just conveyed the results, together with a warning that they would have to analyze a second sample to be certain of the prognosis. But if the result was his old friend's premature death, how could he not be in some way responsible? He wished he'd hidden the results, or at least waited until he'd had both sets. Better still, he wished he'd informed Eliot's regular doctor and let him handle it. Medical men had experience with these situations. He did not. In the normal run of things he didn't have to deal with people, just anonymous samples: numbers, not names. And when there was bad news, it went down the line from one computer database to another. The people were somebody else's problem.

Tate hadn't slept well since before Christmas. He wanted to talk to somebody about what had happened, but that was impossible. Not even Suzy knew the whole story, and something told him it was best to keep it that way. It wasn't that he didn't trust her, exactly. It was just that discretion was not her strong suit. Neither was patience.

His last conversation with Michael had been difficult. Tate had called a few days after their meeting, anxious to know how Eliot was bearing up, whether there was anything he could do. There'd been voices in the background—Margaret's parents, probably—and choral music.

He'd pictured Eliot standing in the kitchen, watching to see if anybody was listening to him. There were going to be some changes, he'd said, although he couldn't say what they were just yet. It turned out that he had decided not to tell his wife about the disease. He was keeping the whole thing to himself, he said, at least for the time being. Tate had agreed that this was the considerate thing to do. There was no point alarming Margaret until they had the results of the second test. But that hadn't been Eliot's concern. He'd wanted to know how long Tate could hold back the results of the first one. Eliot had assured him that, with Christmas almost upon them, it would probably be a couple of weeks before anyone asked for them.

And then Tate had brought up the subject of the missing printouts. He thought perhaps Eliot had taken them by accident, was simply curious. What could he possibly want with them? Eliot had taken a long time to answer. Then he'd said just the one word: *insurance.*

"Insurance against what?" Tate had asked, but suddenly the voices in the background were louder. It sounded like Eliot was being called to supper. He'd said good-bye and hung up. Tate had waited for an hour, then phoned again, but this time Margaret had answered. She'd seemed pleased to hear from him and wished him a merry Christmas. Michael was up in the den with his father-in-law. Margaret said she'd get him to call back. But Michael never did call back.

As it happened, Tate was asked for the test results a lot sooner than he'd expected: the very next day, in fact. He'd tried to stall, but with Pilaski breathing down his neck it had been difficult coming up with excuses. And he wasn't in any position to offend the client.

Tate was still staring out the window when the computer on his desk emitted a series of beeps and a gray panel appeared in the middle of the screen.

NEW DATA ANALYZED
ENTER PASSWORD
TO DISPLAY

The first batch of computer reports didn't usually come through until noon, but things were moving faster today because the volume of incoming material had fallen off over Christmas. Typically Medan Inc. had around one hundred twenty DNA samples under analysis at any one time, a volume of work made possible only by the latest in automation and by the limited nature of the analysis itself. The computer scanned the final stages of the process and reported three times each day. The artificial intelligence it deployed was relatively unsophisticated, and part of Tate's job was to scrutinize the results and have any irregularities checked by the lab staff against the original data. Only when he was satisfied that the findings stacked up did he clear them for release to the client. That, at least, was how he liked it to be. Recently Pilaski had started asking whether they couldn't accelerate the whole procedure: analyze more samples, faster, cut back on the contamination checks and the degree of human supervision. He claimed that he was only concerned with responding to customer demand, but there was no mention of new investment. And if there was no new investment, Tate had pointed out, the result could only be mistakes.

For scientists in the front line of medical research, locating the particular gene responsible for a genetic disease involved painstaking detective work. Genes acted upon the body by producing unique proteins at specific times and places. Sometimes the appearance of these proteins could be tracked back to biochemical activity in individual chromosomes, or even regions of chromosomes. After that it was merely a question of looking for a needle in a haystack, with one crucial difference: the needle and the hay looked exactly the same. What was required were exhaustive comparisons between the DNA of those who suffered from the disease and those who did not, taking one tiny section at a time. Depending upon the complexity of the gene concerned, this process could take many years.

Fortunately for Medan and its customers, once the composition and location of a disease gene had been established, checking whether it was present in a particular sample was relatively simple. At the company's laboratories, screening for nine such genes was undertaken on eight different chromosomes, although this represented an analysis of only a tiny fraction of the genetic information present in the samples. First, the individual chromosomes were identified and separated out using laser technology known as flow-sorting. Next came DNA amplification in which smaller regions of special interest were multiplied millions of times using a catalyst called the Taq enzyme. The resulting soups of genetic material were then introduced to specifically engineered radioactive probes. These probes attached themselves to recognized disease genes, making them radioactive and therefore detectable by photography. These stages had all been successfully automated, but in buying and modifying the technology, Medan Inc. had all but gone bankrupt eight years earlier. Only the arrival of new financial partners had saved the day. That was when Guy Pilaski had been brought in. Tate, a cofounder of the company, had been obliged to accept the position of deputy chief executive (technology).

Tate entered his password on the computer, and the first screen of data appeared. It was simply a list of nine-figure numbers, each one referring to a different, nameless individual. At the bottom of the screen another panel read

SELECT PROFILE OR PRESS
SPACE BAR FOR CURRENT ORDER

Tate scrolled down the list. One of the numbers was different from the rest. He had made it up himself so that he could recognize it easily from the others: AP91919191-9. It was a number for Michael Eliot, the second sample. After a moment's hesitation Tate selected it with the mouse and told the computer to print out the findings.

At first he thought he'd selected the wrong profile. The mutation responsible for Huntington's chorea was located near the end of the short arm of chromosome four. It consisted of an unstable segment of DNA within a gene the function of which was still unknown. In normal people the segment was made up of between eleven and thirty-four repeats of a particular triplet of base pairs. In Huntington's victims the segment was made up of between forty-two and one hundred such repetitions. How this genetic stutter caused the disease's symptoms was unclear. The correlation between the two was not: Huntington's was a dominant inherited ailment, which meant that everybody who carried the faulty gene became its victim, sooner or later.

But this time there was no genetic stutter.

Tate hurried back to the computer and started the routine from the beginning. The same data came up on the screen. Huntington's was one of the diseases Medan routinely searched for. It affected only one person in twenty thousand, but the protracted nature of the illness and the relative ease with which it could be detected made it worth going after. He stood up and walked across to the window, thinking. In spite of everything he'd told Eliot, the second test was little more than a formality. He'd never seen two samples from the same person yield different results, except where the disease in question was caused by a number of different genes—and there the inconsistency usually lay with the computer analysis rather than with the data itself. But this result was different. It said as loud and clear as any microbiologist could want: *Michael Eliot did not carry the gene for Huntington's chorea.*

Tate was suddenly very uncomfortable. He pulled at his tie and unbuttoned his collar. It was hard to believe that the probes would miss the genetic fault on chromosome four, inconceivable that they would imagine it was there when it wasn't. The whole apparatus would have to break down before that happened.

Unless there was contamination. Of course. Somehow one or the other of the samples had become contaminated with DNA from another person. A flake of skin, a drop of saliva, a strand of hair, any of these would do it. It didn't happen very often—hardly ever if you followed the normal procedures—and the presence of two different sets of chromosomes in the same sample would usually become apparent pretty quickly. But it could still happen. Once the wrong chromosomes had been flow-sorted, the procedure would continue as before, only the DNA under scrutiny would simply belong to somebody else.

Tate exited the program and accessed the minicomputer that held all the back data. The analysis of Michael Eliot's first sample was held there. In a few minutes he had the confirmation he was looking for. The two samples were completely different. They belonged to different men. The only question was: which of the two was Eliot?

He put down the printout and sat back in his chair, trying to think it through, trying to be logical. Of the two samples, the more likely to be contaminated was the first. He himself had taken the second in the laboratory, using optimal procedures in optimal conditions. The first sample had been gathered off-site, using generally reliable but far from foolproof methods. If there had been contamination, it was far more likely to have occurred there.

For a moment he felt relieved. It wasn't *his* fault. He had followed the standard procedures. Except that it was he who had given Eliot the bad news—bad news that had not been fully checked out. Eliot had gone away believing he had a fatal neurodegenerative disease that nothing in the world could cure. Ten days later he was dead.

The phone rang. Tate ignored it. He was remembering Eliot's face as he listened to his sentence of death—the fear and then, as the minutes passed, the strange, steely calm. *There were going to be some changes. . . .*

Then another thought struck him: if Michael Eliot didn't carry the gene for Huntington's chorea, then who did?

PART TWO

EVERYBODY KNOWS EVERYTHING

8

Alex slept badly. Every time she thought she was going to drift off, Liz's words came back to her: *he was worth millions.*

She remembered the last time she had seen Eliot, so stirred up, pressing forward to kiss her, the top button of his shirt undone, his tie pulled sideways under the collar. He had put his hand around her waist and in doing so had touched her breast. Hartman had been there, had seen it. A plastic beaker had gone over onto the floor, spilling wine. She had pushed him away then, angry with him for being so brutal, so stupid—angry with herself for letting him do it. But his touch had continued to tingle in the base of her throat minutes afterwards. Later, when she had collected her thoughts a little, she had dismissed it as drunken foolishness, the kind of behavior people indulged in at office parties, but now she saw it as something worse. He hadn't just betrayed his wife, shown disrespect to his wife, he had also been betraying Liz, the woman he was supposed to be running off with. Liz had shown her the plane tickets. Incredible as it seemed, there had been a solid plan of escape.

Alex rolled over in the bed, pulling the blankets close to keep out the cold air. She tried to think of something else, but then she was imagining Liz on the Riviera. She thought about how long it would have taken Eliot to start noticing the local beauties. Liz wouldn't have stood a chance. She was better off without him. The realization that she had just okayed Eliot's death brought Alex upright against the headboard.

The noise disturbed Oscar. He padded across to the window seat and jumped up to look out at the street. After a moment he started mewing to be let out, but Alex was not listening. She was thinking about what Liz had said about Eliot's death. It was too crazy to believe it had been anything but an accident. Okay, the odds were against his electrocuting himself at any one time, let alone when he and Liz were about to make their getaway, but murder? With Mrs. Eliot the killer? The odds against that were even greater. By how much, though? Accidental electrocution against domestic homicide. Alex drifted into a rambling comparison of the different probabilities, and then stopped herself. It was pointless. It didn't matter what the statistical probabilities were. One event required blind chance—simple coincidence—and the other, blind hate. You had to believe that Mrs. Eliot was capable of murder. And anyway, even if she was capable of it, how would she have carried it out? How did you fake an electrocution? You'd have to put a gun to somebody's head, make them hold a wire, throw a switch. . . .

Oscar's steady mewing filtered through to her consciousness. She got out of bed and pulled on a thick sweater.

"What's up, Mr. Cat?"

She picked him up and showed him the fire escape through the window. He loved to get out there. It was the one really catty thing he did. Otherwise he was sociable—friendly like a dog. He loved water and even wagged his tail, albeit in a slinky feline way. It was only on summer nights that he seemed to remember his role in life. He would sit out on the fire escape for hours just contemplating the moon.

"Or maybe drug them," Alex said to herself. "Drug them first and then wire them up."

Of course people had committed suicide that way. She had read about it. They'd connected themselves to the power supply with a timer switch, then taken a sleeping pill. One hour into a pleasant nap and the timer switched on. Alex touched her forehead against the glass. Maybe Eliot had done that, maybe something was going to come out about the money. Maybe he had killed himself, and the wife had wanted to cover it up, had wanted to pretend it was an accident. . . .

*   *   *

On Tuesday morning she found a note on her desk. It was from Randal White, the first sign in quite a while that he knew she even existed. It asked simply if she could find time to see him around nine-thirty. She made herself coffee, checked her e-mail, and then went and knocked on his door.

He was sitting behind his desk, which was partly buried under a heap of documents. It was so unlike him to let his desk get out of control, Alex couldn't help staring.

"I wanted to apologize for not getting back to you on those health-care figures, but as you can see"—he gestured at the desk—"I'm completely snowed under. Janice is after me for ten different things. You know how she keeps a tally."

Janice Aitken, White's personal assistant, had a passion for Post-it notes. Alex noticed a whole row of them on White's dead computer screen. Several bore underlined messages with double exclamation marks.

"Michael's death has . . . I've been having all kinds of meetings, as I'm sure you can imagine."

Alex nodded, though it seemed to her White's neglect predated Eliot's death by several weeks.

"And what with everything else—well, it's turning into quite a busy New Year." White paused for a moment, frowning, then checked his Post-it notes. "In fact, that was what I wanted to talk to you about."

"The New Year?"

He gave her a look, and she saw confusion mixed with the new fatigue he seemed never to shake off these days. "No. Michael. It's his funeral tomorrow, as you may have heard. I wanted to ask if you were planning to go."

Alex frowned. She was conscious of White watching her intently. "Well, I hadn't—"

"I thought you'd appreciate the opportunity, since you two . . ."

White let the phrase hang in the air. Alex had a feeling like missing a step in the dark. Then the realization came to her like a light being switched on: White thought she had been Eliot's lover.

The idea was absurd. Everyone knew about her and Mark. But then again, Mark was not her husband. Maybe White thought she'd decided to move on. Looking at him now, Alex thought that she could see it in his eyes—suspicion, or at least curiosity. She felt the color rise in her cheeks, and immediately wondered if this mistaken assumption had been behind his being so distant in the past few weeks. He thought she was sleeping around, maybe trying to screw her way up the corporate ladder, regardless of whose feelings she might be hurting. First Mark, then Mark's boss—and who next, now that Eliot was dead? The cliquey nature of Providence society meant that the senior execs were in and out of each other's houses on a regular basis. White certainly knew Mrs. Eliot, had certainly met her socially. Alex imagined her crying on White's shoulder, telling him all about Eliot's deceit. For White to feel a degree of animosity towards the "other woman" would be natural.

"Alex, are you all right?"

"Oh—oh yes, sure."

"I mention it because I thought we might go together. It would be a chance to talk about this curious anomaly you uncovered in the data on—what was it?"

"Heart disease."

"Ah yes, that's right, *heart* disease. Of course, if you think you're going to find the service too upsetting . . ."

Alex felt completely confused. But one thought was clear: she mustn't give the appearance of having been affected by Eliot's death.

"No, not at all," she said. "I mean, of course it's all very sad, for Mrs. Eliot particularly. But I really didn't know Michael that well. Not outside work, anyway."

White brought his hands together under his chin, his eyes smiling, his mouth a line. "I see. Well . . ."

"But if you think I *should* go, as a matter of, I don't know, as part of a corporate gesture, I'd be more than happy—"

"Good," said White abruptly. "Good. I'd get into the PrimeNumber issue right now, but—"

The phone rang. White waited for it to stop, but it was obvious that Janice wasn't picking up. Finally he reached under a pile of documents and pulled it out.

"Hello? Oh, Richard . . . Yes, what can I . . . ?"

It was Richard Goebert, the CEO.

Alex looked out the window, trying to gather her thoughts. Clearly if White wanted to discuss the anomaly, she wasn't being marginalized. He couldn't be too bothered about what he thought she might have been up to with Eliot. She felt relieved—and then, almost immediately, pleased that he had taken her comments seriously enough to want to discuss them further.

"Well, actually, Richard, now isn't . . . Yes, yes, I realize that, but . . . well, I'm just having a chat with one of my . . . With Alex Tynan, in fact."

Goebert launched into a long monologue, and White closed his eyes. After a while he opened them, looked at Alex, and shrugged. Eventually he sat forward in his chair.

"Richard, sorry to interrupt, but I . . . yes, yes." He was nodding now. "Surely, of course. Yes, I will. Bye, Richard." He put the phone down. "Richard's thirty-fifth wedding anniversary," he said, as if this explained everything.

The three black limos left the Providence Life building at two-thirty. Richard Goebert, Newton Brady, and Walter Neumann sat stiff and silent in the first; Ralph McCormick of Central Records rode along with Donald Grant and Dean Mitchell, the head of Claims, and Tom Heymann of PrimeNumber. Alex and White rode alone in the third. A pall of freezing fog hung over the city, dissolving the tall buildings on Westminster Street above the fourth floor.

Mel Hartman had been astounded when he learned that Alex was going to the funeral with so many of the senior executives, his confusion becoming alarm when he discovered that she'd be riding alone with Randal White, his idol. His mouth pulled into a half smile as he said he hoped that she and White weren't going to be riding out to Swan Point in her Camry. But through the jokiness, Alex had detected something akin to anger. She explained that she wasn't the only nonexec going to the funeral. Ed Bergen was going from Finance, and then there would be Eliot's family and friends. Hartman had shrugged, saying it didn't matter to him who was going. "Have a great time" had been his parting shot.

Hartman, in his Machiavellian way, had clearly assumed that Alex was being shown a degree of favor. And, making herself comfortable in the ivory leather interior, she couldn't help feeling just a little privileged. After so many weeks of neglect by White, it was nice to be getting his full attention again.

"A very funereal day," he said, looking out at the gray streets.

"They said it's going to snow again," said Alex.

"I don't suppose we'll have much chance to talk once we get to the cemetery," said White. He leaned forward and pressed a button, bringing up a glass screen between them and the driver. He turned and looked at her. "So perhaps you could tell me about this little wrinkle you, um, stumbled across?"

"Well, it's as I said in my e-mail. It's quite a simple thing. The heart attack/convertible correlation is too hard. Every year four-point-two percent of male heart attack claimants own convertibles. There's no variation, not—"

"Yes, I understand all that. Your e-mail was very clear and to the point. I was just puzzled as to how you came to be doing such a bizarre cross-reference anyway."

Alex had prepared for this. She didn't want to talk about the joke she had been planning.

"Well, it was the lunch hour and I just wanted to see how far the data would go," she said. "I mean, we're always telling ourselves how detailed it is, how exhaustive. I thought: why not?"

White looked hard at her. Then he nodded.

"I see. So it was just an accident." He smiled as if he didn't quite believe her. "Well, it was lucky you did pick it out, because obviously in the normal run of things this hard correlation, as you call it, would not have emerged."

He turned away from her. For a minute they rode in silence. Large feathery flakes of snow started to hit the windshield.

"Do you think it's significant?" asked Alex.

"As you know, any mistakes in compiling our actuarial data could seriously affect our pricing. In the end it could cost us money."

"You think that's what this is, a mistake in compilation?"

"Probably."

"Whose mistake?"

White thought a moment. "I think I'd start by looking at Prime-Number. They do most of that stuff for us now. It's cheaper."

"PrimeNumber? I thought they just handled the application forms. Punched in all the raw data for us."

White shook his head. "They used to. Not anymore. They have cheaper premises, cheaper staff"—White shot Alex a disapproving look—"and a lot of computer capacity they don't need. Meanwhile our operations have been expanding. You know how crowded things are getting at headquarters. PrimeNumber has been doing more and more of the grunt work. We've been tied up with them for about seven years. In fact we're pretty much their only customer these days."

"And PrimeNumber compiles our claims data too? Our mortality stats, and everything?"

The thought that something so important, so *central* to ProvLife's business—to its actuarial side above all—should be handled by outsiders struck Alex as a kind of violation.

"Someone has to punch it all in, add it up. It's cheaper to outsource. Although perhaps not so"—White rubbed at the condensation on his window and looked out at the street—"thorough."

He turned to her. "How would you like to go visit PrimeNumber? They're down in West Warwick. It isn't far. We could call it management training. A widening of your operational experience. While you were there you could, let's say, *review* their data compilation methods."

Alex didn't quite know what to say. She was flattered that White was taking the glitch she had discovered so seriously, but a little daunted that he now wanted her to find out who was responsible.

"You mean, you want me to spy on them."

White chuckled.

"Think of it as an audit," he said. "If that makes you feel any better."

9

S wan Point Cemetery lay above the shoreline between the leafy opulence of Blackstone Boulevard and the wide estuary of the Seekonk River. Covering some two hundred acres, its long empty avenues were lined with mature cedars and maples and spruces, its tombstones and monuments hidden among cherry trees and neatly trimmed yews. Especially on the southern side, where most of the land was still vacant, it could easily have been mistaken for a municipal park, except that in a park there would have been people: joggers, roller-bladers, mothers with children, at least footprints in the snow. But at Swan Point visitors were few and literally far between. It was less a city of the dead than an affluent, lonely suburb.

The Episcopalian chapel was a low building built in the old English style, with stone cladding, arched stained-glass windows, and a small lead spire. White's car joined a procession of dark sedans lining up outside, maneuvering with otherworldly patience as they discharged their passengers and retired to a discreet distance. Alex felt a squeeze of tension as they finally came to a halt behind a private ambulance, from the back of which an old lady in a wheelchair was being slowly helped down. She knew nothing of Michael Eliot's family, and this was surely a family occasion, first and foremost. The fact that there were going to be other ProvLife people there made her feel a little easier, but then again they were all so much more senior than she was. They had known Michael Eliot for years. Mel Hartman's surprise—the whole department's surprise by now—was understandable. It was as if she were being singled out for admission to a more intimate circle than her position merited. She'd have felt more comfortable about it if she'd understood exactly why.

By the chapel door two immaculately turned-out men were taking the names of the mourners as they filed past, and handing out orders of service. They wore identical black overcoats with velvet collars and black armbands trimmed with lace. To Alex's dismay, she was left to go in alone, as Randal White paused to exchange a few words with the old lady in the wheelchair. She smiled up at him, taking his arm for a moment, and it was clear she knew him well. Alex asked herself if she could possibly be Michael Eliot's mother.

The coffin lay in front of the altar, covered in floral wreaths. An organ was playing softly. Alex stood for a moment at the end of the aisle, looking for somewhere to sit. East Side society had turned out in force, and most of the pews at the back and the edge of the chapel were already taken. Only the three rows closest to the front were completely empty. Several heads turned to look at her. They would be wondering who she was, a young woman unescorted, no sign of husband or parent. Most of them would probably know she wasn't family. Alex glanced back at the door, hoping that Randal White was about to join her, but there was no sign of him. He was probably greeting more of Eliot's friends and relatives and offering eloquent condolences. Away to her left she caught sight of Ed Bergen. He was hemmed in between a pillar and a tall, silver-haired man with a walking stick. Bergen smiled back at her grimly, clearly wishing already that the whole affair was over. There was no sign of Liz Foster or anyone else from Treasury.

Alex walked quickly up the aisle, aiming for the third row. Her heels clacked noisily on the marble floor. She felt certain everybody was looking at her. Could it be they'd all heard about Eliot's affair at the office? It seemed all too likely. The ProvLife board certainly knew about it, even if they weren't sure about the identity of the other woman. And then there was Margaret Eliot. Could she really have been oblivious to what was going on? And if not, would she have kept the knowledge to herself? The smart end of the East Side was a very small world. Right now half the congregation were probably asking themselves if the blond twenty-something heading up the aisle had been Michael Eliot's secret lover, come to pay her last respects.

Alex was already feeling self-conscious by the time she reached the fourth pew and saw the little white cards with *Reserved* written on them. She felt the color rise to her cheeks. The front three rows were empty because they were for the family, of course. There was nothing to do but to turn around and go back again, her mistake—or would it seem like presumption?—plain for everyone to see. But then she heard the doors opening again, and the next moment the family party was walking up the aisle towards her: the widow, veiled, holding the arm of a tall young man who had to be her son, the old lady in the wheelchair being pushed along by Randal White, a somber middle-aged couple beside them, and then the rest of ProvLife's senior management: Richard Goebert and his wife Eva, Newton Brady, Walter Neumann, Ralph McCormick, and the others. Alex felt trapped. She moved back down the aisle from pew to pew, searching for a vacant space, but no one seemed in a hurry to make room.

Do you think Mrs. Eliot killed her husband?

The question flashed in Alex's mind. Instinctively she turned, only to find the widow staring back at her as she approached. Behind the veil Alex saw her pale face, fine features, beautiful green eyes—eyes that narrowed for a moment as if seeing something they did not want to see. And in that moment Alex knew that Mrs. Eliot *had* heard the rumors, knew there *had* been another woman, and, like everyone else, was wondering who it could be. Alex stood rooted to the spot.

You don't know her, Alex. She'd want revenge.

And then she was gone, lost among the other mourners at the front of the chapel. A bearded man was on his feet at Alex's side, offering her a place to sit. She whispered him thanks and hid herself behind the rows of heads and shoulders, not lifting her gaze again until the service had begun.

For an expert on human mortality, Alex knew surprisingly little about the ceremonial of death. Michael Eliot's was only the second funeral she had ever been to, the other being the cremation of her grandfather seven years earlier. Other relatives had died during her childhood and adolescence, but Alex had never come under any pressure to attend the services. Her mother worshiped regularly at the local

Presbyterian church, and encouraged Alex to do the same. But when it came to disposing of the dead, her enthusiasm for Christian ceremonial deserted her. The whole procedure was just a formality—that was her attitude—something a child could not be expected to understand or appreciate. Alex certainly never got the impression that by not attending she might be showing disrespect to the dear departed, or letting her mother down in any way. So in the end she had always stayed home.

She had suspected at the time that her mother was, in reality, trying to shield her from something she was bound to find upsetting. Partly as a result, Alex had grown up believing that funerals were mysterious, traumatic occasions, windows on a side of human existence best hidden away and not dwelled upon. When she had attended the service for her grandfather, the quiet solemnity of the proceedings had come as a genuine surprise. Yet even now, as she listened to Richard Goebert delivering the address—his theme "the tradition of service" that Michael Eliot "had cherished and maintained," his voice a monotone of institutional sorrow—she still could not completely banish the feeling that behind the evocation of fellowship and redemption, the comforting words of prayer and the singing of hymns, lay something darker and more troubling than the simple fact of death.

There had been no funeral for Sergeant John Tynan, of course. For twenty years and more Alex's mother had refused to entertain the idea that he was even dead. To her, missing in action meant missing—as in *temporarily misplaced*, and *liable to turn up at any moment*—and she ran the house accordingly. As far as Alex could recall, she never went so far as to lay an extra place at the dinner table, but she certainly kept a pair of her husband's clean pajamas folded under the pillow, and laundered them every now and again "to keep them fresh." Some of Alex's earliest memories were of being shown her father's picture in a photograph album, and being told that he would one day come back from the war. Every time there was something in the press about Americans being seen in Russian labor camps or Vietnamese prisons, her mother would cut out the story and read it out triumphantly at breakfast—as if it proved beyond all reasonable doubt that her husband and his comrades were alive and well, and hadn't been killed when their Huey fell out of the sky behind enemy lines in 1972. And even when Alex repeated all the things her mother said, to her uncles and aunts and the teachers at school, none of them ever disagreed, or questioned whether she was in possession of all the facts. They shielded her from the truth—from what the odds really were that her father was alive and would one day return—just as her mother had shielded her from funerals. And so Alex had grown up with the expectation that someday, without warning, a virtual stranger by the name of Sergeant John Tynan was going to walk in through the front door and change their lives forever. Sometimes she wondered if her devotion to the certainties of mathematics, to the science of probability and prediction, didn't owe something to that single, perpetual uncertainty in her childhood.

They sang "Abide with Me" and "Light's Abode, Celestial Salem," assisted by a choir of six. They murmured amen to prayers of commendation uttered by the young minister, and read aloud their responses from the Order of Service: "Enter not into judgment with thy servant, O Lord; For in thy sight shall no man living be justified." And as they were mouthing the Nunc Dimittis from St. Luke, chapter two, the six pallbearers lifted Eliot's coffin onto their shoulders and carried it slowly down the aisle towards a hearse that was waiting outside. Out of the corner of her eye Alex watched them as they went past: they were led by Walter Neumann and Newton Brady, their expressions each a study in dignity in the face of loss. Whatever Liz Foster might say, it was a touching gesture of solidarity and respect on the part of Michael Eliot's colleagues. As she watched the coffin go by, Alex recalled what Randal White had said a few days earlier about how ProvLife was part of the community, not just a mechanism for making money. She felt a momentary glow of pride. Providence Life *was* different. It wasn't just the size of the company or its long heritage, or even the precision and sophistication of its analyses. It was the *ethos* of the place. When she'd left MIT she had been ready to work just about anywhere. She saw now how lucky she had been to end up where she had.

The hearse moved at walking pace to the Eliot family plot, followed on foot by the mourners. Flecks of snow were drifting down from the overcast sky, the tops of the trees hidden in the gathering mist. Alex found herself walking next to Randal White, near the back of the procession. Although the mood was still subdued, the hymns and the prayers—even Goebert's words—had lifted spirits a little, and here and there people were talking to one another, remarking on the aptness of the service or the beauty of the location.

"I'm sorry for abandoning you back there," White said. "I got caught up with Michael's aunt Grace. I haven't seen her for about eight years, but she never forgets a face. A great lady. Ninety-one and sharp as a tack."

Alex smiled. "That's all right, Randal," she said. Usually she felt awkward using White's Christian name, but not this time.

"You should have come and sat up at the front," he said. "There was plenty of room. I could see you stranded there in the aisle. I was about to say something."

"It wasn't a problem. That man made room for me."

Alex nodded towards the bearded man, who was walking a few yards ahead of them. He was easy to spot because, of all the mourners present, he was the only one wearing a beige overcoat. Everyone else was in dark gray or black. He was also alone in wearing brown shoes. White followed Alex's gaze, a faint look of disapproval crossing his face.

"Offered me his handkerchief too," said Alex. "I'm afraid I started sniffling during 'Abide with Me.' It's such a beautiful hymn."

"Yes, it is," said White. "And such a fine text." He looked out across the frozen ground towards a cluster of stone crosses. The remains of an old bouquet were poking up through the snow. " 'Change and decay in all around I see.' Did you know, the man that wrote those words died suddenly the very same night he finished it?"

"No," said Alex. "How . . . extraordinary."

White smiled. "I thought you were going to say improbable."

"Well, that too."

"I wonder if in some way he foresaw his death. Do you think that's possible? Perhaps he wrote 'Fast falls the eventide' because he knew that for him it was literally true."

White fell silent, suddenly lost in thought. For a few moments they walked on together without speaking.

"I don't suppose you know his name," Alex said at last.

"No. He was a parish priest, I believe. Somewhere in England."

"No," said Alex. "I meant the man who was sitting next to me. That man just ahead of us."

"Oh, him." White frowned and looked away again. "Didn't he introduce himself?"

"No. He didn't have a chance, really."

"I can't help you, I'm afraid. I don't think we've ever met."

For some years it had been the fashion at Swan Point to mark each family plot with a single, monumental slab of granite. Four inches thick, with rough-cut edges, it bore the family name in bold capitals that were legible a hundred yards away. The individual graves were arranged around it, with smaller, matching headstones for each. Few of these bore lengthy inscriptions. There were no biographies, no quotations from scripture, rarely even an *In Loving Memory* or a *Dearly Beloved*. Most stones confined themselves to names and dates, as if determined to guard the privacy of the dead. To Alex it seemed that privacy was what Swan Point was all about. Or was that just the way they liked it in Rhode Island? Perhaps part of being small and independent was minding your own business and expecting others to mind theirs.

The Eliots had taken a quiet spot on the northern side of the cemetery, close by a series of older, nineteenth-century tombs, several marked with small Egyptian-style obelisks. The freshly dug grave was flanked by floral wreaths propped up on wooden frames. Every trace of earth was hidden beneath dark green covers. As she stood waiting for the coffin to be carried from the hearse Alex counted seven other Eliot graves, going back two generations. She'd had no idea until then that the Eliots were a Rhode Island family. But then again, it made sense: Michael Eliot's principal supporter at ProvLife had always been Richard Goebert. And there had been Goeberts in Providence for two centuries—all the way back to the slave-trading days when so many Rhode Island fortunes had been made.

They gathered around the graveside and listened to the minister reading the prayers of interment, his voice small in the open air. And it was then, as they were lowering the coffin into the ground, that the irony of it came to her. Michael Eliot's dream had been to leave all this. Almost his last act had been to try and disappear, to sneak away and never look back. And yet here he was, being claimed by his family, his city, his colleagues, surrounded and mourned by the very people he had tried so determinedly to escape. And here he would stay now, forever.

Alex shuddered and looked up from the coffin. Again Margaret Eliot's eyes met hers. Through the shifting folds of the veil Alex thought she could detect the faintest trace of something like defiance. Or was it triumph?

Alex heard the phone ringing and hurried up the last flight of stairs. Oscar, who was sitting on the top step, stared at her nonplussed before darting up a ladder which had appeared in one corner of the landing. Alex unlocked her door and grabbed the receiver.

"Hello?"

There was silence, followed by a sound of someone drawing a long unsteady breath.

"Hello? Who is this?"

The sound became a stifled sob. "It's me. You're home early, aren't you? I thought you'd be back at the office."

Liz sounded upset, shaky. It must have been the funeral that had done it, just knowing that it had taken place. Alex tried to sound cheerful.

"Randal gave me the rest of the afternoon off. You know, as a mark-of-respect kind of thing."

"Did he? That was nice of him."

"Yes, I thought so." She sat down on the sofa. "So here I am at five o'clock. Are you—are you okay, Liz?"

"I should have been there. I shouldn't have stayed away."

"Oh, Liz."

"I should have been there to say good-bye. I should have been. I just thought—"

"Liz, Liz, stop. Don't torture yourself. It doesn't matter. It was just— just a service. That's all it was. A formality."

"I was afraid I wouldn't be able to handle it. I was afraid I'd get too upset and give myself away. I didn't want that to happen—not for me, but for Michael. Because he always wanted things to be . . ."

To be kept secret. Was that what Liz meant? Even after everything that had happened, she was still the loyal PA. But then, how much had Eliot kept secret from her? There was the ten million dollars, to begin with, not to mention how he came by it.

"Liz, I understand completely. It's what he would have wanted . . . probably. I mean, your discretion."

"I should have gone, though, Alex. I had a right to be there. I had as much right as anyone did. More."

"Of course you did," said Alex soothingly. "Of course you did."

For a moment the line was silent. Alex tried to think of something else to say, something that would help.

"What was it like?" Liz said at last. "Was there a good turnout?"

"Yes, pretty good, I guess."

"All those people pretending they care. I can just picture their long faces."

There it was again, the sudden switch from grief to bitterness. Alex felt that Liz was on the defensive. She still didn't know quite how to deal with it.

"I suppose Randal White was there," Liz went on.

"Yes," Alex replied, feeling a little defensive herself. "He was there."

"And Walter Neumann too, I suppose?"

"Yes."

"Of course he was. He wouldn't miss out on that one. They all want Richard Goebert's job when he retires. Did you know that? The CEO liked Michael, so they all have to pretend they liked him too: Brady, Neumann, Randal White. That's why they were there. But they didn't like him, Alex, they didn't like him at all. White *hated* him."

"Liz, I don't think that's completely fair. I mean, *everybody* was there, all the senior people. It was like—like a company thing, in a way. I think they—"

"Michael *hated* the company. He wanted to get out. And someone stopped him."

Alex sighed. "Oh, Liz."

"Did you get a look at her?"

"Who?"

"Margaret. Who else?"

"Yes, kind of. I mean, she was wearing a veil. I didn't get a real close—"

"Do you think she could have done it?"

Alex hesitated. She remembered how the widow had looked at her across the open grave. It gave her a bad feeling. But that's all it was: a feeling.

"I don't know, Liz. I don't think so."

"Did she cry?"

"Liz, I don't—"

"Did you see her cry? You didn't, did you? I bet she barely managed a sniff."

"Liz, why don't you—?"

"Did she?"

"Liz, I don't know! I didn't sit anywhere near her. I couldn't see."

Liz fell silent. After a few moments Alex heard her crying softly. She was as distraught now as ever. And was it any wonder? She was sitting in an empty apartment with nothing to look at but Michael Eliot's luggage, the neatly packed relics of the new life they had planned together. She had come within twenty-four hours of realizing a dream, only to have it snatched away from her. And the worst of it was, nobody could tell her why.

"Listen, Liz," said Alex. "You've got to get out of that place for a while. It's not good, you— Look, why don't you pack an overnight bag and come on over? I'll cook us some dinner and we can get drunk and watch TV. They're showing *The 39 Steps* on A & E."

"Sounds good. But . . . well, aren't you going out with Mark?"

Liz showed up an hour later, by which time Alex was already chopping vegetables, Stevie Wonder playing loud in the living room. They ate early—a chicken stir-fry—and quickly got through two bottles of Chardonnay, Liz drinking most of it. She had calmed down a lot since her phone call. She wasn't tearful anymore, nor angry. She was just very tired, she said.

Alex tried to keep the conversation light. They talked about Oscar, and Mayor Montanelli and Mrs. Connelly's idiot son-in-law. Alex didn't mention Michael Eliot, or his death, or his widow, and even managed to keep off the subject of the ten million dollars. Liz seemed content to do the same. In fact, it seemed as if the whole subject was suddenly closed as far as she was concerned.

10

The pain of loss came as a surprise to Margaret Eliot. Years of deadening routine had reduced her feelings for her husband to a vague dependency mixed with resentment at the indifference he could not be bothered to disguise. Mrs. Ramirez, the cleaning lady, had discovered the body, so she had been spared that trauma, and it wasn't until Michael Eliot was in the ground that the full weight of events bore down on her. After the funeral, after the departure of friends and relatives—after the moody, bitter departure of Peter, her younger son—she sat alone in the living room staring at the wall on which were hung two pictures: one of Peter and Tom, and one of the whole family on holiday in the Florida Keys. It had been taken only twelve years before. Michael had his arms around the boys' shoulders, while she sat cross-legged in a large wicker chair, holding a pair of sunglasses. White, floury sand sprinkled their sun-darkened feet. Michael had taken the boys fishing that day. They had returned smelling of beer, Peter carrying a twenty-pound tuna as though it were a three-hundred-pound marlin.

Now Peter was back in New York—he had left immediately after the service—while Tom was in London where he worked for Citicorp. He hadn't wanted to come home ("What's the point?" he had said) but Margaret knew it was more than indifference that kept him away, it was resentment. Both boys blamed her for what had happened to the family, for Michael's gradual estrangement. They had accused her on several occasions—such things were usually kept for Thanksgiving or Christmas—of being cold and distant. But to her it seemed that it was Michael who had drifted away. If she had changed over the years, it was because of him. Why he had changed towards her, and towards the children, she had never been able to understand. One year everything had been fine, and the next year reserve and distrust had begun to grow like a tumor. The picture blurred as tears flooded her green eyes. What had happened to them all?

At ten-thirty she became conscious of the hands on the long carriage clock, and realized that three hours had passed without her moving. She was hungry, but the sight of the food left by caterers in the kitchen turned her stomach. She folded smoked salmon into a piece of rye bread and then dropped it into the sink, weeping hot tears she was powerless to stop. She lifted her head and looked at her reflection in the darkened window.

"God help me," she said.

Then she took a bottle of scotch from the cabinet, and went up to the cold empty bed.

It was the telephone that woke her. She squinted at the clock and was surprised to see that it was almost ten in the morning. She had overslept. She reached across the bed to give Michael a nudge and then realized with a jolt that he was no longer there, that he no longer would be there—forever. She pressed her eyes shut against an image of frozen earth being shoveled into a fresh grave, then reached for the phone.

"Hello?"

There was no one there. She registered the half-empty bottle of scotch and a broken photo frame on the wooden floor. A band of pain seemed to tighten across her forehead. *"Hello."*

"Mrs.—is this Mrs. Eliot?"

A woman's voice. Vaguely familiar.

"Yes, who is this?"

"You don't know me. You don't know me. Anyway . . . anyway, that's not important."

"Oh?"

She pulled open the bedside cabinet and reached inside for the

Tylenol, then saw with a flash of irritation that there was no water in the carafe.

"What is important—the reason I'm calling—is that I have information."

"Information?"

There was a long pause.

"About your husband," said the voice.

Margaret frowned. She pulled a strand of hair from the corner of her mouth. "What?"

"I said—"

"I heard what you said. What are you talking about, information?" Tears pricked in her eyes. "My husband—"

"Is dead. Is . . . I know."

The voice seemed to falter. Then it was bolder again: "I have information about his finances."

She listened to the voice with her eyes shut, trying to make sense of what was happening.

"Did you realize that your husband left a substantial estate?" said the voice. The woman, whoever she was, sounded like she was reading from a script now, but shakily, as if it were hard for her.

"Who *is* this? I'm going to hang up the phone unless you tell me who you are."

"Did you know he left over ten million dollars?"

The sun came out from behind a cloud. The floor was covered in tiny pieces of glass.

"What—" She found that her voice had gone. All she could manage was a whisper. "What are you talking about?"

"You didn't know?"

"Didn't . . . no, no I didn't know. Who *is* this?"

"Over ten million dollars"—there came an unsteady intake of breath—"in a Swiss bank account."

She shook her head in disbelief and the beginnings of anger. "You're crazy. You must be some sort of . . . you must be ill. My husband was an employee of Providence Life. He earned—well, that's none of your business. He *wasn't* a millionaire."

"He earned slightly over one hundred twenty thousand dollars a year," said the voice.

Margaret tightened her grip on the phone. Michael had earned $123,000 in the last fiscal year.

"How do you—? Who are you? I *demand* to know."

"Of course, last year his money—his Swiss money, his real money—earned about four hundred grand."

She collapsed back into her pillows. "Are you . . . you're not with the IRS?" she said.

There was a burst of nervous laughter at the other end of the phone. This was too much. She swung her legs out of bed and stood up, oblivious of the broken glass scattered over the floor.

"What?" said the voice, vindictive now. "Worried you might lose your precious house? No, I'm not with the IRS. I'm—let's just say I was a friend of Michael's. A *good* friend."

She walked over to the window, thinking now, trying to guess who this woman might be. A sharp pain in her left foot made her look down. There was a streak of blood on the floor.

"Anyway," said the voice, "like I said, who I am isn't important. What I *know* is."

"What—what do you know?"

"I know where the *money* is."

Margaret started to laugh. It was all crazy.

"Come on, Margaret," said the voice. "Don't slip away from me now. Get a grip. I'm telling you I know where the money is. *Your* money."

"My . . . I don't—I'm not sure I—"

"Just *listen*, will you?" Not anger, but impatience, fear. "Michael had ten million dollars in a Swiss bank account. Now he's dead. The money's yours, legally."

"I don't know what you're talking about."

"That's why I'm calling. I have telephone numbers, account numbers, I have all his papers—information that gives you access to what is legally yours."

"Why? Why would you— Why would you do that? Why would you tell me?"

"Simple," said the voice, almost defiant now. There came another unsteady intake of breath, maybe a drag on a cigarette. "I want half."

Margaret stared out at the gray morning. Her foot was stinging, but she had such a powerful sense of unreality, she didn't even look down to see what was causing the pain.

"I can't get the money because I wasn't the wife," the voice went on. "You, as the surviving spouse, get everything. Do you understand me?"

"Yes . . . yes."

"Good. Now listen to me. This is the deal. I give you the information in exchange for half. For *half.*"

"Oh my God."

She covered her mouth with trembling fingers. The voice ground on relentlessly.

"We shared Michael. And now"—it was a cigarette, she could hear the lips smack gently against the paper—"now we share his money. That's fair."

"Shared Michael?"

"You've got the house, haven't you?" It was like she had suddenly touched a nerve. "And the pension and the life insurance policy. But remember, without me, without what I know, you don't get anything else."

"What do you mean, we shared Michael?"

A thought struck home and she sat back on the bed. She recalled the young woman at the funeral.

"My God, it's you, isn't it? At the funeral. You were Michael's—"

"I wasn't at the funeral. Think I'd stand there with all you hypocrites? But don't worry. I'll be saying my good-byes."

Tears flooded Margaret Eliot's eyes. "Oh my *God*. How can you—he's barely in the ground and you're—you're trying to get his money."

"It's mine as much as yours, Margaret. *More* than yours. We were going to share it, the two of us. If he'd lived, you wouldn't have seen a cent of it."

"That's a lie." She was sobbing now.

"He was leaving you, Margaret. That's how he felt about you. The day he died? He was about to walk out the door."

"You're a liar," she said flatly.

"I can prove it. I've got the—"

But Margaret didn't want to know what this woman had. The anger and pain broke like a storm in her head. She split a fingernail slamming down the phone.

11

For a cost-conscious company head, Tom Heymann was pretty generous with his own time. Alex arrived at PrimeNumber on Monday morning and, in the two days she was there, he never left her alone for more than an hour at a time. When she first arrived he invited her into his office for coffee out of a styrofoam cup and "a little chat." He was a small man in his late forties who looked like he put in time at the gym. Light brown hair parted in the middle gave him a kind of Partridge Family innocence, but his eyes, pouchy bruised-looking eyes, were less friendly. It was his eyes that held Alex's attention throughout their uneasy interview. Light gray or light blue, they gave the impression of being lit from behind, and they were everywhere. He smiled as he questioned her, moved his head around in a relaxed we're-just-getting-to-know-each-other fashion, but the eyes remained serious, cutting from her mouth to her hair to her breasts as he talked, as though each part of her was information he'd be reviewing later. Alex couldn't help giving a shudder.

"Cold?"

"No, I'm fine," said Alex.

"We keep it pretty cool in here. Never gets much above sixty-five. Thing is, with all the electronics we're using, there's a tendency for our ladies to overheat. And if it gets too warm they get sloppy. That's when the errors start to creep in."

Alex looked down at her cup. There was a silk-screened logo in a hot arterial red: AT PRIMENUMBER QUALITY COUNTS.

"That's not what this is about, is it?" asked Heymann.

"No, no," said Alex, looking up. "Mr. White just felt that it might be useful for me to get some exposure to the data capture aspects of ProvLife's work."

Heymann's spooky eyes narrowed. "Exposure?"

"Sure. He just felt that I should see exactly how information gets from the applications and the claim forms into the company database."

"I see."

He watched her for a moment, then blinked. He brought his hands together and rubbed them vigorously, obviously a little cold himself.

"Well, let me take you around."

PrimeNumber was located at the end of a cul-de-sac in West Warwick, about seven miles from the center of Providence. It was a bleak area of light industrial units and warehouses, many of which were still awaiting occupation, a testament to the city's faith—or at least Mayor Montanelli's faith—in its high-tech future. The operation was all on one floor packed with cheap-looking desks and partitioned by low burlap screens. There were no corners or houseplants for people to hide behind. Everybody could see everything. Alex guessed that office chitchat was discouraged. Monitors flickered. As Heymann walked her around the floor, one or two heads looked up, but not for long. The sound of keystrokes was like steady rain.

Heymann came to a halt behind a red-haired woman.

"These are the Part Ones."

He picked up a white form with light blue boxes for insurance applicants to enter data. The form was identified by an eight-digit serial number with the prefix AP for applicant and ran to forty-two questions, some of which were broken into subsections. The form asked applicants for basic information such as home address and occupation, whether they wanted a smoker or nonsmoker Basic Plan, and what kind of hospital indemnity coverage they were seeking. The last twelve questions got into more of the underwriting detail and sought to determine if the applicants planned to travel in the next twelve months, what type of car they drove, whether they pursued any hazardous activities such as scuba diving or motorcycle racing, whether they had lost their driving licences or had been convicted of violations while under the influence of alcohol or drugs. Alex watched the redhead's computer screen fill with information.

"We maintain a set of statistical databases down here, as well as inputting the raw data," Heymann explained. "Of course they're all one hundred percent compatible with the Central Records system at ProvLife headquarters. When you guys in the actuarial department go rooting around for numbers, for stats, half the time you're actually on our system. We're fully integrated."

"And how often do you update these databases?"

"It's instantaneous. All the category responses—things other than names or addresses—have a digital tag. So that, for example, when Karyn here—"

At the sound of her name the red-haired woman looked up. Heymann touched her on the shoulder.

"It's all right, Karyn. When Karyn enters an applicant's marital status, the computer recognizes the category and automatically updates the data, just as soon as she gets to the bottom of the form."

Alex nodded. Databases or not, the actual day-to-day function of PrimeNumber was just as White had described it: grunt work.

"And when the claim forms are sent down, you follow the same procedure?" she asked.

"That's right. By compiling and updating the databases on-site we lighten the burden on ProvLife's in-house system. And we've got plenty of spare capacity. That's gonna be even more important when—or maybe I should say *if*—the company moves into healthcare coverage."

Given how close PrimeNumber was to ProvLife, it didn't surprise Alex that Heymann had heard about the health cover issue. But from the way he talked, she had a feeling he knew a lot more about it than she did.

"Say, have you signed up to the pilot scheme?" he said.

"Sure," said Alex. "Just about everyone has. It's better than the old company program."

Heymann smiled. "Then let's take a look. Excuse me, Karyn."

"Sure."

The red-haired woman got up, happy to surrender her terminal for a few moments. Heymann took her place.

"Let's see, now." He began tapping at the keyboard. "I don't suppose you recall your AP number?"

"Er—no, sorry."

"No problem. I'll search by name."

His fingers flew over the keys, and then up came a grid on the screen that mimicked the application form Alex had filled in some six weeks earlier. All her details were there, her job, her years of service, right down to the old Camry rusting in the parking lot.

"We've already set up a new database for the health policies," Heymann said. "It's all up and running."

"That's very impressive," Alex found herself saying.

"Well, if you get hit by a bus tomorrow," Heymann said, looking at her over his shoulder, "at least now it'll show up in the actuarial statistics."

The tour went on for almost another hour. Heymann took her into every section and insisted on showing her virtually every part of the PrimeNumber computer system. By eleven o'clock she was exhausted, and was grateful when he finally headed off to a business engagement. He left her in the hazardous activity section, where she was allowed to sit at an empty desk.

For a while she tried to flip through screens of information on the claims database, looking for inconsistencies or omissions. White clearly suspected that corners were being cut somewhere, perhaps that industry averages were being used to cover gaps, but Alex could find no evidence of that. There was something defensive about Heymann, suspicious even, but at the same time he seemed inordinately proud of his precious computers. Alex's search was made more difficult by the rudimentary nature of the software, which was far less sophisticated than the systems she could employ back at headquarters. There were certainly no user-friendly menus. This was data capture, not data dissemination.

After another hour she leaned back in her chair and let out a frustrated sigh. She looked at the rows of women, their faces lit by the blue glow of the screens. It was curious to see the information she was used to manipulating in large, sanitized blocks being fed in line by line. The handwriting of the applicants, some sweeping and confident, some crabbed and cautious, revealed the reality, the individuality of each of ProvLife's clients.

"You looking for a job here?"

Alex was brought out of her musings by the friendly voice. She turned to look at her neighbor and smiled. The woman was holding a little plastic letter opener in her left hand.

"Oh, no. I work at the company headquarters. In the actuarial department. I'm just seeing where all the numbers come from."

The woman leaned forward and offered her hand. "Roberta," she said with a big smile that was missing a tooth on the left side of her mouth.

Alex reciprocated.

"I'm realizing for the first time what a huge job it is—getting all this information into the system, I mean. How long can you actually enter stuff before you have to take a break?" she asked.

"Two, maybe three hours. There's ladies here go for much longer."

Roberta slit open a new envelope, took out the application form, and put the envelope on a neat stack. They were the same reply-paid envelopes that were issued by the thousand to all ProvLife's policy applicants, but which Alex had laid eyes on for the first time only six weeks before, when she herself had become an applicant for the company's pilot healthcare scheme. At the time her only thought had been how bad they tasted when you licked them. Now the sight of them all stacked up on each desk brought home to her the industrial scale of the company's operations, and all the routine, low-wage work that went with it. Even the letter openers the ladies used were all the same.

Roberta followed Alex's gaze. "Company issue," she said, holding up the white plastic blade. "Just makes the job a lot easier."

"I notice everybody stacking their envelopes, too. I guess you recycle."

"Heymann's very big on recycling. It's a thing you have to learn when you come here. Raymond comes around twice a day with the barrow and all the envelopes go in there."

12

Margaret Eliot sat by the kitchen window listening to the phone ring at the other end of the line. There had been another fall the previous night, and the tall firs in the yard were weighed down with snow, their branches dipping towards the frozen earth. In years past Peter and Tom would have been out there by now, throwing snowballs and making snowmen, or dragging their sleds up the hill towards Blackstone Park. She could picture their flushed faces looking back at her through the glass, woolen hats pulled down low over their foreheads.

But all that was a long time ago. Today the snow lay undisturbed, just like the snow at the cemetery, a pure white dustcover laid across a time and place that nobody had a use for anymore.

The line rang and rang, but no one answered. Slowly Margaret replaced the receiver, letting her head come to rest against the icy windowpane.

The noise of the doorbell brought her to her feet. She looked at the clock on the mantelpiece and remembered that she was expecting a visitor. Harold Tate, Michael's old college friend, had called the day before. He'd wanted to know how she was coping, and if there was anything he could do. He was sorry he hadn't had a chance to talk to her properly at the funeral. She'd been surprised to hear from him, and even more surprised when he offered to come over. It had been a while since she'd seen him. The days when he'd been a regular guest at the dinner table were long past, and she had yet to meet Suzy, his new wife. But then she recalled how Harold had called up before Christmas—just a week or so before her husband's death. And she had always liked Harold, in part because, like her, he remembered the younger Michael Eliot, a person very different from the brooding, taciturn man he had become.

Even standing there on the doorstep Tate looked awkward. Maybe it was just the cold, but with his shoulders hunched and his hands clasped together in front of him, he gave the impression that he had come more out of duty than anything else. There was no sign of his wife, Suzy, but then, she hadn't been at the funeral either. For an instant it crossed Margaret's mind that maybe Tate was having trouble at home.

"I'd have come by earlier," he said, stepping into the hallway and stamping the snow off his shoes, "but I didn't want to intrude. Here, I brought you . . ."

He handed her a bottle wrapped up in blue tissue paper.

"Oh, Harold, you shouldn't have. How very—"

"It's sherry. A *fino*. I seem to remember that you—"

"Oh, I do. I often . . ."

She unwrapped the large brown bottle and made a show of reading the label, trying her best to seem appreciative. It was an unconventional, almost a bizarre gesture, bringing alcohol to a recently bereaved widow. Was it supposed to help her drown her sorrows?

"Gonzalez Byass," she said. "That's—that's very sweet of you, Harold. Do let me take your coat."

Tate seemed to relax a little, pulling off his overcoat with a lot of hearty panting and grunting. With his lined face and close-cropped beard, he looked as if he had just stepped off a fishing boat. Only his deep-set eyes—eyes that were never still—suggested to Margaret a more complex, more highly strung man within.

A few minutes later they were sitting together in the living room, drinking coffee out of her best bone china cups. Outside the clouds were thinning a little, the light growing stronger. The brilliance of the snow made the room seem dark.

They talked about the winter, how it was turning into the coldest one for years. They talked about the trouble people were having on the roads, and the way they kept having to shut the airport, and about past winters that were almost as bad. And then for a few moments there was silence.

Tate looked around the room, taking in the polished mahogany furniture, the silvery green upholstery, the framed photographs of Michael and the boys.

"I'm sorry I couldn't stay after the service, Margaret," he said. "Things have been going crazy at Medan lately. I'd have liked to talk to Peter again, find out what he's doing now."

"He's studying," Margaret said. "Law. He's at a firm in New York. A paralegal, they call it."

Tate nodded. "They grow up so quick, don't they? I guess that's what everyone says, isn't it? What I mean is, I got quite a shock seeing this fully grown man the other day. I still think of him as this kid with freckles and—"

Margaret looked down at the floor. Tate checked himself. He remembered Michael Eliot telling how the boys didn't come to visit much anymore. And why hadn't his older boy, Tom, been at the funeral? London was only half a day away, after all.

"By the way, Suzy sends her apologies. She's come down with the flu, I'm afraid. But she hopes to see you as soon as she's well again."

Margaret didn't answer. She was still staring at the ground, lost in thought. Tate pursed his lips and looked out into the yard for a moment.

"Margaret, it must have been a terrible shock for you. I can only guess at what you've been through these last couple of weeks."

Margaret sighed and nodded. "Yes," she said softly.

"I hope . . . I hope Michael left everything *in order*," Tate said. "You know, his affairs and"—Margaret looked up at him—"and all that kind of thing. I mean, it's amazing the number of people who don't even make a will, or don't get around to updating it when they marry or whatever. Or don't get the right tax advice. I mean, that's critical."

Margaret carried on watching him.

"Yes, I suppose," she said at last.

"So . . . well, if there's a problem I hope . . . if there's anything I can do. I know some very good lawyers—wills and estates people, specialists. I hope you won't hesitate."

He smiled weakly and took a mouthful of coffee. It was beginning to get cold.

"That's very kind of you," Margaret said. "But I don't think there's a problem. Michael and I drew up our wills quite a few years ago. I don't think they've been changed since then. I'm seeing our lawyers later this week."

"Well, that's good," Tate said. "Who are—who is it represents you? If you don't mind me asking."

"No, not at all. Neumann and Klein. That's Walter Neumann's firm. Do you know him?"

Tate considered the question for a moment. Then shook his head.

"He's the chief legal officer at ProvLife, but he has his own private practice too. Tom says that isn't supposed to be strictly ethical these days, but I don't see the harm. Neumann and Klein don't do insurance work."

"Well, I'm glad to hear everything's under control," Tate said, putting his cup and saucer down on the table beside him. He looked about ready to leave.

Margaret studied him for a moment, trying to put together the scraps of meaning she felt were there, trying to see if they added up to something. With his back to the window it was hard to see his face.

"Harold, when was the last time you actually saw him?"

Tate frowned.

"Michael," she said. "My husband."

Tate hesitated.

"We . . . we had a drink together about a week or so before Christmas," he said. "Caught up, kind of thing. Didn't he tell you?"

"I remember you called. Was that—?"

"That was afterwards, a couple of days afterwards. I just called to say Merry Christmas. I only wish . . ."

Tate shook his head regretfully. Margaret fell silent again. She got the feeling Tate was holding something back.

"Harold, you and Michael went back a long way, didn't you?"

"Oh yes. More than twenty-five years."

"Since before he met me, in fact."

"Yes, I suppose that's right."

Margaret nodded to herself.

"Harold, tell me the truth. Was Michael having an affair?"

Tate's expression froze. Then a self-conscious look of dismay came over his face.

"Was he planning to leave me?" she went on. "Is that what you and Michael talked about? I just want to know the truth."

"Margaret, I've really— *No.* Not that I know of. Why do you—?"

"Then how do you explain this?"

Margaret went over to the sideboard. A plane ticket sat propped up against a glazed porcelain figurine.

"Air France to Paris via New York, first class," she said, handing it to Tate. "Second of January. One way."

Tate looked at her for a moment and then opened up the ticket. Eliot's name and initials were there, and the flight details just as his widow had described them. She went and sat back down, waiting for his answer.

"When did you find this?" he said.

"This morning. It arrived in the mail."

"In the mail?" Tate sat up. "You mean, the airline—?"

"It wasn't the airline. It came from someone who knew Michael. Someone who knew him very well. A young woman."

Tate nervously ran his fingertips across his forehead. "Margaret, I—I really—"

"Harold, please don't treat me like a fool, just because Michael did. Tell me."

Tate sighed.

"I . . . I don't know. Michael did talk about making *changes* in his life. There was—I think there may have been—*someone*, Margaret. I'm afraid I don't even remember the name."

For a moment the widow closed her eyes, then forced herself to open them.

"I don't think it was anything serious, really. It sounded like something . . . casual. Not that I'm excusing it, but I don't think he was in love or anything. At least that was my impression."

Suddenly Margaret was on her feet again, her back turned. She had suspected, of course. She had wondered about the late nights at the office and the smell of perfume that drifted up from her husband's clothes when he finally appeared. Perhaps she'd even *expected* him to find another woman. He was still attractive enough. But she had never known. Not until now.

For a moment Tate thought she was going to walk out on him, leave him sitting there alone. But then he realized that she simply didn't want him to see her crying. He felt a sudden rush of sympathy for her. Out of the whole terrible affair, it was she who had been left with the greatest burden: the burden of grieving for an unfaithful husband, of never being able to express her anger at his betrayal, of never knowing whether reconciliation would have been possible. He stood up and went to her side.

"Margaret, listen to me," he said, laying a hand gently on her shoulder. "You don't have the full picture. Michael was under a huge amount of strain when I saw him. A huge amount. Under such circumstances people sometimes do . . . crazy things. Things they wouldn't normally do in a hundred years."

Margaret straightened up, took a deep breath, turned halfway back towards him. She was holding a handkerchief to her face.

"What circumstances?"

"I wasn't sure whether he'd told you. You see, Margaret, he received some very bad news last December. News about his future, about his health."

Margaret sat slowly down again. She took another deep breath, trying to compose herself. Tate sat down beside her, watching her closely.

"He . . . he underwent a genetic test. I'm not sure why. Perhaps he was just curious. The point is, the test showed up positive for a disorder called Huntington's chorea. Have you ever heard of it?"

She shook her head.

"It's a terrible thing, Margaret. A hereditary disorder of the central nervous system. It usually develops in adulthood, between the ages of thirty and fifty most commonly. The symptoms progress gradually and are . . . irreversible."

Margaret blinked. This was new to her.

"What kind of symptoms, Harold?"

"First come slight, uncontrollable muscular movements, stumbling, clumsiness. Then short-term memory lapses, mood swings. That kind of thing."

She swallowed. "And then?"

"On the physical side, eating and speaking become increasingly difficult. There's a tendency to choke on food, and often serious weight

loss. On the psychological side it varies. There's depression. Sleepless-
ness. Some people develop voracious appetites. Sexual, as well as for
food. As the disease progresses . . . Margaret, must I—?"

"Tell me, Harold."

Tate took a deep breath. "As the disease progresses, full nursing care
is needed. Sufferers gradually lose the ability to control any of the muscles in their bodies. And mental faculties often deteriorate further. In
the end, they die."

Margaret looked down into her lap. A black well of despair seemed
to open up beneath her. She began to shake her head.

"And Michael found out he was going to get this disease?"

"Yes. It was just a matter of time. Maybe twenty years, more likely
four or five."

Margaret became quite still. She could not quite believe what Tate
was saying, and yet she saw no reason for him to lie. It seemed incredible that her husband could have received such news, such certainty of
coming misery, and not shared it with her—could even have managed
to hide it from her. Had they really drifted that far apart?

"Of course, one test is never conclusive with these things," Tate
added. "Michael took another, but I'm afraid he . . . didn't live to see
the results."

"Have you?"

Tate shook his head. "You mean the results of the second test? No.
No, I haven't. I—I'm not even sure where Michael had them done. He
just wanted to talk to me about it, me being an old friend and knowing
something about the—the biology."

Margaret nodded slowly. "I see."

Tate smiled gently.

"You can see now why someone might forget themselves under
those circumstances, can't you? I mean, with something like that hanging over you, you'd be inclined to be selfish, at least to begin with. And
besides, Margaret, one little air ticket doesn't prove anything. It was
probably just a whim—a panic reaction, denial. Maybe he was even
planning to take you with him. Have you thought about that?"

Margaret didn't speak for a long time, long enough for Tate to become aware of the ticking of the grandfather clock in the hall, the
sound of his own breathing. He wondered if she even knew he was still
there.

Then she said: "He wasn't going to take me. He was taking her. And he wasn't going to come back. Not ever."

"Margaret . . ."

She shook her head, her eyes closed. Suddenly she felt exhausted.

"It was the woman who sent the ticket, Harold. She said she would. She called me a few days ago. Just the day after the funeral, as a matter of fact."

Tate shifted in his seat.

"She . . . called? Who? Who called?"

"She wouldn't tell me her name. She said we'd shared Michael, and there was no reason why we shouldn't share his money."

Tate sat up. "His money?"

"She said he had ten million dollars in a Swiss bank account. Money I knew nothing about."

"What?"

"She said she had the papers to prove it. All kinds of papers. Proof."

"Proof," Tate said quietly, as much to himself as to her.

"She sent the air ticket because she was Michael's . . . lover. I'm sure there was another one for her."

Tate looked again at the ticket in his hands, and then slowly laid it down on the arm of the sofa.

"Whoever it was, it sounds like a crank," he said, blustering a little. "A crank call. I mean, the whole thing's absurd. It's—it's *sick*."

"I thought I'd dreamt it. When I woke up again, I mean. I've had so many bad dreams since the accident. But then I found the number I'd written down."

Tate was back to fingering the ticket again. He stopped. "The number?"

"We've got Caller ID here. When you dial up it tells you a caller's number. Michael wanted it. Two seven two, five one three one. That's an East Side number."

Tate stared at her, very still.

"I finally got up the courage to call back this morning. Just before you arrived."

"And?"

"No answer. I suppose we could try again now." She reached out towards the phone.

"No!" Tate put his hand over the receiver. "I don't think that's a good idea, I really don't."

"Why?"

"Because . . . because it could be dangerous. This could be some kind of—I don't know, some kind of vendetta, against Michael. You know, insurance companies aren't popular with a lot of people. They make enemies."

"Enemies?"

"Sure. People get mad when they don't get the big payouts they think they deserve. It happens all the time. Listen, maybe this is some employee of the airline, or the travel agency. Maybe their husband had an accident and ProvLife wouldn't pay. Michael was in charge of Treasury. He signed off on the checks. He'd have been an obvious person to blame, a name to grab hold of, and . . . and then they see his name in the papers."

Margaret frowned.

"You think that's possible?"

"Absolutely. Listen, Margaret. Let me take down that number and I'll look into it. No sense in taking any chances." He reached into his inside pocket for a notebook. "Now what was it: two seven two—?"

She had fallen silent again, was sitting on the edge of the sofa, staring out through the window.

"Margaret?"

"She said she wasn't at the funeral."

Tate shrugged. "Well, that figures. Why do you—?"

"I think she was lying. I think I saw her there."

13

On Tuesday evening Alex left PrimeNumber just after five, coming out through the double glass doors with Tom Heymann's team of ladies. Roberta, who had more or less taken Alex under her wing in the two days she had been at the company, gave her a friendly wave as she climbed into her beat-up Orion. Alex waved back and for a moment stood watching as the car pulled away. After eight hours of eye-dimming work Roberta now had to shop, cook, and be a good wife to her unemployed husband, Joey. Alex looked at all the other women and wondered how many of them were on a similar schedule. Exhaust fumes swirled in the biting wind. A horn sounded and was answered by another. Suddenly aware of how tired she was, Alex walked to the end of the lot to her own car and realized it was probably the worst pile of junk out there.

She opened the door and threw in her attaché case. It had been another frustrating day. She was convinced now that if there was a problem at PrimeNumber it had nothing to do with the way the employees entered the data. The occasional error did creep in, but these were usually screened out by Heymann's quality control procedures, with most data being double-checked before being released into the system. More likely it was the computers themselves. If PrimeNumber had been experiencing hardware problems—or possibly glitches in the software—they might have lost data and then taken shortcuts to cover the losses: shortcuts like entering industry averages for car ownership rather than reentering hundreds or maybe thousands of applications. Without being too direct about it, Alex had asked Roberta and some of the other ladies whether the system had ever gone down or thrown up errors, but no one seemed to think so. And after two days of climbing all over the system, she herself had found no sign of any problem.

Alex put the key in the ignition and turned. The starter motor ground for a couple of seconds, then stopped.

"Come on, sugar."

She pulled out the choke a little and pumped the gas with a practiced stab of her foot. With each turn of the starter motor the headlights dimmed. She tried again. Then again.

"Dammit!"

Out in the freezing dark the last of the ladies were pulling out of the parking lot. The only car left now was Heymann's: a Lexus, black and waxed to a high polish like a coffin. Lights were still on in the building, but it was only a matter of time before Heymann came out. The thought of his spooky transparent eyes on her made Alex squirm in her seat. Again she turned the ignition, but the car was dead. Then a van was pulling into the lot. It was the Greenfield Recycling people. Alex breathed a sigh of relief and climbed out of the Camry.

"How're you doing?" said the man, coming across to her with a Maglite trained on her car. Alex recognized him as Raymond, a twenty-something the PrimeNumber ladies said they were all hot for. He was a tall guy with good muscles and a greasy ponytail.

"Car won't start," said Alex. "Don't suppose you have any jumper cables?"

" 'Fraid not. Barney, my partner, he borrowed 'em this morning. Didn't give 'em back." He looked around the parking lot and saw the Lexus. "But that looks like Mr. Heymann's car. He'll have a set in the trunk."

Alex nodded and climbed back into the Camry. "I'll just give it another try," she said.

She pulled the choke out all the way and pumped the gas. Turned the key. Nothing.

"God damn you," she said under her breath.

She turned the key again. The engine coughed, strained, sounded like it was going to take, then died. A smell of gasoline filled the interior. She rolled down her window.

"What's the problem, Alex?"

It was Heymann. He was standing next to her open window alongside the security guard, an amused smile on his pale lips. Alex smiled straight back at him.

"The cold's got to it. Damned thing won't start."

"Flooded her, I reckon," said Raymond. He was staring at the Camry's bodywork in the beam of his flashlight, an appalled expression on his face.

"Sam here says he has no cables," said Heymann. "Me neither. Happy to give you a ride, though."

The Lexus was filled with a new-car smell. Having Providence Life as his sole client was obviously working well for Heymann. Alex wondered what he paid himself in salary. They made their way down to the interstate and turned north. Alex relaxed back into her seat, and realized how tired she was.

"Had a little chat with Newton Brady today," said Heymann out of the blue.

Alex turned and looked at Heymann's face. She hadn't noticed it before, but she could see from this angle that his nose had been broken.

"Really?"

"Yeah. First I called McCormick—I call him pretty regularly at Central Records to liaise, you know—and we were going over one thing and another, and I mentioned White had sent you down to look us over."

Alex shook her head. "Look you over?"

"Just an expression. No, I said you were down here getting some 'exposure'—that was what you said, wasn't it?" His eyes cut across to her face and back to the road. "And he said that was great. Said the more integrated the company is, the more each department knows the other departments' business, the better it is for ProvLife."

Alex looked back at the road. "Makes sense to me," she said.

Heymann turned his hands on the wheel, making a faint squeaky sound.

"So Brady calls me."

Alex said nothing, just waiting now for whatever was coming.

"I guess McCormick must have called him. Brady wanted to know what exactly you were doing," said Heymann. "Wanted to know why White sent you out here."

"But I told you, he—"

"Wants you to get some exposure—yeah, I know. That's what I said to Newt." He looked across at her and smiled. "Hey, it's no big deal. I'm just telling you what happened."

Alex shrugged.

"Makes no difference to me," Heymann continued. "I'm just saying what happened."

Alex started to count the exits: fifteen, fourteen, thirteen. Traffic was light but slow-moving, everybody worried about black ice. Heymann fell silent again. The Lexus was so quiet, Alex could hear him breathing through his nose.

"Company's funny like that, though," he said after a few minutes. "Don't you think?"

"I'm not sure I—"

"I mean the way everybody knows everything. This one did that and the other one did this. Know what I mean? Everybody in everybody else's pocket."

"So what did Brady say? About me being down here."

"Oh, nothing. But I tell you what—the directors are the worst." He put his foot down a little and the powerful car surged forward. "But that's Providence too. You're not from here, though, right?"

Alex shook her head. "Pittsfield, kind of."

"A Yankee," said Heymann. Then he laughed. "Can you believe that? That's what Rhode Islanders call you. Yankees. Like you were from another country." He pushed back a little in his seat. "That's the way it is here. I went out for dinner last week with my wife. Tuesday night. Next day I'm talking to Brad Witney—you probably don't know him, he runs Newport Paper—and he says: 'How was your seafood linguini?' " Heymann looked across. "He *knows* what I had for dinner. Okay, I'm assuming he was in the restaurant, wondering why he didn't come over. Turns out someone he *knew* was there and they'd told him. You see what I'm talking about?"

"I guess Providence is a small place," said Alex, trying to work out why he was telling her all this.

"Sure, but it's more than that. It's like a mentality thing."

He leaned forward a little to look up at the sky.

"Here comes that snow," he said, and then, musingly, but slowly as though delivering a warning: "Everybody knows everything."

Except about Michael Eliot, thought Alex with some satisfaction. Eliot and Liz. They knew nothing about the affair and nothing about the money. It *was* perfectly possible to have secrets from the company. They finally reached exit twenty and turned off into central Providence.

"So, you live on the East Side," said Heymann, his tone brighter now, his little speech over with.

"Just north of it, actually, but you can drop me at the office," she said. She'd already decided she didn't want Heymann driving her to her front door. "There's some stuff I need to do."

Heymann nodded. "Sure, sure. I guess they work you pretty hard up there on the seventh floor, then."

Alex shrugged. Not as hard as he worked his ladies. "Oh, it's not so bad," she said. "They pay us too."

The car turned into Westminster Street and pulled up outside the front door of the Providence Life building. Barely suppressing a sigh of relief, Alex grabbed her briefcase from behind her seat and opened the door.

"Thanks for the ride," she said over her shoulder.

Heymann was smiling, his eyes serious nevertheless.

"Anytime," he said. "You ought to think about getting yourself a new car, though."

14

The following morning White called her into his office as soon as he arrived.

"So you're back with us, then?" he said as he poured them both coffee.

Alex shrugged. "We said I should just give it a couple of days. And to be honest, I don't think there's much to be gained by going back to PrimeNumber. Tom Heymann seems to run a pretty tight ship, and I couldn't find any evidence of a problem with the computers. Since we actually *use* the data back at head office, I think the problem's more likely to have arisen here."

"Here?" said White. "You mean Central Records?"

"Well our systems are older. Maybe it'd be worth talking to Ralph McCormick." White raised his eyebrows as though this was an extraordinary notion. "As head of Data Systems, I mean. Maybe he's aware of a problem."

White sipped at his coffee.

"I'm not sure . . ."—he was choosing his words—"I'm not sure Ralph would be that much . . . help just now."

He looked at his screen. Then, smiling, he reached out and peeled off one of the notes. He dropped it into the bin.

"You've never met Ralph, have you, Alex?"

Alex shook her head. "Not really."

"I've been thinking—in fact, I was thinking about this last night after we spoke—it's time you met the people who run this company. There's a little gathering of the clan planned for Friday night. Just drinks, and I dare say Eva Goebert will have produced a few canapes." He caught Alex's puzzled expression. "Yes, it's at Richard Goebert's place. Why don't you come along? Bring Mark."

Back at her desk, Alex tried to concentrate on the next stage of her healthcare assignment. But it was hard, with everything that was happening. First Mark and now her. That was how it seemed. It was as if they were both being drawn into ProvLife's inner circle. There had been no talk of promotion, true. But first the funeral and now the party—how else could she look at it? She felt like she was being eased into a faster lane. She began to think that her discretionary pay raise might be well worth having. At last she'd be getting her head back above water.

"What's so amusing?"

It was Mel Hartman. He was leaning on her desk, a Styrofoam cup in his hand.

"Pardon me?"

"You were smiling. You know you can't leave me out of your inner life. I have a right to know what's going on."

"Nothing's going on, Mel."

"Is the old man okay?"

"Which old man?"

"Randal A. White. He's acting kind of strange, don't you think? Have you seen the state of his desk?"

Alex felt a flash of irritation. "He's not an old man, Mel. And he's in better shape than you."

Hartman put his hands up in mock surrender.

"Okay, okay. I'm sorry. I didn't know you felt so strongly about him."

"What's that supposed to mean?"

"Nothing. He feels strongly about you. No reason you shouldn't feel strongly about him."

Alex shook her head in disbelief. "What the hell are you talking about?"

"Oh, come on, Alex. What about the night at the office party?"

Alex felt herself flush. All she could think of was Michael Eliot, his mouth pressed to hers, his hands on her body. She looked up at Hartman. He was moving his head around, his tongue pushed into his cheek.

"You mean, you didn't hear?" he said.

Alex looked back at her screen. Now he was going to tell her something scabrous, something she would rather not know. He leaned closer so that she could smell his coffee breath. She tensed.

"We-ell," said Hartman, his voice squeezed into a suggestive whisper, "after that scene with Eliot at the party. Don't tell me you've forgotten about it: when he tried to get hold of you."

Alex looked up abruptly, making Hartman back off a little. But she had only startled him. He wasn't about to shut his mouth.

"After Eliot grabbed you," he said, his eyes dancing, "White and him had words. In the elevator."

Alex shook her head in scorn and disbelief.

"Oh, really? How would you know about that, Mel? Were you up on the roof of the car?"

Hartman smiled smugly.

"Eliot was leaving. White blocked the doors of the elevator and told him what he thought of him. I saw the whole thing."

Despite herself, Alex found that she was visualizing the moment. She couldn't imagine White behaving that way. Hartman touched her on the arm. He hadn't finished.

"So Eliot told him he was an old fart. He said, just because—" He looked furtively around the office and ducked closer. "He said just because White couldn't get it up anymore, that was no reason why he couldn't have a little fun."

He backed up a little to see the effects of his disclosure.

"Can you believe it?"

Alex shook her head. She wanted to know what White had said, but she didn't want to have to ask. Fortunately Hartman didn't require any encouragement.

"And then there was this spooky silence. I was on my way to the men's room, bursting for a pee, when I walked slap bang into the whole thing. There was this spooky silence. I guess White was just giving him the stare, you know. Kind of man to man. Neither of them said anything. Then the doors closed."

"With White inside?"

"Sure, he stepped into the elevator. I wished I'd been able to follow them down."

15

"Y ou're not saying we didn't have a good year," said Newton Brady, popping a nut into his mouth and eyeing Henry Gough, one of Providence Life's eight nonexecutive directors.

Gough raised his shoulders and let them drop.

"No, of course not. Hey, it wasn't a *great* year, but relative to the rest of the industry we did okay. All I'm saying is—"

"*Okay?*" Brady had a way of jerking his head when pretending astonishment that made his jowls shake. "We were two percent ahead of the competition in terms of ROA. Jesus, Henry. It's not like we're a software company or something."

"I know that."

Gough looked around Richard Goebert's spacious, high-ceilinged reception room. It was just after seven, and the party was starting to warm up, the air filled with warm smells of cinnamon and cloves. People stood around in groups discussing the appalling weather, sipping at Eva Goebert's mulled wine. Was it going to be as bad as the winter of '95–96 when they'd had ninety-two inches? The women, without exception, hated it, but for some of the men it was what the community needed every now and then. "Brings people together," said one man. "Everyone out there shoveling."

Mostly in their fifties, they were all Rhode Islanders, several of them from the older Providence families. Gough watched Goebert move among the different groups, a bundle of energy despite his sixty-three years.

"But—well, I'll tell you what it is," said Gough. "We're worried about this testing thing."

Brady waited, a handful of nuts held loosely next to his grease-smeared glass. When Gough saw he wasn't going to get any help, he started to stammer. Brady's implacable stare and heavy, brooding presence always intimidated him.

"I m-mean, isn't the P-ProvLife line a little hard? From what I hear, Randal White's turning this issue into a c-crusade. I talked to someone at Mass General the other day, and they were pretty unhappy."

The thick flesh bunched between Brady's dark eyebrows in an almost theatrical frown. "I don't think the board's position is any different from Randal's or, for that matter . . ."

Brady caught Goebert's eye as he went past.

"Newton!" cried Goebert, giving a little bow. Easily the shortest person in the room, he was nevertheless a distinguished figure. Despite his aging skin and thinning hair he had an aura of intelligent boyishness—a puckishness that was underlined by twinkling blue eyes and pointed, big-lobed ears.

"Great party," grunted Brady. "Where does a guy have to go to get a real drink?"

Still smiling, Goebert brushed at the salt grains Brady had deposited on his sleeve.

"Nuts," he said. Then, smiling at Gough: "Day of the eighty-seven crash, Newton's long IBM or Dupont or something or other. He's shouting into the phone at his broker, and his heart gives out." Goebert tapped Brady's breast pocket with the back of his ancient child's hand. "Refuses to die, of course, needs to close out that damned position first. Doctor patches him up, says keep off the saturated fats, keep off the booze and cigarettes, and *keep off the salt.*"

Brady shot the handful of nuts into his mouth and smilingly munched.

"It was an episode, not an attack," he said through the food. Then, frowning: "Henry here thinks we're going wrong on the testing issue. Worried about Randal going off to Washington on a crusade. I was just telling him how we all feel the same way about—"

"Name Roger Williams mean anything to you, Mr. Gough?" Goebert looked up at him through thickly growing eyebrows.

Gough shrugged. "Sure. I mean, in grade school we—"

"Founded this state. Came into a situation here where land disputes with the Indians were becoming a problem—people calling them savages and so forth. Know what he said about the Indians?"

Gough shrugged and took a sip of his drink.

"He said, 'Nature knows no difference between European and American Indian blood, birth, bodies.' "

Gough looked at Brady. "So?"

"When Williams saw Indians, he saw people," said Goebert. "Now, have you ever heard of Jacob Quinn? No reason why you should have unless you're a historian. A slaver. Big slaver. Slavers made this town, Mr. Gough. Quinn imported molasses from the West Indies, made rum out of the molasses, sent the rum to Africa, where it was used to buy slaves. The slaves went to the West Indies to cut the sugar to make the molasses. Great triangle. Terrific business. Very profitable."

He touched Gough on the sleeve and stared up into his face with his intense blue eyes.

"*People as a commodity,* Mr. Gough. People as things you use to boost your profits." He leaned back and was smiling again, his eyes moving back and forth between the two men. "Two sides of the same community. Now, I happen to think Providence Life is on the same side as Roger Williams. When we look at people we see people, their needs, their responsibilities, their rights. There is a moral imperative—"

"But the technology," interrupted Gough. "How do we protect ourselves against—"

Goebert screwed up his face so that his lips parted, showing oddly lusterless teeth.

"Oh, come on, that's all—" He put his hands on his hips, exasperated. "Newt, what would you call that?"

"A crock of shit."

"There," said Goebert, smiling and tapping his foot, as though Brady had in fact supplied an obscure technical term. "Precisely. This whole protection issue is a—it's a smoke screen. There are people in our industry—the Jacob Quinns, if you will—who want to introduce testing in order to exclude bad risks. They just want the *healthy* blacks. The others can rot in the hold. All they're thinking about is their bottom line."

"But—"

Goebert wagged a warning finger.

"I'm not saying this genetic testing thing isn't going to raise all kinds of challenges, complex issues, but you know what? Taking the line we take, I wouldn't be surprised if we came out ahead anyway."

He brought his elevator shoes together with a light knock, putting an end to any further discussion.

"And where the hell is McCormick?" he said out of the blue.

Brady shrugged and watched Goebert make his way across the room to the double doors of the entry hall, where a young woman wearing a black cocktail dress had just appeared. She had short blond hair and striking dark eyes. Goebert's head disappeared as he bent forward to kiss her hand, and Brady saw Mark Ferulli, a proprietary arm around the woman's shoulder.

"I see you brought your lovely lady friend," said Goebert, coming forward. "What a pleasure to see you, Alex. May I say you're looking absolutely stunning." Alex shrugged and looked down at the unfamiliar sight of her bared knees. "How's life under the Great Illustrator?"

"Oh, he keeps us pretty busy," said Alex.

Goebert smiled at Mark, his blue eyes everywhere at once. "Newton was just telling me what a great job you're doing for us in Treasury," he said. "Not too much pressure, I hope."

"I'm loving it," said Mark.

Goebert looked at him for a moment, flashed another smile, excused himself, and was gone.

"What the hell is *he* on?" said Mark.

"Maybe somebody spiked the fruit cup," said Alex.

She turned.

"I'm glad to hear you're loving the pressure."

"But how do we come out ahead, if we end up taking all the bad risks?" said Gough.

Brady shot more nuts into his mouth, still watching the woman in the black dress. Suddenly he realized he didn't know the answer to

Goebert's question. Where the hell *was* McCormick? He hadn't seen him for at least half an hour.

"Do you know what the budget was for ELSI last year?" said Gough, taking a new line.

"Elsie?" Brady looked distractedly around the room.

"ELSI. It's a program at the National Human Genome Research Institute. It's looking at the ethical implications of the human genome project."

"Oh yeah, right. So many damned acronyms these days."

"Well, do you?"

Brady chewed angrily. "Do I what?"

"Know what the budget was last year?"

"No—no, I don't."

"Six-point-three million. The largest single investment in bioethical research from any one source."

"Really."

"They have funding coming out of their ears, Newton. And they're in cahoots with just about every federal agency you care to name. The Department of Energy, the Centers for Disease Control, the Health Resources Services Administration, the National Science Foundation, the Food and Drug—"

"I heard a great one the other day, at the Capital Grille," said Brady, leaning forward and putting a heavy hand on Gough's sleeve. "What's the difference between a nonexecutive director and a shopping cart?"

Gough frowned, looking down at the thick fingers slick with nut oil and salt.

"Shopping cart's got a mind of its own," barked Brady. "But you can get more food and drink into a nonexecutive director."

He threw back his head and laughed his big haw-haw laugh: "But you can—haw haw, you can get more—food and drink into a—"

"What's all this I-see-you-brought-your-lovely-lady-friend?" said Alex. "What's going on? I thought *I* invited *you*."

Mark shrugged. "What difference does it make?"

"But when I—"

"Look, Newt told me about this a couple of weeks ago. I didn't mention it at the time because . . . Well, what's the difference? It's just a company shindig, for Christ's sake. Goebert uses his wedding anniversary as an excuse to get everybody together. Look, you okay here? I'm going to find us some of that mulled wine."

Alex watched Mark make his way through the crowd, frowning, trying to recall the moment in which she had told him about Randal White's invitation. He had seemed puzzled at the time, then pleased. Why hadn't he told her he had already been asked to come along? She took a drink from a passing waiter and sipped reflectively. Then she decided that it was the same embarrassment he had shown in Hemenway's when she had seen the letters he was juggling to make his password. He was uncomfortable about his new position of power, that was all. He hadn't wanted her to see how well he was doing.

Then another thought occurred: what would have happened if she hadn't invited him? She wondered if maybe he had been thinking about bringing someone else. . . . She was about to go after him when someone tapped her on the arm. She turned, already smiling. It was Tom Heymann.

"Alex, you're looking absolutely wonderful."

"Thank you."

Alex held her smile, but avoided Heymann's hungry eyes. She was self-conscious in the dress she was wearing. Mark had picked it out for her, but she felt like she was borrowing it from someone else. It just wasn't her. She felt exposed.

"How's the car? I noticed you had someone come and tow it away."

"Oh, it's fine," said Alex. "Tom, you haven't seen Randal White, have you?"

"As a matter of fact, I have. Last time I saw him he was trying to eat all the smoked salmon on the buffet."

Alex allowed herself a glance at Heymann's face. He was flushed, and unsteady on his feet. Drunk.

"Oh, really?"

"Yeah. The way he packs it away, he should be two hundred pounds. I don't know how he does it."

His pale eyes drifted down to her throat and breasts and Alex looked away, frowning.

"I thought everybody knew everything in Providence," she said coolly.

It was warmer in the adjoining room. An expensive-looking buffet was getting the earnest attention of a number of guests, but there was no sign of White. Aware of curious gazes, Alex pretended hunger and started to help herself to food, picking up some quiche and salad.

"Looks great, doesn't it?"

A man was standing beside her, his plate loaded with canapés. He pushed out his right hand.

"Brad Witney. You must be Alex, right?"

Alex shook his hand and smiled politely. "That's right. How—?"

"Yeah, Tom told me about you. Tom Heymann. Told me you went down to PrimeNumber to have a look at the way they do things." Witney leaned forward conspiratorially. "Find out anything suspicious?" he said, narrowing his eyes.

Alex took in the small, mobile features that seemed to be pressed into the lower half of Witney's face. He reminded her of a ballet she had seen where the dancers were all dressed as animals. Witney looked like the water rat.

" 'Cause I think they're as suspicious as hell," he said out of the side of his mouth.

"Who's suspicious?" said another man, coming up against Witney's shoulder so that the three of them formed a tight triangle.

Witney looked at the newcomer and pushed a vol-au-vent into his mouth. "How's it going, Dave?"

But Dave was looking at Alex, squinting at her through thick, steel-framed glasses.

"Don't believe a word this man tells you," he said rakishly. Then he shoved his hand out, almost knocking the plate from her grasp. "David Mullins. Ocean State Savings Bank. Nice to meet you, Miss—?"

"Tynan." Alex pressed her hand around fingers that were soft and surprisingly damp.

"This is *Alex*," said Witney, speaking directly into Mullins's ear.

Mullins blinked and nodded. He was wearing a cheap-looking polyester suit which smelled of perspiration.

"So, are you a friend of the Goeberts, Mr. Mullins?" asked Alex.

"Oh yeah. We go back a long way," he said.

Alex watched him bring a piece of food to his mouth and was surprised to see a sleek gold Patek Philippe watch under his shirt cuff. Witney saw it too.

A gust of cold air brought their heads around.

"Christ, are they opening windows?" said Mullins.

Witney leaned back to look through the double doors. "No, it's . . . somebody's coming in." His eyebrows pushed up in surprise. "It's Walter Neumann."

They moved into the doorway and looked across the crowded reception room. Walter Neumann was shaking hands with Goebert and nodding to Eva. Donald Grant slouched next to him, his hands in his pockets. They were both red-faced from the cold, and Neumann's sparse colorless hair lay wet against his scalp. He was a tall man with narrow shoulders. His neck looked like it wasn't strong enough to support the big bony head. As he exchanged pleasantries with the tiny Goebert, his face moved from side to side, the dark almost black, unblinking eyes taking in the room and its guests.

"I thought he wasn't going to come," said Mullins in a whisper.

"They must have got back from Boston early."

Alex took in the two anxious faces. Mullins and Witney looked like kids checking out a difficult parent returned unexpectedly.

Witney gave Mullins a furtive nudge. "Can I have a word, Dave?"

"Sure."

Witney squeezed out a ratty smile for Alex's benefit, and then the two of them went into a huddle next to the dips.

By nine o'clock Goebert's house was uncomfortably full. Squeezed between overheating guests, Alex engaged in polite conversation with a variety of senior execs' spouses, several of whom were three sheets to the wind. Spotting Mark in conversation with an older man, Alex eased her way through the crowd to his side. She grabbed his elbow.

"Hey, honey." Mark gently detached her fingers. "This is Mr. Wickenberg."

"Thomas, please," said the man amiably.

"Thomas, this is Alex Tynan, my . . . partner."

Alex shook yet another hand, and did her best to smile. "I hate that term," she said. "It makes us sound like a business."

Wickenberg looked embarrassed.

"Thomas has been on the ProvLife board for years," said Mark, ignoring the remark, and making Wickenberg sound like he was in line for a Nobel Prize.

"In a nonexecutive role," said Wickenberg. "Since the seventies. Ever since Richard Goebert took over the chairmanship, in fact." He smirked at Alex. "We were just talking cars."

"Really?" said Alex archly. "Let me guess: BMWs."

"Right. Thomas has one of the big ones," said Mark. "The 713."

"Oooh, they're awful expensive."

They all turned. Donald Grant, the boss of Investigations, was standing there holding a scotch and soda in his chunky hand. He nodded to Alex, and Mark made the introductions.

"Real expensive," he repeated when the hellos were finished.

Wickenberg raised his eyebrows and gave an assenting nod.

"Beautiful, though," said Mark. "That money buys you some beautiful engineering."

"Sure," said Grant, looking straight at Mark. "I'm just saying they're a little too expensive."

He was like a roadblock. In a matter of seconds he had brought the conversation to a complete standstill. Alex looked at the fingers around his glass. They were thick, slightly puffy, the nails bitten down to thin ridges of cuticle. He was smiling at Mark, but not in a friendly way.

Suddenly Walter Neumann was looming over them. There were more introductions. Alex had often seen Neumann from a distance, never up close. He was very buttoned up, very inside himself. He gave the impression that he was looking out at you from somewhere behind his eyes. He talked shop with Wickenberg for a moment. Boston business. The way he talked made Alex think of a ventriloquist. His teeth barely parted. He was standing just behind Grant, and it suddenly came to Alex that Grant was the dummy. She laughed, trapping the laughter too late, her fingers pressed against her mouth. The four men looked at her. Mark was frowning.

"Excuse me," said Alex, holding up her empty glass. "I think I'm getting a little punchy."

"I was just saying how expensive those BMWs are," said Grant as if she hadn't spoken.

He addressed himself directly to Neumann. There was an awkward silence in which Alex shook her head. Grant was starting to seem seriously weird. Alex wondered if he wasn't out-of-his-head drunk.

"What do you think, Walter?" asked Wickenberg.

Neumann turned his unblinking eyes on Mark.

"I think that, generally speaking, Donald is a very good judge of value," he said. He said it absolutely straight-faced, as if it wasn't small talk but a pronouncement on the situation in Bosnia.

Goebert breezed past, talking animatedly. They all watched him go.

"I've never seen Richard in such good form," said Wickenberg, obviously wanting to get off the subject of BMWs. "I'll be sorry to see him leave."

"Leave?" said Mark, looking at Neumann. "Is he resigning?"

"No way," said Grant.

"Not for a couple of years, anyway," said Neumann.

"He certainly seems to love the job," said Wickenberg, "and he's in great shape for his age. No, I just meant that *when* he goes—well, it won't be the same. It'll be like a whole chapter of ProvLife's history coming to an end, a great chapter." He smiled at Alex. "You know, we nearly closed down in the eighties. Business was bad and competition was really hitting profits. You know what the burning ratio is?"

"Sure," said Alex, looking at Mark. "The ratio of money paid out in claims to money received in premiums."

"Right," said Wickenberg. "Ours was headed for one to one. And that just isn't supposed to happen in our brand of insurance. We were living on a knife edge."

"One to one," Alex repeated. She was looking at Neumann's oddly inexpressive face. He was staring at a painting on the wall. "I never knew it was that bad."

"Oh yeah. And then there was all that talk about a merger and so forth. It was Goebert who insisted we stay independent. It was also Goebert who said we should stay mutual. Said he didn't want Wall Street telling us how to do our business."

"Must have been a tough call," said Mark, nodding earnestly, checking Grant for his reaction. Grant seemed to be more interested in his drink.

"We stayed mutual and kept slugging away, and here we are ten years later"—Wickenberg held out his hands—"doing fine. You have to credit Goebert for that. He may be a little old-fashioned but he's always been a steady hand on the tiller."

"Well, being old-fashioned isn't always bad," said Mark.

Grant looked up.

"I mean, in the present circumstances," Mark went on, gesturing with his wineglass, "given the challenges facing the industry, focusing on things like your company's responsibility to its clients, the moral imperatives, if you like—concentrating on those issues can't be a bad thing."

"Quite," said Wickenberg, nodding.

The group broke up, Neumann and Grant moving away in search of food. Wickenberg started a conversation about drapes with Eva Goebert.

Alex stifled a yawn, and then started to discreetly pull at Mark's arm.

"That wasn't very polite," he said once they were out of earshot. "Are you drunk?"

Alex put the back of her hand against her cheek. She was burning up.

"Wouldn't be surprising," she said. "I'm bored out of my head. What was all that about BMWs and . . . and moral imperatives? Two weeks ago you were talking brave new worlds."

She looked at Mark's handsome face and suddenly, out of nowhere, had the feeling she was losing him, if she hadn't lost him already. The feeling was accompanied by a powerful urge to lash out.

"And anyway it wasn't very polite of you not to invite me when you had already been invited weeks ago."

"What?"

"Well, don't look surprised. Newt invited you, but you didn't invite me."

"I can't believe you're still harping on that." He looked impatiently around the room.

"I suppose you were planning on bringing Catherine Pell."

"Don't be—"

Suddenly he was smiling falsely. Alex turned and saw Randal White emerging from a group of people. Ralph McCormick, tight mouthed and glassy eyed, followed close behind.

"Having a good time?" said White.

"Great," said Mark. Alex was surprised to feel his arm snake around her shoulder. "It's great to get a chance to talk to so many people."

White considered Mark for a moment as though he had said something surprising.

"Don't you get out very often?" he asked neutrally.

Alex blinked. She looked at Mark's face and could see that he was as surprised at White's tone as she was.

"I mean people with links to the company," Mark blustered, setting his jaw. "The nonexecs and so forth. It's a real insight into local business."

"Pillars," said White flatly, and then by way of explanation: "Of the community."

McCormick laughed—a single hard bark of mirthless laughter. A fleck of spittle stayed on his large chin. " 'Nough pillars to make a colonnade," he said.

As though only now reminded of his presence, White made an elaborate show of bringing McCormick forward.

"Alex, this is Ralph McCormick, our head man in Data Systems," he said. "Ralph, this is Alex Tynan, one of my most brilliant statisticians."

McCormick bent forward from the waist.

"Nice to meet you, Miss Tynan. Randal has been telling me about your interesting discovery in the—"

White put a hand on McCormick's arm. "Let's see if we get through the evening without talking shop," he said.

Alex realized that the music had stopped. People were drifting through to the main sitting room.

"Looks like it's time for Richard's speech," said White wearily. He looked at Alex, his eyes creased with amusement. "Richard always says a few words. Rallying-the-troops sort of thing."

He and McCormick turned away and followed the other guests through the double doors.

"I was *going* to invite you," said Mark, grabbing at Alex's arm.

She pulled herself free and lurched against a woman in a red dress.

"I'm terribly sorry," she said.

Then, with as much dignity as possible, she set off after White and McCormick.

The lights on the chandeliers had been brought up a little, so that the molding around the grand Colonial-style ceiling was picked out in soft shadow. Alex, very conscious now that she had drunk too much wine, made her way through the people towards the front of a rough semicircle that had formed around the fireplace. Goebert was in the process of stacking three large volumes in the middle of a Persian rug. When the stack was complete he stepped up onto it. For a moment he looked down on everybody.

"Goodness me, Newton, you really are losing your hair," he said with an expression of mild surprise.

Brady touched his scalp self-consciously.

"Sign of virility," he said gruffly.

There was some indulgent laughter. The Brady-and-Goebert straight man/funnyman routine was a set piece of ProvLife gatherings. Alex spotted White standing at the front of the crowd, smiling affably. Next to him McCormick stared intently at Goebert's face, moving his tongue over his lips from time to time as if to moisten them. Grant, behind McCormick, was stone faced.

"Ladies, gentlemen, Providential colleagues and friends," said Goebert. "Some of you will know that Eva and I celebrated our thirty-fifth wedding anniversary last week."

He raised his small hands, acknowledging light applause. Eva Goebert, a plump lady in a floral print dress, smiled warmly.

"Thirty-five years," said Goebert, shaking his head. "Can you believe it? It's been entirely wonderful, of course, and I must say I hardly noticed the time go by. The sycamore in the front yard tells a different story, mind you. We didn't plant it, but it wasn't much more than a sapling when we arrived here in 'sixty-five. I was looking at it this morning, and it brought home to me how long we had been together here in this house and how long I had been going in to the office, taking that bracing walk over the hill and across the river."

Alex looked at White, and noticed the man with the thick glasses standing just behind him. Miller? Mellor? Mullins. He was squinting at Goebert, stroking his chin like a Shakespearean conspirator, his right hand tucked into his polyester armpit.

"And goodness me, we have seen some changes," said Goebert. "Changes that come with growth, of course, but changes that come with—well, *change*. And the process doesn't stop. As you may know, our illustration actuary Randal White"—Goebert put out a hand, and White acknowledged the recognition with a tilt of his head—"will be going down to Washington in a couple of weeks to discuss the issue of genetic information and its use by the insurance industry." Goebert paused and checked White's face. "Did I get that right, Randal?"

"On the money as always," said White.

"And it will be left to federal legislators to establish the framework in which we go forward in the future. This will be a change in itself. As you probably know, the industry has enjoyed a degree of autonomy up to now, supervised pretty much state by state. Federal government will have more of a say in the future, that's my guess anyway. But the real change is going to come from the technology itself. This will bring, is already bringing, bigger changes than even I have seen, than I can in fact imagine. And you know what? That worries me just a little."

Goebert's face had lost its friendly, slightly bemused expression. He was looking deadly serious now. He looked straight at Randal White.

"Which is why, when I was looking at that old tree, I got the feeling it was time for me to step aside. To make room for someone more able to cope with the challenges we will soon be facing."

"What?"

It was McCormick who had spoken, his question an outraged shout. Alex looked and was surprised to see Grant come forward and grab McCormick by the elbow. White's face was pale and grim.

"But, Richard, you can't," said Newton Brady.

Goebert stepped down from his books as though abdicating the throne.

"Oh, but I am," he said quietly. "A little earlier than anticipated, I know. But, hell, I'm sixty-three, almost sixty-four. I'm sure the board is capable of voting in a competent replacement."

He was immediately surrounded by people. Alex looked for White, but he was no longer there. There was a buzz of puzzled questioning. Grant was moving McCormick away through the crowd.

"What about Christmas of 'ninety-nine?" said McCormick in a stunned voice.

In the press of agitated people, David Mullins hadn't moved. His left hand still working at his chin, he stared hard at the group that had surrounded Goebert. Alex noticed that he was no longer wearing his watch.

16

On the Wednesday after Goebert's party Alex was working through the ProvLife database, looking at heart disease statistics, when Mel Hartman came and rested his hands on the edge of her desk.

"Get ready, Alex. Are you ready? Because you are not going to *believe* this."

He leaned closer. Alex could smell his sickly-sweet cologne and his coffee-tainted breath. She knew what was going on: Hartman was trying to play Mister Nice Guy, trying to make up for his recent bitchy behavior. He hadn't spoken to her for two days, stewing over her invitation to the party. Now he probably calculated that if she really was a rising star, he'd do better to swallow his pride and keep on friendly terms with her. It was all very well, but Randal White had asked to see her at half past ten, to summarize her findings on the anomaly, and she wanted to be ready in case he asked for specific recommendations. She sighed wearily and kept on tapping at the keys, hoping Hartman might get the hint.

"Sandra, Sandra. Get over here. Come on."

Sandra Betridge was striding past, stirring a mug of coffee with one of the useless plastic sticks that littered the galley kitchen. Hartman waved her over insistently.

"What is it?" she said. "I'm in the middle of something."

Hartman shrugged. "Okay, okay, fine. You wanna be the last to know. . . ."

Sandra looked at him doubtfully, then took a couple of tentative steps closer.

"I hope you're not going to tell me Richard Goebert's retiring, because I heard it yesterday."

Hartman shook his head in disbelief. "Oh, *Sandra*. There are tribesmen in Outer Mongolia heard that yesterday. Inner Mongolia knew a week ago."

Sandra smiled sarcastically. "So who's going to take over? Have they heard that in Outer Mongolia?"

"Sure. Newton Brady's the front-runner, but the odds are shortening on Walter Neumann. But that's not—"

Alex looked up. "What about Randal White?"

Hartman gave her a knowing smile. She immediately wished she'd kept her mouth shut.

"You don't know your stats, Alex. No actuary has taken the CEO spot at ProvLife since the Second World War. Or is there something you're not telling us?"

Alex shook her head.

"I've got work to do," said Sandra wearily.

Hartman held up his hands. "Wait wait wait wait. That's not the thing."

"What thing?"

"Just listen. Just listen. Okay. You know Inés, the little Hispanic lady, the cleaner?"

Alex and Sandra exchanged an impatient look.

"No," they said at once.

"Come on. There's four of them, come in about seven o'clock and empty the trash."

"So you're getting your information from the cleaners now, Mel?" Sandra said, blowing on her coffee.

"Just *listen*. Last night Inés and one of the other cleaners were up on the top floor, outside Central Records. About eight o'clock, this was. Just before." He glanced round at the door and lowered his voice. "Anyway, they're up there mopping the floors or something and there's this *noise* from the men's room. This kind of *bellowing*."

"Bellowing?" said Sandra. "You mean like an animal or something?"

"I mean like a *man*."

For a moment nobody spoke.

"Like, what? You—"

Hartman held up a finger. "So they go in."

"They went into the men's room?" Sandra looked shocked.

"Of course, why not? They're cleaners. You wanna know what they found?" Hartman looked back and forth between them. "Ralph McCormick. Data Systems supremo. In one of the cubicles. And this is the good part." Hartman took another long look at the door. "He was buck . . . naked."

"Naked?" Sandra covered her mouth. Her voice dropped to a whisper. "You mean . . . *completely?*"

"Yep. His clothes were all over. Guy just completely freaked out. Stripped right there in the john."

Alex swallowed. Something told her Hartman might not be making this up. She remembered the way McCormick had been at Richard Goebert's party.

"Je-sus. Was he . . . was he, like, alone?" Sandra said.

"Apparently. This was not a homosexual encounter—as far as we can tell."

Sandra's eyes were bulging. "Ralph McCormick naked. That *is* scary. What did they do, the cleaners?"

"They got the hell out of there. Came running out, screaming. Someone called Security. All hell broke loose. And the next thing they know they're being called into Walter Neumann's office. And he's telling them he's very sorry about any distress, et cetera et cetera, and saying Mr. McCormick's been under a lot of strain lately, and stuffing their pockets with fifty-dollar bills in return for keeping quiet." Hartman folded his arms. "And guess who hasn't come in today. Something about a last-minute holiday?"

"No shit."

"Yep. My guess is it'll be a long one. As in permanent."

"Je-sus," said Sandra, sounding spooked. "He's only been in the job six months. First Ken Miller, now Ralph McCormick."

"Yeah, absolutely," said Hartman. "The curse of Central Records. Maybe all that information is bad for you, destroys your will to live. Like they say: knowledge is a dangerous thing."

"Learning!" Alex almost shouted. Suddenly she couldn't stand to

hear another word. "And it's a *little* learning. 'A little learning is a dangerous thing.' Alexander Pope."

Hartman took his elbow off the monitor. "Well excuse *me*."

"Anyway, this whole thing—it's ridiculous. It's just stupid gossip."

Hartman considered Alex for a moment, one eyebrow raised theatrically.

"Well, Alex, I'm sure that would be the company line. Comrade Ralph McCormick is suffering from a cold and will be returning to state duties in the near future. Heavily touched-up photograph in *Pravda*, page thirty-seven."

Sandra clucked with amusement.

"Very funny," said Alex. "Anyway, what makes you so sure it's true?"

Hartman straightened up. A couple of senior-looking suits from Marketing were coming through the doors, on their way to Randal White's office.

"I have faith in my sources," he said. "Not all forms of knowledge are digital. Maybe you'll find that out someday."

And before Alex could tell him to get lost he was heading back to his desk.

Alex tried to concentrate on her work in the time left to her, but it was hard. She couldn't get the story about Ralph McCormick out of her mind. Mel Hartman and the rest of the department seemed to think it was no more than a huge joke, some executive VP they hardly knew going crazy in the men's room, taking all his clothes off and frightening the cleaners. It was just a touch of color, something surprising in the midst of their all too predictable lives—surprising, but not unique. People went crazy every day. It was right there in the statistics, under *Claims Arising from Mental Illness*. Which was why it didn't mean anything.

But Alex felt sure it *did* mean something. In her bones she felt it was part of a picture, a revelation that was forming before her eyes. If only she could interpret it, see the whole, then maybe she would understand what it was she and Mark were becoming a part of. If only, like the columns of numbers that moment lighting up on her computer screen, she could break the pieces down, add them up, turn them over and over until they gave up their secrets. But she didn't know how. Out of the blue a successful executive decides to abandon his life and start again where no one will find him, using a vast fortune that nobody knows he has. A few weeks later one of his colleagues—another successful, respectable man—suddenly erupts, snaps as if under some unbearable pressure. And all anybody cares about is keeping him quiet. The only man who's smiling is Richard Goebert. The CEO they were going to have to drag out when his time came, so people said. The CEO who has just taken early retirement.

It took Alex a while to notice that the numbers on her screen were different. She blinked, brought her face a little closer to the screen, and then read them again, waiting for her brain to refocus on the problem and tell her why she was not reading them right. But her brain did not oblige. She checked her watch. There were ten minutes before the meeting with White. And she had a problem.

She looked down at the notes she had made, notes that documented—more for Randal White's sake than her own—her step-by-step progress through the Central Records system. It was perfectly clear. The figures before her were a statistical summary, broken down into years, of car ownership patterns among a particular set of ProvLife policyholders: males who had died of heart failure. But the summary had changed since she last accessed it. The last time she had looked, 4.2% in this group had been soft-top owners at the time they filled in their application forms—4.2% every year: a statistical impossibility. Now, inexplicably, the numbers fluctuated as they always should have done, from 2% in one year right up to 7.5% in another.

Alex felt suddenly very warm. Her discussion with Randal White, *his* discussions with Ralph McCormick, her time at PrimeNumber, all of it had sprung from the anomaly she claimed to have uncovered. White hadn't checked the figures himself. He had simply trusted to her analytical competence. But now, it appeared, there *was* no anomaly. She had simply been wasting everybody's time as well as her own. That was what it was going to look like.

"But I know what I saw!" she said out loud.

Immediately the telephone rang. It was Janice Aitken, Randal White's PA.

"Alexandra? Randal's ready for you now. Can you come in?"

White was standing by the window looking out over Dorrance Street towards the distant gray river. He turned as Alex entered the room, and seemed to take a moment to recognize her, or at least why she was there.

"Good morning," she said, feeling intensely awkward. "Is this . . . a bad time to . . . ?"

"No." White gave himself a little shake. "Please. Alex. Sit down. We were going to . . . Ah yes, the—the problem. Would you like some coffee or something?"

"I'm fine, thank you," Alex said, sitting down opposite the desk.

The piles of paperwork had barely diminished, and on top of a stack of files was balanced a big plate of Oreos—an offering to the men from Marketing, no doubt.

Alex knew she should get down to business, but she wasn't ready yet to bite the bullet.

"I enjoyed the party last Friday," she said. "We both did, Mark and I. It was very kind of Mr. Goebert to invite us."

White reached over and switched on his desk light, although it wasn't dark. There was something about his manner that was different, graver. He didn't seem to want to look her in the eye. Alex wasn't sure if he was unhappy about something or simply distracted.

"I'm glad," he said. "It turned into quite a momentous occasion, didn't it? What with the announcement."

"Yes. It was a big surprise," Alex said. "At least to me."

"Oh, not just to you," White said, scanning the surface of his desk for something. "Not by a long way. Still, we'll get by I'm sure." He glanced up at her. "No one's indispensable, after all, are they?"

Alex answered him with a weak smile.

"I had some notes here somewhere. On this anomaly of ours. Okay. Here they are." He pulled out a blue hardback notebook from under an open book. "I finally got around to looking at the data you were talking about."

Alex shut her eyes for a moment. That was why White was unhappy. He had just discovered the same thing she had: that the anomaly she had reported so diligently did not exist.

"Yes, I wanted to talk to you about that. It's very odd, but—"

"Yes, yes, it is. Tell me if I'm missing something, but I simply can't find"—he flipped over a couple of pages in the notebook—"the hard correlations that you mentioned. I assume we have been looking at the same data: ProvLife's own claims records."

"Absolutely. The thing is . . ." Alex took a deep breath. Attack was the best form of defense. "The numbers have been changed."

White looked up at her again, closed the notebook, and dropped it gently onto the desk.

"Changed?"

"Two weeks ago the percentage of convertible and sports coupé owners corresponded every year with the published industry averages."

"Yes, I understand all that—"

"Only now, all of a sudden, the numbers appear perfectly random. They've been changed."

Alex looked White steadily in the eye. She hoped she seemed a whole lot more confident than she felt.

White took a deep breath, his nostrils flaring, and sat back in his chair. "All right. By whom?"

"Well, I guess—I mean, there are two possibilities. First, it might be the computer itself, the software. If there was some data loss, it could be that the system is programmed to cover the gaps with known industry averages." Alex was thinking on her feet, but this didn't sound too silly. "Then, if the data were recovered somehow—say, retrieved from a backup system—the real numbers might go back in."

"In which case the programmer has gone to a lot of trouble for nothing, since real information is all we're interested in where our own records are concerned."

"Indeed."

"And the second possibility?"

Alex bit her lip. White obviously didn't think much of her rogue software theory.

"Well, I guess . . ." She sat up straight. "The second possibility is that someone in Central Records screwed up somewhere, and then tried to cover up."

White stared. For a moment Alex thought he was going to shout at her, but instead he suddenly started to laugh.

"Oh, Alex. I felt sure you were going to fold on me, but I'm glad to find I was wrong. I admire your tenacity. Who ever said actuaries were timid?"

Alex smiled back at him. He'd wanted to believe that the anomaly had really been there, that she was right. But before he said so, he'd wanted to be sure she believed it herself. That was White all over: integrity first.

"So, Central Records it is, then."

"It figures. PrimeNumber enter all the applicant and claims data into the system, and they summarize that data and put it into basic statistical form. But all the industry data—the actuarial data—is kept here. They don't have it down at PrimeNumber, and I'm not sure anyone down there would know how to get it. So if someone were going to consciously substitute industry averages for missing data on real claims, they would have to be pretty familiar with the Central Records system."

White nodded. This he *did* seem ready to believe.

"But why, Alex? Why would they do it?"

Alex already had an answer to this.

"My guess is some data was lost accidentally. Rather than make a federal case out of it, someone in the department simply tried to repair the damage with as little fuss as possible. The only question is: what other data has been lost that we don't know about?"

White let out a long sigh. "I was afraid you'd say something like that."

"You were?"

"Yes. Because my conclusions are the same as yours. And because an urgent reappraisal of our data systems couldn't possibly be a less attractive prospect than it is now."

Alex kept silent. In her mind she had a picture of Ralph McCormick, naked and screaming inside a green Formica cubicle.

"Strictly between ourselves, Alex," White went on, "we've been having some difficulty on the personnel side in that department."

"I had . . . I had heard a few things," Alex said.

White nodded, reading her meaning.

"Well, then you know. Ralph McCormick is . . . not a well man. In fact, to be candid, he appears to have developed a serious cocaine dependency."

Alex stared. This was something even Mel Hartman didn't know.

"And that may not be the whole story. I think the man has psychological problems. Of course, one feels sorry for him, but the fact is, he's in charge of arguably the most important function in the whole of this building. I hate to think what's been going on up there."

"But surely he can't stay in—" Alex stopped herself. "Of course, it's not my place to—"

"Oh yes it is, Alex. It *is* your place. This company's position, its very future depends on the quality of its information. Information is our lifeblood. Without it, we're flying blind. It's an issue that concerns everybody in this company, its actuaries above all."

"Will Mr. McCormick be . . . Will he resign?"

"I don't know. I know he should, for his own sake as much as the company's. But not everyone on the board is anxious to see him go. I can't say I understand it, but our chief legal officer in particular prefers the status quo. But then"—White pushed his lips together as if there were still things he could not say—"I suppose lawyers are paid to be cautious."

17

Harold Tate waited until six o'clock and then left the bar. He drove down the hill past the giant convention center towards the river. There had been no letup in the snow all afternoon and he was obliged to crawl along in second gear just to stay on the road. If Pilaski called him on the mobile, he'd find it dead. Tate had been careful to let the battery run down.

He peeled back the elasticized cuff of his jacket and yanked forward his glove to check the time. But his thick plaid shirt was buttoned too tightly over the thermal underwear Suzy had insisted he wear. Breathing hard through his open mouth, he clawed at it for a moment with gloved fingers, but it was no use. Finally he had to push the fingers of his right hand into his mouth and tear off the glove with his teeth. Cursing steadily, he prized back the shirt cuff and uncovered the watch face. It was ten past. Why the hell had he needed to know that, anyway? He started to laugh, was suddenly laughing so hard he jerked forward against the steering wheel.

At Kennedy Plaza, he turned right, making his way towards Westminster Street, slowing down even more, doing his best despite the snow to be watchful.

He didn't like coming so near the ProvLife building. He'd even thought twice before going to Michael Eliot's funeral, given all the ProvLife people that were bound to be there. But then again, he'd known Michael for twenty-five years. If he *hadn't* gone it would have looked odd, certainly to the widow. He'd called, spoken to her, not ten days before her husband's death. It might even have looked suspicious. Tate waited for the lights to change and then pulled up on the south side of Dorrance. The traffic moved slowly past, the evening rush hour well under way. From the deli down the street came a warm sour-sweet smell of fried onions and hot bread.

When Margaret Eliot had told him about Michael's money, had told him about the woman who had called, he had rapidly come to the conclusion that somehow or other there had been a serious indiscretion. He found it hard to believe that Michael would have been so stupid as to tell the woman where the money had come from, but the fact that she knew about it, the fact that she said she had all kinds of papers and was in a position to substantiate her story with *physical proof*, had seen the return of his sleepless nights. The worst of it was that the physical proof—the papers—had come from him. It was he who had broken the rules, by bringing Eliot to the office, by telling him in person about the results of his test. If he hadn't done that, Eliot wouldn't have run, wouldn't have taken the papers. In fact, when it came down to it, the indiscretion was really his. He had let it happen, and if there was a reckoning to pay, there was a very good chance he would be the one required to pay it. That was why he had to deal with the fallout himself, and quickly.

His first reaction had been to call the number Margaret had traced. Just as she'd said, it was located somewhere on the East Side. He'd called three times, but the woman never picked up. All he ever got was her answer machine, and a cheerful voice that stated the number and then asked for a message. There was a noise in the background. It sounded like a baby or maybe a cat. The third time he'd called, he'd started to say something—*Hello, you don't know me*—but then suddenly changed his mind. If he gave his name he'd only be leaving himself more exposed. He'd slammed down the receiver, his heart pounding in his chest. He realized that, whatever Margaret's assumptions, he knew nothing about this woman, nothing about what she was doing or who she might have on her side. Large sums of money were involved—enormous sums of money—and the careers of determined and, he suspected, increasingly desperate people. If anyone found out about what he had allowed to happen—well, anything was possible. By calling her, wouldn't he just be attracting attention to himself? After all, if it *was* just a question of the money, there was no reason for him to become involved. Any blame would be directed at Eliot, and he was beyond reach. It was the idea that this person, whoever she was, whoever she represented, had *all kinds of papers* that worried him.

He lay awake for three nights, trying to think what to do. Margaret had been quite clear about the woman she saw at the funeral. He had seen her too. During the service she had been sitting in the pew right next to him. He had even lent her his handkerchief at one point when she started to cry. He felt certain Margaret was right: she *was* Michael's lover. Who else could she be? And if that was the case, then she worked at ProvLife, because Michael had said as much. Tate only wished he had pressed him for more details, for a name at least, instead of being so discreet. As it was, he was going to have to find her, recognize her. And then what? Follow her to her home, maybe get inside, find out exactly what evidence she did have? Christ, he didn't even have the nerve to make a phone call. But the more he thought about it, the more he saw that he had no choice.

He had left the lab at lunchtime on Monday and driven up into Providence to walk in the neighborhood of the ProvLife building. On Tuesday, walking along the icy sidewalk, eating a stale hot dog, he had seen the woman come out of a cross street. He'd nearly slipped and fallen. She was with a stylish Italian-looking guy, having some kind of argument, the woman speaking in a low irritated voice and counting off grievances on her fingers. Tate had frozen as she turned to look at him. Then she was gone. He'd walked to the street corner and watched the couple make their way down the next block. At the intersection of Dorrance and Westminster they'd entered ProvLife. Elated and terrified at once, Tate had turned on his heel and hurried back up the street. He was now sure where she worked. All he had to do was wait for her to come out of the building and follow her back to her house.

The ProvLife building loomed above him in the snowy gloom, its absurd masonry looking like frosting on a fat cake. Tate turned up the collar of his hunting jacket and pulled down his cap. There was one thing about the ridiculous clothes he was wearing: no one was likely to recognize him.

*   *   *

Alex Tynan saw him as soon as she came out the door. He was stand-ing on the opposite side of the street next to a blue Pontiac, a half-eaten hot dog raised to his mouth. He was wearing a hunting cap and jacket, and the same silly moon boots she had noticed two days before. She turned left and made her way to the entrance of ProvLife's open-air parking lot, resisting the urge to look back to see if he was following her. Paranoia made it a certainty that this was the same man who had left the strange message on her answer machine. *Hello, you don't know me* . . . but she *did* know him, had recognized him immediately by his beard and sea-dog face. When she had first seen him at the fu-neral he had reminded her above all of a U-boat captain from an old black-and-white war film. When she had seen him in the street, the day of her disastrous lunch with Mark, she had remembered the handker-chief he had lent her, and in the midst of arguing had thought about stopping to thank him, about making an arrangement to return it. But seeing him again, a third time, made her uneasy. It couldn't be a coinci-dence, surely. His intent, scared gaze suggested a purpose. He looked like somebody who was nerving himself up to do something.

Quickening her pace, she looked furtively across to her left to see if Mac was still working. The door to the basement was open but there was no sign of anyone. Light snow continued to fall. She climbed into the Camry and backed out of her space. Pulling out of the lot, she saw the lights of the Pontiac come on. It jerked out into the street behind her and started to follow, fishtailing a little on the icy street.

Alex didn't see the bus until the last moment. It was moving across the intersection. She slammed on her brakes. There was a seemingly endless moment in which it drifted past, and then a throaty clunk as the Pontiac ran straight into the back of her.

Somewhere a horn was blaring. She climbed out of the car. He was already looking at the damage.

"What the hell—" She looked at his terrified face, and felt her own anger expand. "What the *hell* do you think you're doing?"

"I'm sorry. I—I was too close. I was going too fast."

"You were following me," said Alex. "What the hell are you following me for?"

He looked back up Dorrance towards the ProvLife building.

"I don't know if you remember me. From the funeral? From Mi-chael's funeral?"

Alex gave a sharp, dipping nod, her eyes fixed on his face. He kept looking around him as though he were the one being followed.

"Look, can we—is there somewhere we can talk?"

Alex shook her head, and looked at the traffic building up in the street. The bus was gone and the intersection was now clear. A woman in a fur-hooded parka climbed out of a Ford pickup. She was shouting, waving for them to pull over to the sidewalk.

"Get the hell out of the road!"

The man took a step forward.

"If you come any nearer I'll scream," said Alex, clenching her fists.

"For God's sake, you're—you're in real danger here. You understand me? This isn't a game."

Alex stood rooted to the spot.

"I know you have the papers," he said. "Don't try to deny it. I know everything: the call to Mrs. Eliot, the airline ticket, everything. She had your number traced."

"What the—?"

"Listen to me! I don't give a damn about the money. Do what you like with the money. But I must have those printouts."

Alex tried to focus on what he was saying. The sound of horns was deafening. Down the street she could see the turning lights of a patrol car making its way towards them on the wrong side of the road.

"What—what printouts?" She shook her head. "I don't—"

"I'm telling you, you don't know the danger you're in," he said again.

He looked around and saw the police, then dashed back to his car and threw it into reverse. There was a grinding crunch as he backed up. He pulled the wheel hard over and made off down a side street. The last thing Alex saw was his pale face framed by the window. She had never seen anybody look so scared.

PART THREE

HANGED

18

R ichard Goebert's office was the biggest on the eighth floor of the ProvLife building. Walter Neumann, the company's chief legal counsel, had a spacious corner office five floors below that looked down on Dorrance and the pompous facade of City Hall, but Goebert's office was bigger—bigger and better proportioned. It was clear that the architect had lavished particular attention on this room. Looking out through the huge glass window onto the balcony, you felt *right* somehow, properly placed, like the hermit or shepherd in the foreground of a Watteau. That was the way it seemed to Neumann, anyway, as he looked out at the fading light of another gray Providence afternoon. He had long coveted Goebert's office and, since the old man's unceremonious departure, had found it difficult not to wander in from time to time just to gaze at all that newly available emptiness.

He didn't hear Newton Brady come in behind him.

"Hell of a view, isn't it?"

Neumann turned and took in Brady's stout figure framed by the mahogany door.

"Newton," he said flatly, neutrally.

Neumann had a peculiar way of talking that involved never really opening his mouth. It was as if, even in the act of speaking—which he performed with an advocate's fluency and ease—he never quite wanted to commit to having said anything. His clever tongue worked behind closed teeth.

"Bridget said you were down here," said Brady, closing the door and coming forward, staring past Neumann at the balcony and the street beyond.

"Yes, I . . ."

For a moment Neumann didn't know what to say. His big inexpressive face became subtly less expressive as his mind sought a way out of what was a potentially embarrassing situation.

"Bridget thinks we should—thinks that the company should redecorate this room. Goebert let it all go." Neumann pointed to where Goebert's neatly crossed brogues had, over the years, worn an almost perfectly circular hole in the carpet.

Brady stared at the hole as if he expected something to come out of it. "I guess you're thinking of taking the job, then."

He shot Neumann a look, but Neumann was already turning away, going back to contemplation of the balcony.

"Subject to board approval, of course," Brady added sardonically.

"Of course," said Neumann. He smoothed his hair back towards the crown. "Somebody has to do it, and it seems to me that the timing's bad as far as you're concerned."

Brady pushed a thick finger into his collar and pulled.

"Yeah. Eliot's death left us a little short-handed in Finance. It's going to take a while for Ferulli to get bedded in. The way I see it, it's got to be either you or White."

Neumann took a step towards the window. "Was that why you came in here? To discuss . . . ?"

Neumann had a tendency to leave sentences unfinished, a habit that led to misunderstandings. Bridget, his PA, had to make do with hints and nudges, but even she sometimes misunderstood. Not that Neumann minded being misunderstood. The way people mistook things was sometimes revealing. It was a game Brady was more than familiar with. He looked at the back of Neumann's balding head and waited for the man to turn around.

"To discuss the chairmanship?" said Neumann finally.

Brady gave an irritable shake of his head.

"Goebert's gone to the Caymans," he said. "Just for a couple of weeks. He said he and Eva wanted to get out of the cold."

Neumann removed his glasses and started cleaning them with his handkerchief.

"Go on."

"Checked into the Hyatt. They've taken a suite looking out over the golf course."

"A suite."

"That's right. According to Grant, I mean according to his guy on the ground, they went for a little walk in—" Brady frowned and removed a scrap of paper from his pocket. He squinted down at the poorly reproduced letters of a fax. "George Town. That's the capital. They went for a walk in town and dropped in at a place called Colombian Emeralds. It's a jewelry shop specializing in—"

"Emeralds?" asked Neumann, polishing his glasses with an insistent circular motion.

"That's right," said Brady. "Bought Eva two rings. A big emerald set with baguette diamonds and a solitaire in platinum. Twenty thousand dollars."

"How'd he pay?"

"Cash."

Brady waited for a moment, hoping for a reaction, but Neumann kept on polishing, deep in thought. Then he stopped. He put the glasses on and considered Brady's face.

"What does Grant think?" he said.

"Said he thinks Goebert told her yesterday. She didn't leave the room until late afternoon. That's when they went to buy the rings."

Neumann nodded and then watched as Brady pressed the back of his thumb into his sternum.

"Jesus Christ," said Brady, suddenly agitated. He looked around at the empty walls and slotted a tablet into his mouth. "I don't know, Walter. I really don't know. First Eliot, now Goebert. A suite at the Hyatt. And now we have fucking McCormick . . . fucking up."

Neumann blinked at the obscenity, but was otherwise unmoved by Brady's vehemence. He was noticing something about Brady's face, something he had never seen before.

"Did you hear about what happened at the party?" said Brady, still pressing at his heartburn. "I had to wrestle him to the floor. After the old man's farewell? He goes into the bathroom. Not downstairs, thank God. He makes his way upstairs to *Goebert's* bedroom—this is how nuts he is—he goes into Goebert's bedroom, into their bathroom to snort a line. We're on the floor, me trying to get this plastic bag out of his fist."

Brady waited, hoping for once for some sign of disapproval or anger, but Neumann just stared back with his dead eyes.

"He's out of control, Walter! And now he's stripping off in the john. He's running around naked for the cleaners to see."

"I *dealt* with the cleaners," said Neumann.

"You—?"

Brady stopped, staring hard at Neumann's blank face. He sometimes wondered if, behind the steely calm, Neumann was actually worse than McCormick.

"You *dealt* with the cleaners?"

Neumann nodded.

"Walter, that's like saying—"

"'How long have you been having cosmetic surgery?" snapped Neumann, cutting Brady off midsentence.

For a moment Brady was unable to understand the question.

"What?"

"Your veins. In your nose. I can *see* you're having them treated."

Brady touched at his nose, dumbfounded. He started to laugh, but got hold of himself when Neumann's pale face began to color.

"What's it for?"

"Nothing. I—"

"Are you *trying* to draw attention to yourself? Dammit, Newton. We're employees of an insurance company, not—not movie stars."

"It's just a few thread veins," said Brady.

"And what's next? Liposuction?"

Brady's shoulders fell and suddenly he looked like a schoolkid with an eating disorder. Neumann suppressed an urge to slap his face.

"Just stop it," he said calmly. "Whatever it is you've signed up for, just drop it. It's inappropriate."

"But what about Goebert?" Brady whined. "He's running around . . ."

He walked over to the window, breathing hard. He looked out at the gray sky.

"That's a Jack Nicklaus course they have out there, Walter."

"Goebert's out of the picture now," said Neumann. "He stepped out of the limelight. A Caribbean holiday's to be expected. So's a present for his wife. He's just retired. So long as he doesn't go crazy, he can do what he likes. In a couple of months he'll move away from the area. He'll find a place on the West Coast. We won't have to worry about him."

"So why pay a—?"

Brady watched Neumann come to the window and lean his forehead against the cold glass. He had never seen anything quite so spontaneous from the other man, and for a moment he was unable to speak. He watched with horror as Neumann closed his eyes, a look of something like pain seeming to flicker just behind his blank features. Then he knew the answer to his unfinished question. They were paying a private detective to follow Goebert around, had been doing so ever since he announced his retirement, not because they anticipated a problem, but because Neumann wanted to know what Goebert was doing with the money. He just wanted to *know*—wanted, however vicariously, to feel what it was like.

Both men stared at the balcony. A ridge of cloud moved slowly across the window until it was almost dark in the room. Snow started to fall. They stood like that, looking out in complete silence, until streetlights started to glow orange. Brady unpeeled another tablet and slipped it into his mouth.

"White thinks we should send McCormick down to New Jersey to this fancy clinic," he said. When Neumann didn't answer, he went on: "We sure as hell can't have him running Central Records, the way he is."

"Clinic didn't do him any good last time," said Neumann.

"Maybe if you . . . maybe if you talked to him, read him the riot act."

Neumann came away from the glass, shaking his head.

"He's an addict. He'd agree to anything I say, and the first chance he had . . . What about Mary? Can't she do anything?"

Brady turned and looked at Neumann's face, faintly luminous in the gloom, his steel-framed glasses blank squares of dying light.

"I don't even know if she's at home," he said. "I suspect . . . I suspect they're having a little trouble."

Just after five Neumann's tan Lincoln crossed the river into the East Side. McCormick's white clapboard house was on the corner of Everett and Weyland, a short walk from Swan Point Cemetery. Neumann parked in the street. As he made his way up the uncleared path to the front door he thought he saw a face at one of the first-floor windows.

It took McCormick a while to answer. Standing in the open doorway, he looked haggard and scared. He hadn't had a shave for two days and there were deep shadows under his eyes. His weak red mouth twitched in one corner.

"Walter."

"I just wanted to see how you were getting on," said Neumann. "Do you have everything you need?"

McCormick shrugged.

"Sure. That's . . . it's real nice of you to think of me." He looked out at the street, checking for nosy neighbors, then remembered his manners. "Come on in, Walter. Don't stand out in the snow."

Neumann stepped past him into the gloomy interior. The house was heated like a sauna and there was a faint smell of garbage coming through from the kitchen. They walked into the sitting room, Neumann's quick eyes taking in dead plants and overflowing ashtrays. The television was on without sound.

"Where's—?"

"Mary?" McCormick almost shouted his wife's name. "She . . . she's visiting her folks in Newport. Went down there last week."

Neumann turned and watched McCormick as he bustled around, making pathetic attempts to tidy up. Then he stopped what he was doing, a cushion held to his chest. He pointed a trembling index finger at Neumann.

"Coffee?" he said, doing his best to smile. "Or maybe something a little . . . ?"

"Coffee'll be fine," said Neumann through his teeth. "Black."

Neumann dropped the envelope he was carrying onto the coffee table and took off his heavy black overcoat. Then he sat down on the couch, removing a dog-eared *TV Guide* from beneath him. When McCormick came back, Neumann was leafing through a white document with a great show of absorption. McCormick eyed it nervously as he handed Neumann his cup.

"I saw about that Ritter guy on the news," he said, trying to make conversation. "How about that? I didn't think they'd go for him that way. I mean, a civil action."

Neumann looked up. "Well, it's a different burden of proof," he said wearily. "And the prosecution can ask whatever they want. Doesn't mean Ritter's going to pay it. Looks like it's tied up in pension plans anyway."

"I guess it's the lawyers who'll win in the end," said McCormick gamely. "When that guy—what was his name?—when he said his attorneys had been putting in thirty hours a day, nine days a week, I thought maybe there'd been some overbilling."

When he saw Neumann was not in a joking mood, his face fell. He sat down in a battered recliner and let out a long sigh.

"Walter, I just wanted to say—"

Neumann raised his pale hand. "Come on, Ralph, you've known me long enough not to have to . . . I know what you're going through. We're all under a lot of strain, what with Michael's death and Goebert quitting. We just deal with it in different ways."

Neumann watched McCormick's head drop forward, and a look of utter disdain flickered in his cold eyes. McCormick's shoulders jerked, once, twice, and then he was blubbering, wiping his nose on the sleeve of his cardigan, biting his lip.

"I'm not—" He tried to control his voice. "I'm not really dealing with it at all, Walter."

Neumann sipped at his coffee and waited.

"Mary—Mary said she was going to stay at her—at her mother's until I get straightened out."

"Why'd she go?" snapped Neumann.

McCormick looked up, shrinking under Neumann's hard stare.

"Not for any—anything *serious*. We're just not getting on so great. At the moment."

Again McCormick looked at the document on the table. Neumann sat forward, touching the first page with his fingers, as though playing a chord on the piano.

"Yeah, Ritter," he said quietly. "Of course, it's not easy to send a man to his death. I mean, even if they'd had more white jurors at the criminal trial, I doubt they'd have found it any easier to put him in the chair. But money, that's different. Somebody asks you if you think he might have done it or might *well* have done it, and then gives you an indication of what you can make him pay, you feel a little easier about exercising your moral judgment. And the numbers—well, they're kind of meaningless to people on twenty thousand a year."

McCormick nodded, his eyes going from the document to Neumann and back again.

"I . . . I guess," he offered lamely.

"But electrocution," said Neumann. "Did you know they put on that leather mask because the eyes pop out with the pressure?" He shook his head. "Imagine that. I mean, you cook, Ralph. Literally."

He picked up the document and riffled the pages. McCormick read the word AUTOPSY in large black capitals, and then RHODE ISLAND MEDICAL EXAMINER and the names of three pathologists assisting.

"What's the . . . ?"

"This?" said Neumann, as though surprised he should mention it. "Oh, it's just the autopsy they carried out on Eliot. He had a life policy with us. The standard executive thing. Just like you, Ralph."

"Like me? Oh yeah. Yeah."

"The claims department wanted to be sure of all the . . . of all the details. Grant must have left it in my office."

He considered McCormick's face for a moment.

"Did you realize a man's liver weighs about the same as his brain? You wouldn't think so, would you? Look at this." He squinted at the dense type. " *The weight of the unfixed brain is 1508 grams or 53.2 ounces.*' And up here"—he ran his finger up the page—"it says the liver—here it is: *'the liver weighs 1528 grams or 53.9 ounces.'* That's big, isn't it? Like a—well, that must look something like a pig's liver, I guess."

McCormick reached into the pocket of his cardigan and took out a crumpled package of Marlboros. He put a cigarette between his lips and lit it. There was perspiration on his top lip.

"They call the mark," Neumann went on, "the *lesion*—where the current hits the body? They call it the electrical mark." He smiled. "So much for technical jargon, huh? Yes, Grant was telling me all about it. They get quite a lot of electrocutions going through Claims, accidental and not so accidental. Death from electrocution can be difficult to prove, in fact. There may be no mark at all on the skin. When an electrical appliance falls in water, for instance. Then you won't find a mark."

McCormick took an unsteady drag on his cigarette.

"Eliot was pretty straightforward, though," Neumann went on. "Yellow-gray elevated area of skin on his right hand. That's where he was holding that old drill."

He tossed the report down and sat back on the couch.

"That's what I don't understand," he said. "I mean, why use that particular drill? The thing was at least thirty years old. Margaret says she doesn't even remember seeing it before. Admits she doesn't know what-all goes on in the garage, mind you—in his tool box—but all the same seems to think she gave him a new one for Christmas not so long ago . . . He's using this old drill—rubber insulation all shot to hell, of course—he's drilling holes for shelving, poking around in those old walls and—" Neumann shook his head and picked at a loose thread in his pants. "Apparently you can feel a charge at as little as one milliamp. You get to ten milliamps and it *hurts*. Between ten and twenty milliamps, you may not be able to let go. You want to let go, but you can't. The muscles go into an intense cramp. It's like you stick to it, flopping around like a fish on a hook."

He leaned forward and looked along his nose at the report.

"Eliot bit a hole in his cheek. Big chunk out of the inside of his mouth. Says it right here. Cracked a molar. I guess that was—I guess that was the *pain*."

McCormick stood up, his hands fluttering.

"You okay, Ralph?"

"It's not good . . . it's not good for me to get anxious," he said.

"What are you so anxious about?"

"It's not good."

"Sit down, Ralph."

McCormick looked at Neumann's blank face, and slowly lowered himself back into his recliner. He drew hard on his cigarette and blew smoke into the air above him.

"This?" said Neumann, tapping the report with the back of his hand. "Is this what's bothering you? This report? There's nothing here you need to get anxious about, Ralph."

He reached across the coffee table and picked up the remote for the television.

"It just shows you what can happen when you get careless," he said, and he killed the power.

19

Alex dumped more sugar into her coffee and stared at her reflection in the diner window. Even though an hour had passed since the confrontation, she was still shaking. The policeman had wanted a full account of what had happened. She said that some lunatic had run into the back of her and then driven off. The damage to the Camry was minimal, and the young officer had looked relieved when she said she had no intention of taking the matter further.

Now, sitting in the empty diner, listening to an old Bruce Springsteen song, all she could do was think about the stranger's face. What had been most frightening—beyond what he had said, beyond the intensity with which he had said it—was his fear, the fear she'd seen in him. It had been there in his eyes, a startling intensity that was utterly different from anything she had ever seen before, the intensity of a man on the edge of a precipice. And he was warning her, telling her that she should be as afraid as he was.

She didn't know who to talk to. She had tried getting hold of Mark on her cell phone, but he was out of the office, had been out all day at a meeting. She thought about calling the police, but then realized that she had just spoken to the police without saying anything. And what could she tell them? The stranger had committed no crime beyond running into the back of her, and besides, if she were really going to get into it, she would have to tell them about Liz and Michael Eliot and the money, and she'd promised to keep all of that a secret. She even thought about going to Randal White, but there the same constraints applied. And besides, what could he do? He didn't know the identity of the stranger any more than she did. He'd already said so at the funeral.

It was difficult recalling exactly what the man had said, still harder making sense of it. But one thing was clear: he'd made the mistake that many other people at the funeral must have made. He thought *she* had been Michael Eliot's lover. He knew about the bank details, and Eliot's papers, though it was Liz Foster who had those. In which case, was it Liz who was in danger? Or was it both of them?

She tried Liz's number again and again, but there was never any answer. Could she have left town? But that didn't seem likely, because she would have said something. She wouldn't have simply upped and gone without a word. The thought of what *might* have happened began to make Alex uneasy. She hadn't heard from Liz for days, not since the night of the funeral. . . .

She gave herself a shake, decided that Liz was probably just out shopping or visiting friends—maybe had even started looking for another job. She decided to drop by in person, leave Liz a note if all else failed. She struggled to shut out the notion that something bad had already happened.

It was almost eight o'clock when Alex's Camry—complete with its new three-hundred-dollar fuel pump and kinked rear fender—pulled up outside the house. Brighton Street lay still and dark, its curtains and blinds shut tight against the freezing night. A single streetlight burned on the opposite side of the road, leaning precariously against a tangle of telephone wires, casting black shadows across the hardpacked snow.

Alex killed her lights and sat for a moment looking in her rearview mirror. There had been a car on her tail most of the way from Kennedy Plaza, a dark sedan with Rhode Island plates, but it had passed her when she turned down Knight Street, and she hadn't seen it since. It was probably just another commuter, she'd told herself, on his way home to Johnston or Bishop Heights. But the thought hadn't stopped her feeling scared. There was suddenly something hollow about probability. It was as if the rules had changed, as if the straight beam of reason and logic had become scattered, diffracted by some invisible prism.

And the predictability that made life navigable, possible, was gone. What were the chances that a man hoarding ten million dollars would die putting up shelves in a two-hundred-thousand-dollar house? What were the chances that a total stranger you'd seen at a funeral would stalk you like a psychopath, only to warn you that your life was in danger? Above all, what were the chances that he'd be right?

Alex climbed out of the car and closed the door as noiselessly as she could. The temperature was well below freezing, and she found her hands shaking as she pushed the key into the lock. In the distance a dog began to bark. There was an angry shout, a burst of noise from a TV or a radio, then silence. Shivering, Alex hurried up the steps and pushed Liz's buzzer. Up above her one of the windows was a rectangle of dark yellow fabric, but nothing stirred.

"Come on, Liz. Be in."

From the other side of the street the man in the black ski jacket hunkered down behind his steering wheel, watching the woman on the doorstep. He remembered gray eyes staring out of a photograph and a clean smell of lemons.

Hugging herself against the cold, Alex pushed the buzzer again. She couldn't tell if it was making any sound. Peering through the dirty glass panels, she could see the faint outline of the banisters and a diagonal arc of light across the thin red carpet, as if a door at the back of the hall was ajar. She bent down and opened the letterbox.

"Liz? Liz, are you there? It's Alex."

Lights swept across the front of the building. Alex spun around, expecting to see the dark sedan. An old boxy station wagon was turning out of one of the driveways, its chassis bouncing hard as it hit the road. The driver looked at her as he went past, his face a pale oval framed in a fur hood. Alex let out a deep breath and turned back to the door. She banged on the glass. She felt sure the light was coming from Liz's apartment. Maybe the buzzer just wasn't working.

"Liz?"

Still no one answered.

Reluctantly Alex reached into her coat for the ballpoint and the notepad she had brought with her. Leaning against the door, she began to write: *Liz, I need to talk to you urgent* . . .

The door swung open. The catch was on, but it had caught on the edge of the jamb. Warm, sour-smelling air brushed past her. Alex stood peering into the hallway. She could make out the child's tricycle by the foot of the stairs, just where it had been before. Junk mail and free newspapers lay strewn across the mat.

"Is anyone home?" she called out.

Still there was no answer. The draft caught a pair of Pizza Hut fliers and flipped them over. Alex looked around for a light switch, found one beside her, threw it. Nothing happened.

Hurriedly she finished the note. She would put it on the hall table and go. At least that way she could be sure Liz would get it when she got back. Leaving the door ajar, she walked slowly down the narrow hall, one hand running along the wall. She wasn't sure, but she thought she heard footsteps overhead, the creak of floorboards. Or maybe that was the wind too. As she reached the table, her hand knocked against something on the wall, a picture. She grabbed at it to stop it falling, pushing it with a thwack against the wall. Overhead the creak of floorboards stopped. Trying not to make a sound, she put down the note and turned to go. Then she saw that the light *was* coming from under Liz's door. She walked over and raised her hand to knock.

She felt something move. The light at her feet shifted, a broad shadow dividing it in two. She froze. There was someone standing on the other side of the door.

Hardly daring to breathe, she took a step backwards, then another, shifting her weight carefully so that the only sound was the faint rustle of her clothing. If it was Liz, why hadn't she come to the door? Why hadn't she answered? And if it wasn't Liz, then who was it? Through the thump of her own heartbeat the stranger's words came to her. *You don't know the danger you're in.*

The shadow shifted again, growing wider and darker. Alex struggled to control her breathing. From the other side of the door came a faint snap, something being switched off. Then, very slowly, the handle turned.

Alex ran. Immediately her shin cracked against the tricycle. Arms flailing, she grabbed for the banisters, missed, fell to the floor, knees taking the full impact, the tricycle still caught around her legs. Light flooded the hallway. She screamed and twisted around, preparing desperately to defend herself from the blow she felt certain was coming.

"Alex? What the hell are you doing out here?"

Alex groaned with relief.

"Jesus. Jesus Christ, Liz. Why didn't you— Ow, my God." She reached down and gingerly touched her shin. It felt like it had been split in two.

Liz came over and pulled the tricycle away. She didn't look pleased to see her.

"Are you okay?"

Alex took a couple of deep breaths, waiting for the pain to subside.

"I think so. Ow. Nothing broken, I don't think. Why the hell didn't you answer the door, goddammit? I thought you were a . . . Why didn't you?"

"Thought I was a what?" Liz asked, still puzzled—still, Alex couldn't help sensing, *suspicious.*

"A burglar or something. Why didn't you answer me?"

Liz pointed to the headphones hanging around her neck. A portable radio/cassette player was clipped to the top of her jeans.

"Bought myself a little present," she said. "It's got this special Megabass system."

"Oh, Jesus. They should ban those things." Alex climbed slowly to her feet. "And why the hell don't you get the damned light fixed? It's like walking into the black hole of Calcutta."

"Blame the landlord. I'm moving out of here soon anyhow."

"Good idea."

"I was thinking about Newport, actually. That's if I decide to stay around here. What's this?" Liz picked up the note from the hall table.

"I left it," Alex said, tentatively testing her injured leg. "Just before you decided to scare the shit out of me. I need to talk to you, Liz."

Liz read the note and handed it back.

"Oh yeah?" she said. "What about?"

"The guy sounds like a nut, Alex. I wouldn't let it worry you."

They were sitting at the table in Liz's kitchen, Alex still nursing the thumb-sized lump on her shin. The apartment looked much the same as it had during her last visit, except that the luggage and the briefcase were nowhere to be seen. Instead, a number of large carrier bags cluttered up the living room. New dresses, jackets, and skirts were draped over the backs of the chairs and the sofa, some with the price tags still attached. Losing Michael Eliot clearly hadn't dimmed Liz's enthusiasm for the January sales.

"He didn't look like a nut, Liz. He just looked very scared."

Liz scoffed, though to Alex it looked like bluff. "This guy wore moon boots to a Swan Point funeral, and you say he's not a nut?"

"That wasn't at the funeral. That's what he's been wearing this week. At the funeral he wore ordinary brown shoes, if you really want to know."

"Brown? Well, there you go. I rest my case."

"Liz, I'm serious. And I'm pretty sure he was serious too. In fact he was terrified."

Liz poured the remains of her tea into the sink. Alex couldn't understand it: she didn't seem to want to listen.

"Okay, okay, he's serious. But he's seriously misguided, isn't he? I mean, he doesn't know what he's doing, whoever he is."

"Liz—"

"You want a drink? You look like you could use one."

Alex shook her head. "Tea is fine. You go ahead."

"I intend to."

Liz reached into a cupboard for a bottle of Glenfiddich and a glass. Despite the dismissive attitude, she struck Alex as uptight and nervy.

"Liz, the guy just made a simple mistake, that's all. A mistake anyone could have made. He thought I was you."

"What on earth are you talking about?"

"Listen, Liz, your involvement—the fact that Michael was having an affair—wasn't nearly as much of a secret as you seem to think. Everyone knew about it—all the ProvLife executives, for sure. And the way Margaret Eliot looked at me during the funeral, I'm pretty sure she knew too."

Liz was very still for a moment. Then she straightened up and poured herself the whisky.

"And you're telling me everybody thinks he was having it with you?"

"Not everyone, but—"

"But they're only guessing, right?"

Liz turned to face her. Alex frowned.

"What do you mean?"

"I mean, they don't have any *reason* to think it was you? You never slept with Michael or anything?"

Alex blinked. She wondered if she could have understood right.

Liz shrugged. "Hey, I'm just talking here. I heard that you did."

"*What?*"

Liz shrugged again and folded her arms. "I just heard."

Alex was lost for words. How could Liz even think such a thing? All the same, she couldn't help thinking of the office party, the kiss Eliot had planted on her mouth. Who had been there at the time? Who had witnessed it? Probably several people—Mel Hartman for one.

"For Christ's sake, Liz," she spluttered. "I never— It's not *true*."

"That's all right, then," Liz said curtly, and took a sip of whisky. "You don't have to get involved."

Alex placed her bruised leg back on the floor, bracing herself for a moment against the back of the seat. How could Liz be so jealous over a dead man—or was it the man himself she was thinking of?

"Liz, I don't want to be *involved*. I never did."

"Of course not. How is Mark, anyway?"

"He's fine. What's he got to do—?"

"How are things going?"

Alex felt lost again.

"Fine. Why—why shouldn't they be?"

"No reason. I don't know. I just never thought he was really your type, that's all."

"Oh?" Alex's voice hardened. "And just whose type is he, do you think?"

"I don't know. Maybe that new girl. What's her name? Cathy, is it? Catherine? The one with the background."

Alex stood up. She wasn't going to listen to any more of this.

"I just came here to warn you," she said quietly. "I didn't come for a fight."

"To warn me about *what*? You want me to get that latch fixed, I will. I'll even install a chain if it makes you happy."

Alex grabbed her coat. "Have a nice evening, Liz."

"Come on, Alex, come on. I was just kidding around. You and Mark make a great couple. Everybody says so."

Alex reached for the door.

"Alex, come on. Sit down. I'm sorry, okay? Sometimes I think about Michael, and I . . . *Please* don't go."

Alex let her arm relax.

"Okay. Sorry. I guess—I guess you hit a sore spot there."

Liz pulled a weary smile. "Yeah, I know the one. Sure you don't want a drink?"

"Well, maybe just a small one. I'm driving."

Liz reached down another whisky glass. Alex went through to the living room and made room for herself on the sofa between a cream-colored cashmere jacket and a summery-looking evening gown. The price tag on the gown read $1499. It reminded her why she had come.

"Liz, I've been thinking about that money. Michael's money."

There was a moment's silence from the kitchen. Then the sound of a cupboard closing.

"You want ice?"

"No thanks. Liz, if he really had all that money, there has to be a chance that he was involved in something illegal. You must see that."

Liz came over and handed her the glass.

"'If you say so," she said. "You're the expert on chance around here."

"I know you don't want to think about him that way, and I don't blame you, but in itself it's a reason to be careful."

Liz sat down. Alex noticed that she had topped up her own glass.

"Like I said, I'll get the lock fixed."

"That's not what I mean. Liz, tell me: have you been in touch with Margaret Eliot?"

Liz took another sip. She narrowed her eyes slightly and then pushed the hair away from her forehead.

"Now, why would I want to do that?"

"I don't know. Have you?"

"No. Are you saying she's a criminal too?"

"Of course not."

"Then why are you asking?"

"Because . . . because that man said—"

"So we're back with Mister Moon Boots again. Come on, Alex, can we talk about something else?"

Alex studied Liz's face. With her waxy skin and the dark circles under her eyes, she was still a long way from the poised, even formidable woman she had always been in the office. But neither was she the confused, wide-open person she had become in the aftermath of Eliot's death. Alex had the impression that she had charted a new course for herself now, one that didn't depend on anyone but herself. But it wasn't a course she was ready to discuss.

"Liz. There was something else this man said. He said the money wasn't the important thing. He said it was the papers that mattered, papers Michael stole from him."

Liz sighed into her glass. "What papers? I don't know anything about any papers."

"You told me you found a whole bunch of papers in Michael's attaché case, remember? With those bank statements."

"So?"

"So, where are they?"

Liz looked away towards the opposite wall. She was trying her best to seem exasperated, bored, but Alex could sense that it was just a performance.

"Alex, I know I'm only a PA, but I'm not completely stupid. I put the bank statements in the bank. Out of harm's way. Just in case."

"And the other papers?"

"They're nothing. They're just numbers. Pages of numbers. I promise you, they don't mean anything."

Alex let the words hang for a moment.

"They must mean something, Liz," she said softly.

Liz gave her a crooked smile. "Well, I guess you should know, huh?" She put her glass down on the floor and stood up. "I'm telling you they're nothing."

"So why would this guy want them so badly? He's been following me around for days just to get them back."

Liz crossed the room and picked up a magazine. The papers were hidden inside. From where she was sitting, Alex could see they were the kind of scrolled computer paper you used for batch printouts. She saw sprocket holes and faint green bands.

Liz looked at them for a moment, and then shook her head irritably.

"I don't know what they are." She handed them to Alex. "Here. Next time Moon Boots comes sniffing around, you'll have something to give him."

She got home at ten to find Oscar mewing at the door of the apartment. She checked for messages—there were none—fed Oscar, and then slumped down in her comfortable old armchair. She took the papers out of her bag and put them on the coffee table. It was hard to believe that they could represent any serious danger. Not, she realized, because of what they might contain, but because they were on her coffee table, in her safe little room. She couldn't imagine danger entering her life. But the stranger had wanted them. There was no doubting that. To him they mattered more than the money, more than the ten million dollars. He'd believed that she had them and now she *did* have them.

It was just a stack of computer paper, about twenty sheets of it, still joined together in one continuous strip. An uneven crease running down the middle suggested that it had been hastily folded at some time, and along the top right-hand corner the perforated strips were beginning to come away.

A gust of icy wind rattled the windows. Alex took a breath and sat forward to look more closely. She ran her fingers over the grid of numbers, trying to unlock some trace of meaning. Liz had been wrong, of course. Even at a cursory glance there was meaning to be found, not all of it in numbers. At the bottom of the last page was a time, a date, and a word. The data had been put together—or at least printed out—nine days before Christmas, at seven o'clock in the evening. And the person, or the system, or the organization that had compiled it was there in small type at the very end: MEDAN.

The rest of the data was harder to decipher. Each page had an individual reference in the top left-hand corner. The references all began AP and were followed by nine digits. Underneath were two tables of numbers, side by side, under the headings A and B. The numbers on the two tables seemed identical, as if the same series had been generated twice.

Each of the tables was divided into nine columns and eight rows. The rows were numbered, but there were large, irregular gaps in the series: there was no row two or five; a six, seven, and eight, but no nine or ten; an eleven and finally a nineteen. The columns had more complex labels—MCP1B, LQTS1, HTCH4—but here again Alex drew a blank. They were not labels she had ever seen before, and without knowing what they meant, the numbers underneath would remain equally opaque—even the two that were circled in red. She stared at them for several minutes, flipping back and forth from one page to another, trying to discern a pattern, a relationship. But nothing suggested itself.

Alex gave a start as Oscar jumped up onto the armchair beside her.

"Hello, Mr. Cat," she said, tickling him under his chin. "MCP1B. What do you think?"

Oscar replied by climbing onto her lap. With his paws he pushed and prodded at the stack of printouts, as if trying to knead it into something more accommodating. He tried settling down and immediately got up again, his tail twitching with irritation. Computer paper was a poor substitute for the warm wool of Alex's skirt. She tried to tug the stack of paper from under him, but Oscar hung on, balancing precariously on her knees. The printouts tumbled to the floor, unraveling as they fell. As Alex leaned down to pick them up she noticed that a single sheet of paper had flipped out from between the folds. It was different from the others, smaller, plain white, and on it was printed:

41-2328
719

74 21016
74 25184
75 37619
75 40132
75 67801
75 71252

Oscar jumped clear and retreated to the far end of the carpet. Alex studied the paper for a moment and then reached over for her bag, shuffling around inside until she found her Fleet Bank checkbook. Opening it up, she compared the numbers to the ones on the paper. They weren't the same, but the *form* of them matched exactly. The six numbers in the middle of the page were bank account numbers. And the figure above them was the sort code of the branch where they were held.

The windows rattled again, and from the fire escape came an irregular squeak of metal against metal. Alex put down the sheet of paper and went to close the curtains. She felt suddenly vulnerable. The printout was just a mass of figures, figures she could not understand. And if she could not understand them, what threat could she pose to anyone? But the bank account numbers, that was hard information. It could be followed up, investigated, used to pry open Michael Eliot's past. If that was what you wanted to do.

Almost without thinking she picked up the phone and keyed in Mark's number. For a moment she listened to the phone ring at the other end, and then the answering machine cut in. It was ten-thirty and he still wasn't home. They were supposed to be meeting for dinner the following night. Mark was going to cook for her at his place to celebrate a year of being together.

Alex waited for the tone and then spoke. "Hi, sweetheart. Just calling to confirm dinner tomorrow. Should I bring some wine? How about that Amarone you like? Call me when you get back or . . . or call me tomorrow. Hope you're not working too hard. Bye."

She put the phone down, walked over to the door, and checked all the locks. Then she filled the kettle and stood looking down at the buckled linoleum of her kitchenette, her mind going back to the papers. Michael Eliot had been ProvLife's treasurer. He would have personally handled a huge number of disbursements: short-term investments on behalf of the company, payouts to policyholders. Even more than Newton Brady—whose primary responsibilities were long-term investment strategy, corporate acquisitions, and a range of operational matters—he would have had control over ProvLife's day-to-day cash flow. Was it possible that he had been siphoning off money into his own pocket, and that these were the accounts he'd used—offshore accounts perhaps, in the Cayman Islands, maybe, or Switzerland? Alex recalled the story of the bank employee who had become a millionaire by stealing fractions of a cent off every account. It was a story all the actuaries knew. The man had programmed the bank's main computer to round down fractions of a cent every time interest was calculated on any sum, and deposit the difference into his account. Tens of thousands of such calculations were done every day, each one yielding the programmer an average of half a cent. He'd only been caught because he'd started spending the money. Maybe that was why Eliot had gone on living in his $200,000 house, doing his nine-to-five job. He was determined not to make the same mistake.

Alex stood for a long time, thinking it through. It fitted almost too well. Ten million dollars was a lot of money, but compared with ProvLife's total assets and liabilities it verged on the insignificant. The

company had almost four million policyholders paying anything between $1,500 and $20,000 per year in premiums. All that money had to
be invested or paid out again one way or another. After a run of good
years, the annual total earnings ran into billions. And Eliot had been in
his job for all that time. Maybe he'd been running the scam for years,
skimming off a little bit at a time. . . .

Alex was brought back to reality by the sound of the kettle. It was
whistling insistently, filling the kitchen with steam. She gave herself a
shake. She was letting her imagination run away with her. They were
only bank account numbers. For all she knew, they could have been
something perfectly legitimate, something to do with Michael Eliot's
work. They could have been company accounts, accounts belonging to
policyholders or claimants. There was nothing sinister about them. But
then, if they were part of Eliot's work, why had he wanted them with
him in the South of France?

20

Her account manager at Fleet Bank was more than surprised when Alex called the next morning.

"How nice to hear from you today," she said, her corporate-courtesy voice accompanied by the clatter of computer keys. "Actually we were planning to get in touch."

The account manager's name was Ellen Adcock, and for the last eighteen months Alex had been avoiding her. She knew it was supposed to be good policy to stay in touch with your creditors, reassure them that you weren't about to vanish with their money, but the truth was that Alex had made certain assurances about the repayment of her debts, assurances that she had so far been unable to honor. And besides, behind the veneer of politeness there was a kind of impatience about Ms. Adcock, a skepticism that Alex found intimidating. It was as if she couldn't understand why the bank had ever lent Alex any money in the first place, and didn't believe for a minute that she would ever pay it back.

"Well, I just wanted to let you know that things are looking up," Alex said. "I'm on track for a raise in the summer. I've been told."

The clatter of keys continued, then stopped.

"Thirty-five thousand nine hundred thirteen dollars and eighty-five cents," said Ms. Adcock, the courtesy suddenly absent. "That's where we are at present. That's nine hundred thirteen dollars and eighty-five cents *over* our agreed credit limit."

Alex winced. The last time she'd checked she'd been *under* her agreed credit limit, but that had been before the Christmas spending spree. And, of course, the interest had been mounting relentlessly, day after day. Compared with what Michael Eliot had been playing with, the amount had begun to seem trivial, but hearing Ms. Adcock's voice made it seem all too serious once again. Already Alex wished she'd thought of some other way to get the information she wanted.

"Oh dear, I . . . I didn't realize," she said. "Well, I'm sure I can get back inside the limit. I'll—"

"You currently have seven hundred eleven dollars in your checking account. Shall I transfer some of that?"

"Yes." Alex tried to think. There were three weeks until her next paycheck and in the meantime there'd be bills to pay. "Yes. Maybe two hundred . . . and fifty."

"Just two hundred fifty? That still leaves you—"

"Six hundred sixty-three dollars and eighty-five cents over. I know. By next month you'll have it."

There was more furious key tapping. Then Ms. Adcock said: "All right. But we're going to have to talk about the principal sum. This was *not* supposed to be a permanent overdraft."

Alex felt like a schoolgirl being told off for a bad assignment.

"As soon as I get my associateship I can start tackling that. That'll be May. June at the latest."

Ms. Adcock sighed.

"Well, I hope you make it. I really do." The key tapping stopped again. Business was over. Now it was back to corporate courtesy. "Still, Fleet Bank has every confidence in you, and we wish you luck."

"Thanks," said Alex. "As a matter of fact, I do have a question."

"A question?"

"It's for . . . an assignment I'm doing. Banking procedures."

"Banking procedures?" Ms. Adcock didn't seem enthused. "What do you want to know?"

"Sort codes. I'm trying to look one up. Identify a branch."

"That's easy. We just have to check with the clearing department. They have all that stuff on the computer. What's the number?"

Alex gave her the sort code she had found. There was another burst of clattering, interrupted here and there by sighs and impatient mutterings.

"Oh, that's a local one," Ms. Adcock said at last. "On the East Side."

It was a branch of the Ocean State Savings Bank. It stood on the corner of Brook Street and Waterman Street, a couple of blocks from Brown—just a few hundred yards from Michael Eliot's house. The stout two-story building was about a hundred years younger than most of the adjacent properties, 1960s modernist architecture realized in folksy local materials. Despite the tile-hung upper floor and the neatly trimmed box hedge, it looked as if it had been conceived with nuclear war in mind, and the rows of narrow, darkened glass windows did nothing to dispel the impression. Alex had passed by it a hundred times, without ever giving it a moment's thought. Now its very presence in Brown's quiet and civilized environs felt like an intrusion from a darker world.

Alex stood watching from the other side of the street, unsure for a moment whether to go in. A tightening sensation in her stomach urged her to forget the whole thing and return to the safety of the office, to the certainties of her job. She ignored it. It wasn't enough knowing where the branch was; she had to know if the accounts Eliot had listed were in his name. That might be all she needed to blow the whole thing open—whatever it was. Pulling up the collar of her coat, she hurried across the road.

It was a typical bank interior, a little smarter than most, with automatic teller machines, interview rooms, and a line of cashiers behind Perspex windows. A sign pointing down a passageway read SAFE DE-POSITS. Judging from the characters in the queue, the branch did a lot of business with the kids at Brown. Posters on the wall announced special discounts, attractive loan terms, and free gifts for college students. Others boasted about rainforest and Third World charity schemes. The bank's new slogan—*With you all the way*—was everywhere in friendly chalkboard writing, together with pictures of smiling, well-balanced customers enjoying the good things in life thanks to the support of their friendly local savings bank.

The clerk behind the glass looked neither supportive nor especially friendly. He didn't acknowledge Alex, just stared down at the slot below the window like a laboratory animal waiting for its next shovelful of pills. Alex produced her checkbook, together with the deposit slip that she had already filled in with the first of the account numbers.

"Could you—" The slip in her hand was shaking. She passed it under the window and took her hand away. "Could you check that I have Mr. Eliot's account number right? I took it down in a bit of a hurry."

The clerk looked up at her. He was young, maybe twenty-four, with a thin face and watery gray eyes. His name badge read JEFF GILVAR.

"This number here?" he said doubtfully, picking up the slip.

Alex smiled her sunniest smile. "I did promise to pay the money in today."

Jeff climbed off his stool.

"Okay, just one moment," he said, and went over to a computer terminal at the next window. Alex watched him laboriously tap in the seven-digit number, then after a few moments repeat the exercise. On the wall behind him she caught sight of her own image on the TV monitor, and realized with a jolt that there was a security camera just a few feet from her head.

Jeff returned with the slip.

"I'm afraid that account's closed, ma'am. Are you sure you have the right bank?"

"Oh, I think so." *Closed.* Did that mean the account had been Eliot's, or not? "Wait a moment. I do—I did take down another account number for him. Maybe that's the one."

She'd written out the numbers on the back of her checkbook. Jeff pursed his lips and looked over at the line of people waiting to be served.

"Okay, you wanna give it to me?"

Alex went for the last of the six. "Seven five seven, one two five two."

Jeff wrote down the number and went back to the computer terminal. Alex looked up at the TV monitor again. It had switched to a different camera, this one positioned somewhere above the entrance to the safe deposit area. There were two men standing there, talking. One of them had his back turned, but the other Alex thought she recognized. She tried to think from where. Then it came to her: Richard Goebert's party. That was where she had seen the man. She had been introduced to him. She remembered the thick steel-framed glasses and the round, shiny face. His name had been David something—Mullet or Mullins—

and she remembered him saying he worked for . . . *Ocean State Savings Bank*.

Jeff finally returned.

"I'm afraid that account's closed too. I think you're gonna have to check those numbers again, Miss—?"

Alex smiled back.

"They were Mr. Eliot's accounts, right?" she said, trying to sound like a hopeless airhead. "I mean, I got something right, didn't I?"

Now Jeff was looking at her, trying to read her. Alex struggled not to blink.

"Would you mind"—Jeff squeezed out a dreadful saccharin smile—"waiting just a few moments? I think there's someone who might be able to . . . Just, just one second, okay?"

He backed away and was gone. Alex had a feeling she was suddenly in the wrong place. Mullins had to be the manager of the branch. Jeff had probably gone to fetch him. And then she'd be in trouble, because she wouldn't be able to bluff anymore. It was time to leave. She stuffed her checkbook in her bag and walked as calmly as she could towards the exit, keeping her gaze on the succession of posters along the wall. As she reached the door she risked a last look back. Mullins was shaking the other man's hand.

And the other man was Walter Neumann.

21

ark opened the door wearing an apron.

"So where's the car?" Alex said.

They touched lips as she came into the hallway. There was a smell of onions and garlic.

"Yeah," said Mark warmly, "great to see you too."

"I thought maybe it had been stolen," said Alex, ignoring the sarcasm.

Mark pulled a tight smile. "Well, it hasn't. I just sent it back, that's all."

Alex's mouth dropped open. But before she could say anything, he had turned away. She followed him through to the kitchen.

"What do you mean, you sent it back?"

Mark shrugged irritably. "You know. You say, here's the car. I don't want it. I sent it back. Wine?"

Alex put her bottle of Amarone Superiore on a clean work top and slipped out of her coat while Mark went about filling two glasses with Pinot Noir.

"So are you going to tell me about it? What brought about the sudden change of heart?"

He took a gulp of wine and then started to spoon thick green pesto sauce out of the blender. It looked and smelled like heaven. But Mark looked terrible. He was stiff and had a grim look of fatigue on his face.

Alex wondered if he had been having trouble at work. For a moment she even considered the possibility that there might be a link between the BMW's return to the dealer and his appearance. Had he lost his job?

"You just—what?—decided you didn't want it?"

"I *knew* you were going to make a big thing of it."

"I'm not making a big thing of it. I just . . . I'm just curious, that's all." He shot her a baleful look.

"Providence is too cold for a convertible," he said after a moment.

Alex nodded and sipped, hoping for more. But he was busy now, checking crostini, dumping pasta into a steaming saucepan. He opened a bag of pine nuts and spilled some on the floor. There was tension in the kitchen, she could feel it. It was as if they'd had a terrible row. She took a deep breath.

"So how's it going?" she said, trying to start again. "In Treasury, I mean."

Mark shrugged and sprinkled pine nuts into a dry skillet.

"Oh, you know."

There was a silence. Alex decided that the best tack was to tell him about her day. It didn't take long to tell, and he seemed more concerned with getting the dinner right than listening to her.

"Did you hear about McCormick?" she said eventually, falling back on office gossip as if all they had in common was the workplace.

"Sure," said Mark.

"About the incident in the men's room?"

He looked at her, and she could see the dark shadows under his eyes.

"Sure. Who hasn't? You know how people like to gossip."

"You're saying it isn't true?"

Again he shrugged. It seemed to be his new thing, shrugging.

"I'm not saying anything. I'm just saying people like to talk." He stirred the pasta. "If people have time on their hands, they'll sit around talking."

Alex sucked in her cheeks and nodded. "Oh, I see. I guess you're too busy these days for that kind of thing."

He pulled the skillet off the flame.

"Let's not have an argument," he said. "This is supposed to be our romantic evening in, remember? Our romantic Friday night."

He made it sound like something he'd read about in *GQ*.

They ate dinner in the living room. When Alex tried to find out more about the car, Mark just said that driving a convertible had turned out to be less fun than he had hoped. Providence was too damned cold, the insurance premiums were too high, and then there was the risk that some character would sooner or later put a knife through the roof just for the fun of it. It all made sense, but somehow Alex sensed the pressure of some other agenda. It occurred to her that, now that Mark was moving up the company ladder, he might be thinking in terms of something a little less flashy, something gray and corporate—a Cadillac or a Lexus. She recalled the comment passed by Donald Grant at Goebert's party. BMWs were too expensive.

Certainly all Mark seemed prepared to talk about was the office. Apparently Drew Coghill had taken exception to his promotion. According to Art Reinebeck, he'd complained to Newton Brady about a mistake Mark had made in responding to an offer emanating from one of ProvLife's blue chip investments. This after only a couple of days in the job. An opportunity to obtain preferred stock should have been passed on to Brady, but somehow had gotten stuck in Mark's in-tray. Apparently Newton hadn't been too bothered about it, but Coghill had been dancing around like it was the end of the world. All this was recounted with a dull intensity as Mark forked food into his mouth. Alex watched, surprised at first and then increasingly annoyed: she wasn't allowed to talk about statistics, but he was allowed to talk *shop*. At the same time there was a kind of insider's smugness in his manner, which made it all worse. He was giving her the *word*—something to which she, in her subordinate sphere, had no access. She had a powerful urge to tell him what had really been going on over the past couple of weeks, if only to get him to shut up about Drew Coghill.

"So anyway," said Mark, taking a sip of wine and wiping his mouth, "Drew comes in this afternoon, and he says to me—"

"Mark?"

He paused, a forkful of pasta halfway to his mouth.

"Excuse me for interrupting, I just . . ."

Mark lowered the fork to his plate. "What?"

"I know you think it's all just silly gossip, but what do you think is really going on with McCormick? I mean, has Newt said anything?"

Mark leaned back in his chair. "Newt says a lot of things," he said.

Alex waited for him to say more, but it was clear that what passed between SVPs and CFOs wasn't for just anyone's ears. The desire to push him off balance was overwhelming.

"Did you know McCormick has a cocaine addiction?" she said.

Mark blinked. He took another sip of wine.

"What?"

"I said, did you know—?"

"Yeah, I heard. Who told you that?"

She was about to say White, but then decided that the disclosure had probably been made in confidence. She improvised.

"Oh, it's just what they're saying."

"Who?"

"In the office, I mean—the gossip going around. Mel Hartman came up to my desk the other day and—"

"Hartman's a nobody," said Mark hotly. "He should watch himself. He knows nothing. About anything."

"He knows quite a lot about statistics."

Mark smiled and then nodded. "Sure, why shouldn't he?"

His smugness was unbearable.

"So, anyway," said Alex, the color rising in her cheeks. "You don't know."

"Know what?"

"About McCormick. About the coke."

Mark leaned forward, putting his elbows on the table.

"Listen, Alex, it's not something you want to go around repeating."

"Why not?"

"ProvLife's a small company. You know how things get back to people. And then"—he shrugged—"then suddenly you've made an enemy."

Alex had a flashback of Tom Heymann in his Lexus.

"But it's okay between us, right?" she said sarcastically. "I mean we're still friends, right? Even if you are head of Treasury now."

Mark nodded, smiling again. "Now you're being childish," he said.

"Well, you're being mysterious, like—like ProvLife was some kind of secret society."

This was too much. Mark shook his head, giving up on her.

Alex tried to eat, but she was too stirred up. Now that she had started talking about McCormick, she couldn't stop. She realized that she wanted to get everything out in the open.

"Do you think it was related to Goebert's resignation?" she said.

Again Mark paused in midforkful.

"What?"

"McCormick's breakdown. If that's what it was. Okay, he has a co-caine habit, but the business in the men's room, that was more like a nervous breakdown. Do you think—?"

"I understood the question," said Mark, looking up at her from under his eyebrows. "I just don't really understand what you're talking about. How would it be related?" He seemed to reflect for a moment. "Did White say something to you?"

"No. Why would he?"

Mark shrugged and looked away.

"No, it's just something that occurred to me," Alex continued. "Do you remember how he reacted—how McCormick reacted when Goebert said he was retiring?"

Mark shook his head.

" '*What?*' " shouted Alex, imitating McCormick's reedy voice. "He yelled it: '*What?*' Like he was really upset. Like it was really bad news."

"Well, he likes Goebert. He's sorry to see him go."

"It was more than that."

Mark stood up and went out to the kitchen. His voice came to Alex above the noise of the coffee percolator.

"You know what this is, Alex? You guys sit down there on the seventh floor all day, playing with models, creating scenarios. You get out of touch with reality and then you start believing your own projections."

Alex looked at her reflection in the window. She gave a little nod as though confirming a decision.

"Reality," she said to herself.

"Yeah, reality," said Mark, coming back into the room with coffee and a plate of *biscotti*.

"Well, how's this for a little reality?" said Alex. "Did you know Michael Eliot was a multimillionaire?"

Mark put the tray down on the table.

"What?"

"Michael Eliot. The guy who had the job before you. Over ten million dollars in Switzerland."

"What are you talking about?" The color had drained from his face.

"I've seen his bank statements," said Alex, reveling in his astonishment. "Or at least, I know someone who has."

"Know someone? You're not making any sense."

"Mark, I'm telling you, he died a wealthy man."

"But—"

He sat down at the table, and poured coffee into two small cups. Then he put sugar into one and stirred. He couldn't stop shaking his head. It was as if he didn't *want* to hear what she was telling him.

"Mark?"

He looked up.

"You're not—you're not keeping anything from me, are you?"

"But—" He seemed to be struggling with an idea. "But, Alex, why would *someone you know* be looking at his bank statements?"

Alex turned back to the window, looked out at the darkness beyond her reflection. She had promised to say nothing, promised not to mention Liz's name, but her sense of loyalty had taken some serious blows.

"Alex?"

She turned and looked at him.

"Michael was having an affair with Liz Foster," she said.

Mark stopped shaking his head now. His frown intensified into a look of utter disbelief.

"That's—that's impossible. We'd have known about it."

"Who would?"

"What?"

"Who would have known about it?"

"In—in the department. We worked right next to them. We would have known."

Alex pressed a hand against her heart.

"I was Liz's—I'm one of Liz's closest friends, and *I* didn't know about it. They'd been seeing each other for more than a year. They were planning to go away together the day Michael—the day of the accident."

"I don't believe it." Mark pushed his hand into his hair, a look of utter confusion on his pale face.

"Well, believe it. It's true."

"But—the bank statements?"

"He left an attaché case at Liz's house."

"And she opened it?"

"It was all that was left. It was all that she had left—of him. She was devastated. Can you imagine how she felt? She was about to leave for Europe. They were going to live in the south of France."

Mark finished his espresso, and then considered the bottom of the cup.

"So where . . . where is she now?"

"She's still here. In Providence. At least, I think she is."

"But she's not coming in, right? She's supposed to be on vacation."

"I don't know. I don't know what she has planned. She's been acting kind of weird."

Mark nodded. "Well, yeah, I guess she would be."

"She was about to fly away from here to a better life."

"A better bank balance, anyway."

"She *loved* him, Mark." Alex sipped her coffee. "She's not just a—a gold digger," she added without much conviction.

"Is that right?"

Alex set her cup down. She'd broken Liz's confidence, and she didn't feel good about it. But now that the truth was out in the open, she wanted to talk it out a little.

"Well?" she said. "What do you think?"

"About what?"

"About all the money? Why would someone with ten million dollars in the bank keep coming into the office every day?"

"Maybe he liked his job," said Mark, giving her a thin smile.

"I'm being serious, Mark. There's something really . . . I'm thinking maybe he *had* to come into the office."

"What do you mean, had to?"

"Well, look at it logically. What reason would someone with ten million dollars have for coming into an office?"

Mark shrugged. "Well, like I said—"

"No, I mean a *good* reason, a real reason."

Mark said nothing.

"Think about it. What if he was embezzling from the company?"

"Oh, come on."

"What if he had to be in the office to keep an eye on whatever it was he'd set up? He was planning to leave without giving notice, without telling anybody anything. He was going to disappear. Why? Maybe because he'd been—somehow, had been siphoning money out of the treasury and—"

"Alex."

"And he got scared. Maybe some kind of deadline was approaching. Maybe—I don't know, you're the finance wizard, maybe the redemption date on a corporate bond or something like that, maybe it was due, but ProvLife was never going to see the money because he'd already *sold* the bonds. Pocketed the principal. I mean, he was head of Treasury. How difficult would it have been?"

"Alex, Newt runs a pretty tight ship. I think he would have noticed a ten-million-dollar hole."

"Why? I mean, without a proper audit? We've got policy reserve funds, special reserves, surplus funds, not to mention all the real estate, stocks, bonds, mortgages. Our balance sheet isn't exactly transparent. A little creative accounting . . ."

Mark wasn't buying it. He sat back in his chair and considered her as if she were a daffy teenager who had cornered him at a family gathering.

"Okay," said Alex, "what's ProvLife's position in corporate bonds?"

Again he shrugged. It was beginning to get on her nerves.

"I don't know, six hundred million, give or take."

"Exactly. And all small position. Nothing too concentrated."

"That's right. There are rules limiting exposure to any one company."

"Small positions. Ten million here, twenty million there."

"Alex, you can't just take bonds out of your desk and sell them in the open market. There are strict accounting procedures."

"Really? Even the head of the department couldn't find a way?"

"No," said Mark emphatically, but Alex could see he was beginning to consider the possibility.

"All I know is, the money had to be coming from somewhere. If it was his own money, there would be no reason for him to come into the office. If it was money he'd made honestly, he would have told Margaret about it."

"How do you know he didn't? How do you know what Margaret Eliot knows?"

"I don't. That's just—"

Alex hesitated. She felt she'd already betrayed enough of Liz's confidences.

"Alex?" Mark was staring at her intently. "Don't start holding back on me now. This could all . . ."

"All what?"

He stood up and went across to a cabinet that Alex hadn't noticed before. He pressed a button and the doors slid back on a sleek Bang & Olufsen sound system.

"What happened to the Technics?" said Alex, shaking her head.

"It's upstairs. Nothing happened to it."

"So . . . ?"

Suddenly he was furious.

"Jesus Christ, Alex! You're after me every time I get my credit card out. Spending is okay. It's okay to have nice new things. Just because you're broke all the time, that doesn't mean everybody else is."

Alex put a hand to her cheek as if he had slapped her. She had no idea where his anger had come from. It had just spurted up. Mark look shocked too.

"I'm sorry," he said, giving himself a little shake. "*Carina,* I'm sorry. It's just—you know things are pretty crazy at work, and—"

"Sure."

He came towards her. She jerked free of his hands and went upstairs to the bedroom.

She waited for a moment, expecting him to come up after her, trying to get control of herself. Mark knew all about the problems she had had with her mother, knew all about the reasons for her penury. She couldn't believe he had been so insensitive.

For five minutes she didn't move, debating whether to leave or to stay. It was cold in the room, but even colder outside. The thought of getting back into the car made her shudder. She undid her dress and let it drop to the floor, then stood in front of the mirror in her underwear. She was wearing black lace, a Christmas present from Mark. It was supposed to be part of their romantic evening together. The bra pinched under her arms. She took it off with a sigh of relief. She took a clean T-shirt from his chest of drawers, then got into bed.

For a while she listened to him moving around in the kitchen, taking the trash out, loading up the dishwasher. Then she reached under the bed for the alarm clock. She would have to leave early in the morning if she was going to go home and change for work.

The little digital clock wasn't in its usual place. She fumbled. Her fingers grazed something hard and slick. She leaned out of the bed and reached farther into the darkness. It was a stack of magazines, maybe ten of them.

Mark called up from the living room. "Alex?"

He sounded solicitous—probably wanting to make up now. Alex froze, listening, her hand on the cold shiny paper of the magazines. Mark said something to himself in a bitter undertone and went back through to the kitchen. Alex yanked the magazine that was on top of the pile.

It wasn't what she had expected. Not exactly. For one thing, the women wore swimsuits and cocktail dresses, and they weren't on waterbeds or fancy chaises longues. But they were pouting fit to bust, glossed lips pushed forward in the standard poses of provocation, and draped over the bulging hoods of automobiles. Fast cars. Shiny cars. Maserati, Lamborghini, Ferrari. Just the names suggested banked test tracks and the scream of high-performance engines. It was confusing. If Mark was cultivating a new staid corporate self, why did he have magazines stashed under his bed like pornography? She riffled through the pages. A price caught her eye. Then another. She flipped to the back where there were several pages of classifieds. A guy in Manhattan wanted to sell his Aston Martin Volante. He was asking two hundred thousand dollars. A guy in Connecticut wanted to sell his Ferrari Testa Rossa. *He* wanted seven hundred thousand. It was the second ad that was ringed in black felt tip.

She woke at three in the morning, wide awake as if it were the middle of the day.

"Money laundering," she said.

"Wha—?"

Mark rolled over in bed and squinted up at her.

"Money laundering. That's what this is all about. That's what they're up to."

Mark rolled away from her. Alex sat up against the headboard and looked down at him.

"Mark, I think I know what's going on. How about this? The whole problem is, like you say, why hasn't somebody noticed the missing money? Because there *isn't* any missing money. Mark?"

He pushed his head into the pillows and groaned. "What?"

"There is no missing money. Eliot was flowing *dirty* money through the company and taking a cut. He was handling all kinds of transactions every day."

"Alex, for God's sake, go to sleep."

"No. This might be important."

He pulled the duvet up over his ears.

"You know the bank records? The records Eliot left in the case?"

"You mean the bank statements?"

"No. There were other papers too. A list of account numbers."

Mark became very still, listening now. Alex went on.

"I checked them out. The sort code belongs to a branch of Ocean State Savings Bank. It's around the corner from where Eliot lived. On the East Side."

He rolled over and looked up at her. "Jesus, Alex. You haven't been up there?"

She nodded. "Why not? Why shouldn't I?"

"I think the question is, why *would* you?"

"And guess who the manager is?" she said. "David Mullins. Funny-looking guy with glasses. He was at Goebert's party. And guess what else? When I went in there—just to take a look—I saw Walter Neumann. He was talking to Mullins."

Mark propped himself up on his elbows.

"Did Neumann see you?"

"I don't know. Maybe." Alex shivered and got back under the bedclothes. Then she had an idea. "My God, that's it."

"What's it?"

"Of course."

"*What?*"

"Neumann."

"What about him?"

"Well, you know how money laundering works, right? The biggest problem is getting the dirty cash from the street into the banking system. Bankers get nervous about handling suitcases full of dollars, because they're supposed to declare anything that looks shady."

"So?"

"But lawyers, under the rules governing client-attorney privilege, cannot disclose information about their clients' money."

"Alex, I don't see—"

"Clients often open an account with their attorney to cover the expenses of an ongoing suit, say. The lawyer opens a legitimate bank account, deposits the money saying this is from a client, and the banker is unable to ask for further details. That's what makes lawyers a target for money launderers. People pay lawyers to open accounts for them so they can flow their dirty money through them. Once it's in the system, it can be transferred electronically right around the world."

"So where does Eliot come in?" said Mark, looking up at the ceiling. "Neumann wouldn't need him, right? All Neumann needs is a docile bank manager. Assuming he's a money launderer, that is."

"Well . . ." Alex couldn't think of an objection to this. "Maybe it's more efficient to flow it through the company. For some—for some reason."

Mark eased himself down into the bed and pulled the duvet over his head.

"But if you checked out those account numbers," Alex went on. "You could see if there was a trail, if there was something funny going on. See if there was money going into them that shouldn't have been. You've got access to the files now. Mark?"

She shook his shoulder.

"What?"

"I said you need to check out those numbers."

"Yeah, yeah, sure. I'll check the numbers. Now go to sleep."

"Mark?"

He let out an exasperated sigh.

"There's something else. Something I haven't told you."

"*What?*"

"A couple of days ago? This guy followed me yesterday, when I was coming out of the office. He said I should destroy all Eliot's papers. He said I didn't know the danger I was in."

Mark pulled back the covers and got out of bed. For a moment he stood still, looking down at his feet.

"What guy?" he said quietly.

"This guy with a beard. I've seen him before. He was—"

"Where?" Mark stared at her. He looked scared.

"He was at Michael Eliot's funeral."

Then Mark was firing questions at her, wanting the whole story. She told him about the spooky phone call, about how she had seen the guy snooping around outside the ProvLife building and how he had finally run into the back of her car on the corner of Dorrance and Weybosset.

"But the printouts?" he said, stalking back and forth in front of the window now, his hand pressed against his mouth. "You don't mean this list of account numbers?"

"I don't think so. I think he means this batch of computer printouts Eliot had. That's what he had in the attaché case: his own bank statements from Switzerland, and this list of account numbers at Ocean State, and then all these printouts. This guy who followed me definitely said *printouts*."

"I don't understand, though. Why—what makes them more important than—than the money?"

"I have no idea. It's just a load of numbers," said Alex. "Columns of numbers."

"Like what? Like more bank accounts, sums of money, what?"

"No, not like that. There are numbers and letters. Like ABCD1, that sort of thing."

"ABC—?"

"Not ABC, but things like—I don't know, I think one of them is LQTS, LQTS1 or something like that."

Mark pressed his eyes shut, massaging the bridge of his nose with his fingers.

"That doesn't make sense," he said. "What the hell is that supposed to be?"

"I don't know. But I've been thinking—maybe the letters identify a bank. You know, like BNY for Bank of New York, or SBC or CSFB."

"The LQT bank?" he said sceptically. "Lots of Questionable Transactions bank?"

Alex shook her head. "It's just an idea. Like I said, I don't really know what they are."

"And this guy wanted you to hand them over."

"Yes. But if I don't even know who he is, how *can* I hand them back?"

Mark nodded.

"So where are they?"

"In my apartment."

Mark pulled his shorts on and started looking for his pants.

"What are you doing?" said Alex.

"We have to get over there. We have to look at what these papers are."

"Mark, it's four o'clock in the morning."

"So?"

Alex pulled the duvet around her.

"Mark?"

"What?"

"You're frightening me."

He had his pants up around his hips and was about to button them. When he saw the expression on her face, he smiled. He let the pants drop to the floor, and then climbed into the bed.

"Honey, I'm sorry. This is all so crazy. You've got me running around in circles."

She stared hard at his face, trying to read his thoughts. She had expected him to be agitated, but he had been almost frantic.

"Maybe we should call the police?" she said.

Mark shook his head.

"I don't think so. I mean—what are we going to tell them?"

Alex had thought about that too. More than once she had considered going to someone in authority. If White had been around, she would have gone to him. But he had been out sick for a couple of days, and now was about to leave for Washington to attend the NIH forum. She didn't know what she would tell the police. *"Something funny's going on at my company"?* She couldn't see them being very receptive.

Mark leaned forward and kissed her on the forehead.

"I'll tell you what," he said. "We'll try to get some sleep, and then we'll go over to your place tomorrow."

He switched off the light. Alex lay in the dark, looking up at the ceiling. She had the feeling that it was slowly moving down towards her.

22

"Just like you said, there are no amendments. The will's exactly as it was the day your husband signed it."

Howard Sweeting, the most junior of Neumann & Klein's three associates, leaned across the conference table and passed Mrs. Eliot the document. She looked at it for a moment, then slowly, reluctantly, picked it up. The pages were held together with black ribbon, and each one bore the Neumann & Klein stamp together with Michael Eliot's initials. As she reached the last page, she could not help running her fingertips over his confident, flowing signature, as if by following the distinctive pattern of curves and lines she could touch the hand that had made them.

Being inside the ProvLife building, where her husband had worked all those years, listening to his will being read out, she'd begun to feel closer to him than she had for days. It was almost as if he were just outside the room, and might walk in at any moment. Every time someone went past outside she had to fight the urge to look around. She remembered very clearly sitting in this same room, with Michael beside her, seven years earlier. They had made new wills at the same time, just after he'd been made head of Treasury. But that had been the old Michael—the optimistic, good-humored one. The one she had loved. Almost from that moment on, things had begun to change. Day by day, month by month, he'd become steadily more withdrawn, more impatient. He'd stopped telling jokes, become more and more critical of everything, from her cooking to the state of the roads. It was as if he felt he was being held back somehow. But whenever she'd asked him about it, asked what had happened to him, he'd always told her she was simply letting her imagination run away with her.

She opened her bag and took out a handkerchief. If only he had told her the truth, maybe everything would have been different.

"Excuse me," she said, dabbing at her eyes.

Sweeting's mouth puckered into a line. "That's . . . um, quite all right."

A fresh tear ran down her cheek, leaving behind it a faint trace of mascara. Sweeting tried not to look. He was in his early thirties, plump and red-haired, with the sort of blue-white complexion that betrayed the smallest hint of embarrassment. He was self-conscious around women at the best of times, and grieving widows were entirely outside both his professional and personal experience.

"Um . . . is there . . . would you like a glass of water or something?" he said, getting to his feet.

"No, no thank you. I'm quite all right, really."

"You're sure?" he said, hoping she'd change her mind so he could escape for a minute or two.

"Quite sure, thank you."

Reluctantly Sweeting eased himself back into his chair. His face was already a blotchy watermelon red.

"Well, er . . . as I say, I expect we'll get through probate in about six weeks or so. In the meantime, do you have any questions?"

Mrs. Eliot took a deep sniff and folded the handkerchief away.

"Yes, I do," she said. "The will doesn't say anything about . . . off-shore assets."

Sweeting frowned. "Offshore?"

"Yes. I believe my husband had substantial holdings in Europe. In Switzerland, in fact. The will doesn't mention them."

Sweeting cleared his throat and began sifting through the rest of Eliot's file. As he understood it, Eliot had posted up-to-date statements of his holdings with the firm every few years, although his modest stock portfolio would have to be valued by his brokers before its current worth could be established. But in all these statements there had been no mention of holdings offshore.

"Well, er, if he did, there's no . . . I mean, the records we have don't indicate the existence of any offshore holdings as such."

"You're quite sure about that?"

Sweeting turned over a few more pages. The truth was, his experience in handling wills and estates was extremely limited. As a firm Neumann & Klein's main business was industrial and intellectual property law, with a little real estate law on the side. Its most important clients were found among the high-tech companies that had sprung up over the past decade in Cranston and Warwick. It was something of an anomaly that the firm had any private clients at all—a hangover from the days when old Walter Neumann and his now deceased partner Daniel Klein had been grateful for any work they could get. Sweeting just hoped there hadn't been a foul-up somewhere.

"Well, of course, your husband was under no obligation to keep us posted on all his investments," he said. "It's perfectly *possible* that he had some other assets. What sort of sums would we be talking about?"

Mrs. Eliot put the will back on the table and folded her hands together in her lap.

"Several million dollars."

Sweeting chuckled amicably. It was a joke, of course. Then he realized that it wasn't.

"S-several—?"

"Up to ten."

Sweeting was blushing again. He made a little grunt of acknowledgment, nodding in what he hoped was a considered manner.

"Well, that's, er, certainly . . . That would be a major omission. Let me see now, we have the T-bills, the stocks, and the life policies. Altogether they come to well in excess of—well, *half* a million dollars. Could that be what you're—?"

"I know about all that. Michael had those investments for years. I'm talking about money abroad."

Sweeting stuck a finger inside his collar and worked a patch of sore flesh beside his windpipe. How were you supposed to deal with financially deluded widows? Just how long were you supposed to humor them? He wished Neumann had kept the file himself, instead of palming it off on his luckless associate.

"Did your husband indicate to you that he had these assets, Mrs. Eliot?" Sweeting said at last.

"Not exactly."

"Hmmm. But you have some documentation? Some—evidence of some kind?"

Mrs. Eliot seemed to take a long time considering the question. Then she shook her head.

"I just have reason to believe he had it. Offshore. People have told me."

"People?"

"Yes. If he did have it, I'd be entitled to it, wouldn't I?"

Sweeting blinked, then picked up the will again. The widow had made a remarkably swift transition from tearful to formidable.

"Yes. Absolutely. The residue of the estate—that's everything that isn't specifically assigned elsewhere in the will—falls to you. But—"

"Then how would I find out where it was? If the money's mine, then the bank that's holding it would have to tell me. They couldn't just keep it, surely?"

Sweeting tried not to look like he didn't know the answer, but they were into banking law now and that was even more outside his area of expertise than the will.

"I'd have to . . . If you'd give me one minute, Mrs. Eliot. I think maybe I should consult with one of my colleagues on this one. Just bear with me."

He got up from behind the table and hurried out of the room. Margaret Eliot sat waiting for him, staring at the rows of antique prints that lined the walls, listening to the faint sounds of activity in other parts of the building. It had never occurred to her before, but it was strange that Michael should have wanted to put his affairs—and hers—in the hands of Neumann & Klein, of all the firms in Providence. At the time, he'd explained it in terms of the practicalities: the firm offered ProvLife executives preferential rates, and with the offices being in the very same building, it could hardly have been more conveniently situated. And yet, attorney-client privilege notwithstanding, was it normal to trust your private affairs to the vice chairman of the company you worked for? Wasn't that letting the relationship get just a little too close?

As if on cue, the door opened and Walter Neumann stepped into the room.

"Margaret, I didn't know you were here or I'd have— How are you?"

He took her hands as she rose to meet him. His gold signet ring felt cold against her skin.

"I'm fine, Walter, fine."

"*Good.* That's very good. Can I get you something? Some tea perhaps, or—?"

"No, really. I'm just fine."

"Good." He let go of her hands and closed the door. "I've been meaning to call you. But things have been rather . . . hectic. I hope Howard was looking after you."

Neumann sat down in Sweeting's chair and began leafing through the will. It was suddenly as if Sweeting had been nothing more than a temporary stand-in.

"Yes, he was," said Mrs. Eliot. "I had some questions, though. I think he was going to consult with someone."

"Questions?" Neumann looked up, an expression of vague curiosity on his face. "Well, please do fire away, Margaret. That's what we're here for."

Mrs. Eliot cleared her throat.

"Well, it's simply that Michael may have had quite a lot of money in a bank offshore. In Switzerland. Money that isn't mentioned in the will. I wanted to know how I could recover it."

Neumann nodded gently. He showed no surprise.

"Well, of course. If you'd let me have the details, I'll be happy to contact the bank on your behalf."

"But that's just it: I don't have any details."

"But you have Michael's papers? His bank statements and so on?"

"Not those."

"I see. Well, the name of the bank, at least. Michael did tell you that."

"No. Michael never said anything about it. It was"—she looked down into her lap—"not something we ever discussed."

Neumann slowly took off his glasses and put them down in front of him. His head looked massive perched on top of his narrow shoulders.

"Then—forgive me, Margaret—what makes you think this . . . account exists?"

Mrs. Eliot sighed. She'd hoped it would be simpler than this. She'd hoped that Michael had lodged all the details of the money with his lawyers, or that they would at least know about it. She didn't want to talk about her husband's affair, especially not to Walter Neumann. She didn't like the idea of people Michael had worked with all those years—people who had carried his coffin at the funeral—knowing that he'd betrayed her. It was something she wanted to bury, along with her memories of those last bad years. But there was no other way. And anyway, Neumann was a lawyer and she was a client. At least she could count on the information going no further.

Neumann listened impassively as she told him about the phone call and the air tickets and about what they meant. He let her talk, nodding gently, watching her with a stillness and attention that made it hard for her to look him in the eye. She wondered if he already knew about the affair, or whether he was simply indifferent to it.

"Margaret, I'm so sorry you've been put through all this," he said at last. "You can rest assured, I shall find out who's responsible and see that they do not ... bother you again. You were absolutely right to come to me with this. And *very* smart to get that telephone number. With a little luck it may prove absolutely invaluable."

"But what about—?"

Neumann shook his head gravely.

"I'm afraid the likelihood of this money existing is very slim indeed. Frankly, zero. I'm afraid I've had experience of this kind of thing before, in my greener lawyering days."

"Experience of—?"

"Fraud. That's the only word for it. The recently bereaved have long been a favored target for such activities. People who are disoriented, vulnerable. It's contemptible, but true. They—or perhaps in this case, she—promises you a lot of money in return for somewhat less money up front. That's what it always comes down to. It's what they call a confidence trick. How much did she say Michael had in this Swiss bank account? A million dollars? Two?"

"Ten million dollars."

Neumann raised his eyes towards the ceiling. "How ridiculous. I suspect we're dealing with an amateur."

"But this woman, she said Michael was—"

"What she said, I'm happy to say, is of little consequence. She claims to have—how did she put it?—*shared* Michael with you. A lie, I've no doubt whatsoever. A lie, to make you believe she had access to your husband's private affairs. I worked alongside Michael here for twelve years. If there'd been anyone else, I'm sure I'd have heard about it."

She wanted to believe what he was saying, but could it really be as simple as that?

"What about the air ticket?"

Neumann smiled wearily.

"How difficult is it to buy an air ticket? It only takes a phone call. Margaret, I hate to think what this dreadful episode has put you through. You and Michael had a good marriage, a strong marriage. He often said so." He raised a soft white palm. "Maybe he did work a little too hard, stayed late more often than you'd have liked—more often than he should have. God knows, we're all guilty of that here. But that doesn't mean he ever stopped loving you. I don't want you to entertain that idea for one moment."

Mrs. Eliot felt unsteady. For a moment she thought she was going to be sick. She didn't know what to think anymore.

"But, Walter, I *saw* her. At the funeral. I saw her standing next to Randal White. The way she looked at me, I knew it was her."

Neumann slowly shook his head.

"You mean the young lady with the short blond hair? That was Alexandra Tynan, one of Randal's . . . juniors."

"Alexandra—?"

"I can't tell you why Randal brought her along. I thought it a little odd at the time, even a little . . . I don't think she even knew your husband. Between ourselves, I think Randal just wanted . . . the pleasure of her company."

23

They drove back to the East Side after work, Alex in the Camry following Mark. When they got to Phillips Street, Alex found Maeve Connelly waiting, arms folded around her old housecoat, her thin gray hair pulled back with steel barrettes. It was only going up the steps to the front door that Alex remembered she was overdue with the rent. The repair to the car had made her put off paying, and then she had forgotten about it altogether. It was the first time it had happened. She smiled, praying that the old lady wouldn't embarrass her in front of Mark.

"Mrs. Connelly!" she said with a cheerfulness she didn't feel. "How are you?"

"Oh, pretty good, pretty good."

Maeve fixed her pink eyes on Mark, and Alex made an awkward introduction.

"Saw you drive up," Maeve said, once etiquette and her curiosity had been satisfied. "There's something I wanted to talk to you about, Alex, if you don't mind."

Alex pushed her hands deep into her coat pockets.

"Can I just—can I just deal with something, Mrs. Connelly? It'll only take a minute. Then I'll be all yours."

Maeve smiled, showing a dark tangle of ancient bridgework. She looked a little embarrassed herself.

"Well, actually, I'd rather . . . you see, Kenneth is up from Pittsburgh."

The son-in-law. Alex felt her face begin to color.

"Since I have you . . ." said Maeve, making it sound like Alex had been avoiding her.

Alex turned to Mark, who was looking with distaste at patches of damp on the wall.

"Just go on up," she said, handing over the keys.

When she finally joined him twenty minutes later, he was standing in the middle of the rug still wearing his coat. Oscar was walking stiff-legged on the other side of the room, something he did when he had been rejected or told off.

"Missed paying the rent again, huh?" said Mark jokingly as she came in through the door.

Alex took off her coat, still looking at Oscar.

"No, it's just the son-in-law. He's planning on doing some work on the place and he wants Maeve to put the rent up. She wants to know if I'm going to stay on here."

"How much are they asking?"

"Six hundred a month."

"Is that all? Jeez, I thought it was more expensive here."

Alex didn't say that until now she had only been paying four hundred and had often had trouble doing that. Nor did she tell him what she had told Kenneth: she needed time to think about extending the lease. She noticed that the computer printouts were gone from the table.

"Where are the—?"

"The printouts?" Mark reached into a pocket and pulled the papers out. "It's all here," he said, tapping the paper with the back of his hand. "But I don't think you should keep it in the apartment."

He put them back on the table, a neutral I-didn't-mean-anything-by-it expression on his face. But he'd had them in his pocket. Why? Was he planning to walk off before she got back from her talk with Maeve? Alex watched him take off his coat, trying to decide how to react.

"Why shouldn't I keep it here?" she said finally.

He sat down on the couch, looking at her as though she was stupid.

"Alex. Didn't the guy—this guy, whoever he was—say you were in danger?"

"Sure, but . . ." She pulled the printouts towards her and looked at the meaningless information. "I've been thinking about that."

"Good. I think you're right to."

"No, listen to me for a minute. This guy—he appears from nowhere and says, give me the papers, they're dangerous. He doesn't say, give me the papers, they're mine."

"So?"

"So what does that sound like? Remember, he looks real scared. When he sees the police coming along the street, he takes off like a rocket. What's he scared of? Who's he scared of? Not of the papers. He wants the papers even though they're dangerous. So I think . . . I think what he was scared of, in the street I mean, I think he was scared of being seen talking to me. I think the papers are dangerous for me, for him too perhaps, because I'm not supposed to have them. No one is supposed to have them."

"Alex, this—"

Alex pushed both hands into her hair. "I want to know who he was." She picked up the printouts. "I want to know what these are."

Mark opened his mouth in disbelief. "You want . . . Alex, *why?*"

"Because I have to. Getting rid of them won't help me. How could I ever prove I hadn't made copies?"

"You haven't, though. Right?"

"No. I can't even hand them over because this man never gave me his name. It was like he—he *assumed* I already knew it. Like I was already on the inside track."

She put the printouts down and went over to the refrigerator.

"Everybody knows everything," she said under her breath.

"What?"

"It's something someone said to me the other day. Providence is so small. Maybe I *should* know who he is. He was at Michael Eliot's funeral, for God's sake."

"What about White?" said Mark. "Maybe he'd know."

"I already asked him."

"You told him about this?" Mark sounded alarmed.

"No." Alex looked up from pouring milk into a bowl. "He—the spooky guy with the beard, I mean—he lent me a handkerchief at the funeral. I asked White who he was, but White didn't know."

"I don't like it," said Mark, nibbling at a cuticle. "I don't like any of this."

"Maybe he's just a nut," said Alex. She put down the milk and Oscar came padding across the floor to drink. "That's what Liz thinks."

"Why don't we put it in a bank?" said Mark. "In a safe deposit box."

"We?"

"*You,* then."

There was an awkward silence. Then Mark threw up his hands, suddenly exasperated: "Christ, Alex, I'm only trying to help."

Alex shrugged and looked down. "Put it in the bank," she said musingly. "Wouldn't that cost money?"

"I'll pay," said Mark.

"Well, as long as we don't put it in Ocean State," said Alex, looking up, trying to make a joke of it.

Mark didn't laugh.

"Sorry," she said. "It's just I'm not used to being . . . threatened. It isn't the kind of thing that's supposed to happen to actuaries, you know?"

She went over to the coffee table and picked up the printouts again.

"What does all this stuff mean? Why did Eliot want to take it with him?"

Mark came forward. "I think I should take them," he said, the parent getting firm with a difficult child.

Alex gave him a look.

"Is that what you were going to do? Take them while I was down with Maeve?"

He stopped in his tracks, shaking his head in disbelief. "My God, Alex. You're becoming completely paranoid. Did you know that? If I had wanted to take the damned things, I could have walked out of here ten minutes ago."

Alex looked away. "Well, you're not taking them anyway," she said.

Mark pushed out an exasperated sigh.

"I don't understand you, Alex. You tell me all about your problem and then push me away when I try to help."

Alex looked down at her hands. She didn't know what to think about any of it.

The phone rang. She picked up, keeping her eyes on Mark.

"Mom, hi!"

Listening to her mother go through the usual questions, the usual complaints, Alex racked her brains, trying to remember if she was on this occasion guilty of neglect. She realized with a sinking feeling that she could not recall when she had last been in touch.

As usual her mother's central preoccupation was the house. Just keeping the place running took all the money she had.

"So anyway, the sills needed sealing," she said. "All this bad weather is opening up cracks in the wood. So I get John to come around."

Alex looked at Mark. He was backing towards the door, a hand raised in farewell. He had a peculiar expression on his face: a mixture of sadness and irritation. Alex put up a hand, wanting him to stay, listening at the same time to how John had fixed the sills but, by walking on the porch roof, had split the old roof felt and caused a leak.

"They have to replace boards inside the porch where they got wet. It's going to cost me a couple of hundred."

Mark had gone. Alex could picture her mother, sitting by the fire, her swollen feet pushed into ratty deep-pile carpet. She felt a powerful urge to get in the car and drive to Pittsfield.

"Don't worry about the money, Mom," she said. "I'll wire it to your account when I get paid. Just make sure John does a good job."

A half hour later, Alex put the phone down. She looked at the printouts. All the talk of danger seemed absurd. The only reality she could deal with was the leak in her mother's roof. She walked across to the armchair and sat down. Oscar watched her for a moment and then jumped up into her lap.

"Jesus!"

With an irritable jerk, she wrenched him away from her, letting him drop with a thud three feet away. For a moment he looked absolutely stunned. Then he turned his back and silently stiff-walked away.

"I'm sorry, baby. It's just that . . . *Dammit!*"

She snatched up the printouts and stalked across to the swingbin in the kitchenette. But the swingbin was full. Breathing hard, she put the paper on a work top and tried to get a grip on herself.

"Dammit it," she said again, but reasonable now, in control.

She turned the paper around the right way, and stared at the columns of meaningless characters.

"Why generate the same series twice?"

Oscar watched from a distance, full of distrust. Alex looked at him for a moment and then went back to the document. Two tables. A and B. Nine columns and eight rows. MCP1B. LQTS1. HTCH4. CFIB2. Meaningless labels. Dangerous information. Then, at the bottom of the last page, the date and time and MEDAN.

She brought her hand to her mouth, staring at the name as if she were seeing it for the first time.

She pulled the phone book out from under a pile of junk mail. She was amazed she hadn't thought of it before. She knew what Mel Hartman would have said: *Not all forms of knowledge are digital.* She had been too engrossed in the tables to follow the simpler lead. If she could find out what Medan was, she might be able to guess at what she was looking at. She started to go through all the different financial listings in the Yellow Pages, thinking that maybe Medan was some kind of financial information company, like Reuters or Bloomberg—something Eliot would have used in his work. But five minutes later she had found nothing. She flipped to the general section, where residential and commercial listings were jumbled up in alphabetical order.

She found it almost immediately, between Medallion Printing and Medcall Inc.: Medan Diagnostics. Nothing to do with finance—it had to be some kind of lab or clinic. There was a telephone number and an address: 470 Toll Gate Road, West Warwick.

Traffic was light on Route 1 the next morning. It was a Saturday, and most people were heeding the warnings about an approaching snowstorm. Bundled up in her coat and hat, a thick wool scarf pushed up to her freezing nose, Alex crept south with the other cautious drivers, her street map open on the passenger seat. She went past the airport to the top of Greenwich Bay and then followed the signs for Kent County Hospital which, according to her map, was located on Toll Gate Road.

Pretty soon the hospital building itself loomed out of the mist. She saw a street sign and then a number 351 painted on a trash can. A little farther on she saw a closed shop with the number 413 stenciled on the steel shutter. She eased off the gas. Deserted lots and run-down old buildings gave way to the low-rise prefabricated structures of light industry. Here and there saplings had been planted in a half-hearted attempt at landscaping.

Then she was driving past it.

She pulled off the road and looked back over her shoulder. A chain link fence surrounded an area of freshly swept blacktop marked with parking spaces. An Oldsmobile was parked near the double doors of the two-story brown brick building. A small sign by the entrance read MEDAN INC. CLINICAL DIAGNOSTICS. She cut the engine and sat looking through the fence at the recessed rectangular windows, trying to guess what went on inside. What did Michael Eliot have to do with this place? She didn't know what she had expected, but this was disappointing somehow. It was so banal. A scrap of newspaper blew across the parking lot and attached itself to the foot of a sad-looking birch tree.

It was too far away from anywhere to be a clinic or surgery. If this was the Medan that figured on the printouts, then the numbers had been generated by a laboratory. She pulled the papers from her pocket and, switching on the overhead light, looked at them for the hundredth time. Perhaps the repeated numbers related to something physical like a biopsy, something you might examine in a diagnostic test. The numbers on the two tables seemed identical. Had the same material been examined twice? In itself, the repetition suggested an interaction of some kind with the physical world. In the world of mathematics, of pure numbers, the same calculation always produced the same results. There was no need to do it twice.

The distant slamming of a door brought her head up.

A security guard was making his way across the parking lot towards her. Seeing her look up, he raised a hand and smiled. Alex saw his mouth move. He probably thought she was lost. She fumbled for the ignition and started the car.

Half a mile down the road she came to a gas station and pulled in beside a pump. A kid with a stud in his nose came out of the store. She handed him the keys through the window.

"Fill it up, please."

Snow began to fall. Alex leaned back, massaging her sore eyes. The sleepless night had taken its toll. She realized now that she was hungry too. She was leaning forward to look at herself in the rearview mirror, pushing up her woolen hat to see her hair, when she saw the car.

It was the Pontiac. There was a dent in the front fender where he had run into her. It rolled up to the pump just behind her. Looking at her through the snow-flecked windshield was the bearded face.

She froze, unable to think, disbelief giving way to panic. Then she ducked down and started looking around for the kid. But he had disappeared.

"I said, did you want me to check the oil?"

She jumped as the face appeared in her window. The kid recoiled, a startled look on his face.

"How much do I owe you?" said Alex.

"Twelve dollars, ma'am."

She pushed a twenty at him through the window, snatched the keys out of his hand, and pulled away from the pump.

The blood pounding in her temples, she stared out at the cars that streamed by on the road, blocking her in. She checked her mirror, expecting to see the guy out of the car and coming towards her. He was talking to the kid, acting cool. The kid pointed to her car and said something that made them both smile. Alex looked back at the traffic.

"Come on, come *on*."

Unable to wait any longer, she edged out a little into the road. A truck roared past, horn blaring, the words GREENFIELD RECYCLING momentarily there and then gone. The hair stood up on the back of her neck as she watched the Pontiac pull up behind her. If he got out of the car, what should she do? Provoke an accident?

There was a gap in the traffic. She let out her breath and was through.

And the Pontiac was right behind her.

She let her speed creep up, but was almost immediately behind somebody else. She tried to remember if she had seen him on Route 1 or up on the East Side. Had he been parked in the street? How long had he been following? The printouts were on the seat next to her. He would see she was snooping around, trying to find out more. She grabbed at the sheaf of papers and tried to stuff it into the glove compartment, then had to pump the brake to avoid hitting the car in front.

Again she checked her mirror. He looked so cool, so impassive. Biding his time. Then he was slowing down. He signaled, turned. Suddenly the road behind her was clear.

For a moment she couldn't take it in. She drove on a little way, her speed dropping. Then she began to understand. She pulled over to the side of the road. Cars drifted past. It was snowing more heavily now, the flakes thudding lightly against the windshield. After a minute she was looking at a solid screen of white. She pulled off her hat and wiped the perspiration from her forehead. He hadn't recognized her. She was so wrapped up in winter clothes he hadn't been able to see who she was. So he had pulled in behind her purely by chance. It was a garage he probably used all the time Conveniently located. Near his work . . .

She waited for her chance, and then pulled the car around in a tight arc. Now she was going back along Toll Gate Road towards the hospital. As she passed the Medan building, she saw the Pontiac parked next to the Oldsmobile.

"Got you," she said, gripping the wheel.

Back at her apartment she called Mark. But there was no reply. For an hour she walked up and down her living room trying to work out what it all meant. Her stalker worked for Medan, or knew somebody inside the company. *I don't give a damn about the money. Do what you like with the money. But I must have those printouts.* Why? Why had Eliot ended up with the papers? Had he stolen them? She had to find out what they were, exactly what they referred to. A biopsy? A diagnostic test? She needed someone in a similar line to make the guesses.

She remembered Benny.

Benedict Ellis worked at the Arnold Biological Laboratory on Waterman Street. Alex had met him in a student bar when she first came to Providence, and for a while they had seen each other with a group that had disintegrated over the years as people drifted away for employment elsewhere. Although they lived only three blocks apart, they rarely saw each other anymore.

When Alex found him in his front yard, working on a mountain bike, his face red with cold, she remembered why: Benny was strange. He had always seemed odd to her, but over the years the combination of long hours, a narrow field (Benny was a leading light in muco-polysaccharide metabolism), and like-minded friends had taken their toll on his communication skills. His appearance—he had startled green eyes and a constantly smiling mouth—did nothing to dispel the impression of strangeness.

"Alex."

He threw down the spoke wrench and got to his feet when she came in through the gate.

"Hi, Ben. How're you doing?"

He nodded a slow dipping nod, smiling, looking her up and down, obviously surprised to see her.

"Saw Beaner the other day," he said, still nodding.

Alex had no idea who he was talking about.

"How's he doing?" she said, improvising, hoping Beaner was somebody from the old crowd.

"Same old Beaner," said Benny, smiling.

There was a little pause in which his smiling mouth pushed forward into a tight questioning O. "Wha—what's the—?"

"I was just"—Alex pointed back at the street, as if to validate her statement—"walking by, and I thought you might be able to, um, help me with something."

Benny was nodding again, the mouth finding its familiar happy curve.

"I've got this . . . Well, that's the problem," said Alex, showing him the printouts. "I don't really know what they are, and I thought maybe you might be able to tell me."

Benny wiped his hands on his jeans and took the printouts from her. She had forgotten the hands. They were beautiful, with long tapering fingers and almond fingernails, always a little dirty.

"Tags," he said. "Looks like."

"Tags?"

"Yeah. Markers. Identify sites on a strand of DNA—genes. Is that what this is?"

Alex shrugged.

"Yeah," said Benny, smiling, looking as though he was about to laugh, though he wasn't. "You use a probe. That's a radioactively labeled section of DNA. You can buy them. Use them to detect identical sections of nucleic acid by means of pairing. Northern blot, Southern blot. Like a little echo."

He cupped a hand to his mouth, and called: "Helloooo!" and then, in reply, fading away: "Helloooo."

Alex stared, nodding herself now.

"A probe?" she said.

"Yeah, you know, like they use to identify DNA in a criminal trial."

"You mean this is—this has something to do with a criminal trial?"

"Might. Might not. It's just information. Could be used for anything. Depends what you're looking for."

"Could it maybe have a diagnostic application?"

"Sure. You might be looking for some defect or mutation, like in a . . ." He considered the first page of the printout more closely. "I don't know what . . ."

Then he was smiling, looking at her.

"I'll tell you what I'll do. Friend of mine, Beth Klein, works with this kind of thing all the time. She'll be able to tell you what you have here."

"Thanks, Benny. I really appreciate it."

"Sure, no problem."

Alex watched him fold the papers into his back pocket where they stuck out like a tail feather. She wondered if she should tell him they were supposed to be dangerous, then decided that it would only make things too complicated.

"You still living at old Ma Connelly's place?" he said.

"Sure am. Me and Oscar."

Benny frowned, his mouth still smiling.

"Oscar? Oh yeah, the tall guy with the sweaters."

"Little guy with fur, actually," said Alex. "Oscar's my cat."

Benny smiled an embarrassed smile.

"It's been a long time," he said.

24

It was midafternoon when McCormick heard the car pull up. He hurriedly tamped out his cigarette and went over to the window. A black Cadillac was double-parked on the corner, its headlights burning yellow through the falling snow. Neumann hadn't said who would come for him. He'd just said someone would. The Mann Clinic was located somewhere in New Jersey.

McCormick hadn't enjoyed the wait. Ever since Neumann's visit, all he'd been able to think about was Michael Eliot. He couldn't get out of his head the thought of him biting down on the pain, biting into his own cheek, cracking a tooth. He'd even dreamed about it during his fitful dawn-time sleep, had woken up in a sweat, his muscles as rigid as a corpse. He'd known Eliot well. They'd worked together a lot in the early years. He wasn't stupid or weak. He was clever, balanced, *normal*. What could have happened to tip him over the edge? And just how close was he himself? It wouldn't take much to push him over, that was becoming clear. All he had to do was get a little impatient, cut corners, ignore the procedures. And then it would be his turn. One more domestic accident. The kind of accident life insurance companies handled every day.

It was Donald Grant who got out of the car. McCormick felt a tingle of nerves in his stomach. Grant always made him nervous. It wasn't anything he could put his finger on. It was simply the way other people were around him, even people like Walter Neumann and Newton Brady. The respect, the distance. It was infectious. At the same time, talking to Grant, you could never escape the feeling that he knew a lot more than he was letting on, a lot more about you—perhaps more than you even knew yourself.

"Neumann said three o'clock. You're late," McCormick snapped, opening the door.

Grant stamped the snow off his feet and stepped into the hall.

"No, I'm not, Ralph," he said mildly. "You got all your stuff together?"

McCormick sucked his teeth. Technically speaking, Grant was junior to him. Investigations was a subdepartment of Claims, while McCormick had a department all his own. But Grant didn't seem bothered. The corporate hierarchy wasn't what mattered as far as he was concerned and never had been.

"It's all in there," McCormick mumbled, pointing to a brown leather suitcase.

Grant nodded.

"Got rid of all the snow, Ralph?"

"The snow?" said McCormick with a joky shrug, pointing out the door at the snowy gloom. "I'd need a—"

"The cocaine. Did you get rid of it?"

McCormick sniffed. "Yeah, yeah. It all went down the can. Last night." Involuntarily he dabbed at his nostrils. "Hey, it wasn't much."

"Down the can?"

"Yes."

"Last night?"

"This morning. Okay? Last night, this morning, what's the difference?"

Grant watched him for a moment, then pushed the door shut.

"Your wife comin' back?"

McCormick frowned. Grant's tone was beginning to annoy him.

"Of—of course she's coming back. What do you—? She's just visiting her—"

"When?"

"When *what*?"

"When is she coming back, Ralph?"

Grant didn't raise his voice, but he didn't have to. McCormick felt like a worm, wriggling on the end of a hook. He reached for his over-coat and scarf.

"I don't know. When we work it out, I guess. She already knows about my—about the clinic. What's it to you, anyway?"

Grant stepped over and helped McCormick into the coat, giving him a crooked, all-is-forgiven smile.

"Oh, you know how we like to keep everything in the family, Ralph. This is a small town and people will talk. Even wives. You've got a very important job in this organization. We just want to make sure you keep it." He patted McCormick on the shoulder and walked over towards the stairs. "I'm just gonna use your bathroom, okay?"

McCormick turned. "There's one just down here. By the—"

But Grant was already on his way up.

He shut the door and went straight to the medicine cabinet. That was always where coke-heads kept their stashes, hidden among all those prescription bottles and old razor blades. He'd even had a stash of his own there in the old days, before he'd kicked the habit. It was medicine, in a way, at least that was how you pretty soon came to think of it. Helped you forget your troubles. Except what kind of troubles did Ralph McCormick have? What did he want that he couldn't get just by doing nothing, just by sitting there and waiting a few years? He was pathetic. A liability. The clinic might stop him taking drugs, but they wouldn't keep him from wanting to, not for long. You could tell: he was all eaten up inside.

Grant almost laughed out loud when he found what he was looking for in an old aspirin bottle. McCormick really was pathetic. Even his old lady couldn't fail to find it there. It was probably the first place she'd look. He dipped his finger in the fine white powder and tasted it. It was the good stuff, though, no doubt about that. McCormick had got him-self a high-class dealer, paying top dollar without a care. But that was the trouble with dealers, they were not reliable people. You never knew when they were going to slip you something cut with rat poison, or bleach, or worse. It happened all the time. Grant screwed the cap back on the bottle and put it back in the cabinet. Then he flushed the lavatory and left.

25

Mark wasn't in on Saturday night when Alex called. It was after eleven o'clock the following morning when she was finally able to get hold of him. She didn't quiz him about where he'd been, or let him know she'd been trying to reach him, and she didn't say anything about her trip to Medan the day before. After the way they'd parted, she knew that could only make things worse. She just did her best to seem relaxed and reassuring and ended up suggesting she come over that night and cook dinner. He seemed tired but agreed readily enough. It turned out he'd been back at the office until well after midnight, thanks to some problem with the computer system, he said. Alex managed to keep from asking if the problem had anything to do with Ralph McCormick.

She got to his place at seven and walked up the front steps balancing her sack of groceries. There was rock music playing loudly inside, and light from the bathroom was streaming out through a first-floor window. Alex thumped on the door frame with her elbow, but it was obvious Mark couldn't hear her. Fortunately she still had the set of keys he had given her several months earlier, when the talk of moving in had been at its height—when Mark had been the one who was all for it. She fished them out of her coat pocket and let herself in.

He was coming down the stairs as she entered the hall, dressed in a gray jogging suit, his hair still wet from the shower. He looked great.

"I forgot you had keys," he said. "I wondered who the hell it was."

"You gave them to me," said Alex. "You want them back?"

He took the groceries from her, pecked her on the cheek, and walked back through to the kitchen. The rock music was still playing in the living room.

"I just forgot you had them, that's all. So what do we have here?"

Alex took off her coat and slung it on the back of a chair.

"Hoisin chicken," she said as brightly as she could. "It's a great recipe, and dead easy. Spring onions, crushed walnuts, and hoisin sauce. Kind of sweet and sour. I tried it the other day."

Mark fished out the bottle of sauce and started reading the label: ingredients, nutritional information, even the recipe for Chinese barbecued spareribs. It was as if he couldn't think of anything to say, or had something on his mind, something that was squeezing out everything else. Alex felt a flutter of alarm, wondering if he was building up to saying something to her. Something about them.

"I'm having a beer," Mark said finally. "You want one?"

"Sure," she said, though she didn't much like beer and had probably told him so a hundred times. She kept on unpacking the groceries. "I'm going to need an egg white, by the way. You still got eggs in there?"

Mark was crouching in front of the refrigerator, fishing around for his bottles of Michelob. He seemed to be taking a long time to find them. When he finally stood up again there was no sign of the eggs.

"Mark?"

"What?"

"Does that mean you haven't got any?"

"Any what?"

"Eggs. I need an egg."

"I thought we were having chicken."

Alex let out a nervous laugh. "We are, Einstein. But I need an egg white."

Mark frowned. He didn't see the joke.

"Oh, right. Yeah, I got eggs." He crouched down again and started shifting things around in the fridge. Alex watched him out of the corner of her eye. "Yeah. Here we go."

He pulled out an egg carton and put it down on the work top. Alex started making the marinade, adding rice wine and cornflour to the egg white and beating it with a fork. The music came to a stop, but Mark didn't make any move to change it.

"So," he said, handing her a glass of beer but drinking his own from the bottle, "it looks like I'm gonna be away most of next week. I mean, weather permitting."

Alex stopped beating.

"Oh really, where?"

"New York. There's a chance we might get involved in underwriting this brokerage operation. Newt wants it checked out, anyhow."

"A whole week?"

"Flying out Tuesday morning—like I say, weather permitting. There's some other people we're gonna see on Wall Street. Maybe I should go buy myself some scarlet suspenders."

"You've already got some," Alex said. "Left-hand side of the closet."

Mark nodded and leaned against the refrigerator.

"You going alone?" Alex couldn't help herself.

He shrugged. "Maybe."

"What about—?" She stopped herself just in time. This was not the moment for displays of jealousy, especially jealousy that had no basis in fact. "Newton Brady. Is he going?"

"No. Not unless the deal moves real fast, which I can't see happening." Mark took a swig of beer. "So. You get anywhere with those printouts?"

Alex took a moment to focus on the question. She'd already decided to say nothing about it. Things had changed for her since her trip down to West Warwick. The fact that she'd been able to track the stranger to his place of work made her feel more confident, more in control, and every day that went by with nothing happening—nothing menacing or sinister—confirmed her sense of security. And there was another reason for keeping quiet. The way Mark seemed to want to take charge of the whole thing annoyed her. It was as if her taking initiatives was threatening to him somehow.

"No," she said. "I haven't really thought about it. I think that guy I saw was just a nut. Maybe he was just trying to hit on me in some weird way."

Mark took another swig of beer, watching her.

"Yeah, could be," he said. "There are some very weird people in this city."

And half of them work for ProvLife, thought Alex.

"You see him again?" Mark asked.

Alex reached into a drawer for the kitchen knife and began slicing the chicken breasts.

"No," she said dismissively. "If I see him again, I'll call a cop."

Mark let out a satisfied grunt and went and sat down at the table. This seemed to be what he wanted to hear.

"By the way," he said casually. "I checked the payments ledger in the computer for those account numbers you gave me."

Alex put down the knife and turned to face him.

"You did? You mean last night?"

"Yes."

"And?"

Mark sighed and shook his head.

"Those accounts, they're just—they belonged to beneficiaries of ProvLife policies. People who got the money when the policyholder died. Completely routine stuff."

Alex frowned. "You mean, they got money from the company?"

"What else? These people made claims. The claims were settled. End of story."

Alex let her arms drop.

"So then these—" She paused, trying to make sense of it. "These beneficiaries all had accounts at Ocean State, right?"

Mark shrugged.

"Well, that was just a list of ones that did. It is one of the biggest banks in the state, you know."

"So— What? These were all local policyholders?"

"I guess. New England's our biggest market. Nothing unusual about that."

"But why did Michael Eliot take them with him? I mean, these particular account numbers?"

"Maybe he took his work home. Maybe he just left it in his briefcase. Who cares? Listen, I'm still on the learning curve in there, and Eliot wasn't that good at keeping records, lemme tell ya."

Alex couldn't help feeling disappointed. The way she'd found the sheet of paper tucked in among the leaves of the computer printout did suggest that maybe it had gotten in there by accident.

"What size of policies are we talking about?" she asked.

Mark put down the empty beer bottle and got up. He looked fidgety, unable to settle.

"I don't know. You know, routine amounts. A hundred thousand, sometimes less. Anyway, the point is it was all company funds. Completely legitimate. So"—he reached into the refrigerator for another beer—"I guess you can forget about your money laundering idea."

Alex picked up the knife again went back to slicing the chicken breasts. The undersides of them were slick with blood. She could feel it congealing on the tips of her fingers.

"Wait a second." She stopped slicing and looked at her fingers. "I thought the smaller settlements were handled by Claims. I thought only the big payouts were made via Treasury. The half-million-dollar ones and up."

For a moment Mark looked confused.

"What? Who said they were made via Treasury? I told you I just checked the payments ledger. I didn't say which department handled the payments, did I?"

"But, Mark, why would Eliot have a list of the accounts if he hadn't handled the payments?"

"How the hell should I know?"

"But it doesn't make sense. Unless there was something about those payments that was special? Don't you see?"

"No." Mark slammed the fridge door shut. "You're jumping to—you don't know that. It could be . . ."

"Look." Alex stared at the knife in her hand and put it down. "Look, all I'm saying is . . ."

"What?"

"It doesn't matter."

"No, come on. What are you saying? What's on your mind?"

"The names. The names of the policyholders. You have to get them. Or just the policy numbers. Then we can look up the policies themselves and check that everything really is legit."

"What the—?" Mark made to leave the room, then turned in the doorway, gripping the frame of the door with his free hand. "What the *fuck* are you talking about, Alex?"

He blinked, surprised by his own anger. He looked around the kitchen as though trying to see where it had come from.

"Do you have *any* idea what kind of pressure I'm under at the moment?"

"But all you'd have to do is—"

"I'm supposed to be head of Treasury, for God's sake. Do you have *any* idea what that means? I'm supposed to know how to run the *whole damned department*. And you know what? Half of the board probably think I'm not up to it. Do you seriously think I haven't got better things to do than go chasing around Central Records all fucking day? Haven't I done enough already?"

Alex stared, intimidated by his anger.

"Don't curse at me, Mark," she said quietly.

"All because—because you've got some damned fixation about Michael Eliot. Forget Michael Eliot. Michael Eliot is dead. Okay? He drilled through a cable. Now can we get on with our fucking lives, please?"

"Mark, I only—" To her own surprise Alex found herself on the edge of tears. "I only asked—"

"*Only?* You only what? In the first place, Newton Brady came over when I was in the middle of this fucking paper chase you put me up to, and he wasn't very amused when he found I was data surfing on company time."

"What do you mean, company time? It was Saturday night, for Christ's sake. You were on your damned weekend."

"So was he." Mark stabbed at the air with his finger. "So was he. And he couldn't get away until we'd both finished. And, in the second place, as you well know or should know, data on individual policyholders *and* their beneficiaries is restricted for privacy reasons, and not available to just anybody."

"I know the rule. I just didn't know anyone was dumb enough to take any notice. It's about the stupidest thing I ever heard."

"Well"— Mark was nodding, his position justified—"well, if you took just a bit more notice of *stupid* things like your job and your responsibilities, then maybe you wouldn't be living in that rat-infested shit-hole, dodging the landlady when she comes looking for the rent."

For a moment Alex couldn't speak. She felt like she'd been punched in the stomach. The air was sucked out of her. She bit her teeth together, determined not to cry. She wasn't going to let him see that.

"You've changed, you know that?" She was looking him straight in the eye, trying to breathe steadily despite her pounding heart. "Ever since Newt gave you your *encouragement*. You used to be okay. You used to be funny. But now—now I don't know what you are."

Mark set his jaw. She saw him swallow.

"Yeah, and you've been against it from the start, haven't you?" he said. "Why don't you admit it? Even my getting a new car pissed you off. You couldn't be supportive. You couldn't help me take the one—the *one*—big chance of my life and make something of it. You had to sit there and carp, and poke fun. Why was that, Alex? Were you jealous or something? Were you hoping to make SVP ahead of me, via Randal White's . . . good offices?"

Alex stared at him open-mouthed. She could hardly believe her ears. She wanted to hit him, but she could see by the look on his face that he would hit her right back. She turned and reached for her coat. She had to steady herself for a moment against the back of the chair.

"You son of a bitch." It came out as little more than a whisper. "You self-pitying, selfish . . ."

She pushed past him and ran out into the hall. She didn't understand how it had happened, the resentment, the anger. It had come from nowhere. But that could not be. He really *had* changed, for the worse. Something had changed him. She just hadn't seen it happening until it was too late. It seemed to her that ever since Michael Eliot's death everything had been slowly turning bad. And she was powerless to stop it, even to understand it.

"Alex." There was no more than a trace of apology in Mark's voice. Rather, he seemed to be implying that she should grow up. "Alex, come on. I only . . ."

She looked back at him, waiting for him to apologize, to get down on his knees and grovel. But he didn't. He just stood there framed in the kitchen doorway, the unopened bottle of beer in his hand, and sighed.

Alex opened the front door.

"For the record," she said, looking back, "I do not dodge Mrs. Connelly. I pay her. There are *no* rats in that house, and Randal White is one thing you'll never be: a gentleman."

"Alex, I didn't—"

"Cook your own fucking dinner," she yelled, and she ran down the steps towards the car, praying that for once it would start first time.

26

Monday dragged, with Alex's work snagging on unreliable statistics and out-of-date population models. She jumped each time the phone rang. Despite her anger, she couldn't stop herself hoping that Mark would eventually call her. All he had to do was say sorry, and she would have been ready to forgive him. But he didn't call. By six o'clock she was exhausted.

She had hardly slept the night before. After leaving Mark's place she had driven north on the interstate most of the way to Boston, then turned around and come straight back—a two-hour round trip in the freezing dark. She couldn't believe what had happened, couldn't believe how he had spoken to her. It was as if another person had taken over, someone she had never seen before. She hadn't gotten to bed until two o'clock, and had then lain awake, listening to the clock ticking next to her bed, seeing Mark's furious face as he told her what a deadbeat she was, what a loser.

So her plan for Monday evening was to sleep. She got home at seven and, having fed Oscar, went straight to bed.

She was in the middle of a turbulent, suffocating dream when the telephone woke her.

"Alex?"

She didn't quite know where she was. She blinked at the room for a moment, the receiver held against her ear.

"Hello, Alex?"

It was a man's voice. Not the stranger, though. Someone else.

"Alex?"

"Yes," she said. "Who is this?"

"It's Randal, Randal White."

She pulled herself into a sitting position and turned on the bedside light. The clock read half past ten.

"Randal?"

He apologized for calling so late and hoped she hadn't already gone to bed.

"That's okay," said Alex. "I was just . . . I was just reading."

"Oh, really."

He sounded a little sleepy himself. He wanted to know what the book was.

"A Philip Roth novel: *My Life as a Man*."

"Well, I won't keep you long," he said. "I just wanted to ask you if you could do something for me."

"Of course."

"It's something I need for the forum. Can you get onto the system first thing tomorrow, and draw up a year-on-year breakdown for sickle-cell anemia claims? If you don't have any luck nationally, you might find some studies from the southern states—maybe Alabama and Florida. Whatever you come up with, just give it to Janice and she'll fax it down."

There was a long pause. Alex frowned. It seemed like an odd request to be making at ten-thirty on a Monday night.

"I'm flying back tomorrow afternoon," White added, "weather permitting, but I want to leave the figures with someone here. An interested party, you might say."

"Sure," Alex said. "No problem."

There was another long silence.

"How was your day?" White said.

Alex drew her feet up under the covers. This was getting odder by the minute.

"Fine. Well, not fine—not great, actually. How was yours?"

"Not great," he said. "Not so great."

"Oh. I'm sorry to hear that."

"Yes, well," he said. He coughed, and Alex thought she could hear the chink of ice in a glass. "I'm up here on the thirtieth floor, looking down at an intersection of three large roads. All these people streaming back and forth in the dark."

Alex remembered her own journey in the dark: racing along the interstate as though trying to outrun the wave of despair that threatened to engulf her. She was surprised by a sudden urge to tell White all about it.

"Hotels do tend to get me down eventually," said White. "They always make me think of Le Corbusier—you know, what he said about living machines: buildings should be living machines, *machines à vivre* rather than *machines vivantes*. Machines for living."

Alex shook her head.

"Do you speak French, Alex? I just realized I never asked you."

"No," she said. "Not really."

"I like old buildings," he said.

The ice clinked in the glass.

"Me too," said Alex.

"I know this place near Cahors, in the southwest of France, this old convent. Surrounded by vineyards. The main living area has French windows that open directly onto a terrace . . . overlooking the vineyards."

Alex saw sun on hot stone, moving shadows.

"Sounds nice," she said. "I'd like to go to France."

"Would you?"

"Sure. Who wouldn't?"

"It's perfect, Alex. The place I'm talking about. A little piece of paradise. To stand on the terrace in the dawn light . . ."

He let out a sigh.

"Oh dear," he said. "Here I am up on the thirtieth floor dreaming of a convent in the sun. I guess that's a little sad, isn't it?"

"It's not sad," she said. "It's important to have dreams."

"Well, I hope I haven't disturbed you, Alex."

"No. No, not at all. It's nice . . . it was nice to hear from you."

"Good night, then."

"Good night, Randal."

She put the phone down and stayed sitting up in bed. Oscar was watching from his basket.

"What do you think of that?" she said.

Oscar just stared.

27

T he next morning Mel Hartman was telling stories in the kitchen.
"So anyway," he said, pausing to give a good-morning nod as
Alex came in, "he's too ill to talk. There's an embarrassed pause on the
dais and the conference chairman has to step in."

"Did you hear about this, Alex?" said Sandra Betridge.

"About what?" Alex started removing the filter from the coffee
machine.

"About Randal. He got sick at the NIH forum yesterday. Had to go
home."

Alex opened a new package of coffee, trying not to look too concerned.

"I think it was that guy Kenyon from Mass General," said Hartman.

"What was that guy from Mass General?" said Sandra.

"He didn't want Randal to say his piece. Didn't want him to reveal
how the industry's divided on this testing issue. So he spiked his coffee
during the morning break."

Sandra made a face. "Yeah, right."

"What do you think, Al?" said Hartman.

"Which one of the cleaners did you hear it from this time?" said Alex.

Mel sipped his coffee, and smiled at her back.

"It was from somebody at the conference," said Sandra. "A friend of
Mel's. Tell her, Mel."

Hartman frowned, still watching Alex. "Naah. Alex doesn't want to know about this. She's not interested in gossip."

Alex smiled a thin, unfriendly smile, eyes on the coffee machine, waiting for her fourth cup of the day.

"Are you okay?" Sandra asked. "You look tired."

"I'm not . . . I'm not sleeping very well," said Alex.

The truth was, she had hardly slept at all. She had found it difficult to get to sleep after White's call.

"Maybe it was Neumann," said Sandra, lowering her voice. "That got to him, I mean."

Hartman jerked backwards, making the sign of the cross with his fingers.

"No, please—not *Neumann*."

Sandra stifled a guffaw, spilling a little orange juice onto the floor.

"*Yes,*" she insisted. "To get Randal away from the table. They're supposed to decide on the new CEO on Friday. Neumann probably thinks it'll improve his chances if Randal isn't there."

"They'll just set up a conference call," said Hartman dismissively. He stood up straight. "There's no way White's gonna let himself get shut out of that meeting."

Alex turned, sipping at her coffee. "It's the policyholders who decide on the new CEO, not the board. ProvLife's a mutual, remember."

Hartman pushed air out through his nose.

"The board will make its recommendation and the policyholders, as usual, as *always*, will remain silent," he said. "Why'd you think Goebert decided to stay mutual in the first place? For *control*."

Alex walked out of the kitchen, stirring her coffee. She wondered why White hadn't mentioned it to her the night before. She wondered if he had made the call because of the illness. It made sense in a way: alone in his hotel room, recovering from whatever it was, it was only natural that he should reach out to a friend. But she couldn't help being surprised that he would think of her that way. She felt a powerful urge to see him. Would he be flying back immediately? She wondered how he would react to her news about Eliot's money, to her theories about how he might have come by it. He'd said Neumann seemed to be protective of McCormick. Did he have doubts of his own, suspicions?

There was a scribbled note stuck to her phone.

"Who's Bridget Lawrence?" she said to no one on particular.

A head came up from behind a burlap partition. "Neumann's PA. Called about five minutes ago."

Frowning, trying to imagine what Neumann's PA could want, Alex pulled out her phone list and punched in the extension number. A crisp, efficient-sounding voice told her that Mr. Walter Neumann would like to see her in his office.

"May I ask what it's about?"

"I'm afraid he didn't say."

"Oh . . . okay." Alex looked at her desk diary. "I could come by after lunch," she said.

"I think he had in mind right away," said the voice.

"Then I guess I'd better come quietly," said Alex.

Riding the elevator down, Alex tried to decide what it could be about. For a brief moment, walking along the deeper, newer carpet of the third-floor landing, she wondered if it might be related to the Medan printouts, but she told herself she was being paranoid. Even so, arriving at Neumann's office, she felt like she was entering the lion's den.

Neumann was seated with his back to her, a telephone pressed to his ear.

"Mr. Neumann?"

He turned and looked in her direction, not giving the slightest sign of recognition. Alex had a bizarre feeling of being suddenly invisible.

"No, I'm still here," he said into the phone. "Yes, I understand that, but I don't see why you can't seat the senator at the second table." He pointed to a deep leather chair and Alex sat down.

She listened to him talk in his peculiar lock-jawed manner—a ventriloquist without a dummy—her eyes roving over the standard props of the attorney: the ego wall with its framed certificates and selected hand-shaking photographs, the ornamental bronze ink stand, the bookcases up to the ceiling. Why was it lawyers still relied on leather-bound books when everybody else had gone digital?

Neumann finally put down the phone.

"Good of you to find time," he said, barely moving his lips. "I was sorry to hear about Randal. Is he feeling any better?"

Alex wondered why he thought she would be the one to know. She shrugged, following him with her eyes as he walked around the desk to close the door.

"I don't know anything about it. I just heard he'd gotten sick at the NIH forum."

Neumann nodded. "That's right. Sounds like some kind of . . . I don't know. Most inconvenient, what with the healthcare project and . . ."

He sat down and brought his hands together, opposing the tips of his fingers in front of his expressionless face.

"I expect you're wondering why I sent for you. Well, I won't beat around the bush. Providence Life is an old company, some would say old-fashioned, a company that sets itself very high standards of integrity and—"

The phone rang and he immediately picked up, raising a finger to keep Alex where she was—which, she realized with surprise, was on the edge of her seat. Out of nowhere she had a very bad feeling about what was happening, but she couldn't make sense of it.

"Yes," said Neumann into the phone. "Tell him I'll be there in an hour. The Capital Grille, that's right. No, no—I'll be through here in about five minutes."

He hung up.

"I do apologize," he said. Then, frowning, looking at his desk: "Yes, as I was saying, very traditional. As you know, we set the highest standards for all our departments. Perhaps the actuarial department highest of all. Normally, of course, Randal White himself would be discharging this . . . um, this onerous task, but he is ill, and so I have agreed to represent the position of the board in this matter."

He gave her a hard look, and his eyes were like two holes pierced through to a darker space. To Alex it seemed as if his voice were coming from a long way off, as she watched his pale lips move over clenched teeth. *We feel let down . . . to put it mildly. . . . Frankly, your behavior over the past few weeks . . . a kind of ruthless opportunism which . . .*

Then he was struggling to finish a sentence, just shaking his head and looking at her.

"Behavior?" said Alex, her voice sounding cracked and small.

Neumann ran a finger along his desktop and found dirt there.

"I'd rather hoped . . . I can't believe that you are going to protest your innocence in this matter."

Alex was suddenly alive to the danger she was in.

"What matter?" she said. "First—first of all. And—and yes—yes, I am."

Neumann smiled. When he spoke again, it was almost in a whisper.

"Obviously I'm not going to go into detail, but suffice it to say that a client has brought it to my attention that she received a—a rather distasteful communication from you."

Alex waited, but it was clear that he had said all he was going to say.

"Which client?" she said, and then suddenly it clicked. "Mrs. Eliot? Is that who we're talking about?"

The lids came down over Neumann's eyes, just slightly: soft traps, closing on information. Alex felt she had just confirmed her guilt for him.

"Obviously," said Neumann, nodding, "if you want to take this further, that is your right. But I should warn you that I have evidence, documentary evidence provided by a local telecommunications carrier, that this call *was* made, and was made from your apartment."

"Call? But that . . ."

Alex tried to think. Then she realized what must have happened. Liz had called from her place the morning after she'd stayed. Her face was suddenly hot with indignation.

"But that call—I didn't make it."

Neumann raised a warning finger. He looked angry now, not out of control but sternly displeased in a bullying, lawyerly manner.

"Understand something. I did not call you in here to get your version of this business. Whatever arguments you wish to present by way of"—he smiled—"let's call it *appeal*, should be a matter for you and . . . whatever *representation* you can afford. As far as Neumann and Klein is concerned, as far as the management of this company is concerned, this matter is closed."

Alex stayed where she was, unable to speak or move.

"Now. I think you'll agree with me that it is in nobody's interest to have this talked about, um, around town. Providence Life has a reputation, a reputation of which I am very proud. We don't hire *extortionists*. In view of that, we are ready to keep silent on this matter provided you are gone by—" He paused, considering in his best judicial manner the severity of her sentence. "By the end of the day."

He stood up and touched the knot in his silk tie.

"I daresay that Randal White may even be ready to write some kind of letter of recommendation," he said with a smirk. Then the stern look of reproof was back. "If, however, you do decide to take this matter to some kind of tribunal, we will not hesitate to fully publicize your . . . shortcomings. And that could look very bad, *Ms.* Tynan. But then, I'm sure I don't need to tell you what dirt on a résumé does to a young actuary. Which would be a shame, as I understand that you were doing quite well here."

He gave the knot a jerk, and smiled. It was all over, and he had a lunch to go to. She could consider herself hanged.

PART FOUR

ACCIDENTS WILL HAPPEN

28

The elevator lurched to a halt. Alex didn't know what floor she was on. She didn't even know where she'd been meaning to go. All she knew was that she'd been going down, sinking through the building, falling from Neumann's office towards the freezing, cheerless street.

It was a disaster, a catastrophe. Three months from associateship and she was suddenly out of a job. That wasn't something you could explain away. After all the years of study it was . . . *impossible*. Insane. She touched trembling fingers to her forehead and replayed the scene, trying to make sense of what had just happened to her. But she couldn't. All she could see was Neumann's smile as he talked about smearing dirt on her résumé. She would never find a place in another company, because she would never be able to explain why she needed it. And that meant she would never qualify. She would never qualify, she would never get the raise, she would never *be* an actuary. No qualifications, no raise, no job, no apartment. And Fleet Bank on her back for $36,000 that she would never be able to pay back.

She slumped against the wall of the car, her head reeling. Barely a week ago she had been a guest at the chairman's party, Mark's arm around her, safe, secure, a bright young person with a bright future. How could everything change so quickly?

The elevator doors slid open, and she found herself staring at the dirty yellow walls and cement floor of the basement. She was about to press another button when Mac appeared, carrying a tall stack of cardboard boxes and whistling a tune that Alex recognized as Simon & Garfunkel.

"Hello there, Alex." He sounded surprised, pleased to see her. At least someone was still on her side. "To what do I owe this unexpected pleasure?"

"Actually I didn't—I was just—"

She took her hand away from the buttons. She didn't know which one to press anyway. She certainly didn't want to go back to her desk. Mel Hartman probably knew of her dismissal already and was busy making sure everybody else in the department did too.

"How are you, Mac?"

"Stuck on R for Mrs. Robinson, God bless you. But otherwise as right as rain. How about you? You look a little pale."

"I'm fine, I guess."

Mac looked into her face and frowned.

"Are you sure?"

Alex sighed. She didn't have the strength to lie. She didn't have the strength to weigh up the pros and the cons.

"Mac, I just got fired," she said. "Walter Neumann fired me."

The basement was completely deserted. The transfer of ProvLife's old paper records to remote storage had been halted while the remaining asbestos was stripped away from the ceiling and from some of the more inaccessible parts of the central heating system. Most of the space was sealed off behind opaque plastic sheets marked with hazard warnings. In a small windowless room piled high with rolls of fax paper and economy-sized tins of instant coffee, Mac offered Alex a glass of Irish whisky from a bottle he kept, he said, for emergencies.

The whisky helped, but she was still having trouble connecting with reality. It had all happened so fast. She hadn't had time to think, hadn't had time even to react. Again Neumann's dead face loomed, telling her she was finished. The way he had put it made it seem absolutely final. A board decision. But, despite her bewilderment, she could see that that was unlikely. And Randal—she couldn't believe that he'd had any part in it. He'd been in Washington and now he was ill. How had Neumann put it? *I have agreed to represent the position of the board in this mat-*

ter. Was it likely that the matter had actually come up before the board? With Goebert's resignation and all of Ralph McCormick's problems, they had more important things to worry about, even assuming there'd been a meeting. Mrs. Eliot was, apparently, one of Neumann & Klein's clients. Wasn't it perfectly possible that Neumann was taking a unilateral step to protect his private business interests? Even if she had made some *distasteful communication* to Mrs. Eliot, it was hard to see how that was ProvLife's business.

She had to talk to Randal White. She had to talk to him before the whole matter became too public to revoke.

And there was someone else she was going to have to see: Liz Foster. Liz was . . . Alex clenched her jaw and slowly shook her head. She had looked out for Liz, tried to help her, and what had she gotten in return? Lies. With the memory of their last meeting, Liz's suspicion and deceit, Alex felt her despair turning to anger. Liz *had* called Mrs. Eliot. She *was* after Michael Eliot's money. It explained all the little presents she had been buying herself, in anticipation, no doubt, of the gusher she was about to tap. Alex wondered what kind of deal she had offered the widow. How much had she asked for? More than the traditional finder's fee, was Alex's guess. Mrs. Eliot would have realized she was dealing with her dead husband's lover. But, like so many other people in ProvLife's close-knit circles, she had assumed that the lover was Alex Tynan. And what had she done about it? She'd gone straight to her lawyers.

But would Liz help her now? The more Alex thought about it, the more unlikely it seemed. Liz wasn't going to own up. She already had her sights fixed on a share of ten million dollars. What was Alex's lousy job at ProvLife worth next to that? What was their friendship worth? Besides, even if Liz did come clean, would anyone believe her? It didn't seem likely. If Alex wanted to clear her name, she was going to have to take a more direct route.

"Now," said Mac, settling into an office chair that was missing one arm, "tell me about it."

Alex sighed. "Well . . ."

But instead of words, tears came, and she was leaning forward hiding her face in her hands. Mac patted her on the shoulder, said something comforting. After a moment Alex looked up and tried to smile.

"My life is . . . I feel like I just got hit by a truck. I think I broke up with my boyfriend. That was on Sunday. And now . . . there's just been this awful . . . I don't know what to call it. This awful *misunderstanding* with Neumann. At least, I think that's what . . ."

She gave up trying to make sense and just shook her head.

Mac nodded rapidly, searching for something constructive to say.

"Lawyers," he muttered at last, as if that was more than enough.

She had just begun to think that nobody was in, when the door opened. Mrs. Eliot looked very different from the woman she had seen at the funeral. She was dressed in a pair of gray chinos and a baggy plum-colored sweater. She wore no trace of makeup, and her hair was tied back in a knot, so that the streaks of gray were plainly visible. As soon as she saw Alex she froze, her grip tightening on the doorknob. The intensity of her stare was like a physical force, pushing Alex back from the step.

"Mrs. Eliot? I'm very sorry to—to trouble you like this, but I didn't have your number and . . . My name's Alexandra Tynan. I'm—"

"I know who you are."

Alex thrust her hands deep into her coat pockets.

"I—I don't think you do. You see, there's been a terrible misunderstanding. Can you—could you give me just five minutes of your time?"

Mrs. Eliot looked past Alex's shoulders, as if concerned that she might not be alone.

"My lawyers have advised me to avoid all further contact with you, Miss Tynan," she said. "And that's just what I intend to do. I'm sorry."

She made to close the door.

"Please!" Alex stepped forward. "We haven't ever *been* in contact until now. That's why I'm here. I'm not who you think I am. I'm not who Walter Neumann thinks I am."

Mrs. Eliot hesitated.

"You've spoken to Walter Neumann?"

Alex slowly nodded her head.

"This morning. He accused me of attempted extortion and . . . and now I'm suddenly out of a job. All because I've been mistaken for someone else."

Mrs. Eliot looked Alex up and down as if trying to read the truth of what she was saying.

"Mistaken for whom?"

Alex bit her lip. How much *did* Mrs. Eliot know? How much of the truth about her dead husband was she ready to accept?

"For the woman . . . for your husband's lover."

Mrs. Eliot drew a breath and stiffened as if suddenly cold. For a moment Alex thought she was going to slam the door in her face. But then her shoulders relaxed.

"Perhaps you'd better come in," she said.

The kitchen was a mixture of Colonial grace and modern convenience. Dark wood furniture was brightened with checkered seat cushions and a matching tablecloth. Gleaming copper pans and ladles hung from hooks above the range, and thick glass jars lined the shelves. It was the kind of kitchen featured in lifestyle magazines, a perfect setting for those "traditional" family occasions. Alex could almost smell the Thanksgiving turkey and the mulled wine. But it didn't look like Mrs. Eliot had done much cooking lately. Precooked meals had been her staple, judging from the dirty plastic containers stacked beside the double sink.

She told Alex what had happened. Liz had called twice and the deal she had proposed was simple. She would give Mrs. Eliot enough information to access an unspecified portion of her husband's offshore assets. Once this money had been recovered, Mrs. Eliot would hand over half of it to Liz in return for information on how to get the next portion. This would be repeated until all the assets were recovered, although only Liz would know when that was. In this way she would ensure that the widow could not keep all of the last portion to herself. She was determined, it seemed, not to let Mrs. Eliot take a cent more than half the money.

Alex found her anger at Liz's deception giving way to disgust. The audacity, the *greed*! And it seemed to have come from nowhere. Up until Michael Eliot's funeral Liz had been a different person— good-natured, kind, generous.

"I can't excuse what she's done, Mrs. Eliot," Alex found herself saying. "But I know Liz was very upset when your husband died. I think she . . ."

She couldn't go any further. Looking at Mrs. Eliot sitting at the other end of the kitchen table, an untouched mug of coffee in front of her, Alex felt truly sorry for her. For the first time. Being there in that big empty house, she felt the burden of her loneliness. Liz would recover from her lover's death. She would build a new life on new foundations. But Margaret Eliot would always be a part of the family she had lost.

"Michael was very easy to love," said Mrs. Eliot. "Very lovable. It was a talent he had. I guess he got tired of not using it." She straightened up, as if coming out of a dream. "I'm sorry about what happened. I didn't mean to get anyone fired. I don't know why, exactly, but I felt so certain . . . I could imagine you with Michael, I don't know why. When I saw you . . . for the first time it seemed possible that he might love someone else. Probable, even. I saw you and I thought: *of course*."

Alex looked down at her hands, surprised at Mrs. Eliot's candor. Perhaps she no longer had a use for silence or secrecy. Perhaps, since her husband's death, she had come to see what they had cost her.

"You weren't the only one," Alex said. "Half the people at ProvLife got the same idea. I sometimes think they *wanted* it to be true. They wanted something to talk about in their lunch hours."

"I'll call Walter Neumann this afternoon."

Alex smiled with relief. "Thank you."

"I'm surprised at him, though, in a way," Mrs. Eliot went on. "He seemed so certain that you'd never had anything to do with my husband. Now he seems ready to believe the worst."

"I guess my phone number was enough to convince him."

Mrs. Eliot nodded slowly.

But it was true, Alex thought: for a lawyer, Neumann seemed strangely ready to jump to conclusions. She remembered seeing him at the Ocean State Savings Bank—him seeing her too, most likely. Maybe he'd found out what she was doing there, had decided he didn't like it. If so, Mrs. Eliot's protestations might not do her any good.

"He was also very certain," Mrs. Eliot said, "that this money Michael was supposed to have did not exist. He said it was just bait for a confidence trick."

"No. Liz—whatever you might think of her—is not a criminal. She's not trying to con you. She's convinced that the money is there, and she told me she had the bank statements to prove it. That doesn't mean she's entitled to any of it, but I don't think she's just making it up."

"So you're saying . . . In effect, you're saying I should accept the deal? Is that why you're here? To get me to—?"

Alex raised her hand. She knew it might look that way, as if she and Liz were really working together.

"No, absolutely not. I don't think you should touch that money."

"But you can't see any other way for me to get hold of it, right?"

"I . . . I don't know. What I'm saying is, it's probably dirty money. I mean"—she winced at her own tactlessness—"I mean, until you know how your husband came by it, I think you should be very cautious."

Mrs. Eliot got up and went over to the sink. She poured her coffee down the drain and watched it disappear.

"Mrs. Eliot—"

"It's all right," she said. "I've wondered about it too. A month ago I wouldn't have believed it possible that Michael was involved in anything bad. But there was so much I didn't know about him. I haven't got it in me to be surprised anymore. Somewhere along the line he became a stranger."

She stared out into the yard. Outside, the cloud cover was starting to break up. For a few moments the tall firs were touched with gold. But on the horizon a band of layered darkness marked the approach of another front.

"If the money's not clean, I don't want anything to do with it," she said quietly and turned the faucet. "It took my marriage and my family. It won't take me."

"It'll come out in time," Alex said. "Then maybe it will be yours, at least a part of it."

Mrs. Eliot didn't seem to hear her.

"I was going to take a walk," she said, shutting off the water.

They walked up Angell Street towards Blackstone Park. The sidewalks were empty and behind the white picket fences the snow lay undisturbed. It was as if the East Side was in hibernation, sleeping until the winter was over.

"You may not believe it," said Mrs. Eliot, looking out from under the peak of a fur-lined cap, "but ProvLife used to be a good place to work. I remember, when Michael got the job in Treasury, we were really excited."

"It still has a good reputation," Alex said. "It's not glamorous exactly, but it's certainly been around a long time."

Mrs. Eliot shook her head.

"No, I didn't mean that. I meant . . . We used to have friends there. People used to socialize. It's funny, but when the company was struggling—I'm talking about seven or eight years ago, when they had all those big losses—it was better. Everyone was pulling together, that's what it felt like. They were trying to save something worth saving. Michael really enjoyed his work back then. I think he felt that what he was doing made a difference. But when the profits began to recover, it all changed."

Alex frowned.

"But I got the impression . . . I always thought people, I mean senior ProvLife people, were pretty close. Like a community, almost. I mean, at your husband's funeral they all turned out, didn't they?"

"Yes, they all turned out. Officially they were grief-stricken."

"And they even carried—"

Alex didn't pursue the point, afraid she had already been insensitive.

"His coffin, yes, I know," said Mrs. Eliot. "They insisted, and I didn't have the strength to refuse them. Yes, they care about appearances at ProvLife, that's for sure. This is a small town. People talk. Anything out of the ordinary draws attention. Michael was always saying that. But, you know, since the funeral I haven't seen or heard from any of them, except for Walter Neumann. And that was business. Does that sound like a community to you?"

Alex shook her head. At the funeral she had certainly been taken in by appearances. She remembered thinking what a touching gesture it was, Neumann and Brady bearing Michael Eliot away on his last journey. She remembered feeling good about ProvLife because of it.

"Mind you, that was different in the early days, too," Mrs. Eliot went on. "It's a difficult thing to explain, but after the company turned around people started . . . *watching* each other. ProvLife people, I mean. That's what it felt like. And all these petty jealousies started coming out. I couldn't stand it. So I just turned away. I cut back on the company dinner parties and tried to make a life of my own. But it wasn't easy. Up here everyone knows everyone."

Mrs. Eliot looked at Alex and smiled. "Sure you want your old job back?"

Alex thrust her hands deep into her coat pockets. They were passing Aldrich-Dexter Field. A troop of college kids in cinnamon-colored track suits were doing star jumps on the other side of the fence. Some of them wore mittens and old-fashioned woolly hats with tassels on the top. Alex felt a stab of envy. At that moment she would have given anything to be back in college again. Life had been so much simpler then, and so much more promising.

"I don't have any choice," she said. "I'm nearly halfway to qualifying. Without a job I'll never make it. Besides, I need the money right now."

"You said you were an actuary?"

"That's right."

"Michael was always very rude about actuaries, you know. I think maybe that's why he never really got on with Randal White."

"I didn't—I never knew—"

"Oh yes. I wouldn't say they were always at each other's throats, but there was no love lost."

Alex remembered Hartman's story about the row in the elevator. She wondered what had gone on once the doors had closed.

"Michael used to say that actuarial work was for people who found accountancy too exciting."

Alex smiled and shrugged. "That's what everyone says."

"Then why are you doing it, if you don't mind me asking?"

Alex thought back. Her decision seemed so long ago that it was hard to remember a time when it hadn't been made. Yet it was only four years.

"I don't know. I thought about other things, but in the end I decided it was best to go for something—safe, I guess. Stable. Something I knew I could do. So I got an internship at a life company during one of the summer vacations, and the next thing I knew I was filling out the applications. I guess it wasn't such a safe bet, after all."

"And what were the other things?"

"I'm sorry?"

"The other things you thought about for a career."

"Oh. Well . . . there was this guy at MIT. Another mathematician."

"A boyfriend?"

Mrs. Eliot was watching her. Her curiosity seemed genuine. Alex's instinct was to evade the question, but after the other woman had been so open, it didn't seem fair.

"At the time, yes. His name was Robert Halliday. Robby. He was very big on computer software and artificial intelligence. He and some friends of his wanted to set up their own company. You know, right away. They wanted me to join them. I decided it was too risky."

"And what happened?"

"To the company? It went bust a few months ago. Frankly, I'm surprised it lasted as long as it did. And now Rob wants to try all over again. This time it's all about predicting medium-term weather patterns—the software required to set that up. He's just one of life's optimists."

"Doesn't that kind of thing interest you?"

"Sure, but . . . the kind of modeling it requires is unbelievably complex. I mean, natural phenomena? There are so many variables, so many assumptions you have to make about cause and effect. You're always looking for patterns in chaos. Trying to predict the unpredictable. It's certainly more challenging than designing a life policy, but it has to be one hell of a way to try and make a living."

Mrs. Eliot smiled.

"You sound more than just interested. Maybe you should take a closer look."

Alex shook her head. "The company'll just end up the same way as the last one. I know it will."

"Do you? How?"

"The odds of a new software venture surviving these days are pretty small. Something like twenty percent the last time I checked."

"What have the odds got to do with it? I don't understand. If it's something you really want to do . . ." Mrs. Eliot shrugged, and walked on a little. "Well, what do I know? I'm sure you've got your life all worked out."

"I thought I did," said Alex. "Until today."

"Well, that's exactly what I mean." Mrs. Eliot smiled, struggling to explain. "You see, you never know what's going to happen. Let me tell you something, Alexandra. I think . . . I see now that my husband really wanted to get out of here. Out of ProvLife, out of Providence. I think he'd wanted it for years. But he never said anything. He never did anything about it because I think he felt there was no point. I think he felt he was living his life to a plan: work, retirement, then the payoff. And the plan had to be carried out because . . . because the *odds* were worse for him outside it. Do you understand what I mean?"

Alex nodded. "I think so."

"Then one day he found out he had five years to live. He was diagnosed with Huntington's chorea. Do you know what that is?"

"Yes, I—" Alex came to a halt, staring. This was something even Liz didn't know.

"Now, that wasn't part of the *damned plan*, was it?" Mrs. Eliot's eyes were suddenly bright with tears.

"No. I guess not. I'm . . . so sorry."

They were walking again.

"People get into the habit of thinking their life is predictable, but then something like that comes along out of the blue and all your plans are worth nothing. You see what I'm saying?"

Alex nodded. "Yes, I do. Except of course . . ."

"Of course what?"

"Well, it's just that in this particular case the disease *is* predictable. I mean, Huntington's chorea is an inherited disease. If one parent has it, the chances are fifty percent that a child will have it. So you should know if it's worth doing a genetic test."

Mrs. Eliot frowned.

"I'm sorry," said Alex. "I'm just being pedantic. I didn't mean to—"

"Michael's parents never had the disease. I'm sure of that."

"Well . . . if one of them died young you wouldn't necessarily know if they were carrying the gene or not."

Mrs. Eliot shook her head.

"Michael's father was eighty-five when he died, and his mother was—oh, no more than two or three years younger than that. They lived long, healthy lives."

Alex didn't know what to say. She knew Huntington's chorea well. Among diseases that strike in later life, it had been among the first to be genetically identified. As such it had become an early focus for the genetic testing debate within the insurance industry. But the genetic rules were unbreakable: only people who carried the bad gene could pass it on, and if you carried the bad gene, you would sooner or later succumb to the disease. One of Michael Eliot's parents *had* to have been a carrier.

"If you don't mind me asking, Mrs. Eliot—"

"Margaret, please."

"Margaret. Who did your husband's tests?"

"I'm not sure. I only found out about it from Harold Tate. You see"—she looked down at the ground—"Michael himself never told me."

Below them the treetops of Blackstone Park stood out stark and black against the snowy ground. Alex felt again Mrs. Eliot's loneliness, the sense of abandonment.

"I don't think I know Harold Tate," Alex said after a moment.

"Really. I thought you'd met. He was sitting next to you during the funeral service. The man with the beard."

Alex stopped in her tracks.

"What's the matter?" Mrs. Eliot half turned, waiting for her to come on.

"Harold Tate, you said?"

"Yes. He went to college with Michael. He lives down the coast in Wickford."

"And works for a company called Medan, right?"

"Yes. So you do know him?"

"No," said Alex, "not exactly. The thing is . . ." Her mind was racing, trying to fit it all together: the printouts, the warning, Michael Eliot's diagnosis. "Medan. They're a diagnostics outfit, aren't they? Genetic tests must be just the kind of thing they do, right?"

Mrs. Eliot looked at the ground, thinking.

"Yes. Yes, I believe they do."

"Well then, isn't it likely that they did your husband's test?"

"Perhaps, but"—she shrugged—"Harold said quite plainly that he didn't. Michael went to him because Harold knew something about the disease. I have to say, now you mention it, it does seem odd."

And then Alex had it. It all made sense. The printouts Michael Eliot had kept hidden in his briefcase were the results of the genetic test he had taken at Medan, the test that told him he had Huntington's disease. What else could they be? But the results were wrong. Michael Eliot did *not* have the disease after all, and Harold Tate had realized it. That was why he wanted the printouts back: they proved his negligence, or that of Medan. Apparently what Mr. Moon Boots was scared of was a lawsuit. A good lawyer could probably make out a case that Michael Eliot's distress at the bad news was a contributory factor in his fatal accident.

Alex turned to Mrs. Eliot.

"What is it?" she said.

Alex considered the exhausted, melancholy face, and decided Margaret Eliot had suffered enough. It wouldn't be fair to say anything until she was sure of the facts.

"No," she said. "It's nothing."

29

Alex's first thought was to go and see Benedict Ellis and find out if he'd had any luck with the Medan printouts. But back in the car, peering forward through lightly falling snow, it came to her that Tate's misdiagnosis—if that's what it turned out to be—had nothing to do with her problems at work. Her priority had to be to talk to Randal White. Mrs. Eliot was going to call Neumann, and that might or might not help her situation, but White had to be a more powerful ally. She had to be sure he was on her side. That evening she called him on her mobile, and asked if he would mind her coming down. He had just arrived back from the airport.

"What does it . . . What is it you want to talk about?" he asked.

"It's a little complicated," said Alex. "In fact, it's real complicated. I need to see you."

An hour later she was clearing the outskirts of town, snow drifting into her headlights in thick flurries. Conditions were bad and getting worse. At a gas station north of Newport, standing under flickering neon, she seriously considered turning back. And it wasn't just the snow. The relentless cold of the past few weeks seemed to condense inside her as black despair, and she had a nagging desire to call Mark. She needed to hear his voice—wanted to match his voice with the one trapped inside her head. Staring at the spinning numbers on the gas pump, she had to tell herself—literally, her chapped lips mouthing the words—that it was all over between them. Finished. She paid for the gas and pulled back onto the road. Putting on the radio to get the weather, she found herself in the midst of some somber, spiky jazz. It was like the soundtrack of what was going on inside her head. She dabbed at her eyes as she watched the lights of oncoming traffic move across her snow-caked windshield.

Then she was crossing the Sakonnet Bridge, gripping the wheel and trying to believe in a road she could no longer see.

Randal White was the only senior ProvLife officer—certainly the only executive board member—to live outside Providence. There was a small company apartment in the middle of town that he sometimes made use of, but for the most part he drove home every evening, all the way out to his family home outside Newport. Of course, in other parts of the country a thirty-mile commute would not be considered long, but in Rhode Island—in Providence especially—it verged on the downright eccentric.

Newport looked closed down for the winter. Traffic stood at intersections as if the drivers had lost heart and were uncertain about continuing. Alex saw a car abandoned in a drift. Then another. She drove slowly, nudging and coaxing the Camry's failing heater. The freezing salt air of Narragansett Bay squeezed in through the doors, dropping the temperature until she could see her breath.

She went straight past it the first time. Then, realizing her mistake, she pulled around on the empty road. An old tin mailbox sticking up through a drift brought her to a halt. She rolled down the window and checked the painted number. White's house lay a hundred yards up a track, flanked on either side by low stone walls. Squinting through the swirling snow, Alex saw a car in the driveway and a light on downstairs, but no sign of smoke from the chimney. Easing the car down the drive, she took in the weather-beaten brick facade. For some reason she had always imagined White living in a clapboard structure, something sunny and yellow like the Roosevelt house which was a little farther down the road in the Fort Adams State Park. But there was nothing sunny about White's house. Long and low, its back was turned to the east wind like an old barge turned over on its side. Alex got out of the car and stumbled towards the front door, pulling her overcoat against her. The driveway looked as if it hadn't been dug out for several days, and the tire tracks leading to White's Lincoln were almost obliterated.

She stood for a moment, stamping her freezing feet and searching for a doorbell. Then she rapped on the door with gloved knuckles. There was no sound from inside. She stood back and looked up at the windows.

Nothing stirred. Icicles hung down from a piece of broken guttering. She knocked again, thumping hard this time. Then the door was pulled sharply open and she was looking at White's anxious face.

"Alex. Come on in."

With a rush of embarrassment, Alex realized that she had entirely forgotten about his illness. She had been so caught up in thoughts of her job, it had completely gone out of her head. White took a couple of steps back from the threshold.

"Mind the step here. It's all iced up."

She stepped into the house.

"Hi, I . . ." She was unwinding her scarf, clumsily unbuttoning, awkward under his gaze. "I heard about your—about the forum. Are you feeling—?"

"Oh fine, fine. I was just about to . . ." He pushed a hand into his ruffled hair and thought for a moment. "Maybe you could help me start the fire."

They walked through the entrance hall into a spacious sitting room, White switching on lights as he went. Alex took in paneled walls lined with books and watercolor landscapes, a sideboard crammed with framed photographs, crystal decanters on another. The smell of a dead fire tainted the cold air and big, damp-looking logs smoldered in the grate.

"With this wind and snow . . . In the end I gave up," said White. "I don't know what it is, but the darned thing doesn't seem to draw."

The sound of a shrill whistling from somewhere deep in the house brought him upright. He clapped a hand to his forehead.

"Ah yes. That was it. I was making tea. Would you like some?"

"Sure. Yes, please."

When he came back into the room five minutes later, balancing cups and a teapot on a tray, Alex was holding a sheet of the *Wall Street Journal* across the fireplace, and the logs were beginning to hiss and crackle.

"Can you believe this weather?" she said.

White put the tray down on a coffee table.

"And there's worse to come. They said so on TV."

They made themselves comfortable in front of the reviving flames, and Alex asked for details of what had happened at the conference. White said he'd had no warning that anything was wrong. He poured Earl Grey into china cups, smiling at her through the rising steam.

"I just—I don't know what it was," he said. "I think all the upset recently, all the stress, it must have taken its toll. One minute I was standing up, facing the crowd of insurers and politicians, and the next— Terrible timing, really. And not just for the NIH." He gave her a look. "Friday's the big day, you know. We're going to elect the new Pope."

"Yes, I heard."

He sighed. "Still, it isn't the end of the world, I guess."

Alex wondered what he meant exactly. Was he saying his absence wouldn't affect the outcome, or that the outcome didn't really matter? She was about to ask, but White spoke first.

"Alex, I wanted to say—I hope I didn't disturb you last night with that—that call."

Alex was shaking her head and smiling.

"Not at all, not at all. It was nice to here from you. Surprising, but nice."

"I felt stupid afterwards. Rambling on about France. And then giving you that dumb job to do, it was—"

"I didn't get a chance to finish it, I'm afraid. You see . . ."

She didn't know how to continue. A wave of self-pity washed through her and she had to look down at her cup.

"Alex, what is it?"

She took a breath and decided that the only way into it was head first.

"Walter Neumann fired me this morning."

She looked up. An expression of total disbelief had come over White's face. He put his cup down with a sharp click, slowly shaking his head.

"Called me into his office," said Alex, "told me I was guilty of gross misconduct."

"But—what misconduct?"

And Alex told him the whole story, about Liz and Eliot and the money. She told him about her visit to Margaret Eliot, about how understanding she had been.

"She promised to talk to Neumann, but I'm not sure that's going to change anything." Alex put down her cup. "Neumann told me that he was representing the position of the board. That's—that isn't true, is it?"

White shrugged.

"Well, I'm on the board, and this is the first I've heard of it."

Alex let out a breath. It was as she had thought. Neumann had, for some obscure reason of his own, decided to go out on a limb. But why?

"It seems that your friend rather let you down," he said after a moment.

"I'm afraid so."

He looked away, nodding, then shaking his head again, obviously finding it hard to take in.

"Of course I'll—I'll deal with it. Don't worry. I'm sure I can"—he avoided her eye, looking instead towards the fire—"swing it."

It was what Alex had wanted to hear, but somehow she didn't find it as reassuring as she'd thought she would.

"So Eliot had—some kind of liaison with his PA," White said after a moment. "It all seems so—tawdry."

He turned to look at her, waiting, Alex felt, for her reaction.

"These things—well, these things happen, I 'spose," she said.

He nodded and sipped his tea.

"Poor Margaret," he said. "She really deserved a lot better. She wasn't the only one, you know."

"Pardon me?"

"Liz, I mean. There were others. In some ways Eliot was a very— well, *bad* individual. There's no other word for that kind of selfishness."

Alex nodded. She felt awkward talking about Eliot's sexual peccadilloes. She didn't want to recall the incident at the party.

"I have to confess I was more, I don't know, *amazed* to hear about the money," she said.

"Yes," said White, still nodding. "But—surely it can't be true."

"He was planning to go to Europe with Liz," said Alex emphatically. "He had money in Switzerland. Millions of dollars."

"Go to—" White raised his shoulders and let them drop. "But *how*? Where did the money come from? Where *could* it have come from?"

"I don't know. I've been thinking about it—for weeks, actually. I think—"

She looked into White's face and realized that her idea was going to sound absurd. He was used to dealing in verifiable facts, not crazy speculation.

"What?" said White.

She groped for a way to begin. "Have you ever noticed anything? About Neumann or Brady? Or McCormick? Something—not right?"

White stood up and walked over to the fire, where he stared down at the burning logs. A nerve twitched in the corner of his mouth. "Noticed anything?"

"Yes. I mean, I don't really know how to put it, but—I thought I was just imagining things, but this afternoon—Margaret Eliot said—"

"What? What did she say?"

"She told me that after ProvLife's turnaround, people in the company, the senior executives anyway, started to watch each other. Suddenly the mood in the company changed."

White looked at her, a puzzled smile on his face.

"I'm sorry, Alex, I'm not sure I follow you."

Alex shook her head. "No, it's me. I'm trying to express something without—I'm skirting around the heart of it, the core of it."

"Well don't." He came back to his chair and sat down, watching her closely. "Just tell me what you're thinking."

Alex put her hands out in front of her as though presenting an object—a box in which all her jumbled impressions were contained.

"Okay. Okay. Logically. Eliot has—*had*—all this money. There's no doubt about that. There are bank statements, proof."

"You've seen them?"

"Well, no, but—"

She looked at White who nodded, encouraging her to go on.

"So there's this—problem. What we have is this multimillionaire who keeps coming in to work." She shrugged as though what came next required no explanation. "He's either nuts or—"

"Embezzling," said White.

"Exactly." Alex smiled, glad to see him reach the same point so quickly. "It's the most likely explanation. Eliot joined Provlife in 'eighty-five, and pretty soon after that the company started to do better. It started to do better, but something changed. At least according to Margaret Eliot. Michael changed. She dates the beginning of their problems from the company's turnaround. As if something poisoned their relationship."

White blinked, thought for a moment.

"Well, I suppose, if he was taking money from the company, you might expect things to be worse rather than better, and as far as their marriage was concerned. I'm sorry, Alex, but this is all a little vague."

Alex shook her head irritably. He was right, of course: it *was* vague.

"Okay, let me stay with the money for a moment," she said. "Where did it come from? Unless everybody in the company is involved in some kind of huge fraud, which isn't likely, somebody at some point would have noticed the missing ten million. Right?"

White shrugged.

"So," Alex went on, "so maybe the money isn't coming out of the company. Maybe it's going *through* the company. Dirty money. Money looking to get into the electronic banking system."

"Laundering," said White.

For a moment Alex thought he was going to laugh. She sat back in her chair.

"Yes," she said, without much conviction.

"I must say, it is a rather . . ."

He scratched at his cheek, his lips drawn into his mouth slightly. Alex saw that she had lost him.

"So you've never—" She started to feel hot. "You've never thought—?"

"Not really, no." White examined the pattern on the sleeve of his sweater. "Walter Neumann and I—well, we've never really hit it off. But he doesn't strike me as the laundering type. And anyway, the money could have come from somewhere else. *If* this money you're talking about really exists. From a rich uncle or the lottery or something like that."

He laughed and poured more tea. Alex found herself smiling with him.

"But this *misunderstanding*," he said, suddenly serious. "It's worrying. The only way I can make any sense of what Neumann has done is to see it as part of some maneuver, some scheme."

"What do you mean?"

"Goebert's departure brought a lot of tensions to the surface. As I'm sure you can imagine. This business with you and—and Eliot, this mistake—the way Walter has taken it, may well be a reflection of that. Neumann knows how much I value you. The plans I have for you. I have made no secret of the fact that you, people like you, are important for ProvLife's future. Who knows with him? It might be some attempt to discredit the department. To discredit me."

Watching White, Alex wondered how much of his illness was related to the behind-the-scenes struggle for control of ProvLife. It was scary to think that she might be part of that struggle, even as a pawn.

"I wouldn't worry about it unduly," he said. "I shall certainly raise the issue with Neumann myself. There can be no question of you losing your position. My brightest star? No question of it."

He smiled again.

"But what if—?" Alex hesitated.

White finished her question. "Neumann gets to be CEO?"

"I'm sorry. I'm sounding incredibly selfish," said Alex, blushing.

"Not at all. It's quite understandable. You're at a crucial stage of your career. It's only natural that you should be concerned about your future. As for that, er, eventuality—should Neumann win, I mean— well, it's not as if it's going to put him above the law. The CEO has to consider the board's opinion."

Alex could see he was getting depressed just thinking about a ProvLife under Neumann. She was beginning to find it pretty depressing herself.

"Do you think—do you think there's a possibility he might win?" she asked.

White thought for a moment.

"Walter's a formidable person," he said, "but I'm not sure he has the *interpersonal* skills one might want to run such a large company. If he did get the job, I'm not sure how long I'd want to stick around. To be honest, I'd rather jump than be pushed. Of course, that wouldn't have to be immediately." He stood up and kicked at the burning logs, raising a shower of sparks, "Don't worry. I'll see you through your associate-ship at ProvLife. If that's what you want."

He invited her to stay for dinner, which they ate in the huge kitchen heated by an old oil-burning stove. He opened a bottle of Montalcino and, sipping from a huge burgundy glass, opening cupboards and drawers, talked about the house and the area around Narragansett Bay. There had been Whites in Newport for more than a century, and they'd owned that very house for three generations. He himself had been raised there and as a boy had sailed every inch of the bay. Alex had never thought of White as anything other than a middle-aged actuary, and the idea of him looking down into the dark waters of the Narragansett as a young man made her smile. Watching him move around among the pots and pans, sipping at the delicious wine, she found herself relaxing, despite her fraught day. He was making boeuf bourguignon, chopping onions and garlic, searing the meat with chunks of pork, and sprinkling with flour—all with the concentration of a genuine gourmet. He covered the meat with wine, and dropped in a bundle of fresh herbs he had tied together with a piece of string. The kitchen filled with a delicious smell.

When they finally sat down to the table, Alex found that she was ravenously hungry. White watched her eat, a smile on his pale face. When the meat was gone, she tore off chunks of the bread and dabbed at the rich winy sauce. She was in the process of cleaning the last from her plate when she caught the look on his face. She became abruptly aware of the huge chunk of bread between her fingers. She put it back down, shaking her head and laughing.

"God, I'm so sorry. I just haven't eaten anything so good for—well, *ever*. Where did you learn to cook like that?"

"My wife, Harriet, she—she used to like to cook." He looked across at the stove and smiled. "She loved making bread. There were always wonderful smells here."

Alex didn't know much about Harriet White, only that she'd died sometime in the early 1980s. Among the framed photographs in the sitting room had been one of a woman relaxing in an outdoor cafe with her face turned to the sun. That was probably her. She looked pretty in an uncomplicated, outdoor way, and had wavy brown hair tied back with a scarf. Alex wondered why they'd had no children, and what it was that had killed her, but sensed a great sadness there that she ought not to intrude upon.

"I love food, always have," White said after a moment. "It's a real pleasure to cook for someone else."

"So how do you stay in such great shape? I mean, eating this kind of stuff. If I ate this all the time, I'd be—"

She puffed out her cheeks and laughed, trying to keep things light.

White smiled and looked down at his own trim physique.

"I'm just lucky that way," he said. "It must be a genetic thing."

As if to confirm the point, he pulled the dish of meat towards him and set about spooning some more.

"Would you like some?"

Alex stared over the rim of her glass.

"No, thanks. I'm about ready to burst."

White served himself in silence and ate quietly, his eyes fixed on his plate. It was only now that Alex realized that he too had finished his first serving, must in fact have finished it before she did. She watched him eat for a moment. He ate steadily with no sign of diminished appetite. She remembered what Heymann had said about the smoked salmon at Goebert's party. Eventually he looked up and smiled.

"I was just thinking," he said.

"What?"

"About what you said. About how Eliot was planning to run away. Do you know that for a fact?"

"Liz had the plane tickets. One way. To Paris. Then Nice. He was going to run."

White shook his head.

"Can you imagine it, the fuss? People would've thought he'd been kidnapped or murdered or something. Or joined some religious cult. We'd have had to notify the police. The police would've notified Interpol. And even if the truth came out, I don't think Margaret Eliot would've taken it lying down. She'd have had Pinkerton's onto him. Lawsuits for desertion, infidelity, God knows what. She'd have wanted to know what he was living on, for a start, because she'd be entitled to half. I mean, don't you think"—he looked up at Alex, appealing to her—"a man without—*ties*, without responsibilities, a man who *refuses* to recognize that they even exist, is just—just—"

Alex held her breath, waiting for White to pass sentence upon his one-time colleague, wanting to hear what he really thought Michael Eliot was. But instead White grew suddenly self-conscious, as if aware of how close he'd come to speaking ill of the dead.

"Do you mind if we—?" He gestured towards the kitchen door.

glass. I've—I've something rather special you might want

White piled logs onto the fire and stood watching them catch. The damp wood hissed furiously on the glowing embers and then burst into flame. Outside the wind was picking up. A Chopin nocturne was playing. Alex sunk back into cushions on the couch and sipped at the most extraordinary wine she had ever tasted.

"Francis Bacon," said White, "the painter, not the philosopher, once made a stew with a bottle of this."

He was still staring down at the flames.

"Do you know Bacon?" he said, and without waiting for an answer: "Irish. But very English too. Those terrible twisted faces. The studies for a crucifixion. He never worked drunk, or rarely, but he was often drunk when he wasn't working. Anyway, one time he was very drunk and making stew. He wanted to liven it up with a little red wine. So he opened a bottle and poured it in. This stew—it came out wonderfully well. Delicious. Best stew he'd ever made. Afterwards he realized that the bottle he'd used was a Château Pétrus 1958. This was back in the sixties when Pétrus was selling for a couple of hundred dollars a bottle. Bacon said it was a bit of a shame to lose the wine that way, but that the stew *had* been very good."

He turned and looked at Alex, a smile on his face. Alex held up her glass.

"To Bacon," she said.

White raised his own glass.

"Yes. Champagne for real friends, and real pain for sham friends." He saw Alex's quizzical expression. "It was one of Bacon's favorite toasts."

Alex watched him drink, aware, through the haze of intoxication, that he was also a little drunk and quite unlike himself, quite unlike the man she thought she knew. She sipped at the Bordeaux and lay back in the cushions.

She woke up to the sound of a softly played piano. Beethoven now. The fire had burned low. She could hear White moving around in the kitchen. She walked across to the fireplace where a row of silver cups stood on the mantel, trophies for yacht races he had competed in years ago. On an old oak dresser she saw a photograph of a much younger White at the wheel of a boat. He looked vibrantly happy, his hair pushed back from his tanned brow in salty-looking curls. Next to it was the picture of the woman sitting at the table. Alex realized from the background—an old stone wall, green shutters—that it was probably somewhere in Europe.

"Harriet," said White.

He was standing next to her, holding a glass of water. Alex turned and smiled.

"I'm so sorry, Randal. I think the wine finished me off. I haven't been sleeping too well."

He held her eyes for a moment, and then looked away towards the fire. "Me neither," he said simply.

"When was the picture taken?" said Alex.

He picked up the wooden frame. "Seventy-two," he said. "We were over in France on vacation."

"At your convent?"

He shook his head, smiling.

"No. No, that came later. After Harriet died. No, that year we climbed Mont Blanc. Walked, really. It's more of a strenuous hike."

Alex nodded, and took the glass from his hand. "Do you mind?"

"No, I brought it in for you. I thought you might be a little dry from all the wine."

Alex looked at him over the rim of the glass.

"I have to be getting back," she said.

He stared at the dying fire for a moment.

"Don't be silly," he said. "There's plenty of room here. There's a spare room. It won't take a minute to make the bed. It's over the kitchen at the back, so it's always warm."

She went and sat down in an armchair next to the fire.

"What is it?" said White.

Alex looked up. "What?"

"I don't know. You look—are you still worrying about Neumann?"

"No, I—Randal. I just think you should know. About Michael Eliot. I know what he was planning was—well, unfair. But, you see, he thought he had Huntington's disease."

White stared at her, his mouth slightly open. But Alex wanted him to know. He and Eliot may never have been friends, but the thought that White's dislike should continue, even deepen now, when the man was dead, disturbed her.

"I think that was why he was planning to leave Providence," she went on. "He wanted to spend the money before he started to—before the disease took hold."

White looked stunned. "How do you know this?"

"There's a company called Medan. Down in Warwick. They do diagnostic tests using DNA. I think they did a test for Michael. Do you remember that man at the funeral? The man with the beard? I asked you about him and you said you didn't know him?"

White slowly nodded.

"Yes. Yes, I remember."

"He works at Medan. I've seen him go in there."

"You—?"

"Yes. I went down there. It's"—she looked at her clasped hands, pulled them apart—"kind of complicated, but that guy with the beard—Tate, his name is—he came up to me in the street and told me to give him some papers he thought I had. Only I didn't have them. Liz did. She got them from Michael. They were printouts of some kind. I think they were the results of the test. In fact, I think they show malpractice or negligence on the part of Medan."

"Malpractice?"

"One parent has to have the disease. That's how Huntington's works. Neither of Eliot's parents showed any sign of being sick. Eliot couldn't have had the gene defect."

White pressed his hand to his mouth for a moment.

"This—this is all—"

"Terrible. I know. But it helps explain why Michael wanted to run. He thought he was going to die. The test was his death sentence. And not just death. Neurodegeneration. Loss of control. Eventually dementia. Somehow Eliot got hold of a printout from Medan. Tate wanted it back."

"Yes," said White musingly, "yes, I suppose he would."

Alex relaxed. She felt better having shared with White what she knew.

"When this man approached me in the street, he seemed more scared than I was," she said, recalling the moment. "That's the only thing I don't understand. As if there were other parties involved. People he feared."

"Maybe people at Medan," said White.

"Maybe."

"And did you do as he asked?"

"How do you—?"

"Did you give the printouts back to him?"

"No. I gave them to a scientist friend. He's going to tell me exactly what they say."

White looked at her intently.

"Why didn't you tell me about this before?" he said.

Alex frowned and then shrugged.

"Well, I—I didn't know what to do. I still haven't really worked out what to do. And anyway, it's not your concern. I didn't want to bother you."

White nodded.

"Yes—yes, I see. Still, I— And you haven't seen this man Tate again?"

"No. He's disappeared."

"Have you talked to the police?"

"No. Do you think I should?"

White shrugged.

"If this friend confirms my suspicions," said Alex, "I think I should go back to Margaret Eliot. After all, she's the injured party."

"Yes," said White. "Yes, I suppose she is."

30

The snowplows were busy on the roads the next morning, but it still took Alex two hours to get back to Providence. There was nothing for her to do now but wait: wait for Mrs. Eliot to call Walter Neumann, wait for Randal White to do whatever he could, then wait for the phone to ring welcoming her back to her job. She told herself that she could use the time to study for her exams. It was a heaven-sent opportunity to get back on track, maybe even get ahead of the game for once. But as she turned the corner into Phillips Street, and pictured herself creeping past Mrs. Connelly's door, she knew she was kidding herself. How could you concentrate on studying for exams when you didn't know if you would ever actually take them? You couldn't carry on as if nothing had happened when your life was hanging by a thread. Because that was the truth of the situation. The odds were not on her side.

She had thought about it on the long drive up: unless Randal White took over as chairman, unless Neumann was stopped, the chances had to be that she would *not* get her job back. A retreat like that would make Neumann look bad—look weak, just when he was most anxious to look strong. Neumann had taken it upon himself to fire an actuary without consulting the head of the actuarial department. It was something a chief executive might do, but nobody else. If he backed down over the matter, wouldn't it look like he was renouncing his claim? The more Alex thought about it, the more pessimistic she became. Randal White might be on her side, but was that enough? With Neumann in charge, his days at the company would most likely be numbered. *I'd rather jump than be pushed,* that was what he'd said.

Alex made it up to her apartment and set about making herself some coffee. Still in her coat, she turned on the TV and flipped past commercials, talk shows, and children's programs until she finally found herself looking at a weather report on the local cable station. A man with sideburns and a chalk blue jacket was making circular motions with his arms, talking about air masses and occluded fronts. For a moment Alex found herself thinking about Robert Halliday and his latest software venture: computers that could foretell the nature of the seasons. Maybe if she'd taken up his invitation, things would have turned out better. She wouldn't have had to worry about her exams, or about ProvLife, or even about Mark. She'd have been away and clear— just as Michael Eliot had planned to be. But who was she kidding? With all the debts and the bills, she would never have had the courage. Like the actuary in the joke, she was too busy looking at her shoes.

A tapping at the door brought her back to the present. She knew at once who it was.

"Hello, Mrs. Connelly," she said, pulling open the door.

Maeve Connelly offered her a faint yellow smile. She was out of the housecoat this time and into a large pastel pink jogging suit. She handed Alex a postcard with a picture of Brown reproduced in faded inks.

"This came under the door," she said.

Alex flipped it over and read. It was from Ben.

When she finally got through to him at the Arnold Biological Laboratory it sounded like he was standing in the middle of a factory floor. The whine of machinery cut through his reedy voice, and now and again there was a sound of rattling glass.

"I can't believe it," he said. "I think some *moron* sat on my centrifuge." He sounded like he was in the middle of a tantrum. "Can you believe that? All my solutions are coming out looking like vegetable soup."

"Oh," said Alex. "I guess that's bad."

"Yeah, bad."

Benny let out a gruff laugh, suddenly self-conscious. Alex could imagine him blushing at the other end of the line.

"See, see what I want is separation," he explained. "The solutions should end up looking like—well, like consommé. What I've got here is minestrone. And do you hear that noise?"

"I can't hear much else."

"Oh. Sorry. How's that?"

The whining noise faded out.

"Better, thanks. I got your note."

"Yeah, yeah. Right, yeah. How are you, anyhow?"

Alex didn't feel like going into it. "Fine, fine. And you?"

"Oh, great. Apart from my centrifuge." There was a rustling of papers. "Here we go, got 'em right here. Those printouts you gave me? I had Beth Klein take a look at them. I think you met her once, didn't you? Oncologist from Harvard?"

Alex had a faint recollection of a small, softly spoken young woman with a lot of untidy brown hair.

"I think so."

"Anyway, she knew what they were right away. Like I said, it's kind of her field."

Alex found her gaze drifting over to the TV screen. The weather forecast was over now and they were just into the twelve o'clock news. There were pictures of state troopers digging motorists out of snow-drifts and an old woman being evacuated from some remote location by helicopter. Images like that had been on the air for almost two weeks.

"She said they were kind of interesting, actually," Benny was saying. "She wanted to know where you got them."

Alex turned away from the TV. Something in Benny's voice told her he really wanted to know.

"Where I got them? Well, from a friend, kind of. It's really a long story."

"Uh-huh?"

There was a pause on the line. It sounded like Benny wanted her to go on, but Alex wasn't sure she should. According to Harold Tate, the printouts had been stolen, after all.

"I don't really know much about it," she said. "There's some clinical diagnostics company down in Warwick. I think it came from them. What's so interesting, anyway? It's some kind of gene test, right?"

"That's right," said Benny. "Several, in fact. Beth said it was quite a piece of work."

"I'm not sure I understand. What does the test say?"

"Well," Benny said, clearing his throat, "a lot of things. It depends on what you're looking for."

Alex suppressed a sigh. She'd forgotten how pedantic Benny could be when he found himself talking science to a layman like her. It could get very annoying.

"Okay. I'll be specific. Suppose you were running a check on some-one's genes to see if they were going to get Huntington's chorea or not. What would the test say then?"

"Oh, that's easy. Then the tests would say everyone's in the clear."

Alex frowned. "What do you mean, everyone?"

"Well, all the people whose genes have been tested. There are ten different sets of tests here, on ten different individuals. Automated probably. Otherwise why would you need a computer to give you the results?"

"Wait a minute, wait a minute, Benny." Alex pushed a hand through her hair. "You're saying these people, whoever they are, *definitely* do not have Huntington's chorea. None of them?"

"That's right. Remember those tags along the top of each column? HPC1, MCP1B, and all those?"

"Yes."

"Well, one of them refers to the Huntington's gene: HTCH4. And all these people come up negative. The numbers underneath, by the way, they're lumens—that's a measurement of light. When the number's bigger, that means the fluorescence test has shown up positive. And the numbers down the side? They're the different chromosomes where the disease genes are located."

Slowly Alex sat down. This wasn't at all what she'd expected. It didn't fit any of the assumptions she'd made. Why would Michael Eliot steal a whole load of genetic tests belonging to other people, tests that were all negative? What possible value could they have?

"Anyway"—Benny was still talking—"what Beth was interested in was some of these other tags. Like MCP1B. You know what that is?"

"Sorry, Benny, what were you—? You're saying this test is for more than one disease?"

"Sure. Well, for more than one gene *implicated* in disease. Nine, to be exact. You got genes for hereditary prostate cancer, breast and ovarian cancer, cystic fibrosis, Huntington's. All the usual suspects."

There was a brisk snap from the cat flap and Oscar appeared, his fur slick with freshly melted snowflakes. Alex watched him pad noiselessly across the floor and jump up onto the couch.

"Jesus. I had no idea. I thought— But these tests, they all come up negative, right?"

"No, sir."

"No?"

"That's what Beth was curious about. There's one result circled here in red. Remember that?"

"Yes, yes, I do. I thought that had to be the Huntington's thing."

"No." From the other end of the line Alex heard a door close. Benny moved closer to the mouthpiece. "It's a positive result for the presence of the MCP1B gene. MCP1 stands for macrophage chemoattractant protein one. Know what the B stands for?"

"No."

"Bad. It's what we call a polymorphism: a good gene turned bad. People like Beth have been after it for years—on the lookout, anyway. Everyone kind of suspects this gene is out there somewhere in the human genome, but nobody's actually found it yet. At least, that's what we thought. Seems to me this outfit in Warwick have finally tracked it down, whoever they are."

Suddenly Alex understood why Benny had been anxious to get hold of her. Not so much because of what he had to tell her, as what she had to tell him. She'd presented him with evidence of an important medical breakthrough that nobody yet knew about.

"Benny, this bad gene. What does it do exactly? What disease does it—lead to?"

"Well, if the theory's right, it causes macrophages—they're scavenger cells, part of the immune system—to damage major blood vessels. Of course, until we identify the gene responsible, we can't be sure exactly how much more vulnerable it makes people."

"Benny, vulnerable to *what*?"

"Oh. Well, to atheroma, thrombosis, myocardial infarction. Your basic number one killer."

"Number one—? You mean to *heart attacks?*"

"Colloquially speaking, yes."

Alex felt the tension run along her spine. The anomaly she had stumbled across in the Central Records computer, the anomaly that had suddenly vanished, it had involved people who'd died from heart disease. Correlations that didn't stack up. Data that looked artificial— as if someone had just made them up to cover a hole. Was that just coincidence? It had to be, unless Medan and ProvLife were connected. Of course, in one way they were: through Michael Eliot and Harold Tate. But they'd been just a pair of old college friends who'd shared a secret.

"Anyway," Benny said. "I guess Mister AP1005052 oughta go get a checkup and lay off the cholesterol. If this gene's as nasty as some people think, he could go anytime."

"Sorry, Benny. Mr. who did you say?"

"Mr. or Mrs. whoever it is got this number. Every different sheet's got a number here at the top, like a reference number. I reckon the number refers to the person who's been screened. Some kind of ID number. Dunno what the AP stands for, though."

"AP," Alex repeated.

"Yeah. Anxious Person? Acquiescent Participant? Afflicted Patient? Maybe—"

Suddenly it came to her. "Applicant. It stands for Applicant."

"It does?"

Alex shook her head. Why hadn't she remembered before? She had seen labels just like that at PrimeNumber, hundreds of them: they were policy numbers. Every form that was sent out to potential policy-holders had one. And every number carried the temporary prefix AP, to distinguish it from policies that were already up and running.

"So what are they applying for?" Benny asked.

"Life insurance. These must be—I guess these must be people applying for big policies. Several million dollars of coverage, I expect. There's no medical checkup required for ordinary policies, but at the top they're pretty standard. I guess the genetic tests could be part of that, although I don't think we've ever done them at ProvLife. At least not till now."

"Well," said Benny. "Maybe the whole thing's just hypothetical. Like a sort of proposal. Maybe these aren't real tests. Maybe these people don't really exist."

"Maybe not. All the same . . ."

An idea was forming in Alex's mind. If she could find out if the applicants *did* exist, find out who they were, maybe she could find out why Michael Eliot had gone to the trouble of stealing their test results. It was going to be difficult, though.

"Benny, can you give me those AP numbers? It's just possible, I might be able to do some checking."

"Okay, sure."

He read out the ten numbers, Alex taking them down in a notepad she kept by the phone.

"Thanks for everything, Benny," she said when they were done. "If I find anything out, I'll let you know, okay?"

"I'd appreciate it. If it turns out that gene's for real, I think we should be told."

Alex hung up and stood for a moment staring at the TV. Prime-Number downloaded all its data onto the Central Records computer. The computer held complete files on all past and present policy-holders: personal details, credit records, information on claims and payouts, and—now and again, where the amount insured was half a million dollars and up—medical data. The files existed nowhere else. But they were closely guarded, even more closely than the privacy laws demanded. Only SVPs and their superiors had unfettered access—the keys to the kingdom. The question was: did they leave those keys lying around?

Alex picked up the remote and was about to turn off the TV when something on the screen caught her attention. A female reporter in a baggy white parka was talking to the camera. In the street behind her stood fire trucks, an ambulance, its red lights turning, boxy clapboard houses just like the ones on Brighton Street.

"At least one child, a three-year-old, has been taken to Intensive Care," the reporter said, her voice edged with practiced gravity, "and there are as yet unconfirmed reports that a woman's body has been recovered."

The camera panned across the street, picking up another ambulance as it nudged its way through a small crowd, zooming in on the smoking ruins of a house. The pink facade and part of the roof stood intact, clinging to a blackened skeleton of beams and rafters. The sky could be seen through the blown-out windows of the upper stories, and through another, on what was once the first floor, the blackened remains of a child's animal mobile.

Alex knew then for sure: it was Liz Foster's house.

31

No, I know," said Ralph McCormick, nodding vigorously. "I got in an hour ago. There must be about twenty messages on the machine. I didn't mean to—"

On the other end of the line Newton Brady went into a long spiel about all the trouble the company had gone to to get him into the Mann Clinic and how they had expected him to be down there for ten days or at least a week. Of *course* people were concerned.

McCormick massaged his closed eyes.

"I understand that, but, Newt, this program they run there, the treatment—it just makes that unnecessary. I couldn't stay any longer. I'm telling you I feel great."

There was a long pause, and then Newt said some cautionary words about the nature of addiction. McCormick smiled, still massaging his eyes. They obviously thought he had left the program in order to go score some coke. He was, after all, a junky: unworthy of trust.

"No, that's the whole point," he said after a moment. "It's not like— well, you know how I was before. You know how it was the last time. There was always the Demerol, and then, eventually— But this stuff is different. Newt, it actually breaks down the chemical dependency."

Or so the doctors had told him, and he was ready to believe them. To Newt, however, it sounded a little too good to be true. He wanted to know exactly what they were talking about.

"Ibogaine," said McCormick. "It's from some kind of root. Some kind of plant they found in West Africa."

McCormick looked around the room as Newt launched into another monologue. He had been away for only four days, but so much had happened in that time, it seemed much longer. He felt vaguely annoyed that the old newspapers were still on the coffee table, that the house did not reflect the newness he felt inside.

"I know," he said, addressing himself to Newt again, "but I'm telling you, there was no point in staying any longer. I had this— Jeez, I don't know how to describe it. The day before yesterday." He laughed and then checked himself. He didn't want to sound too euphoric, but the relief, his sense of well-being, was making him light-headed. Finally Newt seemed to relax. He wanted to know if McCormick had everything he needed.

"Yeah, there's stuff in the freezer," said McCormick. "I'm starved, as a matter of fact. I was planning on cooking something up."

Newt told McCormick that he wasn't expected back in the office until next week, so he could take a few days off. Then he said good-bye.

For a moment McCormick listened to the silence of the house. This was part of his new self: silence and the sense of slowly unfolding time gave him pleasure. It was as if he had come down off the high wire and could sit back to watch the arena. He smiled at his own thoughts. The answer machine blinked rapidly, retaining its slew of messages. There were calls from Neumann, Brady, White. McCormick wondered how word had got out that he had left the clinic early. Probably one of the nurses had been instructed to give a call. He had been followed all the way to Newark Airport, he was almost sure of that. Nobody trusted him at the company. They thought he was going to do something crazy. Or maybe they thought he was going to try to run.

He ate cannelloni standing under the fluorescent light in the kitchen, the tomato sauce rich and thick in his mouth. It was good, but there just wasn't enough. He needed bread. He pulled a big jar of peanut butter out of the cupboard and broke the seal. He was defrosting a gourmet baguette, staring out at the darkness of the yard and reviewing the past few days, when there was a knock at the front door.

He went through to the hallway. A face loomed against the frosted glass.

"Jesus Christ."

"No, it's his brother, Jerry."

For a moment McCormick didn't recognize him. Then realization dawned.

"Don."

Grant's voice came through the door muffled. "Open the door, Ralph."

"What's—?"

"Your doorbell isn't working. Come on, Ralph, I'm freezing my balls off out here."

McCormick turned the locks and opened up. Grant was wearing a heavy quilted jacket and a hunting cap pulled down almost over his eyes. He looked very unhappy.

"What's the matter?"

"Don't you pick up your messages?"

"Sure, I—"

"You were supposed to call Neumann."

"I was just about to, I—what's the problem?"

Grant walked through to the living room and yanked the drapes together. Then he turned to face McCormick, pulling off his cap.

"He's a little worried about you. Didn't expect to see you back here so soon."

McCormick smiled. "Oh—oh sure. I've just been talking to Brady. Everything's okay."

Grant made a wry mouth. "What's that supposed to mean?"

"Just that—" McCormick came forward, raising his hands. "I had an incredible experience down there."

Grant slumped down in an armchair.

"That's nice," he said. "That's real nice. Incredible experiences are always nice."

"No, but seriously, Donald. I'm serious."

Grant nodded. He still hadn't cracked a smile. McCormick could feel the positive vibes ebbing away just looking at him. He went through to the kitchen where his baguette was still in the microwave. He made coffee.

When he came back into the living room, Grant had taken off his jacket. McCormick handed him coffee.

"You talk to Newton about this?" Grant said.

McCormick smiled. "Well, a little. He doesn't— Nobody believes me."

"Well, you can't exactly blame them," said Grant, looking around the room. "So anyway"—he was losing his thread, obviously distracted—"what happened? You were saying something about the treatment?"

"I was treated with this drug. On day three they gave me a ten-milligram dose. It was incredible. I had insights, Don. Into my life."

Grant bunched his fingers and then pushed his big hands together. He looked very tense.

"It's not unusual, apparently," McCormick went on. "It's one of the effects of the drug. Ibogaine. First—" He pushed a hand into his thin dark hair, remembering. "First I was very calm and relaxed. Then suddenly I started to see images. It was like looking at screens in the cinema. Small and then big. Incredibly detailed pictures. Things from my past. Things from a few days ago. Commercials. I saw grass in a big plain. Just blowing, the wind going across it. I saw a young boy with smooth stones in his hands."

Grant shrugged, a look of disgust on his face.

"So you got high. You could have stayed here to do that. Save the company the plane fare."

"No, no." McCormick shook his head, pacing back and forth. "It wasn't like that. After about eleven hours, the images stopped. These screens, they sort of shrank and disappeared. I came out of it and all I wanted to do was eat. I was hungry. Then I was awake all night long. During the night I had some insights. I understood things about my life that I was doing wrong."

Grant nodded, his hands still linked around his coffee.

"Yesterday I was sleepy all day," said McCormick. "Relaxed and happy. Don, I've never felt like this before."

Grant stood up.

"Great." He moved across to the drapes and peeped out. "So what happens when it wears off?" he said.

He turned and stared at McCormick with hard eyes.

"It won't. The doctors say it won't. It—the Ibogaine, it unravels stuff. Changes the way you are in your head."

Grant nodded as though he'd had enough. "Come on, Ralph. You know you can't kid a kidder."

McCormick backed up a little, shaking his head. "I'm not kidding, Donald. Really. I'm telling you everything's changed for me."

Grant nodded, slower this time, giving McCormick a long evaluative look. He sat down on the couch and swept everything from the coffee table onto the floor, exposing the smeary glass top. Then he took out a little cellophane bag full of white powder.

McCormick gasped.

"Donald—Jesus—Jesus Christ. What are you doing?"

Grant looked surprised. "What—you didn't know? Come on, Ralphy, you think you're the only one likes to have a little fun?"

"No, but—"

McCormick watched Grant sprinkle the cocaine into a little pile, then push it into rows with his credit card. He produced a tiny silver pipe from a pocket in his plaid shirt, then vacuumed up a fat line. He leaned back, dabbing at his nose.

"Oh yeah." He was shaking his head and smiling. "Ralph, if you knew the kind of day I just had, you'd understand exactly how good that feels."

McCormick stared down at him, unable to move or speak. Grant pointed a finger.

"Ralphy, you got that look. Yes you do. You got that hungry look."

"Why'd you come?" said McCormick.

He sat down in an armchair next to the table. The tip of his tongue was tingling.

"Because Walter was worried," said Grant. "Worried about you coming home so soon. Thought you was going to be running around—running around doing your bare-assed thing."

McCormick swallowed.

"That's all finished," he said. "I'm clean now."

"Clean?" said Grant.

He reached across to his jacket and took out a snub-nose thirty-eight. For a moment both of them looked at the gun in his hand.

McCormick shook his head. "What—?" he said.

"Clean?" said Grant again. "You telling me if I looked around this shit-hole of yours, I wouldn't find a stash—a little baggie?"

McCormick just stared at the gun.

"Let's go to the bathroom," said Grant as though the idea had just occurred to him.

When McCormick didn't move, he made an irritable stabbing gesture with the gun.

"I said *move*, goddammit."

They walked up the stairs to the second floor, McCormick walking in front, his hands held up in the air like some hostage in a fifties B movie.

It was crowded in the bathroom. Harsh light bounced off white tile, making McCormick squint.

"Grant, this is—this is silly," he stammered. He knew he was in real trouble, but somehow he couldn't quite take in what was happening to him.

Grant breathed heavily through his nose. In the enclosed space he gave off a bad smell of bourbon and cigarettes.

"Open the cabinet," he said. "Let's see if you got anything hidden in there."

McCormick froze, staring down at the barrel of the gun. Suddenly Grant was against him, pushing him back, using his bulk to flatten him against the wall. Something fell from a shelf. Grant pressed a hard boot down on McCormick's right foot, and leaned all his weight forward. McCormick thought the high, delicate arch was going to split. There was unbelievable pain. Keeping his face close to McCormick's, Grant opened the door of the medicine cabinet and took out an old aspirin bottle.

"Jeez, Ralph," he said, unscrewing the cap with his teeth, "you look all tense and fucked up. Must be the Ibogaine's wearing off already. What the fuck are we going to do?"

McCormick tried to lean away, but Grant had him pinned to the wall. Suddenly Grant pushed back and stood away. He spat the bottle cap into the sink. The pain lanced upward into McCormick's leg. His eyes filled with tears.

"Telling me you're *clean*," said Grant. He held up the bottle. "You're so clean, what's this?"

McCormick shook his head. "I don't know. It's not—"

The bottle was his, but he was sure he'd emptied it. He could see there was a lot of coke. It occurred to him that he hadn't been using as much as he thought.

Grant gave the bottle a little shake.

"Come on, Ralphy, show me how clean you are."

He pressed the gun into his own sternum and pushed his face forward.

"You see, Ralphy, *I'm* clean. I can take a little every now and then. Like today, when I've had a bad day, when things haven't gone the way I wanted. *Then* I can have a little taste. And nobody even knows. You didn't even know. And you know why? Because it makes no difference to me. Because I'm not a poor fucking addict."

McCormick felt the tears start to run down his cheeks.

Suddenly Grant was furious. He cocked the snub-nose and pushed it hard into McCormick's face.

"Don't start your *fuck*ing sniveling. I don't want to see it. You want a taste, go ahead. But don't start fucking weeping."

The air seemed to crackle with rage. Grant held out the bottle. McCormick watched his trembling hand reach out and take it.

32

Brighton Street was a different place. Fire trucks and ambulances stood fender to fender all the way down, colored lights flashing and spinning like a fairground ride's. A jackhammer racket of pumps and generators pounded the air. Long fat hoses trailed through blackened slush. Alex left the Camry a block away and ran back. A thin veil of yellow smoke covered everything, and there was a chemical stink strong enough to taste. The crowd of onlookers had thinned to a dozen or so frozen-looking figures hopping from foot to foot at the far end of the street. There was no sign of the television crew or the reporter in the white parka.

Number seven was a ruin. The fire had started at the back of the building and swept forward and upward, engulfing the upper floors and caving in most of the roof. The whole east-facing wall had collapsed. Alex saw a stove, a refrigerator, an armchair—fabric burned off, metal springs laid bare—perched up on the second floor, open to the sky. In the bathroom next door a sink hung suspended in midair, held only by two copper pipes. Where Liz's apartment had been there was nothing but a heap of charred wreckage.

"Hey, keep back there!"

One of the fire crew was standing in front of her, face smeared with filth, eyes bloodshot. He sounded younger than he looked.

"What—what *happened*? How did this—?"

"Please, lady, behind the rope."

Up above them another fireman was easing his way off the top of a ladder onto the top floor. A section of roof perched precariously above his head, most of the slates hanging loose. A few feet away stood a bed with a pink cover, blackened now with soot, and a dressing table with what looked like a child's soft toy on top of it, still smoldering. Scorched brown wallpaper hanging off an interior wall looked like giant scrolls of parchment.

"I know someone who lives here," Alex told the fireman trying to move her back. "Her name's Liz Foster. She—she lives on the ground floor."

The fireman hesitated.

"Go see that guy over there, okay?"

He pointed across the street to where a police officer was talking to an elderly couple, probably neighbors.

"The woman who was killed," Alex said. "Do you know if it—?"

A sudden shout went up behind her. A cloud of ash and debris came crashing down off the roof, missing the fireman on the top floor by a couple of feet. The whole building looked ready to collapse.

"Please, just get back, okay?"

Alex retreated to the far side of the road. They were still looking for survivors at the top of the house, or bodies, people trapped maybe when the staircase went up. A tangle of twisted metal at the back of the building marked the foot of the fire escape. If that was where the fire had started, it would have been useless to anyone at the front.

"You live here, ma'am?"

The patrolman fixed her with an impatient stare. He had a sandy, sloping moustache and a ruddy face.

"No." Alex tried to stay calm. "It's a friend of mine. She lived on the ground floor. I'm trying to find out if she's okay."

The patrolman turned to the neighbors. "All right, folks, thanks for your help. Better keep clear now." He turned back to Alex. "What's your friend's name?"

"Liz Foster. She's on the ground floor, at the back."

The patrolman shot a glance at the building. Alex knew what he was thinking: there *was* no ground floor at the back, not anymore.

"She work, your friend?" he asked, turning back a couple of pages of a notebook. "Fire started about ten o'clock."

"Not at the moment. They said on the news a woman was—"

The patrolman nodded. "Some old lady on the top floor. Smoke inhalation, looks like. Neighbors here say her name was Samuels."

Alex closed her eyes. It wasn't Liz.

"Thank God."

The patrolman was writing now, the notebook resting on the hood of his squad car, his thick gloved hand making slow, deliberate marks on the paper. Alex had an urge to tell him about Michael Eliot, about the money, about Harold Tate's warning: *You don't know the danger you're in.* But what was the point? Vague accusations of wrongdoing weren't going to carry much weight, especially when leveled against ProvLife executives by a recently dismissed employee. In any case, she still couldn't even say for sure what the wrongdoing was.

"We haven't accounted for everyone yet, I'm afraid," the patrolman said. "Does Miss Foster live alone?"

Alex stared. "You mean, she could still be in there?"

"Not likely. But until we finish checking the place, we can't rule it out. It looks like the fire started at the back of the house. So, she live alone or not?"

"Yes, alone."

"When'd you last see her?"

Alex tried to think.

"It would be—about a fortnight ago, I guess. Look, how long before someone checks back there? She could still be alive."

The policeman held up a hand.

"They'll get to it as quick as they can. Chances are your friend wasn't even in, okay? Just relax."

Alex nodded. "Okay."

"So, any idea where she might have gone? Think she might have left town?"

"It's possible. She has family in Maryland, a sister."

"Okay. What about a boyfriend?"

"Not any—no. Look, do you have any idea how this happened?"

The patrolman shook his head.

"These old buildings. It doesn't take much. All that dry timber goes up in a flash." The radio in his car sputtered into life, but he didn't seem in any hurry to answer it. "One of the guys here says they found an oil heater plugged into a light socket, or what's left of it. My guess is, that'll be what did it."

"An oil heater?"

"Yeah. Your fuse doesn't blow and you've got red-hot wires running right through your house." He pulled open the car door. "And with the state of the wiring in some of these places—"

Alex looked back across the street. Hadn't Liz complained that the landlord never took care of anything? But then again, an oil heater plugged into a light socket? It didn't sound at all like Liz.

"It just seems so dumb," she said.

"Sure," the patrolman said, climbing into the car, "but these things happen all the time. Just ask your friendly insurance company."

Alex was on the interstate heading south towards Edgewood when she realized her mobile phone was ringing. She yanked open the glove compartment and took it out, struggling to press the answer button with one gloved hand.

"Hello?"

A truck slid past her, throwing up slush. The voice at the other end was drowned out.

"Hello?"

"Alex, it's me."

The signal wasn't strong, but Alex knew who it was.

"Liz?"

"Yes."

"Jesus, are you okay? I was afraid—I saw what happened to your house. They told me—"

Then Liz was talking, but the signal kept breaking up. Alex could only make out a few words at a time. She sounded frightened.

"Liz, I can't hear very well. I'm on the interstate. Where are you?"

"I—I left town. I think they were trying to *kill* me."

"Who was? Liz?"

The signal was breaking up again as the road descended into a shallow gully flanked with warehouses and low-rent housing. The outside lane was closed and the traffic was bunching up on the other two.

"Who was trying to kill you?"

"I *told* you. I don't know. I saw them watching the house last night, these guys in a car."

"Okay, just tell me where you are now."

There was a clicking sound. Then the signal cleared.

"I'm in a motel. Some place outside New London."

"New London? What the hell are you doing there?"

"I didn't want to stay in Rhode Island. I wanted to get out of the state. I don't know why, Alex. I saw what they did to the house and I just kept on driving."

Alex hit the brakes as the cars in front pulled up sharply. Her windshield was getting so dirty it was difficult to see out. She turned on the wipers.

"Listen, Liz, they think the fire was an accident." Alex tried to sound calm, tried to sound like she believed it. "I talked to a cop. Someone plugged a heater in where they shouldn't have, and the fuse didn't blow."

"And you think all that was an accident?"

Alex moved over into the slow lane. She felt the front wheels skid as they crossed a band of wet snow.

"I don't know, but apparently—"

"It happens all the time? Come on, Alex. Two weeks ago, you were telling me I had to watch out for myself. Because Michael had been mixed up with some bad people."

Recalling the occasion, Alex was sharply reminded of her own predicament and who had put her there.

"Two weeks ago, Liz, *you* were telling *me* you hadn't been talking to Margaret Eliot. Remember that?"

Liz didn't answer, or if she did, her words were lost behind a crackle of interference.

"Liz?" Alex gave the phone a shake. "Damn!"

A horn sounded behind her. She was drifting between two lanes. She put on her indicator and headed up the ramp on exit sixteen.

"I'm—I'm sorry," said Liz. "I didn't want to involve you. I thought—" Her tone was more defensive than sorry, but then she probably didn't know all the trouble she'd caused. "How did you find out?"

"It's a long story. I'll tell you when I see you. Just don't do it again, okay?"

"No. No, I won't. I think . . . I think we should go to the police. Don't you?" She didn't sound very sure.

"I've thought about it. Somehow I don't think it'll get us very far. Not yet, anyhow."

"But what am I supposed to do? What am I—where am I going to go? I'm scared, Alex." Liz was on the verge of tears. "What if they come after me again? I don't even know who they *are*."

"Just sit tight," Alex said. "Don't tell anyone else where you are, unless you know you can trust them. And whatever you do, don't call anyone at ProvLife, okay?"

"And then what? What happens then?"

"If we can just get a better idea of what Michael was mixed up in, then we *can* go to the police. The thing is, I need evidence."

"Evidence of what, though?"

"Leave that with me. I'm working on it."

"What are you gonna do, Alex? Tell me."

Alex slowed as the road turned downhill along the western side of Roger Williams Park. Mark's house lay a mile away on the other side. Through the scattering of trees she could see the white expanse of Cunliff's Lake, its fringes gray where the ice and snow were beginning to melt.

"Just stay by the phone," she said.

33

Alex pulled in fifty yards down the road from Blimpies and switched off the engine. It was half past ten. Outside, light rain was slowly turning to sleet, making halos around the old cast-iron streetlights. Soon it would be below freezing again and she wasn't dressed for it. She'd gone home and changed into her best work clothes that afternoon—had even put on makeup—all for the bene-fit of the security man who sat behind reception from eight o'clock onwards. She wanted it to look like she'd just stepped out for a bite to eat and was working late. But a knee-length skirt, matching jacket, and silk blouse did not amount to her outfit of choice for an icy February night.

A trickle of people were coming out by the front entrance, hugging themselves against the rising wind. Alex recognized a couple of women from the marketing department and one of the senior managers in Underwriting. She had a good idea what it was that had kept them so late. The company's planned expansion into health insurance had everyone under pressure, and lights were still burning on several floors. Alex waited another twenty minutes, but nobody else appeared.

She picked up her mobile and dialed Mark's number in Treasury. The line rang twice and then she was listening to Mark's recorded voice: *I'm unable to take your call at this time, but please leave a mes-sage after the tone and I'll get back to you as soon as possible.* It was a

message she'd heard many times, but somehow Mark sounded different. In the past she had always been faintly amused at his cold, no-time-
to-waste tone, because she'd felt sure it was an act. She knew the real
Mark Ferulli, the one who used to chase her around the house wearing
nothing but a chef's apron, the one who liked to watch the Cartoon
Network in bed on Saturday mornings. But she wondered now if that
had been the real Mark Ferulli after all. It was three days now since
their last, disastrous encounter, and still he had made no attempt to
contact her. How was that possible after all the time they'd spent together? She wondered whether she had been deluding herself all
along, whether the truth was just the way it seemed: that Mark had
changed the way everything had changed when Michael Eliot died.

Sitting in the darkness, staring up at the rows of dimly lit windows,
she had to fight a sense of bewilderment and despair. A week ago she
had belonged here, been a part of it. The Financial District. The Prov-
Life building. The company. The department. It had all been there for
her. In spite of everything that had happened, she could not shut out a
pang of nostalgia for the way things had been, for the safety and the
certainty—for the belonging. Yet, she reminded herself, the certainties
had proved *un*certain. She was on the outside, more firmly now than
ever. And that meant taking chances. The first chance was that the security man behind the front desk wouldn't know who she was.

Donald Grant was all alone up on the third floor. His team of claims
investigators weren't the kind to spend more time in the office than
they had to, and the rest of the department were administrators,
strictly nine-to-five. And that was just how it was meant to be: everybody carrying out their own carefully defined functions, doing what
they were told to do and nothing more—especially where the bigger
policies were concerned. All claims over $500,000 were passed directly
to Dean Mitchell, the senior executive VP in charge of the department.
If he said investigate, they investigated. And if he said settle, they settled. Where the regular staff were concerned, initiative was not encouraged, and that made Grant's job a whole lot easier. He could concentrate
on the senior management themselves, although lately maintaining dis-
cipline had proved quite an onerous task even there.

Grant was confident that nobody had seen him leaving McCormick's
house. It had been dark and any stray footprints he might have left

would have been washed away by the rain. But that was no reason to get sloppy. He'd sleep a lot better knowing his alibi was in the bag. And that meant doing a little data manipulation on the ProvLife computer. Once he was done, the record would show that he had been in the building all afternoon. Other witnesses would testify to his presence at meetings. The entry log was a detail, but a potentially decisive one. In his experience, people still had a remarkable faith in the objectivity and truthfulness of computers and the information they held. By comparison, the word of a human being was always suspect.

The ProvLife building was equipped with a standard security system. Employees were issued individually programmed sonic-readable cards, gray plastic tags that could be clipped to a lapel or carried inside a pocket. Sensors beside the main entrance, and at the entrance to each department, read the cards and sent the information to a computer. The door would open only if the computer found that the holder of the card was entitled to enter the area in question at the time in question. The files of each individual could be manipulated, so that employees would be allowed access to some floors and not others, and on certain dates and times and not others. In the same way, the computer logged the arrival and departure of staff through the front door.

But, as with all other areas of the ProvLife computer system, this log could be altered, provided you knew how to do it. At ProvLife nothing was ever written in stone, except of course for the rules.

Grant undid his top button and began tapping at the computer keyboard. His head was still buzzing from the line he'd snorted, but otherwise he felt lucid, sharp. In a few seconds his screen was displaying the same information as the terminal in reception: a list of code numbers, names, and times. The file was still active because the day still had an hour to run. At the bottom of the screen a yellow cursor winked expectantly. He would have to copy the file over, alter the data using a utilities program, and then copy it back. It was a tedious job, but he had done it before.

He sighed and stretched. He had earned a few days off, a long weekend in the sun somewhere maybe, a little time with Vera and the kids. But that would have to wait. The last thing he could afford to do right now was leave town. Life went on as normal. Every day was an average day. That was the way it had to be.

The data on the screen shifted as a new entry appeared on the bottom line. It was three minutes to eleven, and according to the sensors Mark Ferulli had just entered the building through the main door. This was fine except for one thing: Mark Ferulli was in New York.

Alex hadn't felt good about letting herself into Mark's house, but she couldn't think of any other way. And in any case, it didn't really feel like trespass. She had spent so much time there, had left so many traces of herself there, that she felt almost entitled—at least to one last look. She was afraid after what had happened that Mark might have changed the locks, but it was clear he hadn't had time for that. Everything was just as it had been on Sunday night. Even the groceries lay where she'd left them on the kitchen table, the spring onions now shriveled and yellowing. After their row, judging from the cardboard box in the trash can, Mark had picked up the phone and ordered himself a pizza. Alex didn't spend long in the house. There was a chance someone had seen her, and besides, it made her sad.

Whenever he went away, Mark left his ProvLife entry card inside a little Mexican pot by the kitchen phone. The truth was, he often forgot it even when he went to work, and had to be buzzed in by the receptionists. Alex had found it there as she'd hoped. If nothing went wrong, she would return it the next morning. That way Mark would never know it had been gone. Only the computer that monitored the entry system at the office would record the fact that it had been used, and nobody ever took any notice of that.

The security guard was leaning back in his chair, chewing on a Snickers bar and reading a copy of the *National Enquirer*. He was younger than the others, with a round shiny face and a seam of angry-looking blemishes around his collar. He looked up at Alex as she held the gray plastic card against the sensor panel, and watched her as she came striding towards the elevators.

"I don't know if I'm working late or starting early," she called out, giving him an ironic smile. "Can you believe this?"

The guard smiled back, taking in Alex's slender figure, and the soft jiggle of her breasts. He wanted to say something in reply, something witty, but his mouth was full of Snickers.

"Them's the breaks," he managed to mumble through a mush of peanuts and nougat.

Alex pushed one of the call buttons and stood for a moment, rock-

ing up and down on her heels. The guard knew he'd seen her around
before. He knew she worked up on the seventh floor because he'd
seen her come out of there once, but he didn't remember her name.
He waited for her to disappear into one of the elevators and then
glanced at the computer screen on the corner of the desk. Apparently
it was Ferulli. The name struck him as odd: she certainly didn't look
Italian.

Alex could feel her heart thumping as the elevator started its climb.
The numbers over the door seemed to take forever to change, and
more than once she felt certain the car was about to stop, that somebody else was going to get in. If it was someone who knew her, knew
what had happened, she was in trouble. They would doubtless smile at
her, say nothing, and then, as soon as they were out of sight, call Security. When the car finally stopped at the eighth floor her forehead was
moist with perspiration.

She took a deep breath and peered out into the landing. In a corner
recessed lamps lit an ugly brass statuette of Atlas with the world on his
shoulders. It was a symbol ProvLife had used back in the forties and
long since abandoned. Alex listened for footsteps, for voices, but the
only sound was a faint hum from the air conditioning units on the roof.

She stepped out onto the polished stone floor and tiptoed towards
the entrance to Treasury. Through the glass panels she could see a
couple of swivel chairs, a big rubber plant, a year planner on the wall.
Dim neon light was coming from somewhere around the corner, but
most of the room was in darkness. She swiped the card. The locks
clicked back.

Inside there was a familiar office smell of chipboard and warm plastic, mixed with traces of stale perfume. The desks stood in rows, like a
small trading room, each one equipped with a computer terminal—in
some cases two. Some screens still displayed columns of market data:
prices, rates, spreads, electronic glimpses of a vast financial traffic that
was as opaque as it was unceasing. The pale blue and yellow digits cast
a faint light across the ceiling. In one corner a fax machine beeped
and grunted, slowly disgorging a long transmission. In the darkness the
room seemed bigger.

Mark's desk was still in the same place, but a wide space had been
cleared around it and wooden partition frames put up on two sides.

Apparently the new head of Treasury was going to have a corner office built around him—one which, unlike his predecessor's, afforded a view across the whole floor. Alex wondered if Mark wasn't trying to make a point, let everybody know he was in charge now and would be watching them. Or was it simply that he didn't want Eliot's old office? Maybe the dead man's shoes were pinching a little.

She stepped through the empty door frame and sat down. She had just switched on the angle-poise desk lamp, pulling it down so that the bulb was just a few inches from the surface of the desk, when the phone rang.

Grant heard the voicemail message begin and hung up. If Ferulli was in the building, what was he doing there? What was it that had dragged him back from New York so suddenly? What was it that couldn't wait until morning? Grant sat for a few moments staring at the name on the screen. Ferulli. The brand-new SVP. New and untested. He'd only been at the company a few years. Arrogant, ambitious, a bit of a chip on his shoulder, he'd certainly seemed a safer bet than Drew Coghill. But how well did anyone know him? Brady thought he could be trusted, but there was too much at stake to leave it at that. Besides, Grant wasn't in the trusting business.

He cleared his screen and took the elevator down to the ground floor. As soon as the security guard saw him, he put down the *National Enquirer* and hurriedly brushed the chocolate crumbs off his lap.

"Evening there, Mr. Grant," he said. "Workin' late?"

Grant planted a hand on the top of the reception desk. Under his cold blue stare the guard felt an impulse to hide the magazine, as if it were something dirty.

"You see Mr. Ferulli come in here?"

"Ferulli? Er—" The guard glanced at his computer screen. "Oh yeah, yeah. Just a couple of minutes ago. That is, you mean—"

"Was he alone?"

The guard looked puzzled. "Who?"

A look of disgust crossed Grant's face.

"Who the fuck are we talking about? Ferulli."

"The lady?"

"I'm talking about *Mark Ferulli*. Thirty-five. Italian. Head of Treasury. Am I going too fast for you?"

The guard looked at the screen again, as if hoping it might help him out.

"I haven't— This Ferulli was a woman. For sure."

Grant took his hand off the desk.

"A woman?"

"Yes, sir. I seen her before, though. I mean, I know she works here."

"You know she works here but you don't know her name?"

The guard could feel himself blush. "Well, I— There's gotta be two hundred people in this—"

"*Where* does she work? What department?"

"I, er—seventh floor. Yuh, seventh floor."

"She's an actuary?"

"Could be. I'm—"

Grant was already headed back towards the elevators. The guard got to his feet.

"Is there a problem?"

Grant didn't answer.

"You want I should come with you?"

Grant turned, holding back the elevator door.

"No. Stay here. If you see that woman, stop her. Think you can manage that?"

There were parts of the Central Records computer Alex knew like the back of her hand, and parts she had never entered in her life. The system in large part reflected the organization of the company, being divided into subsections corresponding to the various departments, with certain key data being held centrally under separate headings. In Alex's experience, you could access the files in your own subsection quite freely, but when it came to other people's, there were restrictions. The company guarded its competitive secrets as jealously as it did the privacy of its policyholders. Unfettered access was not available unless you had the necessary seniority—or the necessary password.

The different subsections were laid out in alphabetical order on the opening screen. Actuarial Services, the part Alex knew best, was at the very top. But for once it was not statistical data she was after. She wanted to turn numbers into names, addresses, *people*: the people whose genetic destiny had been uncovered at Medan, the people whose test results Michael Eliot had gone to all the trouble of stealing. If they were indeed life insurance applicants, then their personal details would be on the system. If she could find the details, then she could find the people, talk to them. There would be no more hiding behind columns of numbers. If she could just do that, she felt certain that the truth would finally unravel.

Alex took out the notepad in which she had taken down the applicants' policy numbers. Then she moved the cursor down the screen until the words CENTRAL RECORDS were highlighted, and pressed Return. A new set of options appeared:

CENTRAL RECORDS DATA
1. Policy files—pre-1990
2. Policy files—1990–present
3. Policy files—all active policies
4. Statistical data
5. Other options

Alex had been this far before. Statistical data on ProvLife policies was the raw material of her work, and was in any case available to all departments. But this time she chose the second option. More than two years at ProvLife and this was the first time she had ever thought of looking up an actual ProvLife customer! It had never occurred to her before, but it was almost bizarre the way everybody was so compartmentalized.

The list of options disappeared and was replaced by just two words in the middle of the screen: ENTER PASSWORD.

Mark had liked her suggestion at Hemenway's. *Celebrates your Italian heritage and all the money you're going to make.* She'd felt sure he would use it. But she'd been sure of a lot of things back then. She took a deep breath and typed in the four characters L-I-R-A.

The computer seemed to take a few moments to think over its response. Then a message she had never seen before came up:

ACCESS DENIED
AUTHORIZATION REQUIRED

"Damn!"

Her voice was loud in the empty office. Alex looked back towards the door, afraid someone might have heard. As she listened she became aware of a faint mechanical hum—the air conditioning again probably, or was it one of the elevators? Hurriedly she returned to the main options menu. It was possible she had the right password, but that it wasn't enough to get her into the policy files. Mark might be an SVP, but his work in Treasury didn't bring him into contact with ProvLife's actual policyholders any more than hers did. His only concern was their money. Maybe ProvLife's need-to-know policy on computer data was even stricter than she realized. In which case there was still something she could check. She reached into her jacket pocket and pulled out her dog-eared Fleet Bank checkbook. The numbers were still written on the back.

Eliot's attaché case hadn't just contained the genetic test results; it had also contained a list of bank accounts held at the East Side branch of the Ocean State Savings Bank. Apparently ProvLife had made payments to the accounts in settlement of successful claims. They were routine payments, Mark had told her, for routine amounts. But that couldn't be. Routine amounts were paid out by Claims, not by Treasury. Besides, if this had been regular business, why would Michael Eliot want to take a record of it to Europe? There had to be *something* special about it. If she could get the names of the account holders, maybe she could find out what it was.

From the opening menu Alex selected the last option: TREASURY OPERATIONS. This time she was asked for a password immediately. Again Alex typed in the four-letter code L-I-R-A. The cursor froze for a second and then Alex was suddenly looking at another list.

TREASURY OPERATIONS DATA
1. LT holdings current
2. LT holdings historical
3. ST & cash positions
4. Transactions record
5. Disbursements ledger
6. Operational projections

She was in. Alex surveyed the options, unsure at first which one to choose. Cash positions, operational projections—everything looked so normal it was hard to believe that anything as exotic as a crime could lie hidden among them. A month earlier she would have found the idea absurd. Like the data she worked with, it was all too sensible, too *dry* to conceal any genuine surprises. The everyday workings of an everyday life insurance company. Yet she knew that couldn't be all. Michael Eliot's death had given her a glimpse beyond ProvLife's numbers, into the lives of ProvLife's people. And a feeling stronger than reason told her that something was wrong.

She forced herself to focus on the present. What she needed were records of ProvLife's major payouts. If they were anywhere, they would be on the disbursements ledger. She moved the cursor onto the fifth option and pressed Enter.

It took a few seconds for the computer to load up the appropriate accounting software, then the data. At last Alex found herself staring at the ledger itself: dates, sums of money, sort codes, account numbers, policy numbers, *and names*. The payments were listed in reverse chronological order. At the very top was an E. A. Daniels who had, one week earlier, been wired the sum of $600,000. But judging from the sort code, he did not bank at Ocean State.

Then Alex saw what she needed: an option at the top of the screen that read SEARCH. She selected it and entered the sort code of the East Side branch she had visited. Immediately the cursor highlighted a payment made at the end of November to one S. D. Bradley. Alex checked the account number against Eliot's list: 75 71252. She searched again and found another payment made three days earlier, this time to a P. A. Trybowski. The account number was also on the list. Alex began writing down the details on her notepad. It was just as Mark had told her, except—

Alex stopped writing. The money wasn't right. Mr. or Mrs. Trybowski hadn't been paid a routine amount, as Mark had said. They hadn't been paid $100,000 or $150,000, the value of an average policy. They had been paid *one million dollars*. Alex hit the search option again. A J. E. Playfer had received $1.2 million, M. J. C. Falkner $750,000, A. M. Moruzzi $1.5 million. These were major payments—not unique perhaps, but of a size that the treasury department alone was meant to handle. Why had Mark told her otherwise? Had he actually checked the payments as she'd asked? Alex brought her hand to her forehead. *He had lied.* He'd just wanted her to drop the whole thing. *I guess you can forget about your money laundering idea.* And when she'd spotted the inconsistency in what he said—the fact that routine payments were made via Claims, not Treasury—he'd become defensive, then angry. She felt sick.

"You son of a bitch."

He'd wanted her to trust him and support him, but was he ready to trust her? No. No further, anyway, than Michael Eliot had trusted his wife. It was an apt analogy, a picture of her future as it might have been. From secrecy to lies, and from lies to betrayal. In Eliot's case the progression had taken years; in Mark's it was already half complete.

She picked up the pen again. In all, the six Ocean State accounts had received a total of just over six million dollars, all in the space of a single calendar month. But what had become of it then? If this was the source of Eliot's fortune, how had he managed to take it? Could she establish that there was even a link? She remembered the night she had first heard about Eliot's ten million, her own disbelief, Liz's certainty: *Money in, bonds purchased, bonds sold. Everything's here. Some of these transactions are only a few weeks old.* The statements were the one piece of evidence Alex had never seen for herself. She picked up the phone.

She didn't notice, as she was dialing the number, that the faint mechanical hum of the elevator had stopped.

Grant brought his face close to the glass, trying to cut out the reflected light of the landing. The open-plan office on the other side lay in semidarkness, the rows of desks and chairs empty. Somewhere around the corner a desk lamp was on, throwing a broad shadow high up against the wall. If there was somebody in there, they were keeping very quiet.

He felt suddenly weary. Someone had borrowed Ferulli's tag. So what? It wouldn't be the first time. Maybe he was letting himself get a little paranoid. The way things had been lately, it'd be understandable. He'd tell the security jerk in reception to search the building. And after that he'd tell him he was fired.

He was about to head back to the elevator when the shadow on the wall moved.

Sandra Betridge let out a shriek as Grant came through the doors.

From the way his hand was hidden under his jacket, it looked like he was about to draw a gun.

"What—what's the—?"

He stopped in his tracks and looked around. Just one junior actuary, working late at her desk. He let his hands drop to his sides.

"Did you just come in here, a few minutes ago?" he asked.

Sandra blinked. "Excuse me?"

Grant managed to check his anger, but there was a precision in the way he spoke that was aggressive.

"I said, did you just come in here? From the street?"

Sandra wasn't sure she was obliged to answer. She wasn't absolutely sure who Grant was, although she knew he was something to do with Claims. On the other hand, he had to be more senior than she was.

"I've been here since eight-thirty this morning," she said, compromising on a haughty tone of voice. "I've got exams coming up."

Grant thought for a moment.

"What other—ladies do you have on this floor?"

Sandra frowned. It came into her head that maybe in some weird way Grant was trying to hit on her, a lone female late at night. She tried to be chatty, buy a little time.

"Well—well, there's—um, Janice Aitken, Randal White's PA. Sue Kaufman. And me. And Alex Tynan, of course, except—I'm not sure she counts anymore. Apparently she's been fired for some kind of misconduct thing."

Liz sounded like she'd been sleeping. Her voice was weak and croaky and it took her a moment to realize who she was talking to.

"Alex? Where are you?"

"In the office."

Liz groaned. "God, you're working late."

Alex still hadn't told her about her dismissal, and now was certainly not the time.

"Listen, Liz, have you still got those bank statements?" she whispered. "Michael's, the Swiss ones."

There was a rustle of bedclothes.

"Yes. Why?"

"They didn't go up in the fire?"

"I had them with me. I always have them with me, as a matter of fact."

"Good. I need you to give me some details. Right now."

Liz hesitated. Suddenly she wasn't so sleepy anymore.

"Why? I thought you said—"

"Liz, I can't explain now," Alex hissed. "Just get them in front of you, okay?"

"All right," Liz said. "What do you want to know?"

"Have you got them?"

There was a noise of something being knocked over. Liz cursed. A few seconds later she was back on the line.

"Yes."

"Okay. I just need to know if Michael received any money in November last year. Can you check that?"

"November, November." Liz sighed, her breath loud against the mouthpiece. "Let me—"

"Liz, *come on.*"

"Yes. Yes, he did. One, two, three . . . Looks like six payments into the main account."

Six. Six bank accounts at Ocean State, six payouts from ProvLife, six deposits in Eliot's offshore account. And all in the same month. At last Eliot's paperwork was starting to add up.

"The amounts, Liz. Dates and amounts."

"Okay. The first was November fifth. That's eighty thousand dollars."

Alex checked the ledger. The first of ProvLife's payouts had been November second, to a T. Sanderson, for $800,000—ten times as much. Alex sighed in despair. It was a very poor match: three days out on the time and ten times out on the amount.

"The next deposit was November tenth," Liz went on. "One hundred and fifty thousand dollars."

Alex scrolled up the ledger. A. M. Moruzzi had received $1.5 million from ProvLife four days earlier. Alex checked the calendar on the corner of the desk: that was three *working* days earlier. And exactly ten times the amount again.

"Keep going, Liz," Alex said, "keep going."

"Okay, then there's . . . seventy-five thousand dollars in on November sixteenth."

There it was again: three working days earlier, ProvLife had paid an M. J. C. Falkner the sum of $750,000.

"Jesus Christ, he was taking ten percent."

"What? What's it all about, Alex?"

"I don't know, I don't know yet, but . . . Give me another—no. No, let me guess. Let's see, okay: November eighteenth, an amount of one hundred and twenty thousand dollars."

For a moment there was silence on the line.

"That's—that's right. How did you know?"

"Because ProvLife paid somebody exactly ten times that amount three working days earlier, somebody called J. E. Playfer."

"I don't understand. Who's J. E. Playfer?"

"Someone with an account at the East Side branch of the Ocean State Savings Bank."

"But who *are* they?"

Alex frowned at the screen. Eliot had gathered all the evidence together. It was almost as if he'd *wanted* someone to piece together the truth someday. Yet every time she found an answer, she was confronted with more questions, questions that got harder and harder. Who were these successful claimants? Why did they all bank at the same branch of Ocean State? And why were they prepared to let Michael Eliot have ten percent of what ProvLife gave them?

"I need to see the policies," Alex said at last. "I need to check them out. And I need to talk to the people who got the money. All these numbers just go around in circles."

"All the policy data should be on the computer," said Liz. "They completed the transfers a while back."

"I know, but I've already tried that. I can't get access. I don't have the password. I don't suppose you—"

"Me? You must be kidding. I never got past the word processor."

"Damn. There are no addresses here. These people could be anywhere." Alex sighed. "I guess I could start with the phone book."

"What about the old paper records?" Liz said.

"The ones in the basement?"

"If these people took out their policies a few years back, their files should still be down there. Mind you, last thing I remember the old records were being shipped out to Iron Mountain. If that's where they are, you can forget about it."

* * *

Grant took the stairs to the ninth floor. He should have checked there first. Ferulli's pass led to Ferulli's office. It wouldn't get you anywhere else except into the conference rooms on the first floor. The guard's stupidity was infectious. He wasn't thinking clearly anymore. It had been a very long day.

On the last flight he reached into his jacket for the revolver. It wasn't normally something he'd let anyone see in the office. It might get people to thinking, and that kind of thinking wasn't helpful. But it was after eleven o'clock and there was an intruder in the building, and he was the head of Investigations, after all. As he reached the landing he noticed that one of the elevators was working. The numbers over the buttons were changing: three, two, one. It was probably the Betridge woman going home. She'd looked pretty spooked.

The doors unlocked with a solid clunk. Silently Grant stepped inside. Everything was dark except the rows of screens, the columns of numbers stark and bright. Otherwise nothing.

He hit the light switches with the flat of his hand. Strip lights flickered to life. Nobody.

He stepped through the wooden frame into what would soon be Ferulli's office. There was no sign of disturbance, no sign that anyone had been there. Grant went over to the desk. There was a faint smell of perfume or shampoo—clean, flowery. He reached forward and touched the top of the computer. It was warm.

The elevator doors closed and there was darkness. It was hot, the air thick with the stink of diesel from the boilers. Alex edged along the wall, feeling for a switch, her foot snagging against sheets of loose cardboard strewn across the floor. She wished Mac were there. She had a feeling he would have helped her if he could, at least shown her where to look.

She hit the switch by accident. A single neon strip cast a film of light over the filthy passageway. A few yards away opaque plastic sheeting covered the entrance to the main storage area. She read a sign: DANGER—ASBESTOS HAZARD.

Alex had forgotten about the asbestos. She didn't know exactly how hazardous it was, only that asbestos and mesothelioma claims had cost

the insurance industry billions of dollars over the years. She had studied the data, but even now she had no idea what level of exposure was
actually dangerous. She had seen the men going in and out of the
building in overalls and face masks.

She yanked back a strip of silver duct tape and squeezed through a
gap in the plastic. On the other side there were rows of tall metal
shelves, the highest accessible via ladders like an old-fashioned library.
More plastic sheeting had been taped over sections of the ceiling,
masking the profusion of pipes and cables. Where the work was going
on, the plastic hung down like curtains at the side of a stage.

Alex walked slowly down the first aisle, a handkerchief clamped over
her nose and mouth. Tiny particles of dust turned in the air, lit from the
passageway behind her. Each set of shelves had a letter of the alphabet
attached to it. Along the left-hand wall the letters ran A to C, on the
right from D back to F. But the shelves were all empty, except for a few
discarded cardboard folders and scraps of loose paper. It looked like
she was too late. The clear-out job had been done. What had Mac told
her a few days earlier? She pictured him standing there by the elevator,
holding a stack of boxes. He'd been whistling something, something
that made her think of Dustin Hoffman in a red sports car.

God bless you please, Mrs. Robinson.

That was it: Robinson. That was as far as they'd got. Alex followed
the letter around to the next aisle: G to J and K to M. Still the shelves
stood empty. She moved to the third aisle. There, next to the emergency exit, partly covered by a dirty white tarpaulin, lay stack after stack
of black cardboard files, ready for removal.

Above the elevator the indicator read B for basement. Grant hesitated, his finger poised over the call button. What would anyone be doing in the basement at eleven o'clock? There was nothing down there
but the heating system, office supplies, and asbestos.

And the old records.

Alex knelt down and opened up the nearest file. It contained a thick
bundle of papers, subdivided into many smaller folders, each one tied
up with red ribbon. Alex pulled out a folder, holding the contents towards the pale light. It was a life policy, maybe twenty years old, in the
name of someone called Taylor. Mac had been hard at work: they'd got

through R and S and now they were onto T. In a day or two they would be finished.

"God damn you, Mac."

Alex pulled the notebook from her pocket and checked the names of the Ocean State account holders. There was a Playfer, a Bradley, a Falkner. It was too late for all of those. Their records were gone. There was a Moruzzi and . . . a Trybowski. Alex moved over to the next stack. She wasn't sure when they'd stopped keeping paper records altogether. If Mr. Trybowski had died just a year or two after insuring his life, then the policy might exist only on the Central Records computer. As she searched she couldn't help picturing him. He would have to be dead now, of course, but how had he died? Who *was* he? A wealthy man, presumably, to have insured his life for a million dollars. He'd probably lived on the East Side—perhaps no more than a few blocks from the Goeberts or the Eliots. Could that have been the connection? Were all these people Eliot's friends?

She pulled open another folder. The name on the policy was Truscott. She threw it aside and dug out another two. Truswell, Truuvert. And then she was looking at it: a policy taken out ten years ago by Frederick P. Trybowski of 14 Claremont Avenue, Mount Pleasant, Providence. The beneficiary, one Patricia A. Trybowski, *née* Lorrimer, was his wife.

Grant was still on the last flight of steps when he heard the sound. Someone was moving around in the old storage area.

He crept along the passage and gently lifted the plastic sheeting at the end. There was a thump, then a metallic rattle. A cold draft moved against his face. He flipped the safety catch off the revolver and eased himself towards the source of the sound. It was dark, but through the lines of shelves he thought he could make out a big white tarpaulin, something moving behind it.

He thought about shooting. The sound wouldn't carry very far. And there would be plenty of time to clean up. But there was still the idiot security guard to think of. He might come down to investigate, and that could make things difficult. If it came to that, he would have to find some other way. Something more . . . probable.

The shelves came to an end. Grant raised the revolver and stepped out into the light.

"Ms. Tynan!"

There was no answer, only another thump as the emergency exit door blew open and hit the stack of files. Papers from a loose folder caught the wind and were flipped over onto the ground. Grant looked out across the parking lot. Through the wire-mesh fence he saw headlamps light up, a car pull out into the road. A couple of seconds later it was gone.

PART FIVE

THE POLICY

34

Number 14 Claremont Avenue was a stucco-fronted house with plenty of what realtors called character. Not a palace, but an acceptable three-bedroomed slice of the American Dream—for someone in middle management. And that was the problem: people in middle management didn't insure their lives for a million dollars. Alex estimated that Frederick Trybowski would have had to be paying premiums of around twelve hundred dollars a month—fifteen thousand a year—which didn't leave much out of a salary of—what? Fifty thousand? Sixty?

She sat behind the wheel of the Camry outside number 20, trying to get up the courage to go knock on the door. That was the plan: go up to the door, say that she was from Providence Life—she'd show her old pass if there were any questions—then explain that there had been a software problem at head office which made it necessary to check records of past disbursements. As plans went, it was a little flimsy, risky even. ProvLife had paid Patricia Trybowski a million dollars. And then she'd turned around and given ten percent of it to Michael Eliot. Other recipients had done the same. Why was that? What exactly had Michael Eliot done for them?

After she had gotten back from the office, she had all but passed out from exhaustion, had barely mustered the strength to undress. But then she had slept badly, waking up again and again, each time sticky with sweat even though her room was glacial. When Oscar had jumped up onto her feet at five o'clock, she'd almost leapt out of bed—her heart hammering, her hair clinging to her neck—and she'd had no idea why. It was as if her sleeping mind had closed like a trap. It had to have been a nightmare. Why else would she have been so stirred up? But all that was left to her was a sense of danger and indefinable *badness*. Something was happening. It touched people's lives and changed them. It had changed Michael Eliot, it had changed Liz Foster, it had changed Mark Ferulli too. Maybe, in ways she didn't know, it was even changing her.

She stared unseeing now as rain slowly blurred the street. She still could not quite believe that Mark had deliberately lied to her. But her attempts to justify his deceit—it had been a misunderstanding, he had misread the data, he had been too busy to really look—all this had given way before the simple fact of his behavior. He had been so anxious to stop her questioning, and had then sought to pacify her with a stupid lie. She couldn't help feeling now that their breakup was also tainted by . . . whatever was poisoning people. He was part of it all, he had to be.

She thought back to the way he had taken over from Michael Eliot. She remembered his smiling face as they sat in Hemenway's eating seafood. He had been so smug, so sure of himself. As if he knew what the outcome would be before any discussion was initiated. . . .

Another thought came to her. She gripped the wheel of the Camry, trying to follow it. Not a thought exactly, not a thought in the sense of an idea, it was more like a bizarre link, an echo. It involved the banker—what was his name?—Mullins, the man from Ocean State. She had a clear picture of his face at the party, how he had stood watching Goebert say his farewell, his left hand stroking his chin, the Patek Philippe no longer on his plump hairy wrist. When she had spoken to him next to the buffet she had been struck by the sight of this expensive gold watch peeping out from under his Kmart suit and his Kmart shirt cuff. It had seemed odd: a twenty-thousand-dollar watch—at least twenty thousand—on a guy wearing clothes worth maybe two hundred dollars, and *old* clothes at that. At the end of the evening he was no longer wearing it. Why? Then there was Mark and his BMW—not a Porsche, okay, not a Mercedes roadster, but a car retailing at over fifty thousand dollars, fifty thousand dollars he didn't have. Of course there were plenty of ways of financing such a purchase, but if he had chosen one of those ways, why had he then given the car back? A Patek Philippe, then no Patek Philippe, a shiny new convertible and then no shiny new convertible. And then there was Eliot, a man living in a house worth—what? two hundred thousand? A multimillionaire who dies putting up shelves in the den.

"Why?"

The sound of her voice brought her back to the street and the rain. And here she was, sitting outside the house of a ProvLife widow, a woman with plenty of money—though not quite as much as she was due—who chose nevertheless to live in a house worth . . .

Alex shook her head. The numbers were starting to drive her crazy. They just didn't add up.

The street was still. Snow had been shoveled off the sidewalks and pushed into gritty piles at the bottom of the driveways. The rain was beginning to cut gullies in the piles.

She had to ring the doorbell twice. Finally there was a sound of bolts being shot back and a gruff curse.

"Yeah, what do you want?" Bloodshot eyes peered at her from behind a door chain.

Alex did her best to smile and look professional.

"Mrs. Trybowski, my name—"

"Hold it right there."

"Pardon me?"

"I'm not Mrs. Trybowski," said the eyes.

Alex let out a sigh of relief. She was only talking to the help.

"Oh, excuse me. Is Mrs. Trybowski in?"

"I don't know, you'd have to go knock on her door."

Alex stepped back, looking up and down the street. Had she mistaken the number?

The door opened all the way, revealing a hard-faced woman who was in the process of knotting the cord of a pink housecoat around what must once have been her waist. She didn't look like the help.

"I'm sorry," said Alex, "I thought—"

"Yeah, well, the Trybowskis did live here. Moved out a couple of years ago."

"Oh, I see."

"It was a repossession."

The woman gave a satisfied nod as Alex's mouth dropped open.

"Could you tell me—" Alex struggled to regain her composure. "Can you tell me where I could find her?"

"I'd be glad to. And while you're up there"—the woman leaned out of sight for a moment and then reappeared holding a stack of magazines and envelopes—"you can tell her to get the mail straightened out. I'm damned if I'm going to keep forwarding it."

Back in the car Alex spent several minutes trying to decipher the woman's writing. When she finally worked out what she had scribbled on the first envelope, her sense of confusion only intensified: Patricia Trybowski had moved to Pawtucket.

Rain and hail whipped against the windshield in violent gusts as she headed east along Chalkstone Avenue. She crawled onto the interstate and started looking for Route 1, which would take her up into the Pawtucket area, all the time struggling to construct a scenario that would make all the elements come together. There were plenty of cases of people who bought a policy at some point in their life and then found it was too expensive to maintain. But in those cases they usually let the policy lapse, they didn't go on paying. Mr. Trybowski had continued to make the payments: he must have, otherwise the company would never have paid the money. But why would someone keep feeding a policy while his home got repossessed?

As she left the highway, it came to her. How many times had people facing financial disaster—owners of small companies, for example, that had fallen foul of the IRS and knew that sooner or later they would go belly up—how many times had people like that taken out a big policy, used their cashflow to sustain it for as long as they could, and then killed themselves to pay for their family's future? They killed themselves rather than let their family down. They had to get it right, of course. Insurers wouldn't pay out in instances of flagrant abuse, but it was possible to beat the investigators. All it required was the courage to drive your car into a ravine. How many times had that happened? Of course there were no statistics available. The suicides who got away with it were never recorded. Their deaths were officially accidental.

Then again, thought Alex, if some kind of fraud was involved, it hadn't worked. You didn't escape to a better life in Pawtucket. As she made her way past McCoy Stadium and found the turnoff into the trailer park Mrs. Trybowski now called home, this became abundantly clear. Fairlawn Park was miserable even by the standards of the neighborhood. Especially under the rain. The dozen mobile homes fringing a loop of buckled tarmac looked like decaying teeth. Between each there was a strip of chain-link fence for privacy, shored up here and there with scraps of plywood and chicken wire.

Alex sat for a moment wondering if it was wise to get out at all. Not that the park looked particularly dangerous. It was simply depressing. She thought of her own apartment as a little on the shabby side, but looking at the grassless, muddy lots and their pathetic trailers, she realized she still had a long way to fall. There was the American dream and the American nightmare. A steady rain drifted across the park. It was only eleven in the morning but the light was beginning to fail.

Alex grabbed up the bundle of mail.

Mrs. Trybowski was in number 4—a ten-by-twenty trailer with a couch and two car seats for patio furniture. Alex stood on the oozy chipboard steps for a moment listening to what sounded like a TV or radio. She rapped on the flimsy door.

"Who is it?"

A querulous, educated voice.

"Mrs. Trybowski? Hello, my name's Alex Tynan. I'm from—"

The door opened immediately, and Alex was confronted by an elderly woman in a threadbare jogging suit and dirty pink slippers. A colorful silk headscarf held back gray hair. There was a smell of fried food.

"Who?"

"Alex—Alex Tynan. I'm with Providence Life."

She expected at least some kind of reaction, but Mrs. Trybowski just stared with her sad brown eyes. She might have been pretty once, but a fold in her cheek pulled her mouth over to one side in what looked like the aftermath of a stroke. She held her chest as she talked.

"Yes. What can I do for you?"

"I'm from Providence Life, the insurance company?"

Mrs. Trybowski nodded.

"If I owe you money, you're out of luck."

"You are the wife—the widow of the late Mr. Frederick—"

"Freddy, yes."

Freddy. The reality of policyholder 8356322 came home to Alex with a little jolt.

"I went to your old address in Mount Pleasant. The lady there gave me some mail for you."

"Barbara Doxopoulis. How is the old harridan?"

She took the mail from Alex's hands as a gust of rain buffeted the side of the trailer. They looked at each other for a moment.

"Why don't you—?"

She stepped backwards and gestured for Alex to enter.

It was surprisingly warm inside the trailer. At one end of the room shelves went up to the ceiling. Alex spotted paperback editions of Tolstoy and Dostoyevsky, a trailing spider plant. Water had started to come in through one of the aluminum window frames. Trickledown. There was a radio. No TV. A couch that must have doubled for a bed was covered with clothing. Mrs. Trybowski picked up a handful of socks and started shoving them into a large rucksack. The joints of her fingers were swollen with arthritis.

"I just got back from doing the laundry. Can you believe this weather? First a freeze and now it's going to flood."

Alex had a flash of her mother taking tea towels out of a front loader. She stepped forward.

"Please don't—please don't tidy up for my benefit. I'll only take a moment of your time."

Mrs. Trybowski paused, a holed sports sock in her hand.

"That's all right, dear. The whole place needs a good cleaning anyway." She said "whole place" as if the trailer were in fact a dude ranch. "So what is it? What is it you wanted?"

"I—well, it's a little delicate. I—we at Providence Life, we've had a problem with one of our computers."

Mrs. Trybowski looked up at her stained ceiling and shook her head.

"Computers," she said. "Freddy used to say that computers were going to relieve us of all the tedious paper-pushing jobs. I used to be a clerk and I hated it. Freddy used to say—to console me, you know, when I was a little down—he used to say that computers were going to take over all the boring jobs, so we'd have more time for the interesting things. But all they've done is put people out of work."

She had hardly taken a breath. She talked like somebody who never got to say a word from one day to the next. She talked like Alex's mother.

"Yes, I know what you mean," said Alex. "Well, anyway, we've had this problem, and I'm checking on certain payments that were made by the company last year. In November of last year, to be exact."

Mrs. Trybowski continued to stare.

"I wondered if you could confirm for me the exact amount paid to you in settlement of your husband's life insurance policy."

Mrs. Trybowski placed the sock back on the couch.

"I'm afraid I don't understand, dear."

"Your husband, he died—"

"Last year, that's right. In January. He didn't have any life insurance. He did have something years ago with—it *was* with you people, now that I come to think of it. ProvLife. But this is years ago when we—" She seemed to think for a moment, her mind wandering back to a time when she had money and a home and a husband. Before the stroke, before everything fell apart. "But the premiums were way too expensive. After he went bust he just—well, he just let it go. When he died I didn't get a cent."

She watched Alex for a moment.

"What's the matter, dear? Why don't you sit down?"

She pointed to a ratty old tub chair that was next to a pile of magazines.

"That chair still has all its legs."

She made tea and they talked for an hour, Mrs. Trybowski giving a detailed account of her colorful life with all its ups and downs. Freddy had been a wonderful dancer, and a partner in a successful firm of heating engineers. In a moment of blind optimism—blind optimism was another one of Freddy's attributes—he had taken out a large life insurance policy so that his beloved wife would never have to worry about the future. Unfortunately the firm had gone bust as the result of a lawsuit—the boilers Freddy fitted used to explode occasionally—and the policy had been allowed to lapse.

As Alex listened, she became more and more perturbed. Finally Mrs. Trybowski noticed something was wrong.

"Dear, if you're worried about your database," she said, "you shouldn't be. These things go wrong all the time. You can take my word for it. Probably just needs its floppy disk cleaned or rebooted or whatever it is they do."

She was running for the car when the thought occurred. It stopped her in her tracks. She turned and squinted back through the freezing rain at Mrs. Trybowski, who was still standing in the door of her sad little home, politely seeing her off.

"What is it, dear? You're going to catch your death."

Alex had to shout above the noise of the downpour. "Mrs. Trybowski, did your husband ever have an account at Ocean State Savings Bank?"

She thought for a moment before giving her answer.

"No. It was Providence Trust," she said. "Always."

Alex sat in a diner somewhere between Pawtucket and the East Side. All around her people were getting out of the rain, digging into pancakes or ham and eggs, getting on with the day as though everything was normal. But it wasn't normal. Just down the road one of Providence's leading corporations was being defrauded of millions of dollars. Freddy Trybowski's life policy had lapsed years ago, but someone had kept it going, someone had seen that the premiums were no longer being paid and so they had started paying them themselves. So that, when the time came—when Freddy died, was it?—they could cash in.

And Freddy wasn't alone. Alex suspected that the accounts on Eliot's list identified other similar cases. How long had it been going on? If money was being siphoned off at such a rate, why didn't it show up in the company's P&L? It was the same old problem. Providence Life was being sucked dry. On top of its regular settlements, a group of people were grafting fake claims—big ones—also settled by the company. So why didn't it show up on the balance sheet?

She sipped at her cold coffee. It all seemed so unreal. One thing was real enough, though: money had been paid into Michael Eliot's account. Ten percent of settlement value, three working days after the initial payout. Who got the rest? Not Mrs. Trybowski. Were there nine other people, each getting ten percent? To defraud the company it would take a conspiracy. No one could do it alone. Alex tried to think it through.

First they found lapsed policies. Why? If you were going to make fake claims, why not write fake policies? But then she knew why. When a new policy was sold, there was always a salesman's or an agent's name against it, commission to be paid, follow-up calls to make. The sales force was numbered in the thousands. But lapsed policies were a done deal, history. The commissions had been paid years ago. Nobody was interested.

Alex nodded to herself. It made sense. The more lies there were, the greater the chance that one would be spotted. Was that why the one policy she'd been able to track down had belonged to a Rhode Island resident? Of course it was. Rhode Island residents often banked at Ocean State. People living in Tennessee or Minnesota didn't—certainly not at a branch on the East Side.

Who would have to be involved? Somebody in Claims, for sure. And Investigations too. The names and departments flashed before her: Ralph McCormick, Dean Mitchell, Donald Grant. David Mullins too, to set up those bogus accounts at Ocean State and wire the money abroad the very same day. And Eliot, of course, the head of Treasury, to write those big checks and ensure no questions got asked. But then Eliot had died. And they'd needed to find a replacement. Someone who'd go along with it. Someone they could trust.

Alex felt the hair stand up on the back of her neck. That person was Mark. Young, greedy, ready to bend the rules a little. The blood was roaring in her ears. That was why they had passed over Drew Coghill: he was experienced, competent, but *too damned honest*.

A guy in a thick lumberjack shirt bumped Alex's table as he pushed past.

"Sorry, honey."

She barely acknowledged him. She had to do something. She had to tell someone. She stood up. But who would she tell?

She thought of the police. Did she have enough evidence to convince them? Enough for them to check out her story, at least? Maybe. Maybe not. The truth was, she didn't have much. Just an old policy that on its own didn't prove a thing—a policy she'd stolen, in fact, while trespassing on the premises of a company that had only the day before found cause to terminate her employment. Besides, if the people inside ProvLife were smart, there would be no paper records. Like everything else in the company, it would have been handled electronically. She had a funny feeling that as soon as the police walked through the doors of the twelfth floor, the Central Records computer would go down.

35

Liz woke suddenly to the sound of wild, almost deranged laughter. She sat up, blinking at the glare of the TV screen. It was a sit-com, one she didn't recognize. A guy in a plaid shirt stood frozen in a comical shrug while the studio audience roared and clapped. She felt around for the remote, found it buried in the small of her back, and hit the off button, only then becoming aware of the hard ache behind her eyes. She squinted at the clock recessed into the headboard. The big red digits said 20:30. She'd been asleep for almost three hours. And no wonder. Between worrying about what to do with her life and the guy snoring in the next room, she hadn't slept more than a couple of hours the night before.

She got up and went into the bathroom. Her skin looked a waxy yellow under the strip light, the flesh around her eyes swollen and purplish. She moaned and flicked the light off again. Through the plasterboard wall she could hear another TV. It sounded like the same sit-com. She felt nauseous, all dried up inside—probably thanks to the scotch she'd started into at half past four. She braced herself against the basin. She'd been getting into a lot of bad habits recently, living like a slob, living as if nothing mattered anymore. She was going to have to pull herself together. She turned on the taps and sunk her head into the water, drinking from her hands.

"Miss Foster?"

She wasn't sure if she'd actually heard it. She turned off the taps and tried to listen through the noise of the TV and the water dripping into the sink.

Someone rapped on the door.

"Miss Foster?"

It had to be one of the motel people. Only Alex knew where she was. Liz grabbed a towel.

"Who is it?"

For a moment there was no answer, just the sound of the traffic on the interstate, the sweep of tires on slush.

"My name's Jackson, Officer Tom Jackson." The voice was polite, efficient, official-sounding. "I'm with the Providence Police Department."

She opened the door a few inches, keeping it on the chain. He was a little younger than she'd expected, taller than average and slim, with thin blond hair, neatly cut. He was dressed in a long overcoat, the collar turned up against the rain. In the shadows she couldn't see his eyes.

"You just came down from Providence?"

"Yes, ma'am."

It occurred to her that he might be about to arrest her.

"But this is Connecticut," she said. "You don't have jurisdiction here."

"I realize that, ma'am." The voice was friendlier now, informal. "We were hoping you might want to help us out anyway. It's just information we want."

"How did you know I was here?"

The man pulled his coat a little closer about him. A truck thundered by, almost drowning out his answer.

"I believe you know Alexandra Tynan?" he said, holding up an ID card that it was too dark to read. "She told us where to find you. I'm sorry to barge in on you like this, but do you mind if I come in? I could drown out here."

Alexandra. It had to be. She was the only one who knew. It was funny that she'd gone to the police without telling her first. Things must have moved faster than she'd expected—or was it just that Alex didn't trust her anymore? Either way, Liz felt relieved. She'd been way out of her depth and it had almost gotten her killed. She didn't want to be scared anymore. She took off the chain and stood back from the door.

Jackson glanced across the parking lot and stepped inside. In the light Liz could see that his skin was pitted and scarred, especially around his cheeks, and his face was drawn as if he'd been very sick not so long ago, and just come through it. He was wearing brown leather gloves, but made no move to take them off.

"We've been looking into certain transactions at ProvLife," he said, closing the door himself. "Illegal transactions. I understand you used to work at the company."

"That's right, in the treasury department. I suppose technically I still do."

Jackson looked at the room, checking out the unmade bed and the litter of a day's snacking. It was a mess.

"You here alone?"

Liz nodded.

"Where are you headed?"

"Nowhere. I'm—" Liz felt suddenly self-conscious. She tucked her shirt in and began looking around for her shoes. "I wasn't headed any-where. I just—decided to leave town. Didn't Alex explain all that? About the fire and everything?"

Jackson nodded. "Yeah, yeah, she explained. Pretty bad luck."

"Luck?" Liz found her shoes by the bed and sat down to pull them on. "I don't think luck was involved, do you?"

Jackson nodded thoughtfully.

"Well, we'll be looking into that too, rest assured."

"Is Alex okay?"

Jackson blinked, then smiled. "Sure. Why wouldn't she be?"

"I don't know, I just— She was looking for—evidence, she said. It sounded dangerous. Do you want to sit down?"

He looked at the nylon-covered armchair as if the issue of whether or not to sit down was an unfamiliar one.

"That's okay," he said. "You knew Michael Eliot, is that right?"

Knew? It seemed a funny way to put it.

"Yes, I—yes, I did. But I had no idea he was mixed up in anything il-legal," she added hastily.

"Of course. I understand he left certain papers in your possession, concerning his financial affairs?"

Liz nodded. That was why Alex hadn't told her about the police. She was probably afraid Liz wouldn't hand them over, that she'd try and hide them someplace. Maybe if she'd been warned, that was exactly what she would have done. An angle on ten million dollars was a difficult thing to give up, even if an angle was all it was.

She reached for her handbag and took out a plain manila envelope.

"Here," she said, handing it over. "So, you got an idea what this whole thing is about?"

Jackson opened the envelope and leafed through the contents, although from the way he did it Liz had the feeling he didn't know what he was looking at.

"We're working on it," he said. "Is this everything?"

"I had some other papers, but I gave those to Alex."

Jackson looked up.

"And what were they exactly?"

"I don't know. I think Alex was trying to find out. Didn't she tell you?"

Jackson tucked the bank statements inside his coat.

"I haven't talked to her myself. One of my colleagues is handling it. She's given us a whole lot of information." He smiled. "We're still on the learning curve here, you might say."

Liz could believe it. White collar crime was probably something of a rarity for the Providence Police Department, and she could just imagine them trying to follow Alex Tynan through the arcane world of life insurance accounting procedures. It was a tribute to her powers of persuasion that she had even gotten them to listen.

"I know it's a little late," Jackson said, "but I'd sure appreciate it if you'd come down to the local precinct and make a statement. We may have to move quickly if we're to get to the bottom of this."

"What, you mean now?"

"I'm afraid so. Money moves fast these days, Miss Foster, and so do people. I'm sure you can appreciate that."

Liz hesitated. Why couldn't they talk right here? Why did it all have to be official?

"Well, I— If there's any question of—of a charge or anything, I want to talk to a lawyer."

Jackson smiled again.

"There's no question of a charge, I can assure you. It's just we may need sworn statements if we're gonna get a warrant." He walked over to the chair and picked up Liz's ski jacket. "We're not talking some two-bit crack den in South Providence here. This is Providence Life. This is a pillar of the community. My guess is old man Goebert knows every judge in town."

"Sworn statements about what?" Liz said. "I told you, I don't know anything about any crime."

Jackson held the jacket open for her.

"We can go through all that at the precinct."

An unmarked Plymouth was parked at the far end of the lot, just behind the bright pink ROOMS VACANT sign. Liz didn't realize there was someone at the wheel until Jackson opened a door to let her in.

"This here's my partner. Say hello, Calvin."

Calvin glanced around and let out a grunt that could have been hello, and could have been the sound of him clearing his throat. By the courtesy light Liz couldn't see much of him, except that he was darker than Jackson and heavier, with a day's growth of stubble and slicked-back hair that hung over the back of his collar. There was a cloying fruity smell in the car, like heavily scented disinfectant.

"Miss Foster here's agreed to make a statement at the precinct," Jackson said, climbing in next to her. "Just like I said."

Jackson sounded suddenly pleased with himself, as if somehow he'd proved a point.

"Calvin here thought you weren't gonna cooperate," he said, by way of explanation. "Isn't that right?"

Calvin didn't reply. He put the car in gear and swung out onto the highway, his front wheels skidding slightly on the ramp. The rain was falling more heavily now, gradually washing away the steep banks of snow piled up by the side of the road. They turned off at the first intersection and headed south towards the shoreline, keeping the phosphorus glow of the town on their left. Gradually the traffic thinned out to almost nothing, out-of-town stores and motels giving way to old industrial properties, some of them abandoned, judging from the boarded-up windows and broken-down fences. High up on a tall red-brick structure Liz saw the words STOKER MARINE ENGINEERING written in faded white paint.

"This is a shortcut we were told about," Jackson said, following her gaze. He leaned forward. "Left up here, okay, Calvin?"

Again Calvin said nothing. By the slow strobe of passing streetlights

Liz could see his eyes in the rearview mirror. She wasn't sure, but she thought he was watching her. She shivered, pulling her coat closer around her.

"So how long were you and this Eliot guy—an item?"

The question seemed to come out of nowhere. It took Liz a moment to focus on it.

"I worked with him for nearly three years."

"Yeah, but I'm not talking about work," said Jackson. "I mean how long were you two—?"

This time Calvin *was* watching her.

"About eighteen months."

"Uh-huh. He ever tell his wife?"

The question brought Liz's head around, but Jackson kept looking dead ahead.

"No. I don't think so."

"Sneaky son of a—" He smiled. "Meaning no disrespect. Kind of played his cards close to his chest is what I mean."

Liz didn't know what to say. Jackson had started polite and friendly. Now he was turning cocky, rude, as if he already had the whole case sewn up and was looking forward to a commendation.

"You want some gum?" He fished out a pack from his coat and offered Liz a stick.

"No, thank you."

Jackson unwrapped one for himself and folded it into his mouth.

"Way I see it, a guy like that"—he chewed hard a few times, making little squelching noises—"a guy who's, like, got it made—it doesn't say a whole lot about his character, I mean his *moral fiber*, his wanting to just walk away like that. I mean, a man has certain responsibilities. Certain obligations. You know what I'm talking about?"

Liz didn't answer. She wanted to say something in Michael's defense, but she didn't know if she should.

"Maybe not," Jackson said. "I mean, you were gonna share all this money, right? What were you gonna do with it? Buy yourself a racehorse, what?"

"I told you. I didn't know about the money until . . . until after Michael died."

"Yeah, right," said Jackson, smiling his infuriating smile. "It was just a love thing."

"Yes, it *was*."

Jackson chewed some more, looking out the window now at a row of brick warehouses with corrugated iron roofs. They couldn't have been more than half a mile away from the river, but they didn't seem to be getting any closer to town.

"Yeah, what a tragedy," he said at last. "All set for the great escape, and then the guy drills through a cable. The thing I can't figure out is, why was he putting up shelves for his old lady if he was just about to leave her? Maybe—" He raised his voice, talking to Calvin. "Hey, maybe he reckoned she'd be doin' a lot more reading when he was gone, was gonna need someplace to put the books."

Calvin let out a low nervous laugh, as if he didn't want to laugh but couldn't help himself. Liz felt suddenly uneasy. Over her shoulder she could see the lights of New London fading into the distance.

"What do you think, Liz?" Jackson said. "You think it could have been something besides an accident? What about suicide?"

"No. Of course not. We were planning to . . . No."

"Then you think maybe someone bumped him off? Like, faked the whole thing? Do you think that could be done?"

Liz swallowed hard. Were they trying to scare her, shake her down? Maybe they were hoping she'd tell them more about the money, confess to something. Maybe they didn't believe everything Alex had told them. Maybe they thought that whatever Michael had been mixed up in, she'd been mixed up in too.

"I—I don't know. You tell me. You're the cops."

She realized, even as she said it, that she no longer believed it to be true. Her heart started to pound in her chest.

"It'd take a little planning," Jackson said, thinking about it. "A little expertise. But it could be done. I mean, that old drill he was using, that was a lethal weapon right there. Metal casing, insulation all shot to hell. I reckon that could have taken care of him right there, if he was, like, made to hold it long enough. The hole through the cable and all that could have been done afterwards. People are always looking to put two and two together, you see what I'm saying?"

"You—you saw his body?"

Jackson looked at her, the faintest beginnings of another smile on his lips.

"Yeah. I'd tell you about it, but I wouldn't want you to get upset."

They were slowing down now. Through the streaming windows Liz could see a dark stretch of water, a canal it looked like, broken slabs of ice still floating on the surface. She couldn't clear her head. Couldn't think clearly about what she *had* to do next.

"What is this?" she said, the fear tight in her throat. "Where are we going?"

They were turning off the road now, down an unlit track. The car bounced over potholes filled with slush.

"Like I said, it's a shortcut," Jackson said and unbuttoned his coat. "Jesus, what a night. This keeps up and there's gonna be flooding."

Liz saw his hand slip inside his jacket. She didn't wait for him to take out the gun. She yanked back the handle of the door and pushed with all her weight. A blur of spray and snow opened up beneath her.

"Hey! What the fuck—?"

Jackson reached over and grabbed her by the shoulder.

"Get in here, bitch!"

Liz looked down at the track, bracing herself against the chassis, unable to let go. The brakes locked, flinging her forward, smacking her head against the door frame. The car did a crazy zigzag, Jackson still shouting and pulling at her shoulder. She lashed out at him, her nails tearing at his face. She heard him scream, and then suddenly she was free. For an instant she saw his staring face, a streak of blood beneath his eye, his hand reaching through the open door. She felt the cold night air blow through her hair. Then she hit the ground: first a lurch like the life being wrenched out of her, then an impact, hard and black.

Calvin got out of the car and walked back to where she was lying, Jackson following, dabbing at his eye with a handkerchief.

"Well?" he said.

Calvin stood for a few moments, looking down at the twisted body. With his foot he pushed her head over to one side. Then, without saying anything, he grabbed hold of her wrists and dragged her to the side of the canal.

"Is she dead?" Jackson demanded irritably.

Calvin looked at him, waiting for him to take her feet.

"What difference does it make?" he said.

Grant was on the stairs when the call came in on his mobile. The voice at the other end didn't identify itself, but Grant knew who it belonged to. The assignment had been carried out, it said, not exactly according to plan, but it was done. Grant wanted to know what had gone wrong, but now was not the time or the place to ask.

"I'll be in touch," was all he said.

He made to switch off the Talk button, but the voice wasn't finished.

"Who told you where to find her?" it demanded.

Grant frowned. A couple of people from Marketing were talking at the far end of the hall. He could understand why people were getting nervous. Things had gotten a little hectic lately, a little exposed. But that was no reason get sloppy.

"No one told me. I heard it," he said, unhooking a set of keys from his belt.

"What were you, listening at a keyhole?"

Grant let himself into the Communications Room that led off the back of Reception. It was where the in-house exchange was located, together with all the monitoring equipment.

"No," Grant said, trying not to let his impatience show. "I was listening to a tape. We monitor our dealers' calls in this company. It makes things easier for the regulator. As a matter of fact, I'm just about to go check on it. Make sure nothing's been *erased*. Are you happy now?"

"No, I'm not happy. The bitch almost took my eye out."

Grant didn't answer. He didn't want to hear this. Not on a mobile phone.

"We're goin' out of town for a few days," the voice said finally. "We'll call you."

36

Alex sat on the couch, mechanically stroking Oscar's velvet-soft ears, imagining what the company would say, imagining what *Neumann* would say if she started making accusations: "You have to understand, Miss Tynan recently lost her position here. In these circumstances I believe it's not *unknown* for . . ."

Neumann would be smooth, detached, devastating. It was the thought of facing him again, even in the presence of a police officer, that had decided it for her. She had to talk to White. That was her only way forward. White was the only one who knew the company—its structure and its players—the only person who knew it well enough to be able to take her discoveries further.

But talking to White was proving difficult. Most of the lines to Newport were down. According to reports on the television the thaw was turning out to be even more destructive than the freeze. Emergency services were out all over Rhode Island, evacuating flooded villages, rescuing people from their cars, clearing roads of fallen trees.

Alex went over to the window and looked out. Ragged patches of snow still clung to the grass, but for the most part the street had been washed clean by the driving rain. In the center of Providence the river had flooded Mayor Montanelli's lovingly restored quays, but up here they were safe.

In spite of this, East Siders were showing their usual backs-to-the-wall solidarity. That morning, while Alex had been driving all over town hunting for the Trybowskis, people from two different community groups had called on Maeve Connelly to make sure everything was okay. One of them had wanted to give her a hot meal, while the other, a man with a sallow pockmarked face, had been concerned about how cold it was in the house. Maeve had told Alex all about it when she got back. The man had even insisted on going through the house to check the insulation, explaining that a number of elderly people had already succumbed to hypothermia. "I told him straight," said Maeve, who had obviously disliked being referred to as elderly, "I said that if I'd been planning to freeze to death, I'd have done it a couple of days ago. I wouldn't have waited for the thaw."

Alex had laughed and had then stood on the stairs for half an hour talking about the terrible weather they were having. She wasn't usually quite so nice to Maeve, but felt it would be useful to have the old woman on her side when it came to explaining why she might not be able to pay the increased rent Kenneth was proposing. The cheerful exchange had left her feeling like Rhode Island's biggest hypocrite.

A gray van was parked on the opposite side of the street and two women in bright blue overalls were carrying foil-wrapped trays and a Day-Glo thermos to the front door of number 27, the home of an elderly couple. Watching them go about their good work, Alex realized that she had missed lunch herself. It was four-thirty in the afternoon, almost dark, and she hadn't eaten a thing since breakfast. She wasn't all that hungry and felt, if anything, a little nauseous. She also had the beginnings of a headache. She touched her brow, looking for signs of fever. All she needed now was to get the flu and her winter would be complete.

Oscar was mewing again. He had been doing it all afternoon, padding back and forth and mewing pitifully. He jumped down from the chair and came over to where she stood.

"What is it, sweetheart?"

She picked him up and started to stroke his head. He was holding himself stiffly in her arms, and flicking his ears as though she were in fact an irritation. She caressed him under the chin, a strategy that usually took about two seconds to turn him into a hypnotized invertebrate. But this time it didn't work. He jumped down and stalked back across the room. He looked at the food in his bowl and then, reproachfully, at Alex.

"It's salmon and rabbit, Oscar. Your favorite."

He then did something she had never seen him do. He leaned against a cupboard—leaned, as if he were tired, still mewing all the same. Alex snatched up the phone and dialed White's number. There was still no connection.

"Goddammit!"

The blood seemed to throb in her temples. Her head was starting to hurt so much it was difficult to think straight. She slammed down the phone and grabbed her overcoat.

She found a convenience store open on Tabor Avenue where she bought bread and cheese and Tylenol. Walking in the fresh air seemed to clear her head. She returned to her apartment just after six, and tried White's number again. There was no answer.

She made herself a sandwich, but when she sat down to eat it she found she still had no appetite. In fact, the thought of putting it in her mouth made her feel physically sick. She sat frowning at it stupidly and got to her feet. She walked across to the kitchenette and dropped it into the trash bin, where it immediately became wedged against the lid.

"Dammit."

It really was turning out to be one of those days. She bent forward to clear the lid, the pain pushing behind her eyes—two distinct points of pressure now. A wad of kitchen towel covered in sooty black marks had caught the edge of the lid and was stopping it from working properly. She pushed it down into the garbage and the sandwich dropped out of sight. She took two Tylenol, standing at the sink, drinking water from the faucet, and then went and sat on the bed.

Oscar was sulking in a corner, not in his basket but wedged between the little window seat and the wall.

"Oscar, honey. What are you doing?"

His eyes were shut and he was breathing in little jerky pulls as if he were having a nightmare. Alex had never seen him fall asleep outside his basket before. She realized that she too was drowsy. She decided to lie down.

It was pleasantly warm in the room.

Directly opposite her bed in the cupboard containing the Mercury boiler, the carbon monoxide was building up. There was no trace of sooty fingerprints where experienced fingers had squeezed and eventually cracked the old rubber seal on the exhaust duct. It was an old boiler. It hadn't even been necessary to starve the burner of oxygen. It burned with the telltale yellow flame and there were even traces of soot around the service door, another sign of defective function. The old lady had never had it serviced, that was obvious. It was an old make, had probably always generated a certain amount of CO—a by-product of incomplete combustion. As long as the system was properly ventilated, as long as the exhaust gases—the carbon dioxide and its deadlier monoxide—escaped to the outer air, there was no danger. But if the exhaust system failed . . . The local police, if they ever bothered to look, would see nothing but another domestic appliance that had gone fatally wrong. Faulty or poorly ventilated heating equipment, blocked chimneys, indoor use of barbecues, use of cooking appliances to heat the kitchen or room—the causes of this kind of fatality were numerous, and insurance companies knew them all. It wasn't something that happened all the time, but it happened. It was the kind of thing that happened to students, or people in low-rent accommodation, people who had a habit of trusting to Providence.

The door to the cupboard was barely open. The gas seeped into the room, three cubic feet with every minute that passed—colorless, odorless, tasteless.

Alex breathed deeply, her lips slightly parted.

She was standing on a sandbar. The sky was gray and the black sea was completely smooth. It looked like glass, but she could see that it was liquid. It was moving slowly, turning, torpid, dimpling on the surface. Mark was in a rowboat. He was reaching towards her. He wanted her to step into his boat. She just stood there, not moving. He started to wave and point at her feet. His eyes were black and glassy like the sea. She tried to call out, but she had no voice. Her heart began to labor in her chest, thumping like it wanted to get out.

The CO whirled and scattered deep inside the tissue of her lungs, a blizzard of molecules seeking out the hemoglobin in her blood, the molecule for which it had a particular affinity. Where the CO molecules bonded with the hemoglobin, the oxygen her body needed was locked out. Alex began to asphyxiate. At blood levels of thirty percent, she would begin to suffer throbbing in the temples; at forty percent, dizziness, nausea, dimness of vision. Sleep would spiral into coma, coma into death.

In her dream Alex saw a name on the boat. She looked up and saw that Mark could see she was reading the name. It took an effort of will to spell out the letters: L-I-R-A. Mark pointed frantically. She looked down and saw that the black liquid was rising—was already oozing up between her toes. It was freezing. She understood that the water was death. She looked back at Mark, but he was sliding away from her, already a long way from her, moving swiftly towards the horizon on the glassy black sea. The boat made no wake. His figure became confused with the boat. Then he and the boat were no more than a point on the horizon. It was only when he had disappeared completely that she realized the name of his boat was not LIRA but *LIAR*. She brought her hands to her face and screamed the word.

And was looking at the room. She was sitting up in bed. A pain like nothing she had ever felt before seemed to split her skull. She touched at her scalp, fumbling, searching for the wound. Her fingers tingled. Then she saw the red fingernails. She blinked, holding them up to her face. They looked as if they'd been painted with Day-Glo nail polish, the kind she never wore. And then, from somewhere deep in her memory, came the understanding of what it meant, a warning: carboxyhemoglobin. She was being gassed. She started to fight. She looked across at Oscar. He was where he had been when she had lain down. But something was different. With a sudden rush of adrenaline and fear, she realized he was no longer breathing.

She got to her feet. The floor seemed to pitch and yaw like the deck of a ship. She staggered across to Oscar and picked up his limp body. His gray eyes were glassy and still under half-closed lids.

A dry sob welled out of her. She staggered backwards, still holding the limp bundle. It seemed to take forever for her to find the door to the landing. Her fingers fumbled on the latch and then it was open, and she was breathing the air of the stairwell.

They want to kill you. The thought came to her as if someone else were trying to explain. *They want to kill you.* She put the bundle down and went back into the room. With both hands she yanked up the sash window, stood there gulping in the air. The freezing rain revived her a little. She pulled her hand across her face.

A spasm of anger went through her. She went directly to the cupboard and yanked open the door. She didn't know what she had expected to see, but here there was nothing. Just a dirty old boiler. Then she remembered the sooty kitchen towel. They had tampered with the boiler and then cleaned their hands. She let go of the door handle. She had to be careful not to destroy any evidence. She reached in and shut off the burner.

She dialed 911. It wasn't until the policeman asked her to calm down that she realized she was crying.

"I'm sorry, I—" She squeezed her eyes shut, pressing out the tears. "I'm sorry, they killed—they killed my cat."

"What's that?" The man sounded angry.

"They killed my cat. Somebody—"

"Listen, lady. If somebody killed your cat you're going to have to come down here in the morning and—"

"No, you don't understand, they tried to kill me."

"But you just said—"

"They *tried* to kill me but they killed my cat."

"Who?"

Alex struggled to clear her head, to make sense. With the window open it was freezing in the room. The table was getting wet.

"Did you see them?" asked the angry voice. "Did you see their faces?"

"No, I—"

"Are they still on the premises?"

"I don't—no, I don't think so."

"Well, listen." He sounded like he had at least two other phones trapped under his chin. "If you can give me your name and address, we'll send someone over right away."

She told him where she was and put down the phone.

"They tried to poison me," she said to the empty room.

She went over to the open window. What would they do now? What would they do now that they had failed? Just come back and shoot her? Looking out at the street, she wondered if they were watching her even now. She looked into the shadows between the old houses, searched for faces in the dark interiors of the parked cars, listened for footsteps through the insistent sound of rain.

She walked out to the landing and picked up Oscar's limp body.

Tears dripped down into his lustrous fur. All the time the question was going around in her head. Who were they? Who was it that wanted her dead? The same people who had destroyed Liz's home? People who knew enough about accidents to plug a heater into a light socket? People who knew enough to fake an electrocution?

The understanding came with a jolt, and she wondered why it had never occurred to her before. Michael Eliot hadn't died accidentally. It had been made to *look* like an accident. Just like her own death would have looked like an accident. Just like the fire at Liz's house looked like an accident. And who knew more about accidents than an insurance company?

37

Harold Tate massaged the flesh between his eyes and forced himself to focus on the light desk again. Lying on top were two black-and-white negatives the size of x-ray shots, each displaying a pattern of blurred black bars arranged in long columns. A stack of similar negatives lay on one side, each protected by a brown paper sleeve. It was after eleven o'clock and the lab was empty. Tate's head ached. He longed to be gone, but there were only a few more negatives to check and then he could finally forget about the whole thing. He could put it down to contamination and stop worrying about it. Because he *had* been worrying.

It wasn't just thoroughness. It was the disease itself. *Huntington's chorea.* The more he'd looked into it, the more alarmed he'd become. People didn't just fall sick and die. First they changed—their personalities, their minds. There were violent mood swings. Often they became paranoid, vindictive. Unpredictable. And somebody at ProvLife had it.

Of course, it might have been just an ordinary member of the staff, someone who knew nothing. It could have been a simple case of contamination. But Michael Eliot was aware of the procedures. Would he really be so careless as to let that happen with his own sample? If not, the possibility existed—a remote possibility, but one that nagged at Tate day and night—that the DNA sample had been switched deliberately. And only someone who knew about the sampling would ever think of doing that.

The electrophoresis equipment was not used much at Medan these days. The automated systems used fluorescent tags that sought out specific gene sequences in solution. Electrophoresis was a more general tool, used to sequence whole sections of DNA and see what they were made of. As such it was often used in forensic science, to identify samples of skin, hair, blood, or semen found at the scene of a crime. Certain sections of DNA, like fingerprints, were unique to the individual. Medan had used electrophoresis in its earlier days, when most of its efforts had gone into original research.

Tate's idea was straightforward. If somebody else's sample had been assigned to Michael Eliot, maybe Michael Eliot's had been assigned to them. He had taken the unusual step of taking a fresh sample from Michael himself—because they were friends—and that had given him what he needed to make a match. If he found one among the ProvLife samples, then the mystery would be cleared up. He would know who had the disease. And if there was no match, it would be safe to conclude that some third party's DNA had somehow found its way into the system by accident.

He leaned closer to the desk, his face a few inches from the dead white light. On one side a shot of Eliot's DNA, a small identifier region on chromosome nine. On the other side a sample assigned to another ProvLife employee, designated with a serial number running up the side. Almost the last in the stack. Using a clear plastic ruler he ran down the columns, comparing the patterns of bars, struggling to keep his eyes from watering. His temples throbbed from the effort of concentration.

They were the same.

Tate stood up straight, blinked, then repeated the exercise, going more slowly this time. He was tired. He could have missed something. But there was no doubt this time: the two strands of DNA were identical. They came from the same person.

He felt a moment of elation. Simple, logical, methodical, he had worked through the problem and been rewarded. Just like the scientist he was, or had been once. He noted down the serial number and hurried to his office. The computer records would tell him who the number belonged to, the person whose sample had been swapped with Eliot's, the person who *really* carried the gene for Huntington's chorea. As he hurried through the necessary commands, Tate made himself a promise: this time he would not call them in, would not break it to them gently, would not offer them advice. He would keep right out of it. Let them find out the truth in their own good time. Let the information stay in the hands of the people who had paid for it. Any other way and things got complicated.

The ProvLife employee file came up. Tate tapped in the serial number, one finger at a time, checking that he had it right. The screen cleared, then up came a list of names in alphabetical order. Near the bottom one of them flashed slowly on and off. It was a name he knew.

Neumann had a foot on the bottom of the stairs when he heard the phone ring. He took it in the study.

"Walter?" said the voice. "It's Harold. I—I hope I didn't—"

"I think you must have a wrong number," Neumann said, interrupting.

"I know," said Tate. "I know all that. But there's something you've got to know, something—terrible. It won't wait."

For a moment Neumann didn't speak. Tate could hear his breath against the mouthpiece.

"Then you'd better come over and tell me about it," he said.

38

She was on the bridge at Fall River when they started putting out warnings on the radio. Several rivers in the north of Rhode Island and in Massachusetts had already burst their banks, and now the police were advising people in rural areas to stay off the roads and to travel only if absolutely necessary. The rain was still falling, not in a torrent but steadily, relentlessly, as if it wasn't ever planning to stop. Alex's dim headlights picked out water sluicing into the road. Muddy streams splashed down from wooded slopes and embankments, cutting through the fast-vanishing ramparts of snow. After the highway Alex went most of the way in second or third, afraid of losing the road altogether. It was almost eleven o'clock, and the police advice seemed redundant. She drove mile after mile without passing another vehicle.

The old center of Newport had never felt more authentic. Dark and empty, lit only by a few dim streetlights, the tourist shops and signs invisible in the gloom, it looked for the first time like the dour New England seaport its founders had created. If anything, Alex felt more vulnerable here, more conspicuous. Driving out towards the sea, she couldn't keep out the notion that she was driving herself into a cul-de-sac, that if they found her here there would be no way out. And no help. She checked her rearview mirror and headed for the waterfront. In the harbor clusters of small sailboats huddled, white masts bobbing, decks covered by tarpaulins. Out on the horizon a single red light winked slowly on and off.

Soon the town was behind her, the road winding slowly around the headland towards Brenton Point. The gate to White's house was shut, and Alex had to climb out of the car to open it. Wet slush lay inches thick on the driveway, spilling over the sides of her boots. As she eased the Camry towards the house, the wheels slipped and drifted, the engine beginning to labor. There was no way it was going to get her home again.

There were no lights. She looked up at the house, praying that Randal was there.

On the spot where the Lincoln had stood there was now nothing but a faint rectangle in the slush. Alex trudged forward, hoping he'd just put the car in the garage. She wondered what she was going to do if there was nobody in. She wasn't sure the Camry would even get back into Newport.

She was still crossing the driveway when the door opened.

"Alex? Is that you?"

It sounded like White, but Alex couldn't tell if it was him for sure. He hung back from the threshold, half hidden by the door. Suddenly Alex felt self-conscious. She hadn't thought how it might look, her showing up like this.

"I tried to call you. I—I've found some things out that you have to know about, Randal. I'm sorry if—"

"Come in. For God's sake, come in."

Alex hurried into the hall. There were voices coming from another room. It sounded like a meeting. Then she realized it was just the TV.

"Did you come alone?"

"Yes, I—"

He closed the door, immediately shooting the bolts. He was dressed in the same green sweater as before, this time with corduroys and sneakers. He was holding something at his side, partly hiding it from her.

White's stare followed hers. It was an automatic, big, black and heavy looking, a Browning or a Beretta. In White's hand it looked bizarre, grotesque, part of some hideous metamorphosis from the cultivated to the brutal. Alex instinctively stepped back.

"Just a precaution," White muttered, embarrassed. "I saw the car from upstairs. There've been some . . . incidents lately."

He seemed edgy, rattled, as if he'd been expecting some far less welcome visitor. He opened a drawer in the hall table and put the gun inside.

"There. My God, you're soaked. Come on through."

He led her into the kitchen, where there was a smell of garlic and the remains of what had once been a whole roast duck sitting on the kitchen table.

"Are you hungry? Have you had any dinner?" he said, gesturing towards the bird. "I could make you a sandwich, or, or—"

"That's okay."

"Then some coffee? Yes, I'll make coffee."

He opened the refrigerator and began moving things around.

"Randal, I think I know—"

"I haven't had a chance to talk to Walter Neumann yet," he said, fishing out a carton of milk and a bag of ground coffee. "About your—case. I—I couldn't quite face going in today, to be truthful. And I think the whole thing's best handled face to face. As soon as I get back to the office, I promise you—"

"That wasn't why I came," said Alex.

White stopped what he was doing and turned.

"I think I know what's been going on at ProvLife. At least part of it. I know how Michael Eliot got that money."

White frowned. He put the milk and coffee on the table.

"You remember that anomaly I found a few weeks back? The funny-looking claims data in Central Records that seemed to have been cooked up?"

"Yes, of course. I asked you to look into it."

Alex nodded. "Yes, that's right. That's the reason I'm telling you all this. I mean, it's one of the reasons."

White blinked.

"Telling me what, Alex? I thought—we agreed the most likely explanation was that real data had been lost, and that someone was covering up."

"I don't think that's what happened," said Alex. "Not anymore. I think there's a whole load of fake data in the system. Policies that don't exist, claims that aren't genuine, payouts that shouldn't have been made."

White looked very pale. He went around the kitchen table and sat down.

"Michael Eliot was resurrecting dead policies," said Alex. "I don't know how he got away with it exactly, but one thing I do know: he couldn't have done it without someone in Central Records helping him. Someone like Ralph McCormick."

White shook his head. She hadn't expected him to like it. He was the company's illustration actuary, its guardian of truth. If its precious data had been corrupted, then it was he who had been duped as much as anyone.

He looked up at her.

"McCormick is dead. Didn't you know? He was found this morning. An overdose. Contaminated cocaine."

Suddenly Alex understood why White thought he needed a gun. Her heart started to pound.

"But—Jesus. Jesus, I—I thought he was in rehab."

"He discharged himself after a few days. Came home again. Told everyone he was over it, apparently. I mean, his addiction."

For a moment Alex was speechless. There were only a handful of people at ProvLife who *had* to be involved in the conspiracy, a few people that the evidence pointed to. And already two of them were dead. Who was left? Someone in Claims probably, maybe Investigations too. But who? And what about Treasury, Underwriting? What about the senior management? The board?

"Randal, I think it's time we went to the police, told them everything we know. Maybe we can—"

"The police? Why should we want to do that?"

Alex came across to the table. She could see that White was nervous, even shaken, yet he didn't seem prepared to accept the truth.

"Randal, you don't really think this was an accident, do you?"

He passed a hand over his face. "Ralph was a heavy cocaine user. He overdosed on a bad batch. It happens all the time."

He got up and went to the sink.

"He and Eliot were mixed up in something," Alex insisted. "Eliot decided to disappear without telling anyone, McCormick took to drugs. They both became unreliable, and now they're both dead. Can't you see it?"

She watched him put two big spoonfuls of coffee into a coffee-maker, spilling some down the side. His hands were trembling.

"Even . . . even if you're right, Alex, what would we say, exactly? That we *suspect* McCormick's death wasn't an accident? On what grounds? Who do we *accuse*, Alex?"

"I don't mean right away. We have to get back into ProvLife first, and get more evidence. Just a little more."

"I know you want your job back, but—"

"That's not what I mean. Something very bad has been happening. I'm talking about fraud, massive fraud. And murder."

White took two mugs down from over the sink.

"It's an interesting theory, Alex, but without evidence—"

"It's not a *theory*." He was starting to annoy her. It was as if he refused to see. "Randal, the treasury department has been settling claims on policies that don't exist, policies that lapsed years ago. I've *got* one of them. I tracked it down. ProvLife paid out a million dollars on a dead policy, a lapsed policy, and Eliot took ten percent. There were six other payments just like it, all in the month of November."

White stayed at the sink looking out.

"Can you prove any of this?" he said.

"I could," Alex said. "Provided I could get the police into Central Records before some convenient data-loss disaster wiped half the files. That's the problem: all the evidence is digital. Even the old policy I took doesn't prove anything unless we can show that there was a pay-out made against it."

White stood very still, bracing himself against the edge of the work top.

"You realize," he said slowly, "to pull off a thing like that, Eliot would have needed more than just Ralph McCormick's help. A lot more. Just about every operational area of the company would have to be involved in one way or another."

Alex nodded.

"That's why Eliot only took ten percent," she said. "The rest was for the others. The only departments he wouldn't need would be Marketing, Underwriting maybe. And ours. Actuaries just manipulate data. We don't check to see if it's genuine."

White's head dropped a little.

"We think we're so damned clever, Randal. But the truth is, when it comes to the real world, we're the last to know."

He turned.

"Then where's the hole, Alex? If we've lost—what are you saying? a *hundred million* dollars—?"

"Over six or seven years, maybe."

"Why haven't we noticed? Why hasn't it affected our profits? Financially we're one of the healthiest mutuals in the country."

Alex sensed this was his last attempt at convincing her—convincing himself—that she was wrong, that the data did not support her hypothesis.

"I don't know, Randal," she said. "I don't know. But I do know fake data when I see it, and I know a fake claim."

He let out a weary sigh. Until that moment it hadn't occurred to Alex to think what it might mean for him if ProvLife were hit by a major scandal. As a member of the board, wouldn't he be certain to face litigation? Would the company even survive? She had simply assumed that the right thing to do was find out the truth, that Randal White would have expected no less. But maybe it wasn't as straightforward as that.

"I still can't believe—I can't—" He slumped down at the table. "I've worked in that place the best part of twenty-five years. I'd be up for early retirement in seven. What am I supposed to do about this?"

Alex reached across the table and touched his arm.

"What do you want to do?" she heard herself say.

White put his hand on hers, looking up into her face.

"I'll tell you what I want," he said, his voice little more than a whisper. "What I want is for you to stop taking chances. This needn't concern you anymore."

"But it—"

"No, Alex, listen to me. I want you to let me handle it from here. I'm in a better position to do it, anyway. If even half of this is true, then we're dealing with some very dangerous people. I don't want them coming after you."

Suddenly tears filled her eyes.

"They already have," she said.

For a moment she was unable to go on. She sat down, pushing the tears from her eyes and clearing her throat. Randal looked stunned.

"This evening my apartment—the air, it filled up with carbon monoxide. Someone tampered with the boiler. I almost—"

She hadn't been sure how or when to tell him. She'd been afraid he'd want to go straight to the police. And she wanted more evidence before that happened. But the news of McCormick's death had changed the equation somehow.

White stared at her for a moment.

"Oh my God," he said. He reached across the table and grabbed her hands. "My God, Alex. Why—why didn't you say something? Why didn't you—?"

For a moment she let the strength of his hand comfort her. It didn't feel awkward. The closeness was suddenly natural.

"I'm okay, Randal, I'm okay," she said. "But I'm sure they were watching. And they'll try again. That's why I—that's why we have to hit back quickly."

Randal looked at her intently. In his blue eyes she saw suddenly something more than urbanity and wisdom, something stronger and more vital. It had been there all along, and yet she had always refused to recognize it—because of the years that separated them, because in the end it could never have worked. She prepared to lean back, to reestablish the distance that had always existed before. But when she felt his grip begin to loosen, she found herself holding on, not wanting to let go.

She lay awake for a long time in the big double bed, listening to the rain outside and the wind moaning through the trees. For a time she slept, the floods invading her fitful dreams. In Randal White's kitchen the water lay waist deep, the kitchen chairs bobbing up and down on the surface. The house on Phillips Street twisted and groaned as its foundations slid slowly down the hill. She saw Oscar stranded at the top of the fire escape, Mrs. Connelly struggling to climb out through a window. Alex tried swimming towards her, but the current was too strong. She clawed at the drowned-out cars and white picket fences. And then she was looking up at the ProvLife building, the water lapping against the plaque that marked the high point of the '38 flood. The great thaw was going to sweep all of Providence into the sea, and her with it. At least Mark would survive. He was safely away in New York. And then it occurred to her that Mark had abandoned her, betrayed her. She pictured him far away in Europe with his ten million dollars. At his side, dressed in her fifteen-hundred-dollar evening gown, was Liz Foster. Alex realized that she had been played for a fool by them both. They raised their glasses to her and laughed.

Then she was awake again, her heart pounding. Mark lay beside her, his breathing slow and regular. She let out a long sigh and slumped back against the pillow, feeling the fear and despair lift from her in a single euphoric moment. It felt as if she'd been dreaming for days. Then, with a jolt, she realized where she was. It was Randal White who lay next to her, not Mark. Because Mark *had* betrayed her, for real.

They had made love. In the near darkness, almost without speaking. She ran it through in her mind, barely able to believe it. He had led her upstairs and she had followed, because that was what she had wanted to do. She remembered the touch of his hands on her body, a gentleness and reverence that Mark had long since abandoned. She remembered a sense of *rightness*, of need overwhelming her doubts. And she remembered pleasure.

She turned and looked at him. One arm lay outside the sheets, its well-sculpted form dark against the linen. She reached over to touch him, but something made her hesitate. What was supposed to happen now? She rolled onto her back and looked up at the pale ceiling. The truth was, she had no idea. There had been no promises, no declarations. Were they supposed to carry on as if nothing had happened? Or was it too late for that? The thought that she had steered her life in some new direction without any idea where it would lead sent a momentary wave of panic through her. What did she *want* to happen?

She sat up slowly and looked over at the window. The curtains were not drawn, and through the silhouette of naked branches she could make out the faint glow of Newport in the distance. She was safe for the moment, that was the main thing. He made her feel safe. She could try living a day at a time for once, take what she could get and move on when and if the time was right. What was the point of making plans when so much hung in the balance? Randal White would understand that. She had a feeling he understood a lot of things.

She eased herself out of bed. She didn't want to go back to sleep, and she badly needed something to eat. She hadn't eaten a proper meal for days. She reached for her clothes, found her sweater and jeans, and slipped into them as quietly as she could.

She was at the bottom of the stairs when she heard it. It was a sound she recognized—always there in the background at ProvLife, part of the permanent ambient noise you learned to ignore: a computer printer. She came to a halt, turning her head back and forth, trying to isolate the sound, unsure if she wasn't just imagining it. She walked towards the kitchen, and stopped outside a door to the right of the corridor. She listened. The noise was barely audible now. Outside she could hear the steady hiss of the rain. Somewhere water was cascading from a blocked gutter. She went back a couple of steps. Looked down. There was a gap in the floorboards. She knelt down and put her ear to the floor. The noise was coming from down in the basement.

It took her a moment to find the stairs. Then she was opening a door and going down in complete blackness. A musty smell rose from the foundations of the old house, slightly sweet like old cardboard. The noise was more distinct now. Her bare feet touched cold cement. Light was coming from somewhere. As her eyes adjusted she could make out a passageway.

White rolled over onto his back and looked up at the ceiling. The bed was empty, and for a moment he thought he must have been dreaming. It was his body that told him what had happened. And her smell. Her smell was everywhere.

"Alex."

He called out softly. Listened for a moment. Then swung his legs out of the bed and stood up.

She moved forward, her bare feet soundless on the cement floor. The printer was still hard at work—she could hear it distinctly now—an ink jet, judging by the staccato nudge of the roller. Then she was standing outside a closed room. She listened hard for other sounds—a rustle of clothes, a breath—but there was nothing. She reached down for the handle.

It was not locked. She pushed gently. The hinges let out a barely audible squeak. She saw metal bookshelves crammed with bound reports, a desk, an angle-poise lamp with a green shade, a computer terminal and keyboard, and then the printer itself on one side. It wasn't the study. That was upstairs. This was more like a workplace.

She stepped inside. The computer and printer were both still working. It looked like data was coming down the line from somewhere, being stored on the hard disk and printed out at the same time. The computer had to be part of a network—like the internal network at ProvLife—unless Randal had logged onto the Internet and forgotten to log off again. She was about to leave when the thought struck her: was this machine *part* of the ProvLife network? When White worked from home, did he have the same access to Central Records that he did in the office? Because if he did, the task of gathering evidence was going to be a lot easier.

She went over to the desk. As if sensing an intruder, the printer suddenly stopped printing, the last sheet of data curling out from under the roller and folding itself neatly onto the top of a waiting stack. On the computer screen a panel read

<u>DATA RECEIVED AND VERIFIED</u>
<u>R</u>EVIEW   <u>A</u>NALYSIS   <u>E</u>XIT

Alex wondered what kind of data came down the line in the middle of the night. Not actuarial data, surely? Actuarial data was painstakingly manufactured from raw data, the latest tables and trends published in industry periodicals. It was statistical, second-hand. She pulled the last sheet of computer paper closer to the light. Immediately she knew she was looking at something familiar. Two sets of identical numbers, rows and columns, headed by their familiar labels: MCP1B, LQTS1, HTCH4. These were the results of another genetic test, just like the one Michael Eliot had taken from Medan. And there was the applicant's number in the top right-hand corner: AP1005178.

She began to feel uneasy. Why was ProvLife's illustration actuary interested in monitoring the results of people's genetic tests? Why should Randal White be interested, when he had said all along that he was against genetic testing on principle?

She turned over another page, and another. Each one held the results of another test, on another applicant. The same format, different numbers. She kept turning and turning. The papers unfurled, falling around her feet in a single continuous ream. There were dozens, scores, hundreds of tests. As many tests in a month as ProvLife had applicants. And then it came to her: these weren't a part of medical tests carried out on the big-ticket applicants, people who wanted a million dollars' coverage and up. There were too many of them. *ProvLife was testing everyone.* Hadn't Benny told her the process looked like it was automated? You didn't automate unless you had an industrial-size workload.

She pressed A for Analysis. For a couple of seconds nothing happened, then a few lines of text appeared at the top of the screen.

No: AP-1005178   Name: T. J. Adair   Sex: M
Batch: 84/98JA1   Birth: 03-17-59

POSITIVES: None   No known risk factors
RISK ASSESSMENT: LOW
                           >ACCEPT<
PREVIOUS   NEXT   SEARCH   EXIT

The applicant number told Alex she was looking at the analysis of the first test results in the batch, those of a man called Adair—a man who, by the look of it, was going to have his application accepted. Nine tested genes, nine negative results. He was a good risk. No Huntington's chorea for him, no prostate cancer, no—what was the gene Benny had gotten so excited about? MCP1B. *Your basic number one killer,* that was what he said. The heart attack gene.

White came to a halt halfway down the stairs. Something was stirring behind the drapes on the landing. He moved forward, his heart thumping in his throat. Someone had gotten into the house. They had taken Alex. He wrenched back the drapes. The wind and rain whistled in through a crack in the glass. The ice must have swollen the wooden frame until it distorted, split. He stared at it for a moment, held by the melancholy sound. Then he moved on down the stairs. He reached the hall table and took out the gun.

Alex lowered herself into the chair. She hadn't thought about it until now, not really. Heart disease was far and away the biggest source of claims in the life insurance business—it accounted for over a third of the total. If you could screen out some of the potential victims, some of those potential claimants, just what would that be worth? How many millions, year on year, to a life insurance company? What would that do to the profits of a company the size of ProvLife?

Her heart began to pound. She reached out to the keyboard again and pressed S for Search. A box appeared in the middle of the screen asking her to specify what she was searching for. She typed in HEART ATTACK.

The cursor winked, then a message appeared:

NO MATCHES—SEARCH AGAIN? Y/N

"Dummy."

Heart attack was not a precise term either for doctors or for actuaries. Alex tried again, this time typing in the words MYOCARDIAL INFARCTION. The cursor blinked again. Then up came another page of analysis.

No: AP-1004812   Name: W. A. HEWITT   Sex: M
Batch: 81/97NO2   Birth: 11-18-55

POSITIVES: 1   MCP1B gene complex
RISK ASSESSMENT: Coronary thrombosis/myocardial
     infarction—HIGH
     Probability death in <10 yrs = 60%
     >DENY<

PREVIOUS   NEXT   SEARCH   EXIT

She called up the next page: another bad gene, another high risk—higher this time because a second gene threatened the onset of something called Long QT syndrome. The third page was like the first, except that this one referred to a woman, her risk for some reason lower. Alex moved through page after page, faster and faster, the names and the verdicts flashing past her: people whose genetic destinies had been unraveled and analyzed and found wanting—without them knowing anything about it. And at the end of each page the same simple recommendation: DENY

For a moment Alex thought she was going to be sick. She brought her hands to her forehead, blinking back the dizziness. She could see them out there, in the trailer parks and the tenements and the welfare lines: the bad risks, the bad stock, the genetically corrupt. Uninsurable. Unemployable. Burdens on the ever-narrowing shoulders of society. It was just the nightmare Randal White was always talking about: eugenics by stealth.

Realization was followed by denial. She didn't want to believe it. Any of it. She sat there stunned, then took a breath, two, told herself to slow down. There was at least one problem with her assumptions. If ProvLife were testing the genes of their new applicants, they would need to take samples—of blood or skin or saliva. And that was impossible. It was true, the big-ticket applicants underwent medicals, but they were a tiny percentage of the total. Normally only the sales force came into direct contact with potential customers. Where they were concerned, the only physical material passing between applicants and the company were the standard application forms, which Alex had seen being processed by the thousand down at PrimeNumber.

She clamped a hand over her mouth, almost laughing at the recollection of it: Roberta and all the other ladies opening the reply-paid envelopes with their little plastic letter openers, neatly stacking them at the sides of their desks, ready for collection. The envelopes. It was the envelopes. *Heymann's very big on recycling. It's a thing you have to learn when you come here.* Tom Heymann had never struck her as the ecological type. No wonder he'd gotten a little jumpy when a trainee suddenly showed up from head office, anxious to learn—how had she explained it to him?—about *the data capture aspects of ProvLife's work.* It was a pity she'd been so anxious to get out of there. Otherwise she might have stopped to ask herself why the trucks from Greenfield Recycling came calling every day, and where they actually went: not to some pulping plant out of state, but to Medan Diagnostics just a mile or two down the road.

And that was what PrimeNumber was for. She saw that now. The outsourcing arrangement had never had anything to do with cost cutting. It was simply safer to have the operation well away from head office, in some cinderblock sweatshop where the ladies did what they were told and no one asked questions. At head office there were armies of middle managers who were paid to arrange things like paper recycling, and who might ask why new applications couldn't be processed a little faster.

How long had the outsourcing agreement existed? According to White, for at least seven years. Had the screening been going on that long—or was it even longer? Seven years ago ProvLife had been struggling, looking to save itself through merger or takeover. And then things had begun to improve, year after year, until the company was one of the most profitable insurers in the country. And it wasn't even illegal—that was the most beautiful part—it was merely unethical. No law said you couldn't analyze someone's saliva if they sent it to you. And thousands upon thousands of people had, mixed with the strange-tasting gum on their reply-paid envelopes. The audacity of it. The simplicity.

And among those thousands one senior ProvLife executive: Michael Eliot. Why had he suddenly become curious about his own genetic destiny after all those years? Why had he waited until last November to take advantage of the company's unique facilities? Alex felt the hair stand up on her neck. She knew the answer to that. In November the company had launched its pilot healthcare plan, the one for employees. Everyone had applied, just like regular customers, except that they weren't being asked to pay. She had applied herself.

The wind was rising again, she could hear it up above. Then there was something else. Was it footsteps? A floorboard creaked overhead. She held her breath and pressed the S key for Search again. This time she typed in the five letters of her name.

The computer seemed to take forever to sift through the records. The hard disk whirred, its green light flickering, then stopped. Alex began to think maybe the line was down, just as the phones had been earlier.

And then suddenly she was looking at it.

No: AP-5000438	Name: A. S. TYNAN	Sex: F
Batch: 80/97NO1	Birth: 06-25-73	

POSITIVES: 1	BRCA1 gene complex	
RISK ASSESSMENT:	Breast/ovarian cancer—EXTREME	
	Probability death in <10 yrs = 85%	
	>DENY<	
PREVIOUS	NEXT SEARCH	EXIT

39

The cars began to arrive outside Neumann's house, the sound of their engines drowned by the rain. From an upstairs window Harold Tate counted them. Six so far. Average sedans, comfortable but not flashy. Grays, blacks, dark blues. Typical cars, average cars. Each one driven by a multimillionaire. Guy Pilaski's Oldsmobile was the only one Tate actually recognized.

The lights of another car lit the base of a small sequoia and then swung around towards the house. A black Lexus. That made seven in all. Tate heard doors slam, and hushed voices. His window didn't give him a view of the front door. He waited, pacing up and down the small drawing room, wondering if he had done the right thing in telling Neumann what he knew, wondering where they went from here. The pit of his stomach told him it might be somewhere he didn't want to go.

Then Neumann was standing there in the doorway.

"We're ready for you now," he said.

They sat around a dining room table under a haze of blue smoke. They looked tired, irritable, anxious. When Tate entered the room, they all looked at him as if he were the defendant in some particularly grue-some murder trial. Tate recognized Newton Brady and Donald Grant, and thought he could pick out a couple of other faces from the funeral, but otherwise they were strangers to him. His contact with ProvLife had always been minimal—deliberately so.

Tom Heymann and Mark Ferulli sat on either side of Brady, while Grant sat opposite with David Mullins, Guy Pilaski, and Dean Mitchell. Neumann took his place at the head of the table and gestured for Tate to take a seat next to him. Somebody out in the hallway closed the doors.

"I've brought Harold in because I think you should hear this directly from him," said Neumann. He turned his dull stare on Tate. "Harold, why don't you just take us through what exactly happened with Michael Eliot's sample."

It took him about five minutes to explain. He went through the safety procedures at Medan, procedures designed to avoid precisely the kind of mix-up that seemed to have occurred. Then he explained about Eliot's tests, and how the second had not matched the first.

"I don't understand why you didn't come to me, Harold."

It was Guy Pilaski who spoke. He peered at Tate over a pair of phony-looking tortoiseshell spectacles.

"I—I just didn't—"

"What the hell are you saying here?" It was Newton Brady. He was smoking a big Cohiba, one end of which was already moist and ragged. "You're saying Michael Eliot never had the Huntington's thing? Is that it?"

Tate nodded. Several people shifted in their seats. Tate had wondered if they knew, if Margaret Eliot had told them. Apparently, she hadn't. That, at least, was something.

"Jesus Christ. Then why did he want to run?"

"He—he *thought* he had it."

"Because you told him," Neumann said. "Isn't that right, Harold?

Tate shook his head. It was a breach of the rules. Officially and personally Medan was to have no contact with ProvLife. At the time he hadn't seen the harm in it. Only now was he beginning to see just how much harm was really involved.

"He was—we were old friends. I felt I—I ought to break it to him personally. Before the test results were sent back to the company. I thought it was only right he hear it first. Nobody saw us."

Tate felt sure Neumann wasn't going to leave it there, let him get away with a mere apology. For a moment there was silence.

"Michael asked you to hold back the test results, didn't he? To keep them from us." Tate had already told Neumann this, but Neumann wanted everyone else to hear it. "He asked you to sit on them until New Year's."

"That's right," Tate said.

"And you agreed."

"Yes."

"Only you didn't keep your word, did you?"

"I didn't think it—"

"*Did* you, Harold?"

Tate shook his head.

"No. Randal White called me. He wanted the results *before* Christmas. He knew we'd done them. I didn't see any way to stall him."

Neumann smiled. He seemed to be enjoying himself, almost.

"You did the right thing, Harold. Thanks to you, we were alerted. We were able to start watching."

Heads went down around the table. People became interested in their hands or their pens or cigarette lighters. Brady tidied up the ash on the end of his cigar. They didn't want to be reminded of what had happened to Michael Eliot, especially not now. Ferulli kept looking back and forth, his face flushed. Neumann noted the response with his all-seeing eyes and continued.

"We wondered what Michael wanted with a brand-new set of luggage. Why he booked himself on a plane to Europe. We wondered if he hadn't found out about his disease some other way, and why he didn't tell us about it."

Tate put a hand across his face.

"All thanks to you, Harold."

"No, I—I didn't—"

"Oh, but you did, Harold. You made up for your earlier . . . indiscretion quite splendidly."

For a moment Tate thought he was going to lose it. Deep down he had always known, but somehow he had never allowed himself to believe it: they had killed him. And he had made it happen. If only Eliot had told him what he was planning, had explained what he was afraid of, then at least Tate would have warned him. But Eliot *hadn't* trusted him. The fact that he had stolen the printouts proved it. He'd wanted evidence, that was clear now—evidence of the screening operation, so that if the others ever came after him he could threaten to blow the whole scheme wide open. And what would have happened to his good friend Harold Tate then? He'd have gone down like everyone else.

"He should've told us," Brady growled. "Michael had it coming." He took the cigar from his lips and pointed at Tate with the chewed end. "I was very disappointed in him. Very disappointed. I thought he had more character. More in the way of—of *moral fiber*. He let us down."

Tate looked up, caught Mark Ferulli's eye, wondered who he was. Besides himself, he was the only person at the table who looked scared.

"So who had it?"

All the heads turned towards Donald Grant.

"Who *did* have the gene?" he said. "If Eliot didn't. You're not telling us your machines just dreamed it up?"

Grant was someone Tate did know. He and Guy Pilaski had been in business together once upon a time, although what kind of business Tate was never sure. In the early days Grant had been the main liaison between Medan and ProvLife, helping to set things up. And everything Grant said, Pilaski did.

Neumann nodded, acknowledging Grant's question.

"Harold thinks Eliot's sample was swapped deliberately, before it got to him. By Randal White."

"Swapped?" Brady demanded. "I don't get it. Whose sample did he swap, for Chrissake?"

"His own," said Neumann coolly. "I expect he simply swapped the envelopes at the outset, sent Eliot the one that corresponded with his own application. Eliot probably didn't notice that the numbers didn't match."

Brady stared, his mouth open, his cigar poised a few inches from his lips. No one spoke.

"So White has the disease," Grant said finally. "Are you sure?"

Neumann brought his long pale hands to the edge of the table and looked down at them.

"Do you remember, Don, that lunch we had at the Capitol Grille? Last November, early November."

Grant didn't reply.

"White canceled. Didn't come in."

"I remember that," said Brady. "He was sick."

"He had an appointment with his doctor that morning. I think that's when they must have given him the bad news."

Someone said: "Jesus Christ." Dean Mitchell. Neumann ignored him.

"Can you imagine how he must have felt? The whole screening operation was his idea. He had all the numbers. He knew what it could save us. Oh, I know Richard Goebert liked to take the credit"—he shot a glance towards Mullins and Pilaski—"but White was the one who thought it up, worked out how it could be done, how it could be hidden. And then one day, after all those years of screening out the bad risks, he finds *he's* about to be screened out. It was all his idea, and yet he was the one person who was never going to enjoy the rewards. All that—that brilliance put to the service of people like Michael Eliot."

"Poor sonofabitch," said Brady, shaking his head. "I knew he didn't like the guy, but—"

"Maybe he thought he was just buying time," said Neumann without much conviction. "Maybe he didn't want us to know, couldn't face the . . . humiliation. If he'd refused to take part in the pilot health-care plan, refused to submit an application, it would have looked very odd. We'd have guessed he was trying to hide something. So he made a switch instead."

"He was very anxious to administer the screening, that I do know," said Mitchell. "He insisted."

"Yeah, you bet," said Grant. "And then he calls up Tate here and says, send me the results of those tests—before Christmas. He knew there was a chance Eliot would run, or screw up some other way, and he wanted us watching. The sick son of a bitch."

"In any event," said Neumann, turning once again to Tate and giving him a thin smile, "if you hadn't been so diligent in carrying out a second test on your friend, on a fresh sample, then Randal's . . . duplicity would never have come to light. It seems we owe you a debt of gratitude once again."

Tate felt a wave of panic. Somehow Neumann was making it sound like it was all his initiative, that the next step—Tate could sense it coming—was his idea.

"Listen, I just thought you should *know*. I take no responsibility—"

"We *all* take responsibility," Grant interrupted, "for everything. Equally. That's the deal, Harold. That's the policy. And you know what else it says? It says we run the scheme until it's time to wind it down.

And then we say our good-byes. One by one. Nobody messes with the schedule."

"Yes, but—"

"No buts, Harold. You signed. White signed. End of story."

Tate fell silent.

"The way I see it," said Neumann, trying to sound more positive, "this is an opportunity to put an unhappy chapter behind us. When you consider it, all our recent difficulties date from Randal's . . . *unhelpful* intervention. To date our strength has always been our forward planning, but in any system there's always the possibility of surprises. The point is, to deal with them."

Grant looked around the table, checking each face, making sure everyone knew where they stood.

Brady sniffed.

"Looks to me like we don't have Randal on board anymore," he said, tapping another inch of ash into the tray. "I think—I think this disease must have gotten to him."

"They do say dementia is one of the symptoms," said Neumann helpfully. "Such gradual mental deterioration can lead to very . . . erratic behavior."

Mullins took out a handkerchief and dabbed at his forehead. He seemed to be sweating a great deal. Grant considered him for a moment.

"Truth is, he probably doesn't give a fuck anymore," he said. "Who can blame him? He doesn't really have a future, does he?"

Regretful murmurs went around the table. Then the room became very quiet. It seemed no one wanted to take the next step.

In the end it was Neumann who broke the silence.

"As usual Don has put his finger on the key issue. The question, the question we have to decide on right now, is exactly how much future we can allow Randal White to have."

40

She hit Print. Then she read through the whole thing once, twice, checking the date of birth and the name as if it might possibly refer to someone else, focusing—her hands were trembling—focusing particularly on her neat new label, the new term that defined her: BRCA1. The tag was compressed, cryptic. It made her think of the tattoos you still saw on survivors of the death camps. It made her think of *Down's syndrome*, of *thalidomide*, of *Alzheimer's*, of *Huntington's chorea*—of all the neutral terms that had ever been used to identify different kinds of waking nightmare. Beyond the tag, hard, specific realities loomed: breast cancer; ovarian cancer. Her future. The way it was going to be. She pressed her eyes shut and squeezed out a low moan of anguish.

"Alex? A-lex?"

White's playful singsong came through the ceiling muffled.

Suddenly she was panicking, snapping off the screen, grabbing up the sliding concertina of printouts, trying to put them straight, trying to make it look as if what had just happened never had, trying to push time backwards. She reached for the light switch, threw it.

She was in darkness, leaning against the door, straining to hear footsteps on the wooden stairs. But there was nothing, just the sound of the rain from far away and her own snagged breathing. Then she saw what she was doing. She wiped a hand across her face and swallowed tears. She was hiding as if what she had done, what she had just found out, was proprietary—somebody else's business. But it wasn't. It was *her* business. It was her destiny and the destiny of others—coming down a conveyor belt like shelled peas that had to be sorted.

White had lied to her. About everything.

She snatched open the door and went back up the stairs, taking them two at a time. There was no sign of him in the hallway or in the sitting room.

She found him standing in the darkened kitchen, his half-naked body lit only by the greenish glow of the open refrigerator. His face was vacant, the mouth slackly open. Alex walked into the doorway, saw the gun. Froze. She was reading everything differently now. The gun was for his own protection, he had said so. But did his saying so make it true? Not anymore.

He seemed unaware of her presence. He was humming something under his breath, staring into the cold light. She was about to speak when his head suddenly snapped over as if he had been struck. She saw tendons in his neck jerked tight like the spokes in a wheel, and his head wrenched painfully sideways. Just as it had started, it stopped. He blinked stupidly for a moment and then reached into the refrigerator. When his hand came back out it was full of something that glistened. He pushed it into his mouth and swallowed, then licked at his fingers and palm, hungrily.

"Randal?"

He gave a start, turned. There was something around his mouth and on his chin. He stared at her for a moment, then looked down at the paper in her hand.

"Alex. What's that you're holding?"

She held the paper out as if it were a malicious note that he would now have to explain.

"My future," she said simply. "It's my future."

White looked at the paper, nodded, touched the gun to his lips.

"I've seen it," he said.

"You lied to me." Alex's voice was barely above a whisper.

"You know—" White frowned and wiped distractedly at his mouth with the breech of the pistol. "You know, there's a lock on that door. I usually lock it. Always. But . . . this, this happened a few days ago. What I'm talking about. It happened a few days ago. And then I lost the key.

Lost the . . . damned key." He tried to smile, but there was a fluttering tension in his cheek that kept his mouth taut and downturned. "I'd lose my head . . . if it wasn't . . ."

He shrugged, giving up on the tired old phrase. He pointed the gun at her—not at her, she realized, at the paper in her hand.

"I'm so sorry, Alex. I was going to . . . It's not my fault. It's not anyone's fault."

Alex looked down at the scrap of paper. Three inches of information ending in the word DENY. She closed her fist on it and screamed.

Then she was clawing at him, punching, kicking.

"You fucking—you *fucking* lying, abject lying—"

He staggered backwards, his arms reaching, trying to restrain her, trying to hold her. They fell against kitchen cabinets, slid sideways. Through the noise of her own sobs she could hear him crying, pleading.

"You have to believe me, Alex—for God's sake—you have to believe me."

Then the strength had gone from her. She collapsed against him, felt his arms close around her, felt the gun against her shoulder.

"It isn't fair." She didn't know if she was saying the words or just thinking them. "It isn't *fair*."

The car went over a ridge at speed so that for a moment they were weightless, straining upward against the seatbelts. The big windshield wiper beat back and across, back and across. Ferulli looked over at Grant's stone-cold baby face. Grant kept his foot hard down, as if he didn't even believe in the possibility of oncoming traffic. He was moving too fast, smiling too much, chain-smoking Kents—speeding, high on something or other.

"Hell of a mess," he said.

It was the first thing he'd said since they'd left Neumann's place—his first words in an hour—and they made Ferulli start.

"What's that?"

"Hell of a mess—this whole thing."

Ferulli didn't know what to say, didn't know if Grant was even looking for conversation. In the end he decided to say nothing, just stared forward through the windshield, watching the headlights suck up the rain. He couldn't believe he had gotten where he was so fast—which was in deep, way over his head, a long way from any land *he* recognized. He was, he realized, exactly where they wanted him. Grant was going to kill White. That was the understanding. Nothing explicit had been said at the meeting, apart from the reference to White's limited future. Neumann had just looked at the assembled faces and then said to Grant: "I think we're all agreed."

It had been Grant's idea to take him along. "I'll take the kid," he'd said, saying it like some spooky old hillbilly. And when Mark had looked at the circle of faces, he knew that this proposal had also met with their approval.

Grant was carrying a gun, Ferulli knew that, and there were two shotguns on the backseat wrapped in a raincoat. But how would it happen? It would be enough for him to witness the killing and do nothing to stop it to make him an accessory. But he had a feeling Grant might want something a little more incriminating than that.

"How . . . ?"

Ferulli didn't know how to put it. Above all—as always, above all—he wanted to look cool, capable.

"How does it . . . ?"

Grant's head snapped around. "What's that?"

Ferulli cleared his throat. "How do we work it? How are we going to work it?"

Grant's smile went tight and ugly. He drew on his cigarette.

"Burn the prints off in the frying pan," he said. "Only take a minute. Cut off the head. Blow the fucker up."

He laughed smoke into the heated air—a laughing baby with a notch in his head like an entry wound.

"What?" he said, astonished. "You never blew up a head? Sure, that's what you gotta do. For the dental records. Shotgun shells in the mouth, superglue the lips together. Pop her in the oven on high. Kaboom." He glanced across, still smiling, sucked smoke deep into his lungs. "Relax, kid. We ain't there yet."

Ferulli could feel it coming now. He knew Grant was screwing with his head, but he could see him putting a bullet into White and then handing him the pistol, making him put another into the body. Something like that. That was the way they blooded people, wasn't it? Guaranteed people's loyalty. His hands were cold in his lap. He couldn't do it. There was no way he could it. He wasn't a killer, for Christ's sake.

What would Grant say if he refused? What would he *do*? He could still hear Newton Brady's words: *Looks to me like we don't have Randal on board anymore.* Ferulli looked out at the dark. Think of the money, he told himself. Think of the money.

It had only taken a month for the first payment to hit his account. One hundred forty thousand. There had been no shortage of advice from Mullins about what to do with it. He already had an account in Grand Cayman. Soon he would have them in Luxemburg, Switzerland. Too many accounts, he thought. But Mullins had been adamant.

"Next month'll be the same," he'd said. "Remember that."

Next month *would* be the same, and the month after that, and the month after that, the accounts steadily building until he was a rich man. It was like a dream come true. In another year he'd be . . . he brought his hands together and squeezed, riding out the wave of frustration.

Since the beginning, everything had been deferred. The first thing they'd done was make him take the car back. Brady had talked to him in his office.

"Buy yourself a Porsche, buy yourself an Aston Martin, buy yourself a fucking *Ferrari*," he'd said, "but do it when the time is right."

But the right time was nearly eight years away. Between now and then he was to do nothing that might draw attention to himself. As he was leaving Brady's office, the big man had said: "In the meantime go get yourself a regular sedan. And, Mark, make sure it's gray or something."

Gray. That was what they wanted. Because that was the way he had to be: colorless, normal, average—just like the performance of Prov-Life itself, right in the middle of the ballpark. So now he couldn't get through an hour without thinking about the way things would be next year, or the year after that, or ten years from now. He'd started to buy magazines, he spent hours staring at brochures, catalogues—his nose pressed to the glossy windows that gave onto his golden future.

But otherwise it was great. Like a magic trick. Nobody was getting hurt. Nobody had been hurt to get the money. It was just conjured out of the air. All they were doing was using the information, screening people out. *They* didn't suffer. They just went elsewhere. The people who got hurt—Eliot, McCormick—that was their fault. They had signed the agreement, they had taken the benefits, and then they had tried to back out. Ferulli frowned, examining his nails. There was no backing out—he was clear about that. His only worry was Alex. What had happened to her was hard to justify. It was wrong. But she was a bright kid, tough too. It wouldn't take her long to get her life back on track. And after all, if it hadn't been for him—for his putting her off the scent— she'd have been in a lot worse trouble. She'd thank him if she knew what he'd done for her. And White—well, White was a liability. He had it coming.

"One hell of a fucking mess," said Grant, back in his groove.

"He's got it coming," said Ferulli, surprised by the edge in his own voice. And when Grant looked across at him: "White, he's—he's crazy. He tried to screw the whole operation. He had no right."

Grant nodded hard.

"I'm glad you feel that way, Marky," he said, and he laughed, his irritating open-mouthed smoky laugh. "It's going to make what you have to do a whole lot easier."

They were sitting at the table, the gun between them, White wearing an overcoat now and drinking Château Pétrus from a long-stemmed glass. They hadn't even bothered to switch on the lights. The refrigerator stood open, humming, casting shadows along the table as if that was the way you always lit a room. White spoke holding the bottle in front of his mouth, his eyes fixed on the grain in the table, like a man in a trance. He wanted her to understand, he wanted to tell her the whole story. Only then would she be able to judge. Alex watched him, numb, drained of energy, grounded in her new reality.

It had started back in '87. ProvLife, its profitability already on the slide, had hit bottom when a series of real estate investments had turned bad. Suddenly the balance sheet was full of holes. There had been talk of converting to a limited stock company, or merging with a competitor. They all knew stock market listing would lead to takeover, while merger would mean that many of them would lose their jobs. Both options were unattractive.

Bringing Medan Diagnostics into the frame had been White's idea. It had been strange—a turning point, serendipitous. ProvLife had taken a stake in Medan at the beginning of the eighties, and the board was well aware of a number of developments in the laboratory there. The company was promising, but commercially a lame duck. It had made breakthroughs with a couple of gene complexes that appeared to code for common forms of heart disease, the biggest source of claims against the insurers. But it was early days, and by no means clear what the applications of the new technology would be, or what kind of regulatory framework it might eventually have to work in. ProvLife increased its stake in the company, then took control. New money led to rapid advances in the diagnostic processes.

"Suddenly—it was as if suddenly we could see in the dark," said White.

Alex remembered what Ben Ellis had said about the printouts, how they pointed to a significant discovery.

"But these breakthroughs," she said. "Why didn't you share them? Why didn't you let everyone know?"

White shook his head and smiled.

"Now, that would have been stupid. Science is business, Alex. It certainly was at Medan. The problem was how to cash in. Discovering a bad gene doesn't always mean you can *do* something about it. The company could have worked for twenty years and come up with nothing. And the truth was, we couldn't afford to wait that long."

Alex didn't answer. She didn't know what to believe. White shifted in his chair and went on.

"On policies worth more than a hundred thousand dollars we'd begun using blood tests for AIDS—and sneaking in analysis for alcohol and narcotics, like a lot of our competitors. It was a simple matter to start using the technology at Medan to enhance those tests. Where we found a predisposition—for heart disease, Alzheimer's, breast or ovarian cancer, prostate cancer, Huntington's—we simply quoted an uncompetitive premium and the business went elsewhere. Claims started to nudge downwards, not by enough to relieve our perilous financial position, but enough for a diligent actuary to notice. It soon became obvious that what we really needed was a way of screening out bad risks across the whole range of applicants. The trouble was, people insuring themselves for less than a hundred grand didn't *want* to give blood samples. There were civil liberties issues—perceived norms of industry practice."

"So you started to use the envelopes," said Alex blankly.

White smiled.

"It wasn't such a radical idea. It was already happening in forensics labs all over the country. You could take DNA from the back of postage stamps. We asked ourselves why we couldn't do something similar. We realized that our kind of life insurance—high-volume, low-margin insurance—was perfectly suited. We reach most of our clients through their employers."

"I know. So what?"

"So the policyholders seal the envelopes themselves, instead of leaving it to their spouses—oh yes, we thought about that. And then we moved on to trials. Harold Tate worked on adhesives giving optimal results for DNA retention. We couldn't change the gum used by the U.S. mail, but we could make our own envelopes. The ProvLife application form was born."

Alex reached for the wineglass and drank.

"PrimeNumber," she said. "All those ladies with the letter openers. You were avoiding contamination, keeping the seals intact."

"It was so simple," said White. "And it worked. Like a dream."

"Like a nightmare."

White nodded, looked down.

"We instructed the ProvLife sales reps to leave the application form with the consumer," he said. "We even made a marketing thing out of it: 'ProvLife reps don't close a sale, they open a dialogue.' Something like that. People could take time to consider the package we were offering. When they were ready, they could just post the form directly to PrimeNumber or hand it over to the rep at the office. That meant they sealed the envelopes. What we ended up with was two sets of data: what they had told us, and the physical data they had put into the gum strips."

Alex began to see it, how it all stacked up.

"Of course there were problems," White went on. "The samples didn't always come through right: there was contamination, or the wrong people sealed the envelopes. It wasn't a perfect system, but it didn't have to be perfect. All we needed was an edge, but we got a lot more than that. We found we could exclude risks on an industrial scale."

"But it's—it's all so—"

"Unethical," said White. He looked at Alex with an expression of bemused sadness. "Of course it was. But the issues were less clear back then. This whole area was just beginning to—"

She wasn't so drained that she'd let this pass.

"Bull*shit*, Randal. You knew exactly what—"

"We weren't *hurting* anybody. Alex, you have to remember that. The people we refused just went somewhere else, and in the meantime—in the meantime we were surviving. ProvLife was surviving."

"But, but, Jesus Christ. What about all your talk of *moral imperatives*, all your *posturing*?"

"Hypocrisy," he said. "Expedient hypocrisy. But the creation of some kind of—I don't know, *underclass*—only becomes an issue if the whole industry starts doing what we did. And who knows what they're doing already? In a way, the fact that we were already screening, the fact that we were making money from that, made it possible for us to embrace an antiscreening, humanistic position."

"A position from which you benefited hugely."

"Yes, sure. It made commercial sense for us to be against screening, but we were still against it."

Alex felt sick. She looked across at the kitchen window, shaking her head. It was all so twisted. And the worst of it was that White could find some way to salve his conscience.

Then something dropped into place. She had been so confused, so stirred up by bad news, she hadn't made the connections, but now she saw how it all slotted together.

"The *money*," she said, still looking out at the rain. "That's where it all came from. You create—you created the fake accounts, the Ocean State accounts, to supplement the claim stream. You were making too much money."

"The screening proved far more effective than we'd ever anticipated," White said. "From lagging behind the rest of the industry, we soon were in danger of outperforming everyone. The burning ratio kept getting stronger and stronger. It threatened to expose us. People were *bound* to notice, bound to ask how. So, in the beginning the fake claims were made just to take some of the shine off our performance, bring the burning ratio back into line. Beat down the flames. We picked out lapsed polices from local clients and doctored their details so all our policyholder statistics stayed in line with the industry norms."

"Statistics on heart disease, for instance."

"For heart disease *especially*. You know, Alex, last year the incidence of genuine heart failure claims was nearly twenty-nine percent lower at ProvLife than it should have been, according to the actuarial tables. Twenty-nine percent."

"It must have been a good year."

"McCormick had to work hard just to make up the shortfall." White smiled out of the corner of his mouth. "Unfortunately, Ralph's understanding of random numbers wasn't nearly as complete as yours."

"He added to the total of convertible owners until it matched the industry average, and left it at that."

"Very sloppy," White said. "I should have checked it myself, but it never occurred to me to attempt such a bizarre cross-reference. Heart attacks and convertibles—"

He shook his head, amused.

"And you sent me down to PrimeNumber to get me out of the way," Alex said. "So you could go into the system and make the numbers random again."

White shrugged. "And to keep Heymann on his toes. I never really liked him."

"And the money?"

For a moment White looked disappointed. He drew an unsteady breath.

"We created a series of bank accounts for the fake claimants—"

"With Mullins."

"It was Neumann who set it up. We had to pay Mullins, of course. What we were asking him to do was—illegal. Then—then, well—"

For the first time White looked genuinely uncomfortable. A pleading look came into his eyes.

"You thought you should get paid too," Alex said.

Grant racked the slides on the pump shotguns and pushed one into Ferulli's freezing hands. He put a handful of rounds into his pockets and made a gesture for Ferulli to keep quiet. They started to move up the drive towards the house. Through the pouring rain it was possible to see a light on upstairs. Downstairs one window was lit a spooky greenish white. Almost immediately Ferulli was drenched. When Neumann had called, he had just slipped on a raincoat and a new pair of bench-made oxfords. The shoes held up for about a minute before his feet were squelching.

Twenty feet from the house Grant stopped and pointed a finger. He said something Ferulli couldn't make out in the noise of the downpour. He had to get up close to hear.

"He's in the kitchen," said Grant, his breath hot against Ferulli's ear. He grabbed his chin and looked into his eyes.

"You stand out here and you wait. I'm going to find a way in. Okay?" Ferulli nodded, blinking the rain out of his eyes.

Grant leaned towards him. "Okay?"

"Yeah, okay." Ferulli had to shout above the rain.

"This is business too," said Grant. "That's all it is."

Ferulli watched Grant walk around the side of the house.

"There were twelve of us to begin with," said White. "Each holding a corner of the net. But even with twelve of us on the payroll, the money just— It was like we'd capped a gusher."

He poured the last of the wine from the bottle.

"It became a problem. We were drowning in money. There was just too much of it. We were clear from the beginning that nobody should know outside the circle, no girlfriends, no wives."

Alex thought of Margaret Eliot. That was what had poisoned the marriage: the money. That was what had changed the mood inside ProvLife: the money. She thought of Mullins with his Patek Philippe. She thought of Mark with his porno car magazines. They were all bursting to spend, but having to do it discreetly, furtively, or not at all. She pointed at the bottle on the table.

"The wine you're drinking, how much?"

White considered it for a moment.

"Alex, I don't think—"

"The price. I'd like to know."

"That bottle? Three thousand dollars."

"Three thousand dollars a *case*?"

"A bottle. My buyer picked it up in London at Sotheby's."

Alex gasped. "That's—that's five hundred dollars per glass, fifty dollars every time you swallow. That's *obscene*."

"Alex, it's just—"

"Just money," said Alex. "Yeah, I know."

White was shaking his head. "Alex, I'm trying to—to explain how it all—"

Her look of contempt stopped him. She waited a moment, then shrugged.

"Go ahead. I'm not going anywhere. Not till the rain stops, anyway."

"Alex, I couldn't have gotten out of it, even if I'd wanted to."

"What are you talking about?"

"I'm talking about the policy. That's what we call it. A kind of a joke, in a way, I suppose. Six years ago there was a . . . a row. Goebert wanted to retire early. The others didn't like it. 'If he can leave, why can't I?' And so forth. We were at Neumann's place. We realized then, that afternoon, that if anyone did leave, we'd have to replace him, and that might prove very risky. Besides, if people started leaving, started *spending* their money, then it might be noticed, questions might be asked. So we drew up an agreement. It set out how long the scheme should be run, how we would all retire or move away from the area at agreed times over the coming years. We each had a date, a release date—something to look forward to. We couldn't all just take the money and run. The thing had to be wound down gradually so that people coming into the company wouldn't see anything. And it would have worked. Over time we just had to let more of the bad risks slip through."

"Bad risks like me?"

White stared, but said nothing.

"But then Eliot tried to run," said Alex.

"That's right. And he was . . . taken care of."

"You mean executed."

"Just as I would have been. He broke the agreement. With no consideration for our exposure, he ran. He only had another five years to do."

"Five years he didn't think he had. Years that became more precious than all the money he'd stashed away."

White gazed into the cold light of the refrigerator.

"Yes . . . yes, I suppose."

"So you killed him."

"*Grant* killed him," said White. "I had nothing to do with it."

"Grant? I thought he was just an accident investigator."

White shook his head.

"He—his résumé is a little more complex than that. They use him because—well, with all his experience, all the accidents he's seen, he's—you could say he's an expert in his field."

"And it was Grant that tried to kill me?"

"Grant or one of his people. Don't you see now? You *have* to come away with me. I can protect you. I can give you whatever you need, whatever you *want*."

Alex laughed. It wasn't a pleasant laugh. It didn't sound like her at all.

"Alex, there's nothing for you here anymore," he said quietly. "There's nothing for you in Providence. Come with me."

"Come where? To France? To your convent?"

"Why not? We would be free, Alex. You would be free."

He was asking her to go live the life of a millionaire in the South of France. It was the same offer Michael Eliot had made to Liz. He leaned forward.

"A few years of happiness, Alex, in—"

A sound from inside the house—a sharp click—brought their heads around. They listened for a moment. White's hand reached for the Beretta. An icy draft had started to blow through from the hallway. White got to his feet, the Beretta in his right hand. He switched on the light.

From where he stood, Ferulli had a clear view of him. He was standing with his back to the window, looking at a doorway that led into the dark interior of the house. Ferulli wondered if maybe Grant had disturbed him. Then he saw the pistol White was holding and froze. He hoped to God that Grant knew what he was doing. He looked down at the shotgun, and realized with a jolt that the kitchen light was also illuminating him. He stepped sideways into shadow. And saw Alex.

"What is it?" said Alex, blinking in the harsh light.

Donald Grant stepped into the doorway and fired. The first charge ripped into White, sending him across the table like a rag doll. Alex screamed and threw herself sideways. Outside Ferulli started running—straight at the window, his weapon raised. He screamed.

"Not her."

Three strides. Two heartbeats. Time stretched. Grant pumping a round into the breech, taking aim, squeezing the trigger.

Ferulli fired first. The window seemed to explode. Wood fragments spiked into the ceiling. Ferulli came up hard against the wall. He pumped and fired, pumped and fired, pumped and fired—three rounds into the square where the window had been. Glass and plaster fragments rained to the floor. Gunsmoke drifted towards the ceiling like a slow lick of flame. There was no sign of Grant.

Ferulli pulled himself in through the shattered window frame.

"Alex?"

She was leaning back against a cupboard, her white face spattered with blood.

"Alex, are you hit?"

She didn't seem to recognize him. She was hyperventilating, her pupils drilled points of terror. She held the gun straight in front of her.

"Mark?"

Grant seemed to come up out of the floor. Ferulli turned, fired late. Grant put two rounds into his body, hitting him in the chest from a distance of three feet, punching him back into the window, dead.

Grant was making a thick gargling sound in his throat. Alex caught a glint of shattered teeth in his ragged, bloody mouth as he turned to find her with what was left of his eyes.

The Beretta jumped in her hand. She didn't stop firing until the clip was empty.

It was raining. It had never stopped. A steady roar. Alex was slumped down on the floor, her legs doubled underneath her. The sound of her own sobbing brought her back into the moment. Rain was drifting in through the rags of curtain. She looked at the gun in her hand. She knew it was White's gun, but she didn't know how she had gotten it. She could not seem to let go. Her knuckles were white with the strain of clutching.

"Axe."

A voice. Indistinct, buried. Like a voice from underground. Alex recognized it. She scrambled across the floor.

He was on his side, his eyes fluttering, struggling to draw breath.

"Alxe."

He was struggling to say her name. She threw the gun from her and put her hands on his face. There was a single deep cut on the bridge of his nose.

"Randal, are you hurt?"

There was blood everywhere. Too much. Blood mixed with grit, glass, plaster, wood. She searched for wounds, but could see none.

"Axe."

She pulled him over onto his back and tried to ease him up into a sitting position. Something ruptured with a soft fleshy pock. A rib showed redly through the hole in his overcoat. The coat was soaked in blood. White gave a violent shudder and snapped his legs out convulsively.

"Alex," he said, his voice perfectly clear now.

"I'm here."

His eyes wandered a little and then found her. Fixed.

"I'm so . . . I'm so sorry. All I . . ."

Alex's vision blurred. He was trying to say something more, but she couldn't hear above the rain. She leaned close to his mouth.

"All I wanted . . ." he whispered.

He tried to moisten his mouth with his tongue.

"Yes?"

"Together."

She drew back and looked into his face. He was slipping away fast. She had to stop the bleeding. She pulled back the coat—gagged. There was a hole the size of a grapefruit. A flap of skin snagged shattered ribs. Blood welled rhythmically.

"I wanted us—" He grabbed at her hand and squeezed.

Alex stared, holding her breath.

"Both," he said. "In the same . . ."

The tongue worked in his mouth. He swallowed painfully and coughed, struggling to draw breath.

"Randal?"

"Both," he said.

A look of profound puzzlement came over his face, and he pushed forward his white lips as though to kiss.

She walked out into the rain. It was coming down like the end of the world—like the final Deluge. She watched it wash the blood from her hands, first the palms and then the backs. The blood under her fingernails made dark crescent moons.

AUGUST
TWENTY-FIRST

Alex watched from behind the wheel of the pickup as Robby and Buck Leith, the guy from the venture capital company, walked away up the narrow track, the wind lifting the tails of their jackets and ruffling the papers under their arms. Robby walked stiffly, still tense from the argument they'd had to cut short so that he could present himself to Leith in a smiling, professional manner. The farmer they had come to see was at work on a big John Deere 530. On either side of him fields of barley shimmered and swayed. Away on the horizon a steel silo stood tall and white against a darkening sky.

Alex bit her lip and prayed for the rain to hold off. Right now rain was all they needed, because according to Robby's projections it was going to stay dry, at least for another week. Humidity was rising, but the dominant air masses over the Great Lakes were supposed to be warm enough still to prevent significant condensation. Of course, statistically speaking, one stray rainstorm didn't mean that the whole Sunscape model was useless, but what good was that to a farmer whose livelihood was on the line—a farmer who wanted to know when best to sow and when to harvest? Sunscape had to prove its value or Leith and his company weren't going to invest.

Since leaving Providence, Alex had been content to bury herself in the world of meteorology and climatology, helping Robby refine the complex computer models that he had constructed over the preceding year. Erratically, to many imperceptibly, the climate in the Midwest was changing. Maximum temperatures were rising. Minimum temperatures were rising even faster, lengthening the frost-free season but also affecting the development of pests and perennial plants. Robby had been right about one thing: the realization that the optimal use of land might be changing was helping to stimulate the market for predictive technology. Half the farmers in Michigan were already plugged into the computer and satellite feeds from the National Climate Data Center.

It had been just the escape Alex needed. Getting into the work, enjoying the space and the freedom of the Midwest, growing closer to Robby day by day—it had felt like a new beginning. But pretty quickly the beginning was over and Alex had found herself in the middle of something her mother would call "a situation." Despite the continued doubts about the company's future—Robby never tired of explaining that it was that kind of business—they had achieved something akin to domestic stability, but perhaps *because* of the unstable nature of the area they were working in, Robby had started to put pressure on her to settle down. Three months into sharing the same bed, it had become clear to Alex that what he wanted above all else was a home, and a wife.

Whenever she expressed any doubts on the matter, he immediately, sometimes ludicrously, took it as a comment on his ability to make his way in the world, to make a go of things, to make a home. She loved him, didn't she? Their reunion after two years apart had been almost comically passionate. So what else could it be? The fight they'd just abandoned had had to do with children, or more specifically a friend's newborn and the example it offered of the merits of procreation. Robby, as usual, had taken the line that the only reason Alex didn't want to make serious commitments was because she saw him as unstable, as a generator of instability.

But there were other reasons, of course.

The night of the killings was one she could recall now only with difficulty. The violence of it had left her damaged somewhere, she knew that, as if a relay had been burned in her brain. Out of nowhere she would get a flash of Grant turning to find her, and feel a jolt of terror as if she were back on the kitchen floor—the same terror, undiluted by the intervening months. Robby told her she was jumpier than she used to be, and she had started to suffer from migraines.

Some moments came back to her again and again. She was standing outside in the rain, shaking—from the cold or the shock or both. Then she was all but overcome with a desire to run, to get away and never look back. It was a sense of revulsion more powerful than any she'd ever felt. Just the thought of going into the house made her feel faint. She was back inside the car, her hand on the ignition key, before she realized what it would mean if she did run: more time for the others to make their escape, to wipe the files and destroy the records. More chance they'd remain free. And then one day it would be her turn again to have an unfortunate accident, one of those accidents that happened every day. She'd reached for the car phone in the glove compartment and dialed 911.

The interrogations went on forever, that's how it had seemed. Car after car had pulled up, red lights flashing. The noise of the rain had been gradually displaced by the sputter and crackle of police radios. Flashbulbs had gone off up and down the house. A succession of strangers had asked her questions, many of them the same ones, as if trying to catch her out. The wail of sirens interrupted her answers. Someone had brought her a blanket. Then a cup of coffee from a thermos. By the time two women officers had escorted her to the county sheriff's office the entire house was surrounded by crime scene tape.

The homicide detectives hadn't been anxious to charge her with murder. There'd been too many guns at the scene and too many bodies for that. By five o'clock they'd stopped asking questions and begun listening to Alex make a full statement, explaining everything she'd learned about ProvLife and its illegal operations. By eight o'clock a string of warrants had been issued for the arrest of several senior ProvLife executives and others implicated in the conspiracy. Alex had finally been driven home at four o'clock the following afternoon. Upon arrival she'd found another police officer questioning Mrs. Connelly about the visitors to her house, and a forensic team dusting her boiler for prints. The following morning Liz Foster's body had been recovered from a canal on the eastern fringes of New London.

Rounding up the main suspects had taken quite a while. The Medan executives, Harold Tate and Guy Pilaski, had been picked up at home; so had Dean Mitchell, the head of Claims. David Mullins had gone in to work as normal at Ocean State, made one phone call, and immediately decided he had urgent business elsewhere. Detectives had met him on his way out. In his briefcase they'd found two million dollars' worth of

European corporate bearer bonds. Newton Brady had been arrested up at the airport after his flight to Montreal was delayed by the bad weather. Tom Heymann's Lexus had been found abandoned at Bradley International Airport, outside Hartford, Connecticut, although his name wasn't found on any passenger records there. It later emerged that he had flown to Canada. Since then there had been no word of him. Walter Neumann had made it all the way to Europe with a false passport, but had eventually been taken into custody in Geneva, pending extradition to the United States. Extradition proceedings were also pending against ProvLife's ex-president Richard Goebert, who'd taken up residence in Venezuela. So far the proceedings had been unsuccessful. As for the two men believed to have carried out Liz Foster's murder, they had never been identified.

The task of laying charges—of fraud, if not of murder—had proved easier. Harold Tate and David Mullins had turned state's evidence, and their knowledge of both sides of the conspiracy—the screening of applicants and the generation of fraudulent claims—together with Alex's testimony, had been enough to complete the picture. It emerged that in the seven years since the operation had begun, ProvLife had made more than one hundred twenty-five million dollars in bogus payouts—while, at the same time, showing a steady increase in profitability. Exactly to whom these hidden funds belonged was a difficult issue. As a mutual, ProvLife had no shareholders, and although technically the policyholders had ultimate title to its assets, laying claim to money obtained in such an unethical way was going to be difficult, especially with the threat of civil litigation still unquantified. In the meantime a series of criminal trials was scheduled to begin at the end of September.

Alex knew she would be summoned to give evidence, probably several times. She had been dreading the return, dreading the memory of that winter, just as she dreaded waking up to the harsh reality of her own predicament. But just like the results of the Medan tests, ignoring it wasn't going to make it go away. The time had come to stop hiding and face the facts.

Two weeks earlier she had gone to a doctor in Rochester and asked for a gene test. It wasn't that she harbored any hope that the results would be different from the ones ProvLife had come up with. It was simply time to thrash out the practical implications with someone who understood them, however unpleasant they might be. And it was time to tell Robby. Until now she hadn't had the courage, but once the information about her future was hers—officially, at her request—there would no longer be any excuse for keeping it to herself. She would have to tell him the truth: that in all probability she would not live to see her fortieth birthday, and that even if she did, the necessary preventive treatment might leave her sterile. And then she would have to leave him. Because however strongly he might protest—and she knew he would protest—she had no right to condemn him to that. Him, or anyone else. It was too much to ask. Whatever future was left to her, she was going to have to face it alone.

That morning the hospital had left a message on the answering machine, asking her to call back. With Robby out trying to impress Leith, she had a chance to do just that. She nodded to herself as she climbed out of the truck, beginning at last to accept what she knew she could not escape. She was going to have to return to Providence for a few days anyway, for the trial. That was where she would make the break, tell Robby that it was over. Then disappear again, maybe home to her mother's. She dabbed at her eyes with the heel of her hand. Her brief, sweet season of wishful thinking was coming to an end.

She walked across the yard towards the farmhouse, keeping a wary eye on the gathering clouds. A collie that had been dozing on the verandah got to its feet and barked a guarded welcome. Alex was about to knock on the door when a woman appeared around the side of the building, carrying a bale of chicken wire.

"Mrs. Harris?"

"That's me," the woman said cheerfully. "You must be one of the weather people. How you doin'?"

The woman put the wire down by the door and offered Alex her hand. She was in her mid-thirties, with long brown hair swept back into a ponytail and pale freckles over the bridge of her nose.

"Alex Tynan."

"Becky. You want a cup of coffee, or a soda maybe?"

"That's very kind, but I'm okay. I was wondering if I could use your phone. It'll only take a minute."

"Surely. Just follow me."

She led Alex into a narrow hallway. Brightly colored boots were lined up along one wall, and a big cardboard box of apples partly blocked the foot of the stairs.

"We're not exactly *Better Homes and Gardens* here." Mrs. Harris chuckled, scooping a rubber dinosaur off the floor. "One day maybe. Phone's over here."

Alex dialed the number for the hospital in Rochester and was put through to Dr. Sussman. From the tone of his voice, Alex could tell at once that he didn't know how best to handle things. He was new in the job, and probably assumed that the presence of the cancer gene was going to come as a complete shock.

"Anyway, the results of your test came back," he said at last, when he'd finished asking how Alex was and telling her how busy things were at the office. "So I thought you'd be anxious to know . . . One thing's been puzzling me, though, actually."

Alex sighed. Why couldn't he spit it out?

"What made you want to take this test? Is there some history of—of any particular illness in your family?"

"You mean cancer."

"Well—"

"Not that I know of."

"Then why—?"

"It's a long story, Doctor. Let's just say it was a hunch. Should we make an appointment to talk about this? About the options?"

Dr. Sussman hesitated.

"Well, of course if you'd *like* to. If you think there are any other reasons for concern."

Alex blinked. "Any other reasons? I don't understand. Isn't the gene reason enough?"

Dr. Sussman cleared his throat.

"What gene would that be?"

"BRCA1. Breast and ovarian cancer. An eighty-five-percent probability, right?"

"Well, I'm—I don't think it's that high. Besides, you don't appear to have it."

Alex reached out to steady herself against the wall. It didn't seem possible. He'd made a mistake. She had seen the results with her own eyes, on Randal White's computer. The screening at Medan had handed the conspirators at ProvLife over a hundred million dollars in excess profits. How could it be wrong?

"Doctor, are you saying I'm in the clear? I don't have the gene?"

"BRCA1? No. No, absolutely not. That's why I was asking about your family. I wondered why you thought there was a problem."

Alex closed her eyes, letting the wave of relief wash over her, feeling it course through her system like some powerful drug. She'd been so convinced that the Medan analysis was correct. Anything that made a hundred million dollars was hard to dismiss. But it had been wrong. And she had been wrong to believe it—just like Michael Eliot.

For a moment she held the receiver away from her ear. In Michael Eliot's case Medan itself *hadn't* been wrong. The samples had been switched before they even got to the lab. By Randal White. Harold Tate had testified to that, it had been leaked to the press. Was it possible . . . ?

In her mind she heard White's last words once again: *I wanted us together.* He'd been trying to explain. Somewhere along the line— probably after the data was on the system—he'd faked the results of her screening. He'd *wanted* her to find them. He'd wanted her to find her world, her future suddenly compressed into a few short years. So that she would do what Eliot had planned to do—what she *had* done: run away. She would run away with him, because the long term wouldn't matter anymore. And because his wealth could buy her whatever kind of life she wanted. What would the alternative have been? To spend her last few years working behind a desk, toiling to acquire qualifications she would probably never have a chance to use. No wonder he'd been in no hurry to get her reinstated at ProvLife. He'd had other plans for her: a life of caring for him at his house in France, her loyalty assured by the prospect of inheriting it all. Maybe he'd even agreed to have her dismissed in the first place, just to add a little urgency to the proposition.

She felt a surge of anger. The selfishness of it was breathtaking.

Dr. Sussman was talking on the other end of the line. Alex put the receiver to her ear.

"Sorry, Doctor. I'm—it's all a bit of a shock. You're right, though, I wasn't expecting a clean bill of health."

She heard him laugh.

"Well, as far as BRCA1 is concerned, you can relax. No question about it." Alex heard him turn over a couple of sheets of paper. "There is, however—let me just find it here. Yep. Yes, if you want the whole picture, I should tell you that we did find a small abnormality on chromosome seven. There's some evidence, admittedly only indicative, that it could lead to—"

"Wait," Alex cut him off short. "Please, wait."

"Pardon me?"

"Don't say another word, Dr. Sussman. You see—you see, the fact of the matter is: I'd much rather not know."

Back in the pickup Robby was fidgety and morose. Alex got the impression that things hadn't gone too well with Buck Leith. It was hard not being able to give him her good news, but it wasn't something she could get into right now. It had been a very big thing, and she had kept it from him. Besides, Robby had other problems on his mind.

"Of course he didn't actually say it," he said as they turned out onto the road. "But I don't think we're gonna see that money."

"Wasn't Mr. Harris enthusiastic?"

"Oh yeah, he was fine. Nice guy. Said anything that helped make sense of all the data he was getting would be welcome. He's no hillbilly. Knows a hell of a lot about meteorology, as a matter of fact."

"So what was the problem?"

"The other guy. Leith. I don't think he *understands*. He kept looking at those big clouds rolling in, and I could tell he was out of his depth. He didn't have anything to measure: no market shares, no cash-flow analysis. If we were trying to sell bathroom tiles, he'd have been a whole lot happier."

Alex watched Robby talk, unable to follow any of what he said, although she had certainly heard it all before. Her mind kept snapping back to the last time she'd seen White. He had sought to manipulate her, to deceive her, as if her life had no importance or value of its own. White. She still couldn't see his name in print without feeling upset and confused. The most disturbing aspect of the whole ProvLife affair had been the news that White had been at the very heart of ProvLife's screening program, and had then discovered that he was himself a genetic outcast, an untouchable. The fact that White was never going to face trial had given certain journalists a sense of licence in dealing with the case. His plight, what Huntington's chorea had in store for him, had been gone into in the most lurid detail. The depth and extent of his suffering, actual and anticipated, made it difficult for Alex, whenever she thought of him, to remain angry for long. He was so much a victim in the whole terrible business, it was hard to think of him as evil. Now that the last link with him—his cruel lie about her future—was broken, all she was left with was a feeling of sadness.

They were stopped at a railroad crossing, while the last few cars of a freight train slid slowly by. Robby was turned in his seat, talking earnestly. Alex realized that he must have taken her distracted silence for more doubts about their future together. He was now talking a blue streak, giving her the pep talk of a lifetime.

". . . to *keep trying*," he said finally. "I know how hard it is for you to live this way, but deep down you know as well as I do that this—with the computing power we now have, with the software we've developed—this thing is bound to work."

The train crossed the crossing, so that for a moment they were looking at the road ahead, spear straight with a hard metallic sheen, dividing the land. Then the clouds broke. A sudden heavens-opening downpour obliterated everything but the yellow X of the crossing signal. Robby stared open-mouthed at the streaming windshield as the rain hammered on the roof. Alex could no longer contain herself.

"Oops," she said, and she began to laugh.

• A NOTE ON THE TYPE •

The typeface used in this book is one of many versions of Garamond, a modern homage to—rather than, strictly speaking, a revival of—the celebrated fonts of Claude Garamond (c.1480–1561), the first founder to produce type on a large scale. Garamond's type was inspired by Francesco Griffo's *De Ætna* type (cut in the 1490s for Venetian printer Aldus Manutius and revived in the 1920s as Bembo), but its letter forms were cleaner and the fit between pieces of type improved. It therefore gave text a more harmonious overall appearance than its predecessors had, becoming the basis of all romans created on the continent for the next two hundred years; it was itself still in use through the eighteenth century. Besides the many "Garamonds" in use today, other typefaces derived from his fonts are Granjon and Sabon (despite their being named after other printers).